## *Dear Reader:*

Our Harlequin Historical romances were launched just last year, and all of you have been so enthusiastic that we thought a good way to celebrate the holidays would be by publishing a special short-story collection.

There's something here to delight every one of you, featuring stories by three of your favorite authors—Kristin James, Heather Graham Pozzessere and Lucy Elliot. From the classic western setting of *Tumbleweed Christmas*, to the war ravaged South of *Home for Christmas*, to a traditional New England celebration with all the trimmings in *A Cinderella Christmas*, Harlequin Historicals celebrates Christmas in the 1800s. Each author has included a special personal note and one of her favorite recipes.

I hope you enjoy this collection, and all of us at Harlequin hope you have a wonderful holiday and a happy and healthy New Year.

Karen Solem
Executive Editor

# Historical Christmas Stories

**KRISTIN JAMES, LUCY ELLIOT AND
HEATHER GRAHAM POZZESSERE**

## Harlequin Books

TORONTO • NEW YORK • LONDON
AMSTERDAM • PARIS • SYDNEY • HAMBURG
STOCKHOLM • ATHENS • TOKYO • MILAN

Harlequin Historicals first edition November 1989

ISBN 0-373-83211-7

Harlequin Historical Christmas Stories 1989
Copyright © 1989 by Harlequin Enterprises Limited.

The publisher acknowledges the copyright holders of
the individual work as follows:

Tumbleweed Christmas
Copyright © 1989 by Candace Camp

A Cinderella Christmas
Copyright © 1989 by Nancy A. Greenman

Home for Christmas
Copyright © 1989 by Heather Graham Pozzessere

# Contents

# TUMBLEWEED CHRISTMAS

## *Kristin James*

This is my favorite of all the Christmas foods my mother prepared. She spent hours peeling and seeding the grapes and slicing them, but now, with seedless red grapes and food processors, it's a fast and easy recipe.

## CRANBERRY SALAD

2 cups cranberries, frozen
2 cups seedless red grapes, frozen
½ to 1 cup pecans, chopped
½ cup sugar

Whipped Cream:
½ pint heavy cream
¼ cup sugar
1 tsp vanilla

Slice grapes and cranberries. (Mother took time to peel the grapes; I don't. The fast and easy way is to freeze them, then slice them with a food processor.) Let cranberries steep in ½ cup sugar.

In a small bowl, whip the cream. Beat in sugar and vanilla. Do not overbeat.

Mix together grapes, cranberries, whipped cream, nuts and sugar.

This dish is handy because it can be made ahead of time and frozen until needed.

# Chapter One

THE HOUSE ROSE up from the dry earth, as stark and bleak as the landscape around it. Melinda Ballard stopped the buggy and sat, simply staring at the house, for a long moment. There were no trees around it to soften its lines or shield it from the harsh Panhandle weather. Undoubtedly once white, the sun, dirt and wind had turned it a muted gray, much the color of the chill November sky behind it. Several shutters were missing, and others hung at a slant. Even the wide porch across the front managed to look unwelcoming.

Melinda's heart sank. She had set out this morning buoyed with hope, thinking that she had found a way to earn the money she and Lee needed so badly. She had been at her wit's end yesterday morning when she'd gone into town to buy flour and sugar and the heavy gloves she would need for this winter. The eggs she had taken in to sell, as she did every two days, had hardly put a dent in the bill she'd built up at the store, and Mr. Grissom had told her flatly that he could extend her no more credit. Melinda had turned away, fighting to keep back her tears.

It had been two years since her husband, Robert, died, and ever since she had been struggling against financial ruin. She hadn't been able to farm their land by herself, even with Lee's help. After all, Lee had been only seven when his father died. She had managed to raise food for them to eat, but not a cash crop. She had had so many debts to pay—not only the costs of Robert's funeral, but also the loan at the bank for seed and expenses that they got every spring and paid off in the fall from their profits, as well as their account at the hardware and grocery stores. Gradually Melinda had had to sell their very small herd of cattle, and even the wagon, plow and mule team, in order to pay off their debts and keep them alive. Now it looked as if they would have to sell the milch cow and chickens, and then what would they have left to sell? Only the land, which Melinda had wanted so desperately to keep for Lee; it was his birthright.

But as she had walked away, blinking back her tears, Mr. Grissom's wife, a kind and sympathetic woman, had hurried after her and told her that "Ol' Daniel MacKenzie" was in need of a cook, if Melinda was interested in work.

Of course she had been interested. She had often tried to think of some way to earn more money than the pitiful amount she got from selling eggs, but there were few jobs for women, and those few, such as taking in laundry or sewing, would have meant buying or renting a house in town, which she couldn't afford to do.

Mrs. Grissom had warned her that she might not find the job to her liking. MacKenzie had a reputation for being difficult to deal with, and it was said that he didn't like women, usually hiring only men to cook for him and the cowhands at the ranch. But Melinda had paid no attention to that. What did it matter if the old man was grumpy and bad-tempered? Her own father had had a volatile temper, and she'd always been able to stand toe to toe with him and argue until they both gave up—laughing, as often as not. In fact, there had been times in her marriage to Robert when she had almost missed those fiery exchanges with her father. She and Robert had grown up friends long before they'd fallen in love and gotten married, and they had rarely fought.

Mrs. Grissom had given Melinda directions to the MacKenzie place, which lay several miles west of town, and had even lent her the Grissoms' buggy to drive out there. This morning Melinda had dressed in a plain, serviceable dark brown blouse and skirt and skinned her hair back into a tight braid, which she wound in a knot atop her head. When she'd looked in the mirror, she had been appalled. She knew the hairstyle wasn't attractive on her, but she hadn't realized how much her dark brown hair had lost its luster during the past year or so. Once it had gleamed, golden highlights glinting within it, but now it just looked plain and dull. And the bare hairstyle, lacking any softening effect, pointed up how thin and worn her face had become. They hadn't had enough to eat for some time, and she had lost weight, particularly in her face. As a result, her large, expressive gray eyes looked sad and too big, and her color was poor, no longer strawberries-and-cream. There were lines of worry etched on her forehead and around her eyes and mouth. She was twenty-nine, but she appeared years older.

She had reminded herself that that was the way she wanted to look. A sober, practical appearance was best when applying for this sort of job. Prettiness or youth would be a detriment, making an employer think that she was inexperienced or incapable, or even that she would be available to his advances. She had to avoid that. Let him think she was older and unattractive. Still, she hadn't been able to suppress a pang at how much she had lost her looks. Once she had been considered pretty.

She had shaken off her mood and driven to the MacKenzie ranch, hopeful that her money problems had been solved and that she and Lee would have a better life. But now, looking at the house, Melinda's heart sank. It looked so desolate, so cold. She suspected that its bleak exterior was a reflection of the owner's personality. She had never met the man, but over the years she had heard things about him, and now they all came flooding into her brain: he hated people, and women in particular; he was mean and angry and harsh; he had a tongue like vinegar and didn't hesitate to use it on whoever displeased him. He wasn't married and he had no children; Melinda had heard that it was because no woman could stand to live with him. She'd also heard that it was because he disliked people so much that he didn't even want a family.

It might be horrible to work for him, worse than anything she'd ever known. Melinda hesitated, her hands clenching and unclenching around the reins. Then she sighed and clucked to the horse, slapping the reins lightly across its back. Why was she worrying about whether she should go on? She had no choice. She was more desperate for the job than MacKenzie was for a cook. Without the money it would bring in, she would have to sell Lee's land, or they wouldn't survive the winter. And she was determined not to do that; the half-section of land was Lee's only inheritance.

She drove the small buggy up to the house and jumped down, tying the horse to the hitching rail in front of the porch. Up close, the house looked even less inviting. She walked up the three shallow steps to the porch and knocked on the door. There was no answer. She waited, then knocked again.

Melinda shivered. It had been cold in the buggy, but at least the vehicle had protected her from most of the wind. But now the freezing north wind whipped around the corner of the house and cut right through her. She had worn Robert's old coat over her dress, having cut up her own woolen cloak to make Lee warm pants and a shirt for the winter. The too-big coat hung halfway to her knees and down over her hands, and she had the collar turned up around her throat, but even its warmth wasn't enough to combat the chill.

She sighed and turned away, rubbing her arms in an effort to warm up. He wasn't home. She'd driven all this way, even borrowed a buggy and horse, and it had been for nothing. She glanced around. There was a small frame house to the side and back of the big house, as well as a barn, a corral and a few sheds. Farther away, past the barn, was a long, narrow building, which she presumed to be the bunkhouse for the cowboys, and across from it lay another house.

That was probably the foreman's house, she thought. MacKenzie obviously had a big spread. But nowhere did she see a sign of people.

Melinda started down the steps toward the buggy, her spirits low. She glanced at the small rise behind the house. There was a windmill at the top of the little hill, positioned to catch the full force of the wind. But the blades of the windmill were not turning, and there was a man working high up on the platform. Melinda brightened. Perhaps it was MacKenzie—or at least someone who could tell her where he was!

Quickly she crossed the yard and climbed the hill to the base of the windmill. She looked up at the man working on it. At that distance and with his face shadowed by his hat, she could see nothing of his features. "Hello?" she called, and the wind snatched away her voice. She cupped her hands around her mouth and tried again. "Hello!"

The man looked down, and though she could not see his face, impatience was evident in his posture, even in the way he turned his head. "Yeah?"

"I'm looking for a Mr. Daniel MacKenzie."

"You got him." His voice was rough and loud, whipped by the wind.

Melinda hesitated. Why didn't he come down so they could talk like normal people? It was difficult to discuss anything shouting back and forth like this. "Uh, I understand you're in need of a cook."

He cupped his ear in a pantomime of deafness. "Couldn't hear you!"

Irritation stirred in Melinda. "I said, I've come about the job of cook!"

"I don't hire women." Daniel MacKenzie stared at the woman below, his mouth pulled into a grimace. Silently he cursed the cook who had quit weeks ago. It was such a damn fool waste of his time to find a replacement. But he had to feed his men, and his foreman's silly wife was digging in her heels about cooking for all of them any longer. If he didn't get someone soon, he just might lose Will, and Will was the best foreman Daniel had ever had.

Melinda's chin came up. She would not back down, no matter how gruff and rude this man was. She had to have this job. She was determined to fight for it. "The way I hear it, you don't have much choice."

She had him there. MacKenzie frowned. Women housekeepers and cooks were trouble. He'd found that out years ago. They cried when you complained about the quality of their work and got a stubborn, muley look on their faces when you gave them orders. Worst of all, if they weren't too old, they got ideas about making the position of housekeeper into the permanent one of wife. Daniel wasn't about to give in to that, of course, but he hated the bother of avoiding their maneuvers and hints and traps. Almost as bad was the fact that if the woman was attractive, he had sometimes felt the stirrings of desire and been tempted to take her into his bed. But that sort of thing could prove to be just as entangling as marriage and wasn't the impersonal, clean relationship he wanted with his housekeeper. Sex was something to be had with the women of the night in Amarillo, a matter of money exchanged for services rendered, with no involvements or pain.

He considered the woman below him. At this distance it was difficult to see her clearly, but she looked neither young nor attractive. Her shape was bulky, her clothes plain and dark, and her face was pinched and colorless. As she'd gazed up at him, her bonnet had fallen off to hang down her back, and he could see her dark hair pinned up tightly in a fashion that aroused not the slightest interest in seeing it down or feeling it glide through his fingers. She seemed a plain and practical sort, not the kind to tempt a man or to try to inveigle him into marriage. She could be a hard worker who would stick to her own business and let him be.

"I'm considered a very good cook," Melinda went on. "You could give me a try, let me cook something and see how it tastes. I can also keep house."

He frowned. Frankly, he was desperate. He couldn't afford to be choosy. Besides, she was willing to clean the house, which his male cook had refused to do. "All right," he said reluctantly. "I'll hire you to cook and take care of the house—as a trial, to see how you do."

Melinda sagged with relief. For a moment she had been afraid that he would say no. And no matter how cold and lonely this house seemed, or how unpleasant he was, or how sure she was that she wouldn't enjoy working here, she had to have the money. "Thank you. You won't regret it."

He grunted, a sound expressive of doubt. "We'll see." He gestured with the wrench in his hand. "I want to make one thing clear—I'm a bachelor, and I like it that way. I've got no plans to marry, and if you're thinking about trying, you might as well forget it."

Melinda stared. The gall, the conceit, of this man! As though she would chase him, trying to get him to marry her! She set her fists on her hips and glared at him. "Well, I'm happy the way I am, too. And you can rest assured that if I were hunting for a husband, you wouldn't be in the race."

MacKenzie blinked, taken aback. A chuckle rose unbidden in his throat, and he forced it down. "You can take the little house in the back. You'll start work tomorrow. I'll send one of the hands to move your things. Where are they?"

"The Ballard farm, southeast of here. It's on the road to the McClure place."

MacKenzie nodded. "He'll be over first thing tomorrow morning."

He turned back to his work. Melinda stood for a moment, still staring up at him. Daniel MacKenzie had to be the rudest man she'd ever met. He hadn't even asked her name or a thing about her. She cupped her hands around her mouth again and yelled, "My name is Mrs. Ballard!"

MacKenzie glanced down at her as though surprised to find her still there. Then he swung around and went to work without a word. It was the first time—but not the last—that Melinda thought she would take great delight in kicking him in the shins.

MELINDA RETURNED to the small sod hut where she and her son lived. Lee was already home from school. She grabbed his hands and waltzed him around the one-room house, laughing. "I got the job! I got the job!"

She didn't tell him that her future employer was so high-handed and rude that she wondered if she'd be able to work for him. *Imagine just telling her that she would move the next morning, without a single by-your-leave or can-you-do-it!* Apparently Daniel MacKenzie expected his employees to jump whenever he said so. It was no surprise to her that he had so much trouble keeping a cook.

But there was no point in spoiling Lee's happiness. Anyway, she had work and that was the important thing. She would be able to provide for herself and Lee and not have to sell Lee's land. And, perhaps best of all, they could move out of this tiny excuse for a house, built half below the ground and topped with sod. A sod hut might be warm and practical in this part of the country where there were almost no trees, but it smelled of dirt, and there was hardly enough room to turn around in. Sometimes, in the winters, when they were imprisoned in the hut by snow or cold weather, she had thought she would go crazy from the lack of space and privacy.

But now they would have a real house to live in. It might be small, but at least it was made out of wood. She had peeped inside it before she left MacKenzie's place, and it had two little bedrooms as well as a living area. Not only that, but it would be fun to cook big, healthy meals without having to scrimp and make do and worry about the cost.

So what if Mr. MacKenzie was rude and gruff? She could handle him—and more than him, if it meant Lee would be warm and well-fed.

Lee shouted, "Yippee!" and twirled with her enthusiastically until they were both so dizzy they had to stop. Melinda flopped down onto a chair to catch her breath.

"Oh, Mama!" Lee exclaimed. "We'll live on a ranch! I've always wanted to live on a ranch. Will he let me help with the horses and the cattle? Did you tell him I helped Daddy with the cattle a lot?"

"No. We, uh, had a rather brief conversation. He just said he'd send a man over tomorrow to help us move."

"That soon? Then I won't have to go to school tomorrow?" Lee's face brightened even more. He had little interest in books.

"No, you won't." A frown creased Melinda's brow. She wasn't sure how often he'd go to school after that, either. He would be too far away to walk to school, and he didn't have a horse to ride.

"Where will we live? In ol' MacKenzie's house?"

"That's no way to speak about your elders."

"Yes, ma'am. Well, will we?"

"No. We'll have a house of our own."

"Really? What's it like?"

"Just a small frame house."

Lee grinned, an impish dimple beside his mouth. "Then at least it's above the ground."

Melinda chuckled. Lee knew her feelings on the subject of living half below the earth. "Yes. And it has its own little porch and a bedroom for each of us."

"Really? Golly! What does MacKenzie's house look like? Is there a big barn? Did you see the horses?"

She shook her head. Horses had become one of Lee's favorite topics of conversation in the past year. One of the McClure boys rode to school on a pinto, and Lee had repeatedly described the horse to her, his voice wistful and admiring. She knew how much he wanted a pony of his own, and it hurt her that they didn't have the money for him to have one. What made it even more painful was that Lee, fully aware of their straitened circumstances, never asked her to buy him a horse. Childlike, he thought that because he didn't ask, she was unaware of how much he ached to own one.

"I didn't see any animals," she said. "But there's a big barn, and a corral. I'm sure you'll see the horses after we live there."

"Do you think he'd let me help take care of them?"

"I don't know. Perhaps, after a while, when he sees how good and careful you are."

Lee continued to talk and ask questions about their new home while Melinda settled down to work. She had to get everything ready to go by the next morning. Fortunately, there wasn't much to pack; they'd had to get rid of the bulk of their possessions four years ago, when they had moved to the Panhandle from their home in East Texas. She had only the bare minimum of pots, pans, dishes and utensils, and she already kept her blankets and linens stored in trunks.

Lee pitched in to help, taking care of most of the evening chores. They ate a quick supper. Melinda watched her son put away his food and smiled. She couldn't ask for a better son, hardworking and obedient—for the most part—yet all boy, too. He was big for his age and already beginning to take on a husky shape. He had done his best to be the man of the family for the past two years. Thank heavens, now he wouldn't have to feel as if he had the weight of the farm resting on his shoulders. He would be free to be a young, curious, active boy.

After supper, Melinda walked the mile to their nearest neighbors, the Hendersons, and asked them to look after her cow and chickens until she could sell them. Then she returned and finished packing. She had to stay up late to do it, working by the light of a wavering kerosene lamp, but at least the next morning, when two of MacKenzie's ranch hands arrived to move her things, she was ready to go. It made her feel as if she had somehow proved something to the nasty-tempered rancher himself.

The two men introduced themselves as Carl and Jimmy, and immediately set about loading her possessions into the large wagon they'd brought. Carl was a friendly sort and kept up a steady stream of conversation the whole time they were loading, telling Melinda how much the men were looking forward to having a lady cook on the premises again. Jimmy, on the other hand, only grinned at her shyly.

Lee ran in and out with the men, holding the door for them and carrying the smaller things. Melinda made coffee, and they drank it with thanks and more assurances on Carl's part that they were glad she was coming to the ranch. They finished the loading quickly, and the four of them climbed into the wagon, the two men and Lee perched on the high seat and

Melinda sitting in her rocker, securely surrounded by her possessions, in the back.

The chair faced the rear, so that she was looking at the farm as they drove away. She had lived here for four years. She thought that leaving it ought to bring a tear or two to her eyes, but it didn't. She had never had any love for this farm; her life here had not been enjoyable. She had been raised in East Texas, with its creeks and trees and the wildflowers blanketing the earth in the spring, and she had found this treeless, dusty land ugly and barren. She had seen no beauty in the reddish dirt or the flat landscape broken by gullies like wounds slashing the earth, or the dusty grays and greens of sagebrush, mesquite bushes, cacti and yuccas. She had loved Robert ever since they were children, but he hadn't been enough to assuage her loneliness at being away from all her family and friends. For the first time she and Robert, always friends, had quarreled a lot, and the sweet love of their early marriage had begun to sour. Then she had lost him entirely.

No, she didn't mind leaving here. Her only thought was that she hoped the Hendersons' daughter would remember to look after the animals.

WHEN THEY ARRIVED at the MacKenzie ranch, Melinda climbed down from the wagon and, for the first time, entered her new house. She loved it immediately. There was a hardwood floor beneath her feet, there were normal walls around her, and the ceiling was high above her head. Everything was coated with dust, of course, but with a little cleaning it would be just perfect.

While the men unhitched the wagon and unloaded the furniture, Melinda quickly swept the dust from the floors. That would have to do for the moment, but later she would scrub the floors and wax them until they gleamed, as well as wash down the counters and cabinets in the kitchen. Last, she would attack the windows with ammonia and water. She smiled, looking forward to the work. It had been so long since she'd had a proper house to work on.

She glanced out the window and saw a man emerge from the barn and walk across the yard to the ranch house. His hat was pulled low over his face against the cold, and she could see no more of it than she had been able to yesterday. But she was sure it was Daniel MacKenzie; she recognized his build and the heavy jacket he wore. He looked once toward her house. He must have seen his hired hands carrying in her belongings, but he didn't come over to greet her and welcome her to his ranch. Instead, he kept walking straight into his house.

Rude. Melinda's mouth twisted. It was obvious that he didn't intend to extend even normal courtesy toward her. She believed the stories she had heard about him hating women. He certainly seemed to have taken a dislike to her on sight. For some reason that idea made her even more determined to do an excellent job for him, to show him just how wrong he was.

When her furniture was squared away, Melinda left her house and walked across the side yard to the back door of the big house. She had plenty of work to do in her own house, and she was sure that Mr. Mac-Kenzie wouldn't expect her to start cooking this afternoon, but she wanted to take a look at the kitchen she would be using. She would be in there bright and early tomorrow morning fixing breakfast, and she wanted to know where everything was.

Melinda knocked on the door and, receiving no answer, turned the knob and walked inside. She stopped, her mouth falling open. She stared around her in disbelief. It was a big kitchen, as befitted the house, with an enormous cast-iron stove. But it was in a state that no self-respecting cook would endure. There was dust everywhere, on counters, the table, even the stove. The stove was also slick with grease and there were stains and blackish lumps scattered over it. The cabinets were in almost as poor a condition. She opened the low cabinets and found pots and pans, most of them dusty and more than one looking as if it had not been cleaned properly. She opened the pantry. There was a flour sack, almost empty, and a sugar sack that was crawling with ants. She could find no cornmeal, no baking soda, no baking powder. There were no jars of home-canned vegetables. The Irish potatoes were so old they had twisted roots growing out of them, and the jar of molasses was sticky on the outside, with only an inch of molasses remaining in the bottom. The honey had gone to sugar.

She left the pantry and simply stood, hands on hips, stunned. She couldn't believe that this was the kitchen of a wealthy, important rancher. Poor white trash wouldn't have a larder like that. How could it have gotten into such a condition?

There were footsteps in the hall, and a man entered the room. Melinda got the second shock of the afternoon. The man was Daniel MacKenzie. She recognized the jacket. But this time his hat was off, and she could see the sharp lines of his face, handsome in a rough sort of way. She could see the blue eyes, startlingly pale and bright against the tanned skin. And she could see that "ol' Daniel MacKenzie" wasn't old at all!

# Chapter Two

"WHY YOU'RE NOT OLD!" Melinda gasped without thinking, then clapped her hand to her mouth in embarrassment. Normally she would not have blurted out the first thought in her head, but his appearance had shaken her out of her usual politeness. From the way she had heard him talked about, she had assumed that Daniel MacKenzie was past his prime, but this man was definitely *in* his prime. His hair was thick and black, as was his beard, with only a sprinkling of gray in either one. Although his face was lined and weather-beaten, that was often true of men who spent their lives outdoors. It was obvious that Mr. MacKenzie was no older than forty, if that much. Melinda decided that she should have asked Mrs. Grissom, not just assumed his age. After all, she was a Texan and knew that "ol'" was a common appellation that didn't necessarily have anything to do with age.

MacKenzie's eyebrows shot up. "Indeed?" His voice was rough, almost rusty sounding, as if he didn't use it often. "Should I take that as a compliment or an insult?"

Melinda's cheeks flamed red. "I'm sorry. I just, well..." There was nothing she could think of that wouldn't make the situation even worse. "I'm sorry."

"You're not exactly what I thought, either," he admitted. His eyes swept down her. It had been only the bulky coat and the angle at which he'd looked at her that had made her look squat, he realized. Up close, he could see that she was short, but with a trim, curving figure. Her clothes were plain brown, but the blouse and skirt couldn't hide the fullness of her breasts or the narrowness of her waist. Her hair was done up in a softer style, and she didn't seem as unattractive or as old as he had thought. His lips tightened with irritation at his misjudgment. "There are eight hands, and supper's at five-thirty," he snapped, his voice sharp with his annoyance.

"What?"

"I said, supper's at five-thirty," he repeated, raising his voice. Was the woman hard of hearing or just inattentive?

"You mean—you want me to begin tonight? With supper?"

MacKenzie frowned. He wasn't an ugly man by any means, but the combination of that frown, the thick black beard and the sharp angle of his face gave him a fierce look that made her forget the general handsomeness of his features. "What the hell do you think I mean? That's what I hired you for, isn't it?"

Melinda stiffened, and her eyes flashed. "Mr. MacKenzie, may I remind you that you're in the presence of a lady?"

"What?" He looked as dumbfounded as she had felt a moment before.

"Your language," Melinda explained.

"What language?" He continued to stare; then his face cleared, and he let out a short bark of laughter.

"You mean 'hell'? Lady, if that's the worst you'll hear around here, you can count yourself lucky."

"I'm not accustomed to being sworn at."

"Then you'd better toughen up. I don't plan to let some prissy old maid censor what I say."

Prissy old maid! He managed to insult her practically every time he opened his mouth. Melinda started to retort, but clamped her lips together tightly. She couldn't afford to get this man angry. She needed the job. And she had known before she started that he would be difficult to deal with.

She drew in a breath and spoke calmly, if icily. "How you speak is, of course, your business. I am here only to cook. Presumably we shall have little need to speak to one another."

He looked a little disgruntled, as though he'd been left with nothing to say. He cleared his throat. "Yes. Right. Then, supper at five-thirty."

Melinda would have liked to give him her opinion of his high-handed ways. How could he expect her to move in and immediately begin cooking, especially in a kitchen in this condition! It was clear that he was a tyrant, the kind of employer who worked his people to death. No doubt that was why he didn't usually hire women, considering them too weak to work as hard as he required. Well, she'd been a farm girl all her life, and for the past two years she'd handled everything on her own. Daniel MacKenzie didn't know the stuff she was made of, but she intended to show him.

"Of course," she answered, her jaw clenched.

MacKenzie hesitated for a moment, feeling strangely as if he'd lost when it was crystal clear he'd won their argument. Melinda spun around and began searching through the cabinets. Behind her she heard him leave the room. When he was gone, she turned around and shot a seething look at the doorway. If she weren't a lady, she thought, she would have turned the air blue with cussing. As it was, she could only content herself with banging boxes and bottles around as she searched for the makings of supper.

She finally found an old box of baking powder. She could throw together some biscuits. And beans. There was a sack of lima beans in the pantry. Of course, to taste their best, they should be soaked all night before they were slowly simmered for a good, long time, but Melinda hadn't been cooking since she was ten without learning a few tricks. She'd let them boil full speed for a while, then simmer, and if she threw in a little salt pork and some spices, they'd be edible.

She pulled out a huge cast-iron pot and set it in the sink. There was a pump handle at the sink; indoor water was something she'd never had before. She pumped it cautiously and water trickled out. Melinda smiled and pumped harder. She scrubbed the pot thoroughly, then filled it with water and dumped in the beans. She found a rag that looked as if it had been washed in recent memory, dampened it and wiped off the stove. She would have to save a thorough cleaning for later. There wasn't time now. She stacked the wood—at least the wood box beside the stove was full—in the fire door of the stove, added some pieces of kindling, stuffed in crumpled newspaper and set it alight. Not for the first time she longed for the variety of wood they'd had back home. What she needed now were some splintered pine logs to make a quick fire. But here one didn't have a choice of oak for a long fire or pine for a quick fire. There was only mesquite wood or the little knobby logs of what was called shinnery, or, occasionally, the broken limbs that had fallen from the cottonwoods and larger oaks by the creek. She had learned to make do with what she had.

Once she had the pot of water and beans boiling, she went in search of meat. There was none in the kitchen, so she looked outside. One of the small sheds had a pipe sticking out of the roof; it must be a smokehouse. She went to the shed and opened it. Inside it smelled deliciously of meat juices and mesquite smoke, baked into the very wood of the structure. Long strings of beef jerky hung from the narrow rafters, as well as an assortment of hams, sausages, slabs of bacon and ribs. She carved off a slice of salt pork and cut down one of the large hams. Back in the kitchen, she tossed the chunk of pork into the beans and set about slicing away the thick, salted rind of the ham. Then she took out two large skillets, cleaned them and set them on the stove with a large blob of grease in each. When the grease was sizzling, she cut off thick slices of the ham and laid them in the skillets.

While the ham fried, she found a flat cookie sheet and a large mixing bowl and, after washing them, she mixed the biscuits, rolled them out and cut them with a small glass, being unable to find a tin biscuit cutter. She laid the flat biscuits on the greased sheet and popped it into the oven. She couldn't locate a tablecloth to protect the long wooden table in the kitchen, so she set the dishes on the table itself. It had obviously been eaten on that way before, judging by the stains, scars and burned rings on the wood surface. She only wiped the dishes, not having the time to wash them thoroughly. Presumably the men had eaten on them in this condition before; once more wouldn't hurt.

She put the food in serving dishes and set it on the table, then turned her attention to brewing a pot of coffee. Last, she made a big bowl of red-eye gravy from the meat drippings left in the skillets. She was carrying it to the table, holding it with her skirts in lieu of cloth holders, when she heard the scrape of boots on the steps outside, and the cowhands began to stream in the door.

The first one in was Carl, and he grinned and sniffed the air appreciatively. "Oh, ma'am..." he breathed. "I knew I was going to like you the minute I set eyes on you."

One by one the men filed in after him. Like Carl, they were dressed in heavy flannel shirts, denim trousers and jackets and dirty, work-scarred boots. Two pairs of boots clanked with spurs. Mentally cringing, Melinda thought of what the spurs must be doing to the wooden floors. Now she understood why the floors were so pitted and gouged. All the men pulled off their hats, smiling at her, some shyly and others boldly. Melinda smiled at the shy ones and favored the bold ones with a cool stare that soon had them dropping their gaze. There were eight of them in various sizes and shapes, some with beards or mustaches and some without, hair and eyes in all shades, but all of them were hard, spare and browned by the sun into a kind of sameness.

They introduced themselves to her politely, but their eyes kept sliding over to the table. Melinda smiled. "Go ahead and sit down. Would anyone like some coffee?"

"Yes, ma'am." They were quick to follow her suggestion, scrambling for seats at the table.

Most of them wanted coffee, and she went around the table, pouring the coffee from the enameled pot, a small rag wrapped around the handle to keep it from burning her fingers. The men dug into the food without ceremony, heaping their plates. They began to eat, and all around the table came a chorus of, "This sure is good, ma'am," and, "Awful good cooking, ma'am."

The inner door opened, and Mr. MacKenzie stepped into the room. The hands barely paused in their eating to glance up and nod. MacKenzie looked at the table, and Melinda thought she saw a gleam of interest enter his eyes. He sat down and speared a piece of ham, then ladled red-eye gravy on top of it. Like the others, he cut open two biscuits and doused them with the gravy, then began to eat. Melinda waited expectantly for him to tell her it was good, as the others had. He didn't say a word.

Melinda walked over to him. He looked up questioningly, and she resisted the urge to dump the coffee in his lap. Instead she smiled stiffly and asked, "Coffee, Mr. MacKenzie?"

"Sure." He held out his cup. When she had filled it, he returned to his eating.

Melinda set the pot on the table and went to the sink. She set a large dishpan in it and pumped it half full of water, adding a few chips of soap, then began to wash the pots and pans she had used to cook in. Earlier, before the men had come in, she had prudently set aside two plates of food for herself and Lee. They would eat when the men had left. She had not been asked to join them, and she would never think of plopping herself down at a table full of men uninvited.

It didn't take the men long to finish. They went through the food like a swarm of locusts through a wheat field, and there were several hopeful inquiries as to whether there were any more biscuits. Obviously she would have to make more biscuits next time. The men sat back, chatting, enjoying their last sips of coffee.

"Sorry there wasn't any time to make dessert," Melinda apologized as she began to pick up their plates and carry them to the counter.

"Oh, ma'am, this was wonderful," Carl assured her, and there was a general chorus of assent. Melinda was watching Daniel out of the corner of her eye, and she noticed that he made no comment. He was probably blaming her for not being able to whip up a nice apple pie in the past hour, too.

One of the younger men jumped up to help her clear the table, and she smiled and thanked him. Two of the others quickly rose to help. MacKenzie stood up.

Just at that moment, the back door burst open, and Lee tumbled in. "Mama? Can I eat yet? I'm about to starve."

Melinda held up an admonishing hand. "Quietly, Lee. And it's 'May I eat?' Just let me get the table cleared."

"You have a son?" MacKenzie's voice was quiet in a way that stopped all movement and chatter in the room.

Melinda turned, her stomach doing flip-flops, her fingers curling into her skirts. "Yes."

"You didn't say you had a boy." Her employer's face was hard and cold.

Melinda swallowed. She thought he would have looked the same way if he had accused her of being a thief. "You didn't ask me. I presumed it wasn't a matter of importance."

The cowhands began to stir, reaching for their hats and mumbling their thanks, shuffling out the door. Melinda wondered whether their departure meant they judged the threat of storm to be over—or just beginning. Lee came up beside Melinda, and she sensed protectiveness as well as fear in the rigid set of his body.

"I wouldn't have hired you if I'd known you had a child," MacKenzie said flatly.

Melinda bridled. "Lee's a good boy. He'll be no trouble to you or anyone else."

"I don't want children in this house."

Tears sprang into Melinda's eyes. She wasn't sure whether they were from anger or hurt. Maybe it was both. Her voice trembled despite her effort to keep it even. "Then I promise you that Lee won't set foot inside it again. My son and I will take our meals in my house."

She whirled and strode toward the door, pulling Lee along with her. She twisted the doorknob and pulled the door open, but MacKenzie was there in front of her, his hand flat on the door, pushing it shut.

"Don't be any more of an idiot than you have to be. I'm not exiling you to your house."

Melinda lifted her chin and stared straight at him. She refused to let this man intimidate her, especially when it came to her son. "No? Then what are you doing? Telling me I can no longer work here?"

Daniel looked at her. He would have liked to tell her exactly that. "No children" was a rule that was never broken in his house. Even Will's children kept scrupulously out of his way. This woman was already a burr under his saddle. He knew life would be easier without her. He felt tricked and deceived. She was younger and shapelier than he'd thought. She had a child. And her eyes were huge and a clear, soft gray, rimmed with thick lashes. They were lovely eyes, even if they were too big in her thin face.

His mouth twisted, and for a moment Melinda thought he would tell her to leave the ranch. But instead he sighed gustily and turned away, muttering, "Hellfire and damnation!" He stalked off toward the door, then swung back. "No, I'm not telling you you can't work here. My men would probably rise up in riot, after that meal tonight." He would never tell her so, but even he, who usually didn't care what he ate, found his mouth watering at the thought of her next meal. "You can stay. But I don't want him underfoot. Is that understood?"

"Perfectly." Melinda kept her expression as cool and regal as she could make it. MacKenzie looked at her for a moment, then jammed his hands into his pockets and walked out of the room, muttering again.

Lee turned his wide eyes up to his mother. "Mama, what's the matter with him?"

"I haven't the slightest idea," she replied crossly. "I think maybe he was just born mean. But I'll tell you one thing. We're going to save every penny I make, because you and I aren't going to stay here a day longer than we have to!"

MELINDA AROSE EARLY the next morning. The sky was still dark when she left her house and walked across the cold yard to the big house. Work began early out here, and the person who cooked breakfast had to be the first one up. She slipped softly into the house and laid the fire in the stove, then prepared the biscuits and coffee. While the stove heated, she went back to her house and shook Lee awake, instructing him to go to the barn and milk the cow while she gathered the eggs. He nodded, rubbing his eyes sleepily, and obediently climbed out of bed.

Melinda walked to the dilapidated chicken coop, swinging the basket she had brought from her kitchen. Stooping, she opened the door and stepped inside. There was only a trace of the pungent odor of a henhouse. And there were no hens sitting in straw. In fact, there wasn't any straw. She glanced around. No chickens? No eggs?

She stepped out and surveyed the yard. There was no other building that could be the chicken coop.

Shaking her head, she went to the smokehouse. Obviously there was going to be nothing but meat this morning, so she took a large slab of bacon as well as two rolls of sausage.

As she walked to the house with the food, Lee ran up to her. "Mama! Mama! You won't believe this, but I promise it's the truth. I looked all over that barn, and there's no milch cow."

"No cow?"

He shook his head. "I swear. I checked every last stall."

"Don't swear," she replied automatically. "I believe you, sweetheart. This place is a disgrace."

She whipped up a respectable breakfast of bacon, sausage and biscuits. Once again, the men gulped it all down and told her how good it was. "Eatin's never been this good on this place," one of them commented. Mr. MacKenzie didn't say a word.

After the men had left, Melinda opened the door from the kitchen to the rest of the house and walked inside. She felt vaguely guilty as she walked down the hall, as though she was sneaking in somewhere she didn't belong. The house was so still and quiet it was unnerving. She found herself walking on tiptoe.

With a grimace, she stopped herself and firmly set her heels on the floor. She had a right to be here; after all, Mr. MacKenzie had hired her to clean the house as well as cook.

Something felt gritty beneath her feet, and she glanced down. There was dried mud on the floor. There was also dust along the baseboards, and in the corner she spotted a cobweb. Automatically she looked up. Yes, cobwebs in the corners of the ceiling, too. She opened one of the closed doors lining the hallway, thinking that it wouldn't be so gloomy if only MacKenzie would open the place up a bit.

The room was dark, shrouded with heavy drapes. Melinda crossed the room and opened them. Dust fell on her, making her cough. The windows behind them were dirty, but at least they let in the light. She glanced around the room and shook her head in disbelief. No wonder MacKenzie kept the room closed up; the sight of it would horrify anyone. It was a formal dining room, obviously unused. Dust coated every piece of furniture, and she could see the tracks of her feet in the dust on the floor. Cobwebs decorated the baseboards, ceilings and legs of the furniture. A glass chandelier hung over the massive dining table, dulled by an accumulation of dust and tangled with cobwebs.

She plopped down on a chair, and a puff of dust rose up from it. Melinda hopped up and wiped at the dirt on her dress. Anger rose in her. The place was furnished beautifully. The table was mahogany under its coat of dust, and the drapes were velvet. The rug that covered the center of the room was Persian. It was a crime to let everything go to ruin like this!

She went through the rest of the downstairs, fueling her anger. It was all in as bad a state as the kitchen was. The leather couch in the sitting room had a rent in it, no doubt from a careless spur. The draperies were thick with dust—as was every other surface in the house. The floors didn't look as if they'd been waxed in years—or even cleaned, probably. She didn't have the heart to go upstairs.

How could even Mr. MacKenzie neglect a lovely house so? His solution to the mess seemed to be to close the doors.

The last straw was when she discovered mouse droppings in the parlor around a chair, then found that the mice had chewed through the cushion of the chair, no doubt to make a nest. It was a chair that was covered in what had once been beautiful, expensive damask.

Melinda made a noise of frustration deep in her throat and charged out the side door, grabbing her coat as she went. A glance at the hill showed her that MacKenzie wasn't working on the windmill today. She strode across the yard and into the barn.

"Mr. MacKenzie? Mr. MacKenzie!" He wasn't in there, either. She went out and looked around, shielding her eyes. She caught sight of him standing by the corral, one foot on a slat of the fence, watching the horses milling around. Two men stood beside him— one of the hands who'd eaten her breakfast and a man she'd never seen before.

Melinda marched toward them. "Mr. Mac-Kenzie!"

All three men swiveled to look at her. Daniel MacKenzie's eyes widened, and he couldn't keep a grin from sneaking across his face. His new housekeeper was stomping toward him with the light of battle in her eyes, but the effect was spoiled by the coat hanging ludicrously big on her, its sleeves so long her hands disappeared, and by the fact that her face was smudged with dirt and her hair was tangled and coated with dust, half of it falling out of its careful roll.

Beside Daniel, Will Moore, the foreman, murmured, "That woman looks madder'n a wet hen."

"She's riled about something," Strack, the hand, agreed on the other side of him.

"I believe I have some work to do back at the house," Will decided. He'd seen that look in his own Lula's eyes, and he wasn't about to stick around to catch a lecture that didn't even belong to him.

"Uh, yeah." Strack sidled away. "Just remembered something I gotta do in the barn."

"Cowards," MacKenzie muttered as the two men melted away. The grin kept twitching onto his face, and he felt a certain sense of anticipation as he straightened, facing her.

Melinda saw the grin, and it stoked the fires of her irritation. What in the world did he find funny when she was so mad she could spit? She stopped two feet away from Daniel and planted her hands on her hips. "Mr. MacKenzie, your house is a disgrace!"

"I beg your pardon?"

"You have a beautiful house, and you've let it fall to rack and ruin. I've never seen such a pitiful sight."

"I'm sorry it doesn't meet with your approval," he commented dryly.

"It wouldn't meet with anyone's approval, unless they were blind! It's filthy! How you could allow a lovely place to get into such a state, I'll never know. There are mice—mice!—setting up house in your front parlor! And your kitchen is deplorable. You don't have the most basic staples. The flour is gone, the potatoes have sprouts as long as my hand, and the sugar is swarming with ants. There are no chickens in your henhouse, no milch cow in your barn, and not a single canned vegetable or even a jar of fruit preserves anywhere! How do you expect me to cook a meal? I couldn't even feed one person supper tonight, let alone a whole ranch full!''

''Why the devil do you think I hired you?'' MacKenzie retorted. ''Clean the damn place!''

''I don't have anything to clean *with*! There's not a single bottle of ammonia in the house. It's obvious that there hasn't been in quite a while. There's no wax, no—''

''Then get some! Get all the flour and whatever else you want. What are you crying to me for? You're the one who's in charge of all that. Make a list of what you need and give it to one of the men, or have one of them drive you into town.''

Melinda opened her mouth to say something, then stopped. She was still sizzling, and she would have liked to continue to argue, but she realized that Daniel had pulled the rug out from under her. She had expected him to grumble and gripe about having to buy a whole batch of supplies, to defend the state of his house and larder. Instead, he'd simply told her to buy whatever she needed, somehow making it sound as if she were incompetent. It was completely irritating. ''I still need some hens and a cow,'' she said finally, her expression mulish.

He grinned again. She looked just like a little girl who'd been caught grubbing in the dirt. ''Then get them. I'm sure somebody around Barrett has a few chickens and a cow for sale.''

She thought of her own livestock. ''Well, actually, I have some back at my farm.''

''Then send one of the hands for them. Now, are we finished? May I return to work?''

Melinda's eyes flickered toward the corral. She would hardly call standing around watching a bunch of horses ''work.'' But she swallowed her words and said only, ''Certainly,'' in a voice like ice. She swung around and walked away, lifting her skirts up a little from the ground.

MacKenzie stood watching her until she reached the house. He wished the jacket she wore weren't quite so concealing. Then, catching the direction of his thoughts, he turned to the corral, scowling.

# Chapter Three

MELINDA STORMED into the kitchen, closing the door after her with a resounding thud. She would have liked to shake it off its hinges. Daniel MacKenzie was an infuriating man.

She went around the kitchen, jerking open one drawer after another, searching for paper and a pencil to write the list of goods she needed from town. Typically, she could find nothing. Finally she stormed out and went across the yard to her own house, where she dug a sheet of paper and a small pencil stub out of the bottom drawer of the dresser in her room. She straightened up, glancing into the mirror above her dresser as she did so. What she saw there stopped her in her tracks.

A wild woman stared back at her, eyes wide with horror. Her hair was twisted and tangled, half undone and covered with dust. There were smudges of dirt on her forehead and cheeks. No wonder Mr. MacKenzie had kept smiling. It was a wonder he hadn't burst out laughing! She thought of how she had stood there, ranting at him about the untidiness of his house, and all the time she had looked like this!

She stared at herself, her anger wavering, and suddenly she began to laugh. She laughed until her sides hurt and she had to wrap her arms around herself and struggle to regain her breath. She sank down on the floor, giving herself up to her hilarity. Finally her laughter subsided, and she leaned against the dresser. The tension of the last two days had drained out of her, along with her anger.

Melinda sighed. Mr. MacKenzie was right. It was her job to get things in order; that was what he had hired her for. Naturally he would expect her to purchase whatever she needed. It would be fun, actually, to stock a kitchen from scratch without having to worry about pinching pennies.

She cleaned herself and redid her hair. Next she went to her own kitchen and got an apron, a few dishcloths and her basket of cleaning materials. She wasn't about to wait for MacKenzie's hand to get back from town with the supplies before she started cleaning that house.

She returned to the big house and drew up a long list of urgently needed supplies. She gave the list to Carl and instructed him to go out to her farm afterward and bring back the chickens and the milch cow. With that done, it was time to attack the kitchen.

Soon the kitchen was filled with the acrid scent of ammonia. First she cleaned away years of accumulated grease, dirt and burned food from the huge iron stove. Next she scrubbed the cabinets, pantry shelves and counters. Finally she tackled the floor, getting down on her hands and knees with a tough-bristled brush and working carefully over the entire floor. By the time she finished, she ached all over and her head hurt from the ammonia fumes, but the kitchen was gleaming. Wearily she took her last panful of ammonia water outside and dumped it in the yard. As she did so, she saw a woman walking across the yard toward her. She was tall and raw-boned, with a cheerful, lively face.

The woman called and waved a hand, and Melinda waved back. "Come in and visit." She would be glad for the chance to rest and chat.

The woman climbed the three wooden steps to the small side porch. "I'm Lula Moore, the foreman's wife."

"Mrs. Moore. It's a pleasure to meet you. I'm Melinda Ballard."

"Call me Lula. We'll get to know each other well enough. We're the only women for miles around."

Melinda opened the door and ushered Lula inside. Lula stared around the kitchen in amazement, then let out an unladylike whistle. "Land o' Goshen, girl, you've managed a miracle!"

Melinda chuckled. Only another woman would appreciate what cleaning up this kitchen had involved. "Thank you." She put a pot of coffee onto the stove to brew, and she and Lula sat down at the table, smiling at each other. "It will be wonderful to have a woman close by."

"Isn't that the truth? Sometimes I get so tired of nothing but men and young 'uns and cows that I could scream." Lula grinned at her conspiratorially. "I didn't plan on coming over this morning. I was going to let you settle in first. But then Will told me about that fight you had with Mr. MacKenzie, and I just had to come up and meet you. I've never met a lady—or many men, for that matter—brave enough to take on Daniel MacKenzie."

Color rose in Melinda's cheeks. "Oh, dear. You must think I'm awful, creating a scene like that. I should have waited to speak to him in private. My wretched temper got the better of me. It's not the first time."

Mrs. Moore chuckled. "Don't go apologizing for it! It's the best thing that's happened on this ranch since Jimmy killed a seven-foot rattler. It's the first time Daniel's ever met a woman who'll stand up to him. I remember when Will and I first came here, there were about three women housekeepers in a row, and when Daniel barked at them, they just cried or quit, or both. They say there was one who was tough enough to tell him off, but she got so disgusted that she up and left. She said she didn't plan to spoil her widowhood arguing with another man."

The two women giggled. "That's why it's been men up here ever since."

"I know," Melinda commented dryly. "I could tell from the condition of the house."

Lula shook her head. "Poor thing. I don't envy you cleaning it up. Tell you what, I'll send my oldest girl, Opal, up here to help you for a couple of days."

"That's very kind of you."

Lula made a dismissive gesture. "No trouble at all."

The coffee finished brewing, and Melinda got up to pour them each a cup. For a moment they were quiet as they sipped their coffee, but Lula Moore wasn't one to let a silence last long. Soon they were talking about their children, the ranch, Lula's husband and whatever else came to their minds. Before long the conversation turned naturally to Daniel MacKenzie. Melinda related how harshly he had reacted to finding out that she had a child.

Lula shook her head, her face sad. "He's got no fondness for children, that's a fact. But it isn't that Daniel's mean, or that he's got anything against your boy. It's just—well, I don't mean to gossip, but I reckon you ought to know about Daniel, so you'll understand. Maybe you won't get so riled up about the things he does and says if you know what happened to him."

Melinda's eyes widened. "What happened?" Her voice lowered, and she leaned forward, as did Mrs. Moore.

"Well, this took place a long time before Will and I came here, so I only heard the story secondhand myself. Daniel was one of the first ones to settle in the Panhandle, way back in the late seventies. He was a young man, not even twenty. His father was a wealthy man back East, I understand, and he sent Daniel to stay with some cousins who had a ranch south of here. Daniel had always been kind of sickly, and—"

"Sickly?" Melinda echoed in astonishment, seeing MacKenzie's broad shoulders in her mind's eye.

"Hard to imagine, isn't it? He's tough as a cedar post now. Apparently fresh air and sunshine and plenty of hard work were what he needed. He loved it here and decided to stay. He bought some land and started ranching. He worked for years, building it up, buying more and more land, until the Lazy M is one of the biggest ranches around. Not like the XIT, of course, but big and prosperous. His father died when Daniel was about twenty-eight or so, and he went to the funeral and to settle the estate and all, and he stayed there a few months. Well, while he was back East, he fell in love."

"Mr. MacKenzie?" That was another thing Melinda had trouble believing. She couldn't picture him as anything but angry or remote.

Lula nodded, smiling, caught up in her romantic story. "They say she was beautiful, blond and dainty, like a porcelain doll, and she dressed in the most beautiful clothes. Daniel got engaged to her, and he came back to the ranch and built this house for her. Brought in lumber, fancy chandeliers, expensive furniture. He didn't spare any expense, and of course he could afford it. So he married her and brought her home. That must have been, oh, ten years ago, about 1885. There still weren't a lot of people living around Barrett."

"What happened to her?" Melinda asked, thinking of the beautiful, fragile young girl, dressed in elegant laces, satins and velvets. No doubt she had come from a wealthy, sheltered background in some cool, green flowering place back East. What must she have thought when she arrived in the Panhandle and found this flat, empty land? How had she felt when she heard the wind whining around the corners of the house, or saw the snow driving down endlessly in a blizzard? Melinda was washed with pity for the girl. No matter how much she had loved Daniel—another thing Melinda found difficult to envision—she must have been lonely and unhappy.

"Well, for two or three years, they were happy. They were young and in love. She had a baby, a little boy, and they say Daniel was mad about the child. He carried him with him everywhere and was always talking about teaching him to ride when he was older and showing him the ranch and all. But when the baby was only three years old, Daniel's wife went into town one day in winter. It started to snow real hard, and they should have stayed in town, but the girl insisted they leave for the ranch. She was sure they could make it before the snow got bad, and she didn't want to be separated from her baby. It was a servant she'd brought out from the East who was driving her, so he didn't know any better than she did. They set out, and the snow turned into a blizzard. They drove off the road, and when Daniel and the men found them, they'd both frozen to death."

"Oh, no!" Melinda felt tears starting in her eyes for the girl she hadn't known, but for whom she felt much sympathy. "The poor thing."

Lula nodded. "Yes, but that wasn't the worst. That very same winter, only a month or so afterward, the baby got pneumonia and died, too."

"That poor man." Melinda's heart stirred with pain and empathy for Daniel MacKenzie.

"It was a terrible tragedy. It scarred him. They say he's been sour on life ever since. That's why he never married again and why he can't bear to have children around."

"Oh, yes." Tears glimmered in Melinda's eyes. She was a woman of ready feeling, and if her temper was often right below the surface, so were warmth and sympathy. "I can understand." She had often thought that if Lee died, she would not be able to bear it. She had been delivered of a stillborn child once, and it had almost broken her heart.

Besides, he had lost both a child and a wife. Daniel MacKenzie was a man to be pitied, not disliked. Now that Melinda knew about his past, it was much easier to understand him—and not to blame him. No wonder he had closed off those beautiful rooms with the elegant furnishings he had bought for his beloved bride! No wonder he didn't want women and children around!

"Thank you for telling me," Melinda said to Lula. "It explains so much."

Lula nodded. "Yes. It's a sad story." She sighed. "So tragic. So beautiful and romantic."

Melinda wasn't sure how beautiful and romantic it was to have one's life wrecked by the deaths of a beloved wife and child, but it was certainly tragic. From now on, she vowed, she would have more patience with Mr. MacKenzie. She wouldn't let herself be wounded by his gruffness or lack of gratitude. She would keep a lid on her temper and not blurt out the first thing that came into her head, as she was wont to do. She would keep Lee out of his way, and she would try to steer clear of anything that would remind Mr. MacKenzie of his loss. It might not be easy at times, but she was sure that with patience and perseverance, she could bring about a more comfortable relationship between herself and her employer.

WHEN CARL RETURNED in the middle of the afternoon with Melinda's supplies, she stored them away happily in the spotless kitchen. It gave her a feeling of pride, almost of ownership, to see the results of her labor, as if her work had somehow made the place her own. Then she set to work on supper, whipping up a huge meal of chicken-fried steak, mashed potatoes, gravy, biscuits and a mess of greens. There was even time to make a deep-dish apple cobbler for dessert. She had found a clean oilcloth during her cleaning, and she laid it on the table before she set it. It wasn't very attractive, but at least it would protect the table from further scarring.

When the men came in, the way they sniffed the air and closed their eyes in a pantomime of ecstasy was enough to make her fast, furious efforts worthwhile. Many of them noticed the change in the condition of the kitchen. Even Daniel glanced around the room in a bemused way, then dug into his food with a hearty appetite. He had a second helping of the cobbler, too, she noticed, though, typically, he didn't say a word of thanks or praise. The other men made up for that, however, lauding her cooking skills until she had to laugh and blush at their extravagances.

The next morning after breakfast Melinda made bread. After first mixing, then kneading, she finally stuffed the dough into bread pans and set it aside to rise, covered with dishcloths, while she prepared the noon meal. When the bread had risen, she adjusted the oven to exactly the right temperature through the judicious use of wood and the damper, then put the loaves in to bake to a golden brown. While they were cooking, she started on her second batch, this one of sourdough loaves and rolls, made from the starter that she had brought with her from her own house.

When the hands trooped in for the noon meal, they found a platter of succulent roast beef, a bowl of brown gravy made from its drippings, a platter of sourdough rolls and a sliced loaf of golden-brown bread, both fresh from the oven and smelling heavenly, as well as bowls of potatoes, carrots and green beans. To top it all off, there were two sweet-potato pies on the counter, cooling.

The men attacked the food as if it had been weeks since they'd eaten. Melinda went around the table filling up their coffee cups, then returned to the counter to slice the pies and dish them up onto dessert plates. She also put a second pot of coffee on to brew, having learned that the men used up one pot quickly and wanted another to drink with their dessert. She glanced at the table and saw that the bread was gone, so she took another loaf, sliced it and carried it over.

She picked up an empty serving bowl and was just turning away to carry it to the counter when Mac-Kenzie's voice stopped her. "Why the devil do you keep jumping back and forth? Sit down and eat."

Melinda assumed that this was Daniel's ungracious way of issuing her an invitation to eat with them. She faced him and replied calmly, "I'll eat after you all have finished."

He grimaced. "Stop sulking and sit down and eat. I don't have the foggiest idea what you're mad about, so your show is wasted."

"Sulking!" Melinda's eyes flashed, and she set the serving dish on the table with a clatter. "I am not sulking. My job is to cook, not to eat with you!"

Daniel glared at her. "Well, you've finished cooking. Why the hell won't you eat like everybody else?"

"An employee doesn't just plop herself down to eat at the same table with her employer if she hasn't been asked."

"I'm asking you now!" he roared.

Melinda set her hands on her hips pugnaciously. Daniel's own hands were clenched tightly around his knife and fork. They leaned forward, each one's eyes boring into the other. All around the table, the men watched interestedly. It wasn't often that they had a delicious meal as well as a bang-up fight.

"And I refuse," Melinda replied. "I am free to eat whenever I please, and I'll wait to eat with Lee."

"Lee? Who's Lee? There's no one—"

"My son." Melinda clenched her jaw, waiting for him to fly off the handle again about her child. She didn't care if he did have a tragic history, if he said so much as one bad thing about Lee, she'd—

"The boy?" Daniel's eyebrows lifted in surprise. Then he scowled. "What the devil is he doing out of school in the middle of the day?"

"It's too far for him to walk!" Melinda snapped. She waited, her heart in her throat, for MacKenzie's suggestion that she board him in town during the week. It was what some people did who lived too far away from the school. But Melinda couldn't bear to have him gone that much.

"Well, for—" Daniel began in exasperation. "Why didn't you say anything about it?" He glanced down the length of the table. "Jimmy, find a horse for the boy to ride." He glanced up at Melinda. "Can he ride?"

"A little." His father had started to teach him, but after his death, they'd had to sell the horse.

MacKenzie turned back to Jimmy. "Give him a gentle one. And teach him to ride."

Melinda stood looking at him, dumbstruck by his generosity. Of course, lending one horse probably wasn't much to a man who owned as many as Daniel MacKenzie. But considering how he felt about Lee's being here, it was amazing. It would mean so much to Lee to have a horse to ride and someone to teach him. "Thank you," she said, her voice low and earnest. "That's very kind of you."

MacKenzie waved away her thanks, looking slightly embarrassed.

Later, when dinner was over and the other men had left, MacKenzie lingered behind. He held his hat in his hands, sliding it around and around through his fingers, and he kept looking down at it as though it held some wisdom. Melinda glanced at him questioningly. First generous, then embarrassed, now ill at ease. She would never have imagined Daniel MacKenzie being any of those things. What had come over him?

"Mrs. Ballard..."

"Yes?"

"I'm not a tyrant."

"I beg your pardon?"

"I wouldn't make a woman and a little boy wait to eat until the rest of us are finished. What I said the other day—well, I didn't mean he couldn't sit at the same table with me. I just—"

Knowing what had happened to him, Melinda's heart was touched with sympathy. "I understand."

"Do you?" His words sounded bitter.

"I think so. After Lee, I had a stillborn baby."

His eyes narrowed, and his face, which had looked almost human before, turned cold and closed. He made no comment on her words, just snapped, "I expect you and the boy to eat at the table with the rest of us. Is that understood?"

Melinda resisted an urge to salute. His reaction had squelched her sympathy. It was like offering friendship to a porcupine. "Yes. Perfectly. And 'the boy' is named Lee."

Daniel didn't reply, but simply walked out of the kitchen.

AFTER DINNER, Lula's daughter Opal arrived, as promised, and they started cleaning the house. It was a lengthy process and one that took several days to complete thoroughly. They swept, mopped and waxed the hardwood floors until they gleamed. They dusted and polished the furniture and the banister on the stairs. All the baseboards and windowsills were washed. The rugs, both elegant Persians and simple braided ones, were carried out and the dust beaten from them. The drapes were taken down and treated in the same fashion. They dusted the valances and all the cobweb-holding corners of the rooms. Every dish in the china cabinet and every knickknack on the tables and mantels was washed thoroughly, as were the windows. Melinda even had one of the hands take down the crystal chandelier in the dining room, and she washed each delicate prism until it sparkled.

One by one she opened the rooms as they finished cleaning them. She drew back the heavy draperies so that the sunlight could stream through the now-sparkling windows, giving the house light and warmth. She waited warily for some comment from Mac-Kenzie about her opening the rooms he had closed off, but he said nothing about it.

They started on the second floor. The only bed-room that was actually used was Mr. MacKenzie's, so Melinda set about making it habitable first. It gave her an odd feeling to enter a man's bedroom, as though she were doing something slightly wicked and excit-ing, despite the fact that she had a perfectly legiti-mate reason to be there. It was even more peculiar to wash his clothes, to handle the shirts that had lain next to his skin or the sheets upon which he slept. His things still smelled faintly of his scent, a mixture of horse, tobacco, sweat and leather, and she found it disturbing—but not exactly in a bad way.

There was a kind of intimacy implied in the task, as there was in entering his room. He was a stranger to her, really, yet she knew how his bedroom was ar-ranged and where his brush and comb lay on the bu-reau. She had ironed his shirts, and she had seen the indentation where his head had lain upon his pillow. It gave her a funny, shivery feeling.

After Mr. MacKenzie's bedroom, they cleaned the upstairs rooms one by one, leaving them in the same pristine condition as the lower floor. Melinda drew back the curtains and drapes and opened the doors into the hall, so that it was no longer a gloomy tunnel. The only exception was the second room down the hall from MacKenzie's. The day she opened its door, tears sprang into her eyes. It had obviously been a small child's room. There was a small bed, and in one corner sat a cradle. A rocking horse stood in the center of the room, carved out of oak and beautifully painted. A tarnished silver-backed baby brush and comb lay on a tray on the dresser, and there was a wooden spinning top on the chest of drawers. A painting of a child at his prayers hung on one wall.

Melinda swallowed hard and set about dusting and cleaning the room. After that, she always made sure the room was kept clean. But she left its door closed, as it had been for years.

# *Chapter Four*

DANIEL MACKENZIE was aware of the house changing around him. At first it was only the food. Once they had eaten dry, tasteless stuff, sometimes burned, at other times almost raw, even now and then bizarrely both, but now, instead, their meals were delicious and savory. The vegetables were seasoned and not boiled to death; the rolls were light and flaky and not black on the bottom; the sourdough biscuits practically melted in his mouth and were accompanied by pale yellow butter in molds.

They continued the custom of slaughtering a steer every week for the large ranch population, but in the past the men had barbecued the animal and eaten the barbecue every night for a few days. But now they cut up the beef and stored it in the cool cellar dug into the side of the windmill hill, and Melinda cooked several different, interesting meals from it—barbecued ribs and briskets, stew, roast, pan-fried steaks, ground hash, pieces of round steak breaded and fried. There was always some kind of gravy from the meat drippings, too. Now and then, just for variety, she served up fried chicken or maybe a ham or fried pork chops. The crowning touch, always, was one of her sweet desserts, like apple dumplings or big pale sugar cookies or sweet-potato pone.

The men made pigs of themselves—including himself, Daniel was forced to admit. Meals were a delight to be looked forward to now, not simply a chore to get through in order to fill an empty belly. And it wasn't only the food. There was something about having a lady at the table. Suddenly the men were coming to the kitchen scrubbed and clean, and their language improved. They made an effort to keep the conversation interesting, instead of just discussing their work. It was pleasant to look down the table and see Melinda's pretty face and soft form, to hear her quiet laughter over some joke. It made Daniel feel a little confused and disturbed, yet he always looked forward to seeing her.

Then she started changing the house. He was so used to the place being dark and closed up, as his insides had been since the day Matthew died, that at first he didn't notice the difference, just walked through the house and out without glancing around. But gradually he began to notice that the place was somehow lighter. He began to look around, and he saw the scrubbed and shiny floors. He saw the rooms opening up, more every day, clean and filled with light. He glanced around him at the gleaming fine wood and the sparkling glass of the chandelier and oil lamps; he stared through the spotless windows at the unending stretch of land outside them.

The house was once again as clean and rich as it had been when Millicent was alive and had her servants scurrying around—except that there was more light, for Millicent had hated the sight of the flat land outside and had kept the heavy curtains drawn. The sun hurt the furniture, she said, and perhaps it did, but there was such freedom in being able to look out and see clear to the horizon. Nor was the house as formal as when Millicent had been there, when Daniel had felt uneasy about setting a cigar down in one of the elegant china or glass dishes and had always seemed to be stumbling over some maid or other.

Daniel told himself that he didn't like the way Mrs. Ballard had changed the house. She was pushy, a bossy female who took too much on herself and didn't know when to keep her mouth shut. None of his other women housekeepers had dared to argue with him or to tell him he was in the wrong. Unfortunately, those women, like Millicent, had had a remarkable tendency to cry over the slightest complaint or terse order, or to tighten up and get that wounded female look on their faces, as if he were a snake that they were forced to put up with. He had always felt guilty after he yelled at them and, perversely, that had made him even angrier.

But with Melinda, there was something enjoyable about exchanging hot words. Afterward he felt a pleasant sense of release, and he found himself thinking back on what she'd said and how her eyes had flashed, and he smiled. He wasn't left feeling as if he was a brute who had picked on a weaker creature. Melinda Ballard could stand toe to toe with the best of them, he thought, and as like as not come out on top. It seemed crazy, and he didn't like to admit it, but he rather enjoyed arguing with her.

If he was honest, he had to admit that part of that enjoyment was in seeing her fire up. Her big gray eyes turned so clear and sparkling, in contrast to their usual softness, and her cheeks flushed with color. There was always an electricity about her when she got her back up, and he was reminded of those hot, velvet black nights in the summer when lightning crackled across the sky in the distance.

But then, she was a pleasure to look at anytime. She had changed almost as much as the house. Proper nutrition and an abundance of food had taken away the gauntness in her cheeks and put back the natural luster of her hair and the tone of her skin. In a matter of weeks she had gone from being a woman he thought old and plain enough to be his housekeeper to being a young woman who was too lovely for him to feel comfortable with her around all the time.

He found himself thinking about her far too often—in the day while he worked, in the evening when he read or caught up on his book work, at night as he lay in his bed, trying to go to sleep. In his mind, she was Melinda, not Mrs. Ballard, and he was afraid he would slip and speak to her too familiarly. He day-dreamed about her big gray eyes and her rich brown hair, worn now in a softer, fuller style that made his hands itch to touch it. He thought about the womanly curves of her body, the full breasts and little waist, the swell of her hips hidden beneath her full skirts. At night his thoughts turned downright inde-cent, imagining what her legs looked like beneath her skirt or picturing her clad in only a lacy chemise that barely covered her breasts, veiling but not concealing the deep rose-brown circles of her nipples.

It was a mistake to start thinking about her like that, because then he couldn't stop. He couldn't work, couldn't think, and he would lie awake for hours. Invariably the next morning he was at his crabbiest, barking at everyone, but especially at Melinda.

It irritated him excessively that he should feel desire for her. It wasn't as if she displayed any interest in him. Indeed, unlike most of the younger housekeepers he had hired, she hadn't shot him a single coy look or given him a flirtatious smile. She hadn't even tried to maneuver him into a situation where they were alone. Besides, even if she had seemed to like him, he couldn't have let himself take advantage of a woman who was both under his protection and under his power—though, God knows, one would never know it by the way she acted!

So he could not have a brief, purely physical encounter with her, and he certainly wouldn't consider anything more than that with any woman, no matter how desirable she was. He had tried marriage once, and he was positive that the state was not for him. He had neither the patience nor the good temper to live with a woman, and he had found out with Millicent how quickly the sheer veil of love was ripped away by the struggle of daily living.

And, as if Melinda wasn't bothersome enough, there was her boy. Melinda had maintained her word and kept him out of Daniel's way, but he couldn't help but see Lee around the place, following one of the hands around or playing or riding a horse. He was also at the table every morning and night, where Daniel couldn't miss him. No matter how hard he tried,

Daniel couldn't keep his eyes from drifting over to the lad. Lee wasn't of the coloring that Matthew had been, and he was far older, but every time he saw him, Daniel thought of Matthew. They would have been about the same age now, if Matthew had lived. And Matt would have been running around, learning all about the ranch, too, except that it would have been Daniel, not Jimmy, whom he would have tagged along behind. Just the thought of it reawakened the old pain, long ago put to rest, and though it wasn't as severe and slashing as it had been once, Daniel hated even the memory of his past loss.

It was, all in all, a damned nuisance having Melinda Ballard here. He ought to fire her, but he couldn't bring himself to do it. It would be unfair, considering how well she performed her work, and besides, he would probably have a mutiny on his hands if he took those delicious meals away from the men. He kept hoping that Melinda would quit, as the others had. But she showed no signs of that, even when he was in his surliest moods. She just ignored him when he was like that, which made him feel even more irritable, or she snapped right back at him and they wound up arguing, and then he was left with a bubbling, unfinished excitement inside.

Daniel would have been amazed to learn that he was often on Melinda's mind, too, and in ways that surprised her. After she had learned the sad story of his family from Lula Moore, she had felt more kindly disposed toward him, even when he barked at her or fixed her with one of his black looks. One Saturday morning she was gazing out the kitchen window at her son, whom Jimmy was teaching to ride, when out of the corner of her eye she saw Daniel step onto the front porch. He started toward the yard, then stopped when he saw Lee and Jimmy. For a moment he stood there motionless, his eyes on the boy on the horse, and Melinda saw such bleak pain and longing in his eyes that it made her heart twist within her. Then he turned abruptly and stalked through the front door. He was in one of his foulest moods for the remainder of the day, but Melinda held her tongue.

That wasn't the case often, of course. When he snapped at her, she usually answered him back in kind. She had never been a timid woman, but sometimes her tart retorts surprised even herself. There were times when she thought for sure that he would release her from his employ. But he never did. It made her wonder if perhaps he secretly enjoyed their spats. Melinda knew that she often experienced a certain tingly excitement during their arguments; they could be oddly invigorating. There were even moments when, facing his bright blue eyes, his body taut with anger, she had felt, deep in the pit of her stomach, a stirring that was—well, frankly sexual.

She wouldn't have admitted that to anyone, of course, any more than she would have admitted that she thought Daniel MacKenzie was handsome, or that she enjoyed looking at him. Considering the way he felt about her and how much they fought, she knew she shouldn't like him in any way. Yet she found herself stealing glances at him during meals, and more than once she went to the kitchen window to watch him cross the yard when she heard the closing of the front door. She liked to see his long legs striding across the ground, firm and tight inside his heavy denim trousers. She liked the set of his shoulders and how he carried his head. She even liked the way he tilted his hat down in front over his forehead.

He had wonderful hands, large and strong, with long, supple fingers. They were tanned and callused, the nails short and blunt, the backs lightly sprinkled with silky black hairs. Masculine hands. Melinda often looked at them; she especially liked to see them curled around one of the blue enameled coffee cups. She would think of the roughness of his palms and fingertips and imagine how they would feel upon her skin. Would his fingers be tender when they curled around a woman's breast?

She rebuked herself for thinking such things. It wasn't proper. And it wasn't possible, either. Daniel MacKenzie would never dream of touching or kissing her. He disliked her thoroughly. And, of course, she wouldn't permit such a thing, even if he did want to. Still, sometimes after she went to bed at night, she lay looking out the window beside her bed at the big house across the way, all silver and shadow in the moonlight, and she would think about Daniel. Her breasts would ache a little, her nipples tingling, and she could feel heat spreading through her. Her lips would feel alive and tender, and she would lightly rub her fingers across them, wondering what his lips would feel like. Would his beard scratch? If it did, she didn't think she'd mind. Embarrassingly, moisture would start between her legs, so that she pressed her legs together hard to stop it, but that didn't work.

Once she ran her hands slowly down her body, over her nightgown, touching her sensitive breasts and sliding down the plane of her stomach to her legs. Her eyes drifted closed as her body clamored for the touch that would ignite it. It had been two years since Robert died, two years since her body had known a man's hands. But she hadn't missed it until now, hadn't thought about it until she came to Daniel MacKenzie's house. She didn't know why he affected her this way. She didn't even like him. She wondered if she was turning into a loose woman. Could that be something that crept up on one unexpectedly? Could she change overnight from a lady into a slut? It seemed absurd. It couldn't be true. But why then was she suddenly man-crazy?

No, not man-crazy. It wasn't any man who stirred her. It was just one man. Daniel MacKenzie. Daniel MacKenzie, with his vivid blue gaze and his thick black hair, his hard, strong body. Daniel MacKenzie, who didn't even like her.

It puzzled her. It annoyed her. But she enjoyed it.

EARLY IN DECEMBER Melinda was awakened one night by the sound of hundreds of little taps against her window. Foggily, she came awake and lay listening to the tiny popping sounds. Sleet, she thought, and snuggled deeper into her covers. The sound meant bitter cold outside, and she shivered, thinking of it, and was glad for the warmth of her quilt and blankets.

The next morning her room was so cold when she made herself leave her bed that her teeth chattered.

She wrapped the heavy robe around her and thrust her feet into her slippers, then hurried straight into the main room of the house to light the Franklin stove. She stirred the banked coals to life with the poker and shoved in kindling and heavier logs, as well as shavings to bring the red coals to life. The fire flamed up, and Melinda adjusted the damper. Sleepily, she huddled in front of the stove for a moment, seeking the warmth that would soon be pouring from the small metal furnace.

But she knew it would be some time before the stove became really hot, and she had no time to waste. Morning was her busiest time; that was why she rose so early, before dawn was even streaking the sky. Wrapping her arms tightly around herself, she dashed into her bedroom and pulled out her hairbrush and the clothes she would wear today. Then she ran back to the stove and laid the clothes over it to warm while she took down her hair, brushed it out and pinned it up. She had done it so many times she didn't need a mirror. She pulled on her woolen stockings, long-legged pantalets and petticoats without taking off her nightgown and robe; it was far too chilly, even by the now-roaring fire, to disrobe. Finally, however, there was no choice, and she had to let her robe and nightgown drop so that she could slip on her chemise, blouse and skirt. Last, she sat down on a footstool, pulled on her shoes and laced up the high tops.

Fully dressed, she returned to her bedroom. She broke the thin layer of ice in the wash pitcher and poured a bit of water into the bowl. She dipped her washrag into it and, grimacing, swiftly washed her face. She dried it with even more haste, then brushed her teeth with baking soda.

Her personal chores completed, she went into her son's small room and gently shook him awake. She sympathized with his groan and mumbled protest, but he had to get up. He had to leave for school early, and before that there was milking to be done. When she was sure that he was indeed awake and groping his way out of bed toward the stove, she left him. Her husband's heavy coat hung on a rack by the front door, and she pulled it on, buttoning it all the way down. She wrapped a long knitted scarf over her head and around her throat and opened the front door, pulling on her gloves as she started out. Then she stopped and stared at the scene before her. Even though she had lived in the Panhandle of Texas for over four years, she had never seen anything like this.

Icicles of various diameters and lengths hung from the roof of her porch and, across the way, from the roof, shutters, railings and gingerbread trim of the main house, as well as from the barn and all the outbuildings. All the walls of the buildings and the ground itself were covered with ice. Each twig of every branch of the mesquite bushes and twisted little shinnery trees was encased in ice, and from them dangled thousands of tiny icicles. Ice also covered the yucca plants, the scattered cacti and the blades of the low clumps of grass. Even the line of tumbleweeds that had blown up against the corral fence and lodged there was coated with ice and decorated with icicles.

The sun, rising palely in the east, touched the ice all across the yard, and it sparkled like prisms in the sun.

Melinda stared. It looked like a fairyland, so delicate, crystal-clear and gleaming. She had never imagined that this bleak place could look lovely and enchanted. She smiled and went to the edge of the porch, gazing around her in delight.

A noise from the direction of the main house brought Melinda back to what she was supposed to be doing. Beautiful as the scene was, she still had breakfast to make. She wrapped one gloved hand around the narrow wooden porch column and ventured cautiously onto the ice-slick step. With the same slow movements, she stepped onto the ground. She was used to icy stairs; she had encountered them before. She was not used to ice so thick that it didn't crunch and break beneath her feet. She felt her feet slip with her first step, and she slid, her arms flailing for balance. Fortunately, she didn't fall, though she wound up several feet away in a direction she hadn't intended to go.

Determinedly, she turned toward the main house and began to make her way toward it. She walked with her arms outstretched, her eyes fixed on the ground, her steps small and tentative. Her feet slipped and skidded so much that she appeared to be doing some outlandish dance, but she kept on.

Daniel MacKenzie, who had come out of the side door of his house on his way to the barn, paused to watch her. She was wearing that coat again; the sight reminded him of how much the garment irritated him. It was way too big for her, and the cut was mannish, as well. She needed a woman's coat or a cloak, something warm and feminine, as befitted her. He wondered what she had done with her own coat; obviously her financial straits had been the cause of it, whatever it was. Why hadn't her husband provided better for her? It wasn't right that a lady like Melinda should be reduced to having to become a housekeeper for some churlish, ill-tempered man.

Frowning over his thoughts, MacKenzie went down the steps and started across the icy ground. He, too, stepped carefully, although his greater weight and the heels of his boots kept him from sliding as much as Melinda. He was walking past her, a few feet away, when suddenly her feet went flying, and without warning she slid across the ground and slammed into him. Instinctively Daniel's arms went around her, and he battled to steady them both. For a moment they were flat against each other, his arms encircling her, her hands clutching at the front of his coat.

Then his feet slipped, too, and suddenly he landed flat on his back, with Melinda stretched on top of him. They lay staring into each other's eyes. Though their heavy winter clothing made it impossible for them to actually feel each other's bodies, they were both intensely aware of their position. With their faces only inches apart, Melinda could feel Daniel's breath on her skin. She had never been this close to any man except her husband. She couldn't keep from thinking about his arms, his legs, his chest pressed against her body. Beneath all the layers of clothing, her nipples started to tingle, and her thighs relaxed and grew warm. Her eyes widened at the sensations budding within her. Then she realized with horror how long she had been lying there on top of him, staring and making no effort to remove herself. A blush started in her cheeks, adding to the rosiness already put there by the cold.

She began to struggle to get up at the same time that he did, but all they accomplished was another fall. This time when they landed, it was MacKenzie who was stretched out atop her. It was, if possible, an even more suggestive position. His weight was heavy on her, pushing her into the chilling ground, but Melinda felt no pain, only a delicious heaviness in her abdomen and legs. Her skirt had become rucked up, and she could feel the coarse material of his trousers against her stockinged legs. She gazed up at him, her breath coming fast and hard in her throat. He could feel the quicker movement of her chest against his, see the heightened color of her cheeks. His eyes went to her mouth, pink and moist, lips slightly parted, and he could not look away. Melinda could see his eyes darken. Unconsciously she sucked in her lower lip. His eyes followed the movement, and he moved his legs apart and down on either side of hers, clamping hers in between them. His head lowered, and for a wild, brief instant Melinda thought that he would kiss her.

Then a child's laughter erupted from the porch of her house, and Daniel's head snapped up. He scowled over at Lee, who had come outside and had seen them go tumbling twice. When Daniel glared at him, Lee clapped both hands over his mouth, but even that couldn't stifle his laughter. Daniel looked back down at Melinda, and his frown grew even fiercer. He rolled away from her, and she tried to scramble to her feet. She managed to make it to her hands and knees before MacKenzie, also trying to rise, went sprawling on the ice and knocked her legs out from under her. Irritated, she rolled over to her back to try to get up that way, and as she turned, her elbow slammed into Daniel's side. He grunted, clutching his side, as he fell again.

"Damnation!" He glared at her. "Are you trying to kill me?"

"Kill you!" Melinda retorted heatedly. "Who just knocked *me* to the ground?" She tried to jump up indignantly, but her feet skidded out from under before she could get even halfway up, spoiling the pose.

"You came barreling right into me, not the other way around!"

They bickered as they thrashed around, unable to get a purchase on the slick ground. Melinda slipped, and her foot jolted the back of Daniel's knee, sending him tumbling; he rolled just as she reached out to steady herself with a hand on his shoulder, and she went sprawling. It seemed as if any progress either of them made was immediately ruined by the other one's flopping around.

Up on the porch, Lee abandoned any attempt to hide his laughter. He doubled over, shrieking with merriment. Melinda, struggling vainly to rise on the slippery ice, wasn't sure whether she wanted to hit him or MacKenzie more. Daniel got up on his hands and knees, but he couldn't haul himself to his feet, because his hands and knees kept slipping with every movement he made. Melinda, looking at him, was reminded of a dog she'd once had that would run onto a freshly waxed floor, then scrabble frantically to stay on his feet. She began to giggle; then she was laughing. Suddenly her irritation and frustration exploded into hilarity.

MacKenzie shot Melinda a black look and started to explode into a tirade concerning her lack of respect and general want of sense, but just as he opened his mouth, his hands and legs began to slide slowly in different directions. He was powerless to stop them, and Melinda, watching him, wrapped her arms around her waist and laughed even harder. Suddenly, unexpectedly, Daniel grinned. Melinda had never seen him smile, *really* smile, and it almost took her breath away. The next thing she knew, he was lying flat on the ground and had given himself up completely to laughter. She thought she had never heard anything so wonderful.

## Chapter Five

MELINDA PUSHED ASIDE the heavy curtains and looked out the parlor window. The ice had made it impossible for the children to go to school, and they were celebrating the unexpected holiday by sliding down Windmill Hill. She smiled, listening to their shrieks of laughter. They had better make the most of it today, for the sun was out and already at work melting the icy wonderland.

She watched one of the foreman's boys zooming down the hill on a sheet of tin. Lee was struggling to make his way up the hill, having already slid down. His feet seemed to slip back as much as they went forward, and he was making his way primarily by pulling himself from one skinny tree or bush to the next. His feet slipped out from under him, and Melinda winced. But he clambered to his feet, laughing.

She thought about Daniel and her struggling on the ice early this morning, and a chuckle rose in her throat at the memory. Her face softened as she thought of their hilarity. She didn't think she had ever heard Daniel laugh before. Oh, sometimes his mouth twisted into a sarcastic smile, or he let out an ironic chuckle, but never a deep belly laugh of pure fun.

Smiling, Melinda tied back the heavy draperies and began to dust. The cold and the shrieks of laughter from outside made her think about Christmas. It was already December, so the season was getting close. She needed to make the fruitcakes soon; they required several weeks to set. And she should ask Daniel—that is, Mr. MacKenzie—to bring out the Christmas decorations. Melinda's smile grew wider. It would be fun having a big house to decorate again, and enough kitchen and storage space that she could make a real Christmas meal. Christmas had been so cramped and awful those years in the sod dugout. This year, at last, she would have some money to buy Lee toys. She had gotten her first month's salary, and just this once she planned not to save a bit of it, but to splurge on Lee for Christmas. He'd been so good the last two years, never complaining, even though she hadn't been able to buy the set of tin soldiers he wanted.

Well, this year he would get them. She'd seen a lovely set of British soldiers in the hardware store, their coats a shiny red and their guns deep black. She could get him a chess set, too, and—oh, there were so many things. It would be fun to prowl through the stores, not the agony it had been last year.

Humming, she finished her household chores quickly. By midday she was through, and after the hands had eaten and she had cleaned up the dishes, she sat down with the makings of fruitcake and several large metal pans. She poured a pile of pecans onto her chopping block and started chopping. Sacks of pecans had been one of her first purchases after she arrived at the ranch, for she had known how many would be needed for the various Christmas and winter dishes. Practically every evening she and Lee had shelled pecans when their other work was done, picking out the meats and storing them in tin cans. There was still plenty of shelling left to do, but at least she had enough nuts for the fruitcakes.

When she had chopped up the pecans, she started on the citron, dates and candied orange peel. It was a long, tedious process, her least favorite in the fruitcake making, for the candied fruit was sticky and messy, clinging to the knife, the board and her hands, and clumping up in the bowl. As she worked, her thoughts strayed back to East Texas and the Christmas celebrations there, and she sighed wistfully. She remembered the sounds of the pecans plopping onto the roof in November. When she had awakened to those noises as a little girl, she had known that it wouldn't be long until Christmas season. Soon after, there had been the pecan gathering, when they had spread bed sheets and blankets out on the ground and shaken the trees, then picked up the pecans and poured them into gunnysacks.

She remembered the way the cold had crept up on them more gradually than it did here, and as it had gotten colder, her excitement had grown. Melinda's hands stilled, and she leaned back in the chair, thinking of the hot kitchen at home, the windows fogging over from the cold outside. Mama and Gran had bustled around, making the oyster stuffing from the recipe that had been handed down through the family clear back to Gran's grandmother, who had grown up in coastal Georgia. A couple of weeks before Christmas, Daddy, who had already scouted out the best pine or cedar tree in the long woods between their farm and Uncle Clinton's place, would come in one day carrying the tree. After that, the children's excitement had been almost more than they could contain.

She and her older sisters had fashioned swags of evergreen and decorated the mantels and doors. They had made strings of popcorn and cranberries, and paper chains, to hang on the tree with the ornaments, and on top there had always been an angel with hair like spun sugar and gossamer wings. Daddy had brought home a box of oranges and a big clump of bananas, as well as a sprig of mistletoe shipped in from Central Texas. He would always tiptoe in the kitchen door, hiding the mistletoe behind his back, and sneak up behind Mama and hold it over his head while he stole a kiss from her. It made the children squeal with laughter, and Mama would shake her finger at him and pretend that she was angry, but everyone knew that her face was flushed more from pleasure than from the heat of the stove.

Melinda remembered their stockings hanging from the mantel and the excitement of sneaking downstairs at dawn the next morning to look with wonder at all the gifts. Then, when the presents had been opened, they had trooped into the kitchen for crisp golden waffles and bacon, and Daddy had read the Christmas story from the Bible before they ate. There had been mountains of food the whole day through, and in the afternoon, the house had swarmed with relatives and friends who'd dropped in to visit. By evening all the aunts and uncles and cousins were there, and when it got dark they'd set off the fireworks. Gran was a staunch Rebel still, who often reminded them that Gramps had fought under Stonewall Jackson, so their family hadn't gone in much for fireworks on the Fourth of July. It was Christmas when they set them off. She remembered running across the lawn in the dark, a sparkler fizzing in her hand and firecrackers popping in the background, the cold stinging her cheeks. It had seemed as though nothing in the world could be more wonderful.

Tears gathered in her eyes. Suddenly Melinda realized that she was sitting with her hands idle, crying over Christmases past. She shook her head and straightened, blinking the tears from her eyes, and went back to work.

She was surprised a few minutes later when there was a knock on the door and Mrs. Moore bustled in, wrapped up in heavy coverings from head to toe. Lula giggled as she began to unwind the woolen scarf from her head. "Do I look like a woolly bear? It's still cold as floogens out there, even if the sun is shining. So I figured I better wrap up, 'cause I knew it might take me a while to get here." She stepped out of the man-size boots she wore over her shoes and untied her cloak. It took some time before she was free of her outer garments.

"Whew!" she exclaimed, plopping down across the kitchen table from Melinda and automatically taking up a knife to help work. "What an undertaking. But I had to get out of the house. Will doesn't have anything to do outside. It's too slippery to even ride out to check the stock. He's been prowling the house all day long, until I was ready to go out of my head. I had to get out of there."

Melinda smiled. "I'm glad of the company."

"Making fruitcake?" Lula asked, nodding toward the citron, dates and candied peel.

"Yes. I figured I'd need to make a lot, considering that crowd of men."

"They sure can eat," Lula agreed. "I'll have to start on my fruitcakes tomorrow, I guess. I've been working the past couple of days on Opal's and my dresses to the Cowboys' Christmas Ball. What are you wearing this year?"

Melinda paused in her work and looked at the other woman. "You know, I hadn't even thought about it. I haven't gone the past couple of years, since Mr. Ballard died." The Cowboys' Christmas Ball was a huge party and dance held every year by Austin Carter, the owner of the Barrett Hotel, on the Saturday before Christmas. It was the major social event of the year, and people came from miles around. Despite its name, everyone was invited, not just the ranchers and their people, but the townspeople and homesteaders, as well. Melinda, Robert and Lee had attended the first two years they had lived here.

"But you'll go this year, won't you? Daniel never goes, but all the hands do, and so do Will and I and the children. You can ride with us."

Melinda thought about it. It would be fun to go to a party again, to dance and talk and laugh. It would be a rare occasion to dress up, as well as a chance to get together with other women and chat. Living out here, where there were often miles and miles between neighbors, could get very lonely. "I'd like to...." She hesitated.

The problem was a dress. She had only one nice dress, a blue wool, Sunday-go-to-meeting kind of dress. Not only had she worn it on every special occasion for the past few years, but it also wasn't really a dance dress, for it was high-necked and rather plain. The first two years when she had gone to the ball, she had worn a green velvet party dress that she'd brought with her from East Texas, but it was old and its nap had become worn. She'd had it for ages, and it wasn't new and stylish, and she—well, face it, she wanted to look pretty and special.

"Then it's settled," Lula went on assuredly. "You'll have a grand time. I always do. Will won't dance, but there's plenty of other men that do." She grinned meaningfully at Melinda. "A lot of unattached men, too."

"I'm not in the market for a husband."

"Pooh." Lula waved away that objection. "What single woman isn't?"

They continued to talk as they prepared the fruitcakes. Melinda discovered that Mrs. Moore's fingers moved as fast as her mouth, and by the time Lula left that afternoon, eight fruitcakes had been mixed and put into deep, narrow cake pans. After Lula's departure, Melinda cleared a space on the pantry shelves for several wide, shallow biscuit tins, into which she poured steaming hot water. She covered the fruitcake pans with clean linen napkins and set them into the biscuit tins for the slow steaming they required.

As she worked she thought about the upcoming Christmas dance and what she could wear to it. The more she thought, the more she wanted to go. However, while she had enough money to buy Christmas things for Lee with her first month's salary, she couldn't afford the yards of expensive material she would need for a ball gown, too. And Lee came first.

When dinner was over, she went to her house and looked through her clothes, as though something would pop out that she had forgotten. Unfortunately, they were all the same: serviceable dull black, brown and blue skirts and blouses. She sighed. She didn't have time to make anything, anyway, even if she had the money. She would be busy with her normal work, which was exhausting, as well as the extra Christmas tasks. She would just have to wear her blue Sunday dress. That was more befitting to a widow who had a child and wasn't young anymore.

As she turned away, she caught sight of a big brown box on the top shelf of the wardrobe. She stopped. She had forgotten about that. When they had moved here, she had been unable to throw away her wedding gown and had brought it with her. No doubt it had turned yellow and was falling to pieces by now. Melinda hesitated, then stretched up on tiptoe and pulled down the box. She untied the string that kept it tightly shut and opened it. Lace and satin cascaded out. She pulled out the gown and spread it on the bed. The style was too old-fashioned, of course, and the color was all wrong. But it was beautiful, expensive material, suited for a ball gown, and if she dyed it another color and did extensive alterations . . .

Melinda smiled. She could make something of it. It was probably unfeeling of her to use her wedding dress for a mere party dress, but she couldn't help it. The idea of having something pretty and new to wear was too tempting.

Smiling to herself, she found a piece of paper and began to sketch what she would do.

TWO NIGHTS LATER Melinda sat in her parlor beside the Franklin stove, her head close to the kerosene lamp to catch every bit of its light, cutting and stitching on what would become her ball gown. It was after ten o'clock, and she should have been in bed, for her mornings always started early. She had undressed and put on her nightgown and bed robe, and her hair hung loose around her shoulders. She had been on her way to bed, in fact, but she hadn't felt very sleepy, and she had been unable to resist doing a little more work on her dress.

The wind whined around the corner of the house; it was a lonesome, chilling sound, and Melinda shivered, even though she was warm enough beside the metal stove. The sun had shone brightly for the past two days, melting the ice except for the patches protected by shade, but the temperature continued to be cold, especially at night.

There was a sound outside, and she paused with her hand over her dress. She sat motionless, listening. It had sounded like a shout. There it was again, only closer. She stood up, leaving the dress on her rocker, and went over to the window to pull aside the curtain and peer out. It was a dark night; there was no moon. For a moment she could see nothing. Then she detected a flash of movement on the porch of the big house, and suddenly the bell that hung there rang out.

Melinda jumped, startled, and one hand flew to her heart.

The bell ringing at night could only mean that there was some sort of emergency. Was someone sick? No, there would have been no need to awaken everyone on the ranch for that. It must be something that required help. The bell continued to clang. Lights sprang to life down in the bunkhouse and the foreman's house. She saw the front door of the ranch house open, and Daniel emerged holding a kerosene lamp. His hair was rumpled, as though he had been asleep, and his shirt-tails hung down outside his trousers. She watched as the cowhand left the bell and ran to Daniel. He gestured in an agitated manner and pointed toward the barn. Daniel whipped into the house, then came out again without the lamp, and the two men ran toward the barn.

Melinda could see nothing unusual. She hurried to the front door and opened it. There were men running toward the barn from all over now. Behind her she heard Lee's sleepy voice, "What is it, Mama?"

"I'm not sure." Then she saw a peculiar glow at the far end of the building, and she gasped. "Oh, my Lord in Heaven! It's a fire! Quick! They'll need everybody's help."

Melinda ran into her bedroom and exchanged her soft at-home slippers for her work shoes. She didn't take the time to change into a dress. Every minute counted with a fire. Instead, she just threw her coat on over her robe and gown and grabbed a pail from the kitchen. She ran out the door and across the yard toward the barn, the bucket bouncing against her leg. Lee was right beside her.

Some of the men, including Daniel, were wearing bandannas over their faces to protect them from the smoke and were bringing the fear-maddened horses out of the barn and turning them loose. Will Moore ran to the corral gate, where the horses were already shifting around nervously and whinnying. He flung it open and let the animals out. Other men hurried back and forth from the small round metal stock tank inside the corral to the barn, carrying buckets of water to throw on the flames. It was obvious to Melinda that the water in the tank would not be nearly enough, so she went to the pump handle and began to pump vigorously. Lee took the bucket, scooped up a pailful of water and ran to join the men in the barn.

Melinda pumped and pumped until she thought her arms would fall off. When she could do it no longer, Lee switched places with her, and she carried the bucket, heavy with water, to the fire. Before long it was clear that the barn could not be saved, and Daniel shouted at the men to leave it. They concentrated on wetting down the corral fences and the ground around the barn. After that, the side of the bunkhouse and the outbuildings were soaked with water. The worst was not losing the barn; that could be rebuilt rather easily, considering the number of hands who worked for Daniel. The real danger was that the fire might spread from the flaming barn to the surrounding buildings and destroy them or, worse yet, spread to the grass and blaze across the prairie.

She traded places with Lee again and continued to pump. Now and then she paused to straighten her back and rest her hands and arms. Even accustomed as she was to hard work, her muscles were crying out in protest, and she could feel blisters forming on the palms of her hands. She wished she had thought to grab her gloves when she ran out the door. Whenever she stopped, her eyes roamed over the men until she found Daniel. He wasn't hard to find, for he was always in the thick of things, shouting orders and throwing himself into whatever needed to be done. His face was lit eerily by the glow of the fire in the dark night. Sweat shone on his skin, and despite the cold, dark patches of wetness had formed on his shirt. He looked hard and strong and competent.

As she watched him, Melinda's heart squeezed within her chest, and she felt as if she were suddenly spinning crazily. She bit her lip and returned to her pumping with renewed vigor, her irritation with herself pouring into work. It wasn't love, she told herself sternly. She couldn't possibly have any feeling for a man like Daniel MacKenzie. Desiring him was one thing; he was, after all, a handsome, powerful man, whatever his faults. But his faults were plainly there, and surely she wasn't foolish enough to ignore them. He was rough, rude and hard; he disliked women, and he didn't want her son around.

But then she thought of the piercing blue of his eyes and of his thick black hair. She thought of the warmth that always started in her stomach whenever he looked at her. She remembered the tragedies that had marred his life and thought that perhaps they had soured him, that he hadn't always been like this. She remembered his laughter the other morning and his unexpected, flashing grin, and she thought that perhaps he was changing. Might not that hard shell crack and fall away under the warmth of a woman's love?

Her hand slowed on the pump handle. She realized what she was doing and shook her thoughts away. Sternly she returned to pumping. She looked up when she felt a hand on her arm. Lula Moore stood beside her. "They've just about got everything watered down," she told Melinda. "They're starting to dig a fire trench around it now. There's nothing you can do here. But you could make some sandwiches and coffee. I have a feeling that when this is over, they're going to be mighty hungry."

Melinda nodded, grateful to give up the job. She walked up to the ranch house while Lula returned to her own home. Inside the kitchen, Melinda peeled off her coat. The fire and hard work had made her hot, and she was grateful to get out of the heavy garment. She would have stripped it off outside, she had grown so warm, but it had seemed too bold, considering that she had on only her nightgown and robe underneath. She started a fire in the stove, then washed the dirt and soot from her hands. She prepared two pots of coffee and put them onto the stove to boil while she began to make thick sandwiches for the men.

When she had a tray piled with sandwiches, she called Lee and gave it to him to pass around. She put her coat back on and carried out a tray of cups and the coffee. The men grabbed the sandwiches and ate hungrily, then gulped down the coffee. They were almost finished with their task, and they returned to it with renewed energy now, with food and hot coffee in their stomachs. Melinda went back to the house to replenish both pots of coffee. At the porch, she turned and looked back. The barn was burning fiercely against the black sky, casting a red, flickering light over the toiling men. It reminded her of a scene from an illustrated book of Dante's *Inferno* that she had seen in her parents' house.

But she could see that the fire wasn't spreading, no matter how awful it looked. The men were winning the fight. She pulled herself away from the scene and went inside to wash out the pots and make more coffee.

She was standing by the stove, her coat off, waiting for the coffee to finish, when the side door opened and Daniel walked in. His clothes were stained with sweat, dirt and soot, and his shirt hung open down the front, the tails outside his pants. His sleeves were rolled up, and he had obviously washed his face and arms under the pump outside, for they were clean and still damp. His face was weary and marked by sleeplessness, but he was smiling.

"You did it!" Melinda guessed.

He stopped, as though surprised to see her there. He stared at her, and Melinda was suddenly very aware of her state of dishabille. Heavy and unrevealing as her gown and robe were, they were still nighttime clothing, not the kind of thing to be wearing in front of a man. And her hair was unbound. No man except her husband had seen her with her hair unbound since she was fourteen. Nervously she pushed it back from her shoulders. If only he wouldn't stare so!

"Yeah." Daniel's voice sounded a little rusty. Frankly, he was surprised he'd even been able to say anything. He hadn't expected to see Melinda in his kitchen; he had thought she had finally gone back to bed. But here she was, in his house, standing there in her nightclothes. They covered up more of her skin than lots of evening dresses, but somehow the knowledge that this was what she wore to sleep in, that only one layer of cloth lay between that robe and her bare skin, made his own skin feel as if he were standing in front of that fire again.

Her hair hung loosely around her face and down to her waist, thick and soft and dark. He had never seen her hair down before; it was a husband's privilege. His fingers itched to reach out and touch it. Almost involuntarily he moved toward her. "Yeah, we stopped it," he told her, hardly aware of what he was saying.

He stopped only a foot away from her. Melinda was startled by how close he had come, but she didn't step back. A frisson of excitement ran along her skin, sparking a warmth deep in her abdomen. She could smell the smoke on him; she could see the drop of water, like crystal, that nestled in the hollow of his throat. She thought that she would like to lick that drop of water from his skin with her tongue, and she pressed her lips together tightly. What if he read her thoughts on her face?

But Daniel had no interest in trying to interpret her expression. He was too lost in her big gray eyes, too busy grappling with the violent emotions churning inside him. When he'd come in he had been tired but elated, charged with their successful escape from danger. Somehow, when he saw Melinda, the elation had exploded into something else—an eager, electric, intensely sensual excitement. He wanted her, right here, right now, as badly as he had ever wanted any woman. Maybe worse.

He reached out a hand to her hair, and his fingers skimmed lightly over it. The silky strands caught and clung to the calluses on his fingertips, and it was like fire licking through his abdomen. God, her hair was lovely, so thick and soft. He wanted to sink his hands into it; he wanted to bury his face in it. He could see his fingers trembling slightly, and he didn't know if it was from the physical strain of what he'd done tonight or from sheer desire.

"I saw you earlier, pitching in to fight the fire. You're a brave woman."

Melinda gazed up into his face. His touch, the expression in his eyes, the heat of his body so close to her, made her feel weak and liquid. Her thoughts were scattered and confused; she struggled to pull together a coherent sentence.

His hand slid down her hair and onto her arm, then to her hand. His fingers grazed one of the raw places on her palm, and she winced involuntarily. He frowned and lifted her hand to look at it. "You hurt yourself!"

"Just some blisters." She offered a small, self-deprecating smile. "I forgot to put on my gloves."

"I'm sorry."

"It's not your fault."

"You hurt yourself trying to save something that was mine." He didn't tell her that the thought made him feel both angry with himself and yet fiercely proud and possessive.

Daniel led her to the sink and gently washed her hands, cleaning the raw places with infinite care and blotting them dry. He took an unguent from the medicine box in one of the cabinets and spread it over the reddened and blistered skin. Then he wrapped gauze carefully around each palm and tied it.

They stood there for a moment, her hands resting in his. Slowly, never taking his eyes from her face, Daniel raised Melinda's hands to his lips and gently kissed each one. She stared at him, her eyes huge, her chest rising and falling with her rapid breathing. She was filled with yearning and anticipation, hardly daring to breathe or move, lest it break the enchantment lying over them and make Daniel leave.

Instead, he came closer, his head lowering to hers, and Melinda went up on tiptoe to meet him. His hands slid down her arms and sides, brushing her breasts in passing, and stopped at her waist. He pulled her up and close to him, and her arms went around his neck. Their lips met and clung as his arms slid around her, squeezing her to him, and he deepened the kiss. His mouth was hot and urgent. Melinda's lips opened beneath his insistent pressure, and his tongue moved inside her mouth, wet and velvety. He explored her mouth, arousing wild, tingling sensations that shot all through her as his harsh, rasping breath sounded in her ears.

Melinda shivered and clung to him. She felt dizzy and breathless, as though sparklers were shooting through her. Her tongue touched his, and she felt

Daniel shudder. His skin grew hotter, and he pressed her more tightly against him. His response was like a match to the dry tinder of Melinda's desire. She was suddenly aflame, conscious of nothing but heat and urgency. Her tongue stroked and tangled with his, and he groaned. Feverishly his hands ran down over her buttocks and back up, bunching up her robe.

There was the sound of feet on the wooden steps outside, and Lee's voice called, "Mama? Are you in here?"

They sprang apart, and Melinda whirled away. Her hands flew to her burning cheeks, and she wondered if it was clear from her face what had been going on. She heard Daniel's boots crossing the floor, and then the sound of the outside door opening.

"Mama?" Lee came into the room, babbling excitedly. "Did you see it? We stopped it. I watched that ol' barn burn, and oh, boy, was it somethin'!"

Melinda drew a deep, calming breath and turned around. Lee was chattering and reaching for one of the leftover sandwiches, hardly even glancing at her. Except for him, the room was empty. Daniel was gone.

# Chapter Six

MELINDA AND LEE returned to their house, but after she lay down, she tossed and turned, too keyed up to sleep. She couldn't stop thinking of what had happened between her and Daniel. She blushed at the thought of how boldly she had behaved, and she wondered what he must think of her. But then she remembered the force of his own passion, and she giggled, smothering the sound with her pillow. Surely, with the way *he* had kissed *her*, he wouldn't think her forward. She was amazed when she remembered how hungrily he had kissed her, how his hands had moved over her back and hips. She had thought he didn't even like her!

Just tonight she had realized that she was beginning to feel too much for the man who employed her, and then he had taken her in his arms and kissed her like that. It must mean that he cared for her. And yet...the idea was absurd. How could he care for her? He'd hardly spoken two civil words to her the whole time she'd been here. But then, she reminded herself, it seemed just as unlikely for her to feel anything for him. Yet, crazily enough, she knew she did. She thought about him almost all the time; her hands lingered longer than was necessary over his clothes when she folded them; she cleaned the two rooms that were most particularly his, his bedroom and the study, more often than any other rooms in the house, except the kitchen.

When he had taken her into his arms, it had felt so right, so wonderful and exciting. She couldn't remember ever feeling that kind of wild, leaping desire, even with her husband. Certainly she had never kissed Robert with such fervor. The intensity of the sensations she had felt stunned her. Could this be love? It wasn't at all what it had been with Robert. She and Robert had been friends all their lives, long before they grew to love each other. Their love had had a solid basis of friendship, respect and shared memories. Their courtship had been sweet and innocent, and on their wedding night he had been gentle and slow with her. They had argued, of course. What married couple didn't? But their arguments had been quiet differences of opinion that were usually resolved with a kiss and a hug. And if at times they had grown a trifle bored with each other, well, that was the way life was. That was the way love was. Wasn't it?

Was it possible that the wild and stormy feelings that Daniel MacKenzie engendered in her were also love? All the bright, burning anger, the desire bursting in her like fireworks when he kissed her, the excitement that rippled through her whenever he was around—were those surging, conflicting emotions love?

Melinda didn't know what to think. She didn't know what to expect from Daniel. She didn't even know what she wanted. But she knew she could hardly wait until the next day to see him again.

MELINDA AWOKE FAR LATER than usual the next
morning. She ran anxiously to the big house to prepare breakfast and was relieved to see that the ranch
hands weren't sitting there waiting hungrily for their
food. After the hard, late night they'd all had, everyone must be sleeping late. She scurried around, getting breakfast, her ears cocked all the time for the
sound of the inner door opening and Daniel entering
the room. But it didn't happen.

Some time later, when the food was prepared and
she had rung the bell calling them to eat, the ranch
hands began to file in. Daniel was among them. He
must have been out working already. Melinda turned
toward him, her heart rising in her throat, waiting for
a smile or a special look. But he didn't so much as
glance at her. She sat down at her place, feeling sick
inside, and pushed her food around. It was all she
could do to hold back the tears.

Later, when the hands had left, Daniel lingered,
standing behind his chair, his hands clenched on the
wood so hard that his knuckles turned white. Hope
began to rise in Melinda again. Perhaps he had been
embarrassed to show anything for her in front of the
men. That made sense. She went to the table on the
pretext of carrying some dishes to the sink. In fact,
what she wanted was to be close to Daniel, to give him
an opportunity to speak to her. Her heart was pounding like mad with anticipation. She lowered her head,
suddenly too shy to look into his face.

Daniel cleared his throat. "Uh, Melinda . . . that is,
Mrs. Ballard. I . . . I apologize for last night." His voice
was as stiff and cool as if she were a complete stranger

instead of the woman he had fervently kissed only a few hours ago. "It was inexcusable of me. It was late, and we had all been working hard. I fear that my jubilation carried me away."

So! It wasn't any feeling for her, or even desire, that had made him kiss her. It was simply that his excitement about their victory over the fire had bubbled over, and she had happened to be the only person around to kiss. Melinda kept her head down. She couldn't bear to let him see the tears forming in her eyes. She refused to let him know how he had hurt her.

"Of course," she replied, pleased that she could keep her voice so steady and cool. "I understand. No doubt it was the same for me."

She turned and walked to the sink. She scraped off several dishes and set them into the soapy washing pan, all the while keeping her back to Daniel. He stood for a moment without saying anything. Then she heard the sound of his boots on the floor and the inner door swinging shut. He was gone. Melinda went to the table and carried another load of dishes over. She worked quickly and efficiently, as she always did. But now, as she scraped and washed and rinsed, tears poured silently down her cheeks.

MELINDA TOLD HERSELF that she was no worse off than before. She had never believed that Daniel wanted her until that kiss. Now she knew for sure that he didn't. Or if he *had* wanted her, even a little, he must have been disgusted by the forward way she had flung her arms around him and kissed him back. But her life was not changed. She still worked here, still

had her son, still had—well, whatever she had had
before. At the moment she was experiencing some
difficulties in counting her blessings, but they were
there, she knew. Things were the same. *She* was the
same.

The only problem was, that was a lie. She wasn't the
same. She was hurt, confused and angry. And she
couldn't forget the taste of Daniel's mouth on hers or
the strength of his arms around her—or the wild feelings that had risen up in her in response.

For the next few days Melinda avoided Daniel as
assiduously as he avoided her. They were together only
at mealtimes, and then neither one of them looked at
or spoke to the other one. If a dish of food was sitting
in front of Daniel, Melinda would have starved rather
than ask him to pass it to her. She talked to the other
men as she always did, laughing at their jokes and listening to their stories, doing her best to pretend that
she was not hurt.

Unfortunately, she knew she could not avoid Daniel much longer. She had to ask him about the Christmas tree and decorations. She refused to let her
feelings of shame and hurt keep her from putting on
a proper Christmas for Lee. She would have to brace
herself to talk to Daniel, and soon. There were only
two weeks left before Christmas.

She realized that it would be easier to speak to him
with other people around. At least it wouldn't appear
as if she wanted to steal a moment alone with him.

So, as dinner was ending one day, she summoned up
her courage and looked down to the other end of the
table. "Mr. MacKenzie."

Daniel's fork clattered onto his plate, and his head snapped up. He was grateful for his beard, because he was afraid he was blushing. Hearing her speak his name, which hadn't happened in three days, had startled him, but even more upsetting was the response that shot through him. He was hungry, shamefully hungry, for any word or look from her. If she had shown him even a smidgeon of encouragement, he thought he would have gone down on his knees to her, begging her for her love.

Oh, damn! There he went again. His lips tightened, and the familiar self-anger surfaced. He hated himself for kissing her. He hated himself for feeling this way. Why was he such a fool where women were concerned?

It had been contemptible of him to kiss her the other night—and he knew how much farther he would have gone, blind to anything but his lust, if her boy hadn't barged in on them. Melinda Ballard was not a woman of light virtue. He couldn't just take her to his bed and enjoy her, then cast her aside, as he could the women in the red-light district in Amarillo. He couldn't ease his hot, surging desires with her soft, womanly flesh. She was a lady, a woman to be loved and cherished and married, as well as to take pleasure from. He had been close, dangerously close, to doing all those things.

But he knew that falling in love with Melinda would be foolish in the extreme. He had sworn after Millicent died that he would never love another woman, never marry again. His own bitter experience had taught him what a mistake love was. He had fallen head over heels in love with Millicent, carried away by her feminine sweetness and beauty. He had married her and brought her proudly to this home that he had built for her. But their love had died, crushed under the sledgehammer of reality.

He wasn't meant to be married. He loved this land; women hated it. Millicent had cried for hours when he brought her to the ranch, and she'd never adjusted to it. She had wanted desperately to leave, and after a few months he had been willing for her to go home to Maryland. Standing in the wreckage of his hopes and dreams of love, he had agreed to a separation, but then she had found out that she was pregnant. After his son was born, he couldn't bear to lose Matthew, so he had refused to let her go unless she was willing to leave Matthew with him. They had continued to live together in a loveless, miserable state. Then she had died. The land she had hated so much had killed her. He had killed her by refusing to set her free.

Daniel had tried to tell himself that it was just Millicent who had hated it here, but he knew it wasn't true. This was a harsh, hard country, unsuitable to a woman's soft nature. He had heard many other women complain about the Panhandle—the loneliness, the hardships, the weather, the bleak, flat landscape. One afternoon a week or so after Melinda came to the ranch, he had overheard her in the kitchen talking to Lula Moore, extolling the virtues and beauty of East Texas. She had told Lula that her dream was to save enough money to move back there. She hated it here, just like any other woman. Just like Millicent.

But it wasn't only the land that had killed his love for Millicent. She had, quite frankly, irritated him with her weakness, her vapors and her ceaseless complaining. She had had no interest in him or the ranch, only in dresses and hairstyles and gossip. It seemed as though she knew how to do nothing useful. Of course, that was the way women were supposed to be. He remembered finding her idle chatter charmingly girlish before they were married, and he had smiled indulgently when she'd pouted prettily and begged him not to talk of business and "such man things." At that time he had been eager to talk instead of the glory of her blond curls and the glow of her skin and the velvet beauty of her eyes. He had been happy to shelter her from the silly little things that frightened her.

But the charm had quickly turned to irritation when she had cowered under the bed covers during a thunderstorm or squeaked with horror at the idea of riding around the ranch with him or refused to take her meals with the "rough, wild men" who worked for him. Her sweet, maidenly shyness had turned out to be coldness and repulsion in the marriage bed. At first he'd felt like an ogre for wanting to take her sweet young body, but desire had rapidly turned into indifference.

Daniel's wayward heart kept telling him that Melinda Ballard was different. He'd never seen anyone who worked harder—and without complaints. He remembered how she had pitched in and fought the fire the other night with him and his men, pumping water until her poor hands were raw and blistered. And he thought of the way she had kissed him back; there had been no coldness in her. She wasn't like Millicent. Maybe if he allowed himself to love her, it wouldn't turn sour and hopeless.

But the familiar guilt flooded him when he compared Melinda to his late wife. It hadn't been Millicent's fault that she hadn't lived up to his expectations; it had been his fault for dragging her out here, for putting too many burdens on her, for wanting too much. He had killed her with his selfishness, and he couldn't forget that, couldn't explain it away. It could happen again. What would he do if he fell in love with Melinda, married her, then found their love crumbling around him as the other had? He couldn't allow that. He couldn't bear it again. Fear and doubt and guilt mingled in him, and somehow they all turned into anger—anger at himself, at Melinda, at the world.

He forced himself to look at her with polite indifference as he answered her. "Yes, Mrs. Ballard?"

"It's only two weeks until Christmas."

"Thank you for keeping me informed of the date," he returned, his roiling emotions seeping out in sarcasm. He disliked himself for speaking to her this way, yet he could not help it. It was all he could do not to explode into a rage, churning as he was with so many combustible emotions.

Melinda crossed her arms and set her mouth. He was as cantankerous as always. You'd think he was an old man, given the joyless, nasty way he responded to everything. Her voice was icy as she went on. "I merely wanted to remind you to get out the Christmas decorations. And we need a tree. I should start decorating as soon as possible."

Daniel's brows drew together. "I have no Christmas decorations," he snapped. "Nor will there be a blasted tree in this house."

Melinda's anger rose up to meet his. She wanted to scream at him, but she struggled to control herself. After all, she must remember that memories of Christmas with his dead son must hurt him. "I always celebrate Christmas," she said through clenched teeth.

"It'd be nice to have Christmas." Corley, one of the younger hands, spoke up. "I remember Ma always had Christmas cookies settin' out, and those red flowers she'd buy in town—" He stopped abruptly, silenced by one fierce glance from his boss.

"Of course it would," Melinda agreed stoutly. "No one," she said significantly, fixing her gaze on Daniel, "gets too old or too *mean* for Christmas."

Daniel's eyes flashed and his fist thudded down on the table. "Damn it, woman, I said no! This is my house, and I'll not have you or anyone else telling me what to do." He stood up, and his chair shot back and turned over with a crash.

Melinda jumped up, too, planting her hands on her hips. "Someone needs to tell you what to do! You're too stubborn and cranky to see sense!"

He wanted to roar. He wanted to grab her and shake her. He wanted to kiss her and go on kissing her forever. "I won't have Christmas decorations hanging around, getting in my way, and I will not have a Christmas tree in this house!"

Melinda glared at him, too choked with rage to get anything out. Daniel stared at her for another moment, then growled and stomped out of the room, nearly crashing the door off its hinges as he slammed it behind him.

Melinda wanted to throw things at him; she wanted to scream. She would have Christmas. She refused to let some bitter, nasty-tempered man ruin the holiday for her and everyone else on the ranch. They all deserved to have Christmas, including the cowhands. If Daniel MacKenzie wouldn't help, well, that was fine. She would do it without him. He couldn't keep her from cooking Christmas cookies and candies or a feast of a meal. Let him refuse to get out the Christmas ornaments. She would make her own. And if he wouldn't have a tree—well, she would figure something out.

Right after dinner Daniel saddled his horse, packed a few supplies and rode off to visit the north-line shack for a few days. He said he was going to ride the fence, although he and everyone else knew that the hands regularly rode along the barbed wire fence all winter long, checking for breaks or fallen posts. No one would have dared to mention that fact, however.

Melinda turned to cleaning the dinner dishes with such vigor that by the time she was through she had broken one pottery serving bowl and two glasses, bent a spoon and dented one of the enameled metal coffee cups. Then she marched out onto the porch and surveyed the countryside. What was she going to do for a tree? She had to find something to hang the ornaments on, something that would satisfy the letter of his law, but that would also show him that she meant what she said.

Her eyes happened to hit on the northwest side of the corral, where several tumbleweeds had piled up, and she stopped. A grin spread across her face. Now she knew what she was going to do. Still smiling wickedly, she started off across the yard toward the fence.

DANIEL SPENT two miserable days riding the fence and sitting alone in the line shack, staring at the wall and listening to the December wind whistling around the corners of the little house. Finally he decided to return home. He was still irritated with himself and Melinda, but not nearly as irritated as he was lonely. After two days of thinking about Melinda as he rode through the cold, he figured that if she was going to be constantly on his brain, he might as well go back where he could actually see her and hear her voice— and live in a clean, warm house while he was doing it.

He amazed himself, he thought as he rode into the ranch yard and dismounted. For seven years he hadn't cared that he lacked creature comforts, hadn't even noticed, really, that the food was always cold or burned, or that dust balls gathered beneath the furniture and along the baseboards, or that the laundress in town starched his shirts too much. He hadn't missed the comforts any more than he'd missed the company of ladies or the sight of a woman's lips curling into a smile or the sound of her laughter. Now, in just a few weeks, Melinda Ballard had spoiled him until it seemed that he not only didn't *want* to live without those comforts, he damn well near *couldn't*.

When he had unsaddled his horse and turned him loose with the others in the corral, Daniel walked across the yard and into the house through the kitchen door. He told himself that he hadn't entered through that door in the hopes of seeing Melinda, it was just the easiest way. But he couldn't deny the fizzle of excitement in his stomach as he took the steps two at a time or the disappointment that pierced him when he found the kitchen empty.

The house smelled deliciously of vanilla and hot cookies. All along the table cookies were spread out on racks and brown paper to cool. They were cut into Christmas shapes of stars, trees and bells. Two small bowls of red and green icing stood at one end of the table, with paper cones beside them. Some of the cookies were already iced.

The rich, warm scent teased at Daniel's nostrils, and a nostalgic longing darted through him. He felt strangely as if he wanted to both cry and smile. Melinda was having Christmas no matter what he'd told her. It didn't surprise him—but, oddly, it didn't really displease him, either. The pantry door opened, startling him, and Melinda stepped out. She stopped abruptly when she saw him, a little gasp escaping her.

"You're back."

Daniel looked at her, feeling absurdly ill at ease. He took off his hat. He didn't know what to say. "Yes." He continued to stand, just gazing at her, until he realized that he must look like an idiot. He supposed he ought to say something about her baking, ought to point out that she had ignored his orders, but he suspected that if he did, he would manage to appear even more foolish. It was best to ignore it.

"How were the fences?"

"The what? Oh. Oh, they were all right. In good condition." It had been only two days, yet he couldn't keep from staring at her as if he had been gone for weeks. He thought of the last time they had been alone together in the kitchen, when he had kissed her.

He stepped back, almost as though he could physically avoid the thought. "Well. I, uh, better see to some, uh...paperwork."

Daniel left the kitchen and strode down the hall. He didn't know where he was going. He had no paperwork to speak of, except the bookkeeping that he was always behind on—and he had no intention of doing that. He could go down to the barn and inspect what the men had done. Or he could talk to Will and find out what had gone on in his absence. But he had just told Melinda that he was going to do some paperwork, and it would look crazy for him to leave the house now.

He headed for the study, casually glancing into the parlor as he walked. He passed it, then stopped and backtracked to the door. He looked inside again. His eyes hadn't been playing tricks on him. There was a large tumbleweed sitting on a table in the center of the parlor. Strings of popcorn and cranberries and brightly colored paper chains were looped around it. Bows in various colors, materials and sizes adorned its dry, flimsy branches. A homemade felt angel was balanced near the top. The woman had made a Christmas tree out of a tumbleweed.

"Well, I'll be damned."

Melinda, who had followed Daniel into the hall, a little leery of his reaction to her tree now that the time of discovery was upon her, let out a sigh of relief. He didn't sound furious.

Daniel heard Melinda's sigh and swung around to face her. "A tumbleweed."

Melinda shrugged. "It's not a tree."

He struggled to keep his mouth from twitching into a smile. "You're one determined lady."

"I've been told that."

"Oh, hell." He moved away, slapping his hat against his thigh. He paused partway down the hall and glanced back at her. He should get mad at her now. He should tell her what he thought of her flouting his authority. But he couldn't find any anger or indignation in him. He felt too funny inside, too inclined both to laugh and cry, as he'd felt in the kitchen, smelling those cookies. He sighed and turned away, heading for the front door. Melinda barely caught his words as he walked away. "I might as well give up and get you a tree."

He stalked out the door. Melinda stood, staring after him, and began to smile.

It was after dark when Daniel rode in again. Supper was through, and Melinda had finished the dishes and was sweeping when the kitchen door opened and Daniel walked in, a short, scrawny juniper tree hoisted on his shoulder.

"What are you still doing here?" he growled. "Don't you ever go home?"

Melinda just smiled. "I was finishing up. I kept you some supper." She motioned toward a plate on the counter, a napkin over its contents.

"You work too late. Whatever happened to Will's girl, the one that used to help you?"

"Oh, that was a welcoming gesture on Mrs. Moore's part. I couldn't presume on her."

He grimaced. "No presumption. I'll pay the girl. She ought to do it willingly enough for money."

Melinda stared at him, not sure she'd heard him right. "You mean you want to hire her? To help me?"

"That's what I said, isn't it?"

"Well, yes, but..." Melinda's voice trailed off. She wasn't about to argue against having someone to help her clean. The big house and cooking for so many men made for exhausting work, and she was usually running behind. She smiled. "All right. Thank you."

Daniel looked uneasy with her thanks. "Where do you want this thing?"

"In the parlor, I guess." He'd already nailed crossed wooden planks to the bottom of the trunk for a stand. Melinda thought of the Christmas tree skirt in one of her trunks. She hadn't been able to use it with the bottom-heavy tumbleweed.

She followed him into the parlor, where he unceremoniously dumped the tumbleweed on the floor and set the low tree on the table. Daniel stepped back and looked at it uncertainly. "Scrawny thing, huh?"

It was indeed. It was little more than a bush, and there were big gaps in the branches. But at least it had green needles on it. At least it was a tree. It was the only kind of evergreen tree she'd ever found out here, except where someone had planted a row of fir trees for a windbreak beside their house.

"It'll look fine," she reassured him. "Where'd you find it?"

"In one of the breaks over in the southwest quarter. They grow on the walls of the gullies sometimes. Stubborn things." He grinned, and his eyes slid to her. "Like some people."

Melinda grinned back. She would have liked to hug and kiss him for bringing her the tree, but there was no indication on his part that it would have been welcome. They both looked at the tree.

"I brought another one, case you needed it," he continued, studying the tree. She knew that he was embarrassed at revealing any kindness. "I left it outside. Thought you might want it in your house."

Her smile turned a little wobbly, and tears shimmered in her eyes. "Yes," she said softly. "Yes. Thank you."

OVER THE NEXT FEW DAYS the house seemed suddenly filled with Christmas. The delicious smells of Melinda's baking and candy making hung in the air. The men couldn't resist popping in now and then throughout the day to grab a cookie from one of the full jars or a piece of candy from a glass dish. Once Melinda heard one of the hands joke that her candies had even sweetened ol' MacKenzie's disposition.

Daniel did seem milder, more ready to smile or even laugh. Though he often snapped at people, as he always had, the perpetual frown had eased from his forehead, and his voice was no longer heard rising in anger all over the place. To everyone's slack-jawed amazement, he shaved off his beard, keeping only the mustache. When Melinda saw him, she almost didn't recognize him. He appeared younger, not so hard and far more handsome. Every now and then he would come into the kitchen in the late afternoon or evening, while Melinda was working, and he would sit at the table, sipping a cup of coffee. Much to her surprise, he even chatted with her in a normal way, without flaring up into argument.

He climbed into the attic and brought down two big boxes of Christmas decorations, telling her in his usual gruff way that she might as well use them, they were just gathering dust. Use them she did. She had hung the strands of popcorn and cranberries and the paper chains on the tree Daniel had brought, but she didn't have enough ornaments at home to do justice to two trees, so the poor thing had had a rather naked look. Inside the boxes she found dozens of beautiful ornaments, fragile glass or delicately carved wood or daintily sewn tiny cloth dolls. There were green and red bows, both large and small, made out of velvet, grosgrain and satin. She pulled out garlands of tinsel to hang on the tree and festoon the mantel. There was a large, handsomely carved and painted nutcracker and a delicate porcelain crèche. She even found a mistletoe ball made of two small, crossed, ribbon-covered hoops to hang in a doorway. Of course, there was no mistletoe to put in it, but Melinda hung it anyway, and in her mind's eye she pictured Daniel catching her beneath it and kissing her.

However, she was careful not to let herself think that way too often. After all, he had made it clear that he had no intention of following up on that one kiss. She wondered if her kiss had repulsed him. Had she seemed too bold? Or was it that she wasn't skilled enough? Or perhaps he had found their kiss lacking in the love that had been there with his wife. The possibilities were inclined to sink Melinda into a most un-Christmaslike state of unhappiness. She tried to make herself concentrate only on the observances of the season and not on Daniel MacKenzie.

Despite the crush of work, she had more free time now that Daniel had hired Opal to help her, so she was able to use most of her evenings to work on the gown she was making over for the Christmas ball. When she finished it, two days before the ball, she tried it on in front of the mirror, turning this way and that to get the full effect. It had turned out beautifully. She had done away with most of the lace overdress, leaving only the satin gown with just a few rows of lace around the hem. Then she had dyed it a pale, dusky pink that did wonderful things for her eyes and skin. She'd taken the skirt in so that it had the new, slimmer silhouette, and she'd ripped out the lace sleeves and inset at the neck to make the neckline fashionably bare. The dress showed off her white shoulders and neck to advantage, but even though it was no more daring than the pictures in the women's fashion books, she had made a small lace shawl to drape over her shoulders. The result of all her work was a simple but stunning dress, and she knew that with her hair artfully swept up and decorated with a few pale satin rosettes, she would look the best she possibly could.

It was disappointing in the extreme to think that Daniel wouldn't even see her in the gown, for everyone had assured her that he never attended the Christmas ball.

However, the next morning, much to her surprise, as she was standing at the sink washing dishes, Daniel walked into the room and asked abruptly, "You going to that silly Christmas ball in Barrett?"

Melinda turned, her eyebrows lifting. "Yes."

"Figured as much. Well, long as I'm going, too, you might as well come with me."

Melinda's jaw dropped. She didn't know if she had ever heard a less graceful invitation, but she couldn't think of one she'd ever wanted more to accept. However, she couldn't think only of herself. "Lee is coming with me."

"Bring the boy, too."

Melinda stared. "Well . . . well, all right, then."

"Be ready at seven o'clock sharp."

THE NIGHT OF THE CHRISTMAS BALL, she prepared a quick, early supper. Since everyone on the place was attending the ball, they were all in an equal hurry to eat and get ready. For the first time since she'd started working there, Melinda left the supper dishes to soak and hurried over to her house. There wasn't much time. Knowing that, she had already bathed and washed her hair early this afternoon, brushing her hair dry in front of the fire. Now she took it down, brushed it again and piled it on top of her head in a fuller, more elegant style. On one side she fastened a cluster of satin rosebuds dyed to match her gown. Then she dressed as quickly as possible.

The knock on the door came promptly at seven, and Melinda almost ran to answer it. It was foolish to be so excited, she knew, but she couldn't help herself. She draped the lacy shawl around her bare shoulders, holding it closed at her breast, and opened the door. Daniel stood outside, stiff and nervous-looking and unbelievably handsome in a dark suit, with a blazing white shirt beneath and a narrow black string tie. His boots were polished until they shone, and the black Western hat in his hand looked as if it had never before been taken out of its box. His eyes swept over her, taking in the bare shoulders with their filmy covering and dropping to the white tops of her breasts, barely visible above her dress.

"You look beautiful." He said the first thing that came into his head, his voice slightly shaky.

"Thank you. You look quite good yourself." Melinda felt as if she were bubbling, effervescent with excitement and happiness. "Come in." She stepped back and called, "Lee, it's time to go."

"Coming, Mama."

Melinda reached for her coat on the hook near the door. It would look awful with the dress, spoiling the effect, but it was the only one she had, and she had to wear something or she would freeze on the long drive into town.

Daniel reached out a hand and stopped her. She glanced up at him in surprise. "No, wait. I just thought. There's something in the house I need to get. I'll be back in a moment."

Curiously she watched him trot across the yard. Lee joined her at the window. "Where's Mr. MacKenzie going?"

"I don't know. Now, Lee, I want you to promise you'll be on your best behavior tonight." She turned to him and bent to button up his coat. "No horseplay. Mr. MacKenzie isn't used to being around children, and this will be your first time alone with him, and I—"

"No, it isn't."

"Isn't what?"

"My first time around him. He took me riding with him three days ago. We went clear down to the breaks and back."

"What?"

He looked at her strangely. "I just told you, he took me—"

"No, I heard. It's just that it's . . . I can hardly believe it."

"Yeah. I was kinda surprised, too. I know he didn't like me at first. But sometimes he comes around when Jimmy's working on my riding, and a couple of weeks ago he even came over and showed me how to do something. He was nice when we went riding. He told me all kinds of neat stuff about the ranch, and when we came back, he told me he enjoyed it. He said he'd let me help when the roundup comes in the spring. Can I, Mama?"

"I suppose so, if it's all right with Mr. MacKenzie," Melinda replied absently. Daniel was changing even more than she had realized.

Daniel returned in a few minutes, a large, wrapped box in his hands. He held it out to Melinda. "Here.

It's your Christmas present. I want you to open it early."

Melinda reached out to take the box with suddenly trembling hands. She hadn't even dreamed that Daniel would give her a present. Carefully, she opened it, knowing that she was so foolishly in love with him now that she would save all the wrappings. She lifted the lid. Inside lay something made of thick black material. She lifted it out. It was a heavy cloak, one that fell all the way to the floor. The inside was lined with black satin, and it fastened at the neck with a silver clip. She held it up, staring at it, and tears gathered in her eyes and rolled down her cheeks. A cloak. He had seen her in her coat, and he'd understood why she wore it. He had cared enough to notice and then to want to change it. Melinda stroked a hand down the cloak.

"I meant it to make you happy," Daniel said, his hand coming out to touch her wet cheek.

"I am. Oh, I am," she replied, her voice thick with tears. She turned and let him slide the cloak around her shoulders and fasten the clip. For an instant she stood within the circle of his arms, his gift heavy and warm around her, enveloping her, and she was utterly, blissfully happy. "Thank you. Thank you."

He smiled slowly and held out his arm, elbow crooked, for her to take. "Then let's celebrate."

# *Chapter Seven*

THE BARRETT HOTEL was festively decorated for the Christmas ball and packed with merry people, all dressed in their finery. A band consisting of a piano, fiddle and guitar played away at one end of the open room that was normally the location of the hotel's restaurant, but at the opposite end, in the lobby, nothing could be heard of the music because of the hubbub of laughter and talking. Melinda supposed the party was lovely and enjoyable; she didn't notice. She was too busy floating on a cloud of her own. Men paid her compliments, and she smiled in return. But she didn't really hear what they said to her. She could think of nothing but sitting beside Daniel on the long ride into town, their thighs touching, with only the material of their clothes between them, the lap robe across their legs enclosing them in their own warm, private cocoon. Wherever she was and whomever she was talking to or dancing with, her eyes sought out Daniel.

Melinda had so many invitations to dance that she wouldn't have had to sit out even one if she hadn't wanted to, but afterward she couldn't remember any of the dances except the three she had had with Daniel. It had startled her when he asked her to dance. She hadn't seen him with anyone else, and he didn't seem to be the type to dance, but when he swept her out on the floor, she found that he moved well. More importantly, his arm was around her waist as they waltzed, and he was gazing down into her eyes. They were only a breath away from each other, their embrace just shy of causing comment. She could feel the heat of his body; she could see the pulse in his throat. His eyes were hot and probing, and she felt as if she were melting. She was in love with him, and she couldn't keep hope from rising within her.

Melinda wasn't sorry when the evening ended. She looked forward to the ride home. Lee, who had been running around all evening, stuffing himself with treats and playing with the other children, was exhausted. Not long after he climbed up into the buggy seat behind Melinda and Daniel, a heavy blanket across his lap, he was sound asleep.

The night sky was as clear as it could be only in the Panhandle, pure black except for a thin slice of pale moon and the faraway white light of the stars. It was cold and utterly beautiful and, snuggled safely under her lap robe, Melinda gazed at the view in delight. Once or twice Daniel glanced over at her, and a small smile touched his lips. She could see the beauty in this fierce, huge land. Perhaps she didn't hate it as much as she said.

When they reached the ranch, Daniel stopped the horses in front of Melinda's house and jumped down to help her alight. They looked into the back seat, where Lee lay sound asleep, stretched out on the seat with the blanket wrapped around him. Melinda hated to wake him up to get him out, but he had gotten far too big for her to carry, so she leaned forward to shake him awake. Daniel stopped her. He nodded toward the house. "You get the door."

He scooped Lee, blanket and all, up in his arms and carried him onto the porch. It took a stunned moment for Melinda to realize what he was doing; then she darted to the front door and opened it for him. Quickly she preceded him into Lee's tiny bedroom and turned down the covers of his bed. Daniel laid the boy down on the bed and bent to remove his boots. Then he pulled the covers up and, for a moment, stood gazing down at Lee. Melinda watched, seeing pain and pleasure mingle strangely on his face.

When he turned and left the room, Melinda followed him, closing the door behind her. Her throat was choked with sympathy and regret, but she didn't know how to express them. Daniel was not a man who welcomed sympathy. She came up beside him and laid her hand on his arm. He looked down and smiled.

"Would you like some coffee?" she asked, reaching up to unclasp her cloak. "I could fix us some. Or how about hot chocolate?"

Daniel lifted the cloak from her shoulders, his hand grazing her bare skin. "I don't want anything to drink," he said, his voice low. He tossed the cloak onto a chair and stared down at her as his hands came up to touch her throat. "You were beautiful tonight. Did I tell you that?"

Mutely Melinda nodded her head.

"I rarely tell you, do I?" he admitted, his fingers drifting down over her shoulders. "It's one of my many faults. I'm too rough, too blunt, lacking in the social graces."

"I didn't say that." Melinda's voice came out breathlessly.

"Oh, yes, you have. Many times. Perhaps not tonight." He paused. "You are beautiful. I kept watching you all evening, dancing...talking...laughing. And I wanted you so badly I could hardly remember where I was." His fingertips slid across the smooth white skin of her chest down to the quivering tops of her breasts, exposed by the low neckline. "God, you're lovely."

He bent and brushed his lips against the soft flesh. Melinda drew in a sharp breath, part surprise and part sharp delight. "Daniel..."

His lips trailed kisses across to her other breast, sending shimmering sensations through her. Her knees went weak, and she gripped his arms tightly to stay steady. His mouth worked its way upward, tasting her skin from her breasts to her throat. Melinda let her head fall back, offering up more of herself for his delectation. Daniel's hands went to her waist, his fingers digging in as though to keep her from moving away from him. He murmured her name, his breath ragged and hot on her flesh, exciting her almost as much as the touch of his lips.

Melinda moved restlessly, and her hands went up to Daniel's head, weaving into the thick mass of his hair. Shamelessly she tugged at his head, urging him upward to her mouth. Smiling, he kissed her. His kiss was long and deep, compelling. Melinda felt as if her bones were turning to wax and melting away beneath her. She swayed against him, and Daniel answered by squeezing her body more tightly to his. He still wore his heavy overcoat, and the thick material frustrated her desire to feel his hard, masculine body against hers. She wriggled against him, and her nipples tightened in response to the friction of the cloth across them.

Daniel kissed her again and again, his tongue plundering her mouth. He kissed her face all over, hard, quick kisses, always returning to her mouth. His tongue traced the whorls of her ears, and he nipped gently at the lobes. He pushed the narrow straps of her gown off her shoulders and down her arms, freeing her breasts from their restraint.

Melinda had worn a corset on this special occasion, to make her waist infinitesimal, and it had the effect of pushing up her breasts so that they swelled above the frilly white cotton chemise, only the deep rose nipples still covered. Daniel stared down at her, his breath rasping in his throat. Slowly he reached out and took the chemise between his fingers and gently pulled it down. The material scraped over her sensitized nipples, making them harden and swell even more. Lush and erotic, her breasts thrust up at him, the nipples pointing provocatively. The blood pounded in his head as he reached out a forefinger and lightly touched one nipple. He circled it, watching the bud tighten beneath his touch. He went to the other and worked the same magic on it. Melinda sucked in her breath, and Daniel glanced at her face. Her eyes were closed, and her lower lip was pulled in, her teeth biting down into it, her face a mask of ecstasy.

Daniel shuddered and pulled her to him. His mouth fastened on hers, and he kissed her as though he would never stop. His hands cupped her breasts between their bodies, his fingers teasing and stroking her nipples, until Melinda moaned at the devastating pleasure and moved her hips against him, blindly seeking fulfillment.

He bent, sweeping her up into his arms, and turned to carry her into the bedroom. As he did, his eyes fell on the door to Lee's room. Her child was here; he had forgotten that. He could not take her with the child lying only a room away. It was too crude, as though he did not value and respect her. Daniel stopped.

Melinda opened her eyes and glanced questioningly at him. Her eyes followed his gaze, and she, too, came back to reality with a thud. She was a mother, not a wanton strumpet who didn't care where she coupled.

Slowly, regretfully, Daniel set her on the floor. Melinda's hands flew up to her breasts, quickly tugging up her chemise and dress to cover them. A blush stained her cheeks.

"I'm sorry—I—oh, hell!" Daniel turned away and strode out of the house.

Melinda watched him go, then sank into a pile on the floor, her knees too weak to help her stand. She felt hot and aching and thoroughly frustrated. Yet at the same time she couldn't stop grinning like an idiot. Daniel wanted her. He wanted her almost past reason.


FOR THE NEXT FEW DAYS Melinda was so busy that she had almost no time to think about Daniel. Almost.

Nothing, not even the preparations for a huge Christmas feast, could completely take her mind off him. She was too lost in love. She thought about the way he smiled, the things he said, the wild, marvelous sensations his kisses evoked in her. She wanted to be with him, wanted him to make love to her. It was obvious that he wanted her, too. However, it was equally obvious that he had no intention of making her his wife. He hadn't spoken one word of love when they had kissed. He had said nothing to her of commitment or marriage. No doubt he still cherished the memory of his late wife too much to put another woman in her place. He obviously desired her, but he was fighting it, because he didn't want to seduce a woman whom he considered a lady. He knew that her only position with him could be that of mistress.

Melinda would lose whatever position and respect she had in the community if she became his mistress. People would whisper about her, and when she went into town, she would be the target of sidelong glances and leering grins. There were times when she desired Daniel so much that she thought she would be willing to undergo those things. She was afraid that she could put aside her moral beliefs if that was the only way that she could have him. But then she would think about Lee, and she knew that she couldn't do that to him. Whatever she did would taint him as surely as it did her. How could he grow up here with people calling his mother a whore?

She tried hard to suppress her desire, to take her mind off Daniel, and so she threw herself into her work. She chopped, sliced, seasoned, baked, boiled

and, most of all, cleaned. The entire house had to be
sparkling for Christmas Day, and the good china,
crystal and silverware had to be taken out and cleaned
of the dust and tarnish that had accumulated on them.
And, of course, with all the cooking and mixing that
she was doing, she was forever washing dishes.

She didn't see much of Daniel, fortunately. But
sometimes she would glance up during a meal and find
him looking at her from the opposite end of the table.
His blue eyes would be filled with smoky secrets, and
her pulse would leap, and she could do nothing but
stare at him, all her senses thrillingly alive. At night,
after she went to bed, she found it difficult to sleep, no
matter how tired she was. Her mind always turned to
Daniel, and soon her body would be thrumming with
desire, with no hope of satisfaction. And always there
would be the little flicker of hope, the irrepressible
desire that Daniel would change, that he would grow
to love her as well as want her, that he would ask her
to marry him.

After all, Daniel *had* changed already. He talked
and laughed and joked more. Two days before
Christmas he went into town and returned with crates
of oranges and apples, boxes of Christmas candy and
sacks of nuts more exotic than the pecans they were
used to. By the way the men stared, Melinda could tell
that it wasn't a Christmas custom at the ranch. He also
brought in a sprig of mistletoe, shipped in by train
from farther south, and placed it in the mistletoe ball
Melinda had hung in the doorway of the parlor. One
day when she had carried a dish of fudge into the parlor and was turning to leave, Daniel surprised her by

stepping into the doorway and stealing a kiss from her beneath the mistletoe. Then, just as quickly and quietly, he had stepped back from her and left.

Finally Christmas Eve came. When Lee had complained that there was no chimney for Santa Claus to come down, since Melinda's house was heated by an iron stove, not a fireplace, Daniel had graciously offered to let Lee hang his stocking from the parlor mantelpiece in the ranch house. After supper on Christmas Eve, Lee hung his stocking under his mother's watchful eye. Afterward he put on his coat and ran down to the foreman's house. As a special treat, Lula Moore had invited him to spend the night with her youngsters and join them in popping corn and roasting nuts. After all, she told Melinda, as wild as her children were on Christmas Eve, she wouldn't notice one more, and Lee's absence would free Melinda for the massive work she had to do for the meal tomorrow.

Melinda spent her evening making cakes: one Lord Baltimore cake and two coconut layer cakes. She had already baked the pies this afternoon, and the pie safe in the corner of the kitchen was full of apple, pecan and mincemeat pies, six in all. By ten o'clock she was done with the cakes, too, and after she checked to make sure that everything that could be done ahead of time for tomorrow's meal had been, she left the big house and hurried to her own cabin. High on a shelf in the wardrobe closet of her bedroom was a big bag, which she pulled down and carried across the yard to the ranch house.

Quietly, thinking that Daniel might already have gone to bed, she slipped down the hall to the parlor. To her surprise, she found him sitting there with the lamps lit. Her surprise must have shown on her face, for he chuckled and said, "I've been waiting for you." He nodded toward the limp stocking hanging from the mantel. "I figured you'd be back to fill that."

Melinda smiled, pleased that he had wanted to be with her. She took her presents out of the bag and laid them beneath the tree, feeling both awkward and pleased at having Daniel's eyes follow her movements. She remembered what had happened the last time they had been alone together, and a tingle ran through her. She glanced over at him and saw the same hot memory in his eyes. She looked away, very aware of how quickly she was breathing and how fast and furiously the blood was pumping through her veins.

She went to the stocking and dropped nuts, an orange and an apple to fill the toe. Then she began to stuff in the little goodies she had bought: a whistle, some marbles, a small ball, licorice whips, a few hard candies, a new slingshot. Daniel came over and squatted down beside her, so close to her that their arms were almost touching.

"I thought you might want to add these things," he said, holding out his open hand.

Melinda looked at him in surprise; then her eyes dropped to his hand. He was holding a jackknife that would delight any boy and a pair of child-size spurs. Melinda stared. He had bought them for Lee. "Why, Daniel!" She looked at him, her face warm with gratitude and love. "You didn't have to...."

He shrugged. "It's not much. I got him a real present for tomorrow. But I thought he might like these, too."

"He'll adore them." Melinda took the knife and spurs and added them to the stocking. She turned to Daniel and smiled warmly at him. "Thank you. It was very kind of you."

He shook his head, a little embarrassed by her thanks, and looked away. "I—I had a child once, a boy. He died when he was very young. I thought—that I could never love anyone again. I thought that I was dead to emotion." He paused. Melinda stayed very quiet, afraid to speak or even to move for fear she might break the fragile moment. "That's why I didn't want children around here. They made me think of Matthew. But I've found that I don't mind so much. At first, whenever I looked at Lee, I felt that old pain, but then the longer I was around him, the more I saw him as a person, as himself, and not just some reminder of Matt. I like Lee. I enjoy being with him."

"I'm glad." Melinda put her hand on his arm.

He looked at her, then bent down and kissed her once, briefly and hard. She felt the familiar surge of longing, and an ache started deep inside her. She swallowed, wondering if she would be able to resist him if he began to kiss and caress her.

But Daniel did not kiss her again. He stood and took her hands in his. Melinda stood, too. She wasn't sure whether she was relieved or disappointed. "I have something I want to give you. Now, not tomorrow, when all the others are here."

Melinda looked puzzled. "But, Daniel, you've already given me my Christmas present. Remember?"

"This is something different." There was a strange look in his eyes, hesitant and hopeful and, strangely, almost frightened. He released her hands and moved away. He took a small box from the mantel and handed it to her.

Melinda looked at it. The box was so clumsily wrapped in red tissue paper that she was sure Daniel must have wrapped it himself. Giving him another puzzled glance, she unwrapped it and lifted the lid of the tiny box. Inside, lying on a bed of cotton batting, was a woman's ring. In the center was a large, square-cut emerald, and all around it in a sparkling circle were small diamonds. "It's beautiful!" she gasped and looked up at him.

What did it mean? Was this the sort of gift with which men paid their mistresses? Her heart tore within her, and she found herself begging inside, *Please, oh, please, don't let him be asking to set me up as his kept woman.* No matter how many times her desire had led her to consider the possibility of accepting that role, she realized now that it would break her heart to have him ask it of her.

He saw the questioning in her eyes, and although he did not realize why she was confused, he explained. "That was my mother's ring, and before that, my grandmother's. If you don't like it, I'll get you another. It's just that it's a tradition in my family, the betrothal ring of the first son."

"Betrothal?" she breathed, her chest tightening. She hardly dared to believe that it was true. "You're asking me to marry you?"

He nodded. "I never thought I'd ask that again. When Millicent died—well, frankly, our marriage had been so wrong, so disappointing that I—"

"Disappointing!" Melinda's jaw dropped. "But I thought you loved her terribly! That you built this house for her!"

"I did love her, at first. But then, when we lived here together—well, she hated it here. We never seemed to agree. It wasn't right between us. Millicent was desperately unhappy, and I grew to dislike her. It was my fault, all my fault. She died because of me. I didn't want her to leave, you see, and take Matthew from me. I practically forced her to stay. Then she died."

"Oh, Daniel, no!" Melinda went to him, wrapping her arms around him and laying her head against his chest. "You mustn't blame yourself because she died. None of us choose the way we'll die—it just happens. It was out of your hands."

"Perhaps. I don't know. But I decided that I wouldn't marry again. After Matthew died, I didn't want children. And I'm not good with women. I'm blunt and ill-tempered. I don't know the right things to say, and I always wind up hurting their feelings. I love this country—it's the only place I want to live. But women hate the loneliness and barrenness. For a long time it didn't matter. I didn't feel capable of love anymore. It was easy to avoid it."

He sighed. "Then you came here. I couldn't avoid you. I couldn't run from you or push you away. You just stood your ground and gave back as good as you got. You were so damned beautiful, so desirable. You turned me inside out. You lit up everything in my life and made me see how cold and lonely I'd been for years. You made me want to have more than that. Melinda, I love you. I can't bear to live without you. I want to marry you. Will you? Could you bring yourself to—"

He looked down at her with such hope and trepidation that Melinda had to laugh. She threw her arms around his neck. "Yes! Yes, you silly man. Of course I'll marry you. I love you."

He grinned, then forced his face into sober lines. "Are you sure? I know you don't like the Panhandle, but I—"

She chuckled again. "As you might say, 'I don't give a damn where I live.' I just want to be with you. That's all that's important. Besides, I've even gotten to think it's kind of pretty—in its own strange way."

Daniel grinned, and his arms went around her hard as he bent his head and kissed her, his lips moving over hers slowly and lovingly. But then the pressure increased as passion took him, and she parted her lips to grant him possession of her mouth. Their tongues met and twined in a dance of love until his skin grew searing hot and his breath ragged. Finally he pulled away and looked down at her, a faint question in his eyes.

In answer, Melinda smiled up at him and pulled his head down to hers again. He kissed her thoroughly, then lifted her up into his arms and carried her out of the room. Up the wide staircase he carried her and into the bedroom that was so masculinely his, where she had often worked and dreamed, but had never been with him. He set her down tenderly by the bed, and his hand went to the row of buttons down the front of her dress. Eagerness and passion made his big fingers clumsy, and Melinda, smiling, took his hands away and began to unfasten the buttons herself.

Daniel stepped back, his eyes on her hands and what they gradually revealed, as he, too, unfastened and removed his clothing. His garments fell scattered on the floor, and he stood before her naked and powerful. But Melinda was no longer a girl, and though her cheeks might color a little at the sight of him, she did not take her eyes from him, but looked her fill. The desire on her face when she gazed at him naked was too much for Daniel, and he had to go to her and take her into his arms. He kissed her as his hands swiftly removed the last of her light cotton undergarments.

He jerked down the covers on the bed, and they lay back on it, their hands and mouths eagerly exploring each other's bodies. Melinda sighed shakily, afire with sensations she had never known before. She hadn't known it could be like this, not just sweetness and love, but fire and storm and raging need, too. She reveled in the differences between them, his hardness against her pillowy softness, the hair-roughened skin that abraded her sensitized nipples and tender flesh, the aggressive thrust that found eager acceptance in her.

His mouth was hot on her breast. His hands found the soft, secret places that aroused her into almost mindless passion, and her hands played over him, delighting in discovering him, urging him on until they were both writhing and panting in their urgent need. When he came into her, she welcomed him, wrapping her arms around him and moving with him in the timeless rhythm of passion. Together they vaulted to the heights and slowly, gently, came fluttering down to earth again.

With soft murmurs and kisses, they separated; then Daniel settled her into the crook of his arm, and they lay together, dreamily quiet. Melinda had never felt so content, so happy. She thought about the next day—well, this day, really, for it was past twelve o'clock. Christmas Day.

She thought about the morning that would come—the eager unwrapping of presents, the huge breakfast with its reading of the Christmas story, the surprise when they announced their marriage plans—and she smiled. She knew that she and Daniel would have many more Christmases together. There would be more children, and they would make new customs and traditions, and in time there would even be grandchildren around them to share the joy.

But there would never be a Christmas more special than this one. For this night, they had both given and received the greatest gift of all: love.

# A Note from Kristin James

I grew up in the Panhandle of Texas, where this story is set, and so did my mother. The ice storm, the wind and cold, the shock of moving from the vegetation of East Texas to the vast, flat, treeless landscape of the Panhandle (as my mother's family did) are all quite true. The Windmill Hill mentioned in the story sat on my grandfather's farm, a small rise in the flatness where he placed the windmill to catch the most wind.

Many of the Christmas customs mentioned in the story are ones my mother told me about. Her father used to bring home a crate of oranges and bananas as a treat at Christmastime, as well as hard candies and walnuts and pecans. They spent the chilly winter evenings sitting around the fire cracking the nuts for the various dishes (and eating quite a few along the way), popping popcorn and stringing it for the tree, stringing cranberries and making paper chains.

When I was little, we always went to my grandmother's on Christmas Eve, then had Christmas Day at home, where we opened our presents, got our stockings and had a big feast. My mother would spend much of November and December making fruitcakes, candies and fudge for Christmas, as well as whatever parts of the dinner she could make in advance and freeze. I would hang around the kitchen, hoping to get to lick the spoon or bowl when she was through. But I enjoyed even more going to my grandmother's house before Christmas, because she still followed the old traditions of making paper chains and strings of cranberries, and she would let me help her. Most of my family would gather at our house on Christmas Day for the noontime meal, and I remember that later in the day other relatives and friends would drop by for a visit, so that the house was always full of people.

By the time that I was born, they shipped trees in from elsewhere for Christmas, so I never saw a tumbleweed used—or even one of the scrub junipers. But my sister used to make beautiful wreaths and centerpieces for Christmas using the dried native plants and weeds, such as yucca pods, devil's heads and branches of tumble-weed, which she dipped into aluminum paint. One of the cutest such wreaths I've seen was a ring made of old, rusted barbed wire decorated with prickly pear cactus and centered by an old boot. Talk about a Western Christmas!

I hope your Christmas memories are just as special, and that these Christmas stories become a part of your holiday tradition.

*Kristen James*

# A CINDERELLA CHRISTMAS

## *Lucy Elliot*

*To Les, with love*

We make these spicy, crunchy cookies both to eat ourselves and to give as Christmas-tree ornaments. Before we cook them, we poke a hole at the top of each through which we can insert a string afterward. We decorate the cookies to look like whoever they are going to be given to. The one for Les, my husband, always gets a tie and an attaché case.

The real Petra, who is Swedish, uses blackstrap molasses, which gives the cookies a slightly bitter taste and an almost black color. We prefer to use half blackstrap and half regular molasses, which adds sweetness to the cookies and a rich gingerbread color. Kept in an airtight container, these cookies will last for several weeks.

## PETRA'S GINGERBREAD MEN

| | |
|---|---|
| 5 to 6 cups sifted flour | 1 tsp cinnamon |
| 1 cup molasses | 1 tsp cloves |
| 1 cup brown sugar | ½ tsp salt |
| 1 cup shortening | ½ tsp nutmeg |
| 1 egg, well beaten | ½ tsp cardamom (optional) |
| 1 tbsp baking soda | |

In a heavy saucepan, bring molasses, sugar, shortening and baking soda to a boil, stirring constantly. Boil 5 minutes. Remove from heat. Cool thoroughly.

Sift together 5 cups flour and all spices.

Add flour mixture and beaten eggs alternately to the cooled molasses mixture. Dough should be very stiff. If not, add more flour, but do not exceed six cups in total. Chill 2 hours.

Preheat oven to 350° F. Roll out dough to ¼" thickness. (For crispier cookies, roll out thinner.) Cut out cookies in favorite shapes. If dough gets sticky, chill again. Bake for 8 to 10 minutes. Allow to cool.

Decorate cookies with topping.

Makes about 4 dozen cookies.

## COOKIE TOPPING

*1 egg white*
*1½ cups confectioners' sugar*

Beat egg white until frothy. Add confectioners' sugar, ½ cup at a time. Beat for at least 5 minutes.

# Chapter One

OUTSIDE THE SNOW WAS FALLING, drifting down through the gaslit evening onto the trees in the yard. Already the spruce by the window was frosted with a thick powdering, and the maples at the gateway had become webs of spun-sugar lace. Below, on the wide street, a carriage appeared; there wasn't enough snow yet to support a sleigh, but the driver, moved perhaps by the spirit of the snowfall, had fastened bells to the horses' bridles. They jingled as they trotted past, leaving behind two sets of tracks to be filled in by the snow.

At last, thought Mary Hillyer, leaning closer to the tall window to watch the carriage pass. And about time, she added, for beneath this first soft fall lay only the bare frozen ground and last summer's yellowed grass. It was the fifteenth of December, ten days until Christmas, and despite the frigid temperatures no snow had fallen until now. The first flakes had begun during supper, to everybody's joy; Eveline had rushed outside and returned with wet drops on her face and a prayer that enough would come down to last until Christmas Day.

The room was very hot. Pressing her forehead to the cool glass, Mary watched as the world was transformed from a well-kept New England avenue to a fairy wonderland. The echoing bells and the whiteness stirred old memories, of sugaring and sleigh rides, and tramping the woods with a sack to fill with holly and mistletoe and pine boughs to carry home. It had been years since Mary had had time for any of those things, but the images, being precious, had remained indelibly sharp. Even now, in this close room, she could feel the tingling of frozen cheeks, the brittleness of the holly breaking beneath her hand; even now she could smell the fragrance of the cloud of steam rising from the kettles of boiling sap as the farmer dipped a tin cup for them to pour onto the snow, loops of golden sweetness that melted on the tongue.

Yes, sugaring was magic, but she'd liked the sleigh rides best of all: tinkling along through the snow-draped night, burrowed down in a nest of fur robes, with baked potatoes in your pockets to keep your fingers warm. And afterwards there would be hot cider with cinnamon sticks and your whole body throbbing from being indoors again.

The carriage had vanished, and the tinkling of the bells. Mary's sigh of reaction clouded the windowpane. She raised her hand to rub the glass. Then, on impulse, she reached up instead, unhooked the latch and threw up the heavy sash. She felt a rush of elation as the cold air enveloped her, and leaning out, she drank in the wonder of the night.

And it *was* wonderful, silent and yet alive. The sky was that particular shade of pink that comes only with Christmas snow, and the air was piquant with the tang of damp pine and the promise of things to come. Closing her eyes, Mary felt her heart swell with happiness, but with a yearning as well—a longing so deep and aching that she feared that if she let it grow it would finally consume her, tear her heart in two. And yet she could not stop it, could not turn away from this night. Was it only the coming of Christmas? It felt so much more powerful, as if something buried deep within her were struggling for release. As if—

"Hell's fire!" snapped a voice from behind her, shattering her thoughts. "Close that infernal window, girl, before you freeze us all to death!"

For the space of a single heartbeat, Mary remained as she was, watching the images fading and feeling her heart contract. Then, with a sigh, she straightened. Drawing back into the room and refastening the window, she turned to the old man in the bed.

"I'm sorry, Grandfather." Her smile held only the faintest regret. "I only wanted to smell the snow."

"Smell!" Isaiah Hillyer snorted, his expression disbelieving beneath the gaunt crag of his brow. "Smell is it, girl? And I thought you were different— thought you had some sense. Now I see you're no better than the rest of the family! As if it doesn't cost enough to heat this old barn without your trying to heat the rest of Northampton, as well!"

"Yes, Grandfather," murmured Mary, lowering her eyes to repress a gleam of amusement at his characterization of the house, which was generally considered one of the first in the town. Isaiah himself had built it to be the very first when his factories along the river had made him a wealthy man. Before that, for a century or more, the Hillyers had lived in the old family homestead, which still stood at the edge of town. As she thought of the Old House, Mary's lips curved in an unconscious smile. I'll bet it looks pretty now, she thought, with the snow falling down. How nice it would be in the parlor with a fire to keep you warm.

Her thoughts were broken by a wail rising from the hall, followed a moment later by her sister, Eveline, her pretty face screwed into an expression of disgust.

"Mary," she demanded, "where is my gold locket? I've searched everywhere for it, and it simply can't be found! I can't go without it, and I'm already late!"

Eveline was eighteen, five years younger than Mary, and in coloring and disposition she was her absolute opposite. While Mary's hair was pure brown, the same color as her eyes, Eveline's curls were golden, and her eyes a bright cornflower. Since dinner Eveline had changed into a full evening dress, a billowing rosetted confection of dark green silk. Clouds of light green netting draped the heavy underskirt, looped down to be drawn back in a deep-bustled pouf. A dozen white tea roses were woven into her chignon, and from her ears dangled heavy gold earrings.

Mary, by contrast, still wore the dress in which she had dined, her hair arranged simply and devoid of all ornament. Her eyes chided her sister affectionately, but she merely said, "I haven't seen your locket since you wore it last. Perhaps if Mother is somewhere about she could help you look."

"Oh, Mother!" Eveline rolled her eyes. "She's deep in a séance with Mrs. Parker's niece. Mary, if you don't help me, I'll be hours late and Justin Harris won't have a single dance left for me. Oh, Mary, do help me look!"

"Who's that? Eveline?" Isaiah twisted his head towards the door, but Eveline, with the skill of long practice, had remained just beyond his view. "What's that addlepated ninny fussing over now?"

"Just a locket, Grandfather." Mary smiled soothingly. "I won't be a minute. Then I'll read your Mr. Boswell to you." Moving as she answered, she managed to reach the hall just as she finished speaking so that she was out of the room before he could protest.

And, of course, he did protest. His querulous voice pursued her past her own neat room and into Eveline's chaotic one.

"Worthless!" he complained. "You're worthless, all of you! But what else could you expect from that jellyfish son of mine? Married a silly woman who believes in ghosts, then didn't have the gumption to outlive his old man!"

"The old frog!" Eveline whispered, pulling shut her door.

"Now, Eva." Mary began to sift through the clutter heaped high on the dressing table. "It's only his being an invalid that makes him irritable."

"He was irritable before," Eva retorted, pausing to smile at her reflection in the wardrobe mirror. "Except that back in the old days, when he could walk, he had more people to scold. I can hardly wait until I'm gone from this house! I think that when Justin proposes I shall marry him." Her smile deepened, then faded as she shook her head. "I don't know how you do it, putting up with him day after day!"

"Well, someone has to do it, and I guess that I'm the one. Here, is this what you want?" Straightening,

Mary held up the oval of gold. Eveline clapped her hands.

"Yes, yes, now quickly, where's the ribbon that goes with it? Oh, from all that fussing, look what I've done to my hair!" Her hands flew to her carefully arranged curls, then stopped. "Is that someone knocking at the door? Perhaps it is Justin, stopping on his way.... Why doesn't Emily answer?"

"Because it's her evening off, and Betty is with her mother, who has come down with a putrid throat." Mary slipped the locket on the ribbon with a sigh, and Eveline snatched it from her and pushed her towards the door.

"Then you must go down! Tell him I won't be a minute, I'm just fixing my hair. And hurry, or he'll think that I've already gone."

"Yes, all right," said Mary, hurrying towards the stairs; but, though his legs were useless, Grandfather's ears were razor-sharp.

"Ho, now! Is that Mary, trying to sneak out?" he called. "Likely off to meet some fellow and leave me here to die! If it weren't for my money, you'd have left me long ago! I know what keeps you, don't think that I don't!"

"Oh, dear!" murmured Mary, catching up her skirts to run down the stairs. If only Grandfather had been born with one ounce of tolerance—or if only Mother took as much interest in the living as she did in the dead. If only, if only... Harassed and distracted, she crossed the hall to the door just as the knock was repeated with a vigor that rattled the knob. Turning the lock, she pulled the door open, one hand on the knob . . . and the other pressed to her forehead, which was beginning to pound.

AND THAT WAS HOW Jack Gates saw her first—a slender brown-haired woman in a deep mauve dinner dress, her hand held to her forehead, in evident distress. He stepped forward instinctively, thinking to render aid but, startled by his movement, she stepped away, her hand dropping to her throat, and he saw her eyes widen as if she had had a shock.

Brown eyes, Jack noted, his own eyes resting upon her face. Eyes the same brown as a newly plowed field after the sun has warmed it through the heat of the day. In the instant between heartbeats he felt the sun's good warmth, smelled the richness of the land so soft between bare toes. He had known such pleasures as a boy on his family's Wisconsin farm, in the happy thriving years before his father had fallen ill. And even after that, during all his failing struggles to hold on to the farm, still there had been moments when he had paused in his work and looked up, letting his eyes absorb the quiet beauty of all he saw. "Yes," he had thought at such moments. "Yes, this is worth everything. To hold on to this quiet beauty is worth any sacrifice."

How strange to think of such things now—after so much time and so many changes—staring at this woman, here on this snowy porch. Indeed, this New England mansion was about as far away from the old Gates farm as you could get! Almost as far as the successful young lawyer he had become was from that farm boy. Jack shook his head sharply, as if to clear his thoughts, and the sharpness of the movement seemed to snap the spell that had held them both in thrall. The woman blinked, as if waking from a dream, and her gaze quit Jack for the young man at his side. Jack saw her brown eyes sparkle as shock turned to delight.

"Gray!" Mary exclaimed, still half caught in her daze. But her older brother left no time for recovery; he bounded forward to wrap her in a warm embrace. "But Gray," she protested as he swung her around, "I thought you'd written that you would not come until Christmas Eve!"

"We had thought so too," agreed Gray Hillyer with a grin. "That is, until they gave us time off for good work—and a handsome bonus, too!" Two years Mary's senior, and the sole son among the five Hillyer children, Gray shared Eveline's blond good looks and imperious ways. But tonight he was jovial, and he released Mary to declare, "You are looking, my dear sister, at the two brightest rising stars in all of the Boston bar! May I present my friend and fellow lawyer, Mr. John Franklin Gates. Jack, my sister Mary— the rock and foundation upon which the family stands. Nothing can be so wrong that Mary cannot set it right!"

"Miss Hillyer."

"Mr. Gates."

He took the hand she offered, and as their fingers touched she felt her heart lurch, just as it had when he had stepped towards her with concern in his eyes. As his warm, strong fingers closed about hers, she felt a sense of awakening, as if all her life until this point had been but a dream.

What was it about him that caused this sensation...that made her heart lurch so and her legs tremble as if they would give way? What was it about this man she had never met before that claimed and held her gaze even when she wanted to look away? She scanned his features, searching for some clue.

He was very handsome. The eyes that held hers were a dark, clear blue, deeper and truer than Gray's, their clarity enhanced by thick fringed lashes the same color as his hair, a rich, untinted brown so dark as to be almost black. A lock of hair had fallen forward when he'd removed his hat; now he pushed it back from his forehead with a quick carelessness that tugged at her insides.

But it was not just his good looks. She might not have beaux of her own, but between Gray's friends and Eveline's admirers she had been exposed to her share of handsome men, and she had never before felt this instantaneous stir of recognition. This was something deeper and more intimate, as if in some secret way she were connected to him. And then he smiled. She felt its warmth as it lit upon her, powerful as a theatrical spot lighting the grand entrance of the evening's heroine. For a moment she felt special, treasured, important, as if the smile were meant for her and her alone.

Eveline's voice, calling, reached them from the landing above.

To Mary, the hall lamp seemed to darken as Jack's eyes rose from her to gaze with admiration at the picture Eveline made coming down the stairs.

"Why, Gray, you trickster!" she scolded as she came. "What are you doing here so soon? And just in time for the Woodcrosses' party. I hope you're dressed right now, for I've already ordered the carriage, and I won't wait for you to change!" From the rise in her inflection Mary knew without looking up the exact moment at which Eveline had seen Jack.

"The Woodcrosses' party— What a stroke of luck!" cried Gray. "Of course, we shall go directly, they shall have to take us as we are! Come, Eva, don't dawdle making eyes. Jack, my baby sister—the one I warned you about. Eveline, Mr. Jack Gates."

Mary had to move back to make room for Eveline's full skirts; she watched from the shadows as Mr. Gates took Eveline's hand with the same smile he had shone upon her. Eveline was carrying her wrap upon her arm, and he took it from her. As he laid it upon her shoulders and smoothed it with his hands, Mary felt her own shoulders rise in response to his imagined touch.

A voice came from behind them. "Mary? Is someone here?" A small woman, her light hair laced with grey, stepped forward tentatively, blinking as though her eyes were unaccustomed to the light.

At the sight of her, Gray called out, "Mother! You see, it is I, come home for two weeks, vacation. I hope you haven't let the spirits set up camp in my room!"

"Oh, no," she shook her head. "They only seem to want to come to the back parlor. I've a new one, you know. A Centius Brutus, a goldsmith in ancient Rome. Mrs. Parker's niece helped me to locate him. She is a wonderful medium. Perhaps you will sit with us one night."

"Not I." Gray shook his head. "Not with the Spirit of Christmas Past skulking about the streets."

"Oh, do you really think so?" For a moment Mrs. Hillyer seemed to consider this, but then, with a gesture between a wave and a shrug, she turned and disappeared in the direction from which she had come.

"My mother," Gray explained for Jack's benefit. "She's not much on introductions. Too much on her mind. But here's Tom with the carriage, so it's on to the Woodcrosses'. Jack, Eva . . . out you go!"

Jack's attention was fixed upon guiding Eveline down the snowy steps, so he was in the carriage before he realized that they were only three.

"But what of Miss Hillyer?" he asked, glancing back towards the front door, which had closed behind Gray.

"Who, Mary? Oh, she had to stay with Grandfather. Wait until you meet him. He's a positive bear!" Gray growled in imitation.

Eveline, laughing, explained. "Mary never goes to parties. She likes to stay home."

"Does she?" Jack recalled the range of expression Mary's brown eyes had held. Those eyes had spoken to him—telling or asking, he could not be sure which—and for a moment he pondered, trying to understand. But then Eveline's hand upon his arm claimed his attention, and the gaiety of her laughter rose to sweep him on towards the merriment ahead and away from the one they had left behind.

MARY WATCHED THEM LEAVE. Pushing back the curtain from the window beside the door, she saw Jack take Eveline's arm to help her down the stairs, saw the ease with which he handed her up into the barouche. Watching, she imagined how it would be to feel the firm pressure of his hand, to feel the warmth of his smile for hours together. She heard or imagined she heard the peals of their laughter as Tom mounted the driver's seat and laid the reins on the horses' backs, and within her she felt rising an unaccustomed pang. It really was not just Jack Gates's looks that struck a chord within her, it was something deeper—the grace with which he moved, the sureness and conviction, as if he knew where he was going and that he would arrive, as if he found great satisfaction in everything he did. Watching, Mary wondered what it would be like to spend an evening with him—to have him smile down at her as he had in the hall, to have his arms around her as he led her in a dance. She didn't wish for a lifetime, only for one special night; she wasn't Cinderella, she was just plain Mary Hillyer.

The carriage left the yard, its wheels trailing twin furrows in the deepening snow. No doubt, thought Mary, Eveline was already in love with Mr. Gates. Eveline fell in love with every man she met, and a goodly number of them fell in love with her, as well. Perhaps Jack would propose to Eveline, and perhaps she would accept. Then they would be married and go off to Boston to live, as her sister Sophia had done.

Sophia, who was twenty-eight, had been married for ten years. She had five children, and Florence, who was twenty-one, already had two. It was only a matter of time until Eveline, too, had a husband and children whom she would bring to spend Christmas with their spinster Aunt Mary.

When had it happened? When had everyone begun thinking of her as an old maid? Surely there had been a time when she had expected another life, a home of her own, with babies and a wonderful man to love. When had her bright dreams faded, and what had caused their death? Had it been Florence's marriage, the knowledge that her younger sister had passed ahead of her? She had thought then that it was. But now, looking back, she saw that it must have happened earlier than that, and more subtly, as well, the slipping from girlhood into her present role.

Was it something physical? She couldn't believe it was. She wasn't a blond beauty like Eveline, but still, she had never been displeasing to the eye and she could have named a dozen girls whom she had known in school who could not claim beauty among their attributes and who were nonetheless long since married and raising families. What then could it be that turned men away? What was it that had sent Jack Gates off without a backward glance tonight? Had he seen something when he looked at her, some invisible message that had said she belonged at home and not out beside him, not dancing in his arms.

A thin voice from above broke into her thoughts. It was Grandfather, outraged at her continued desertion. Outside, the snow had already erased the carriage tracks, and the yard stood still and lovely beneath its blanket of white. What foolishness was she thinking, going on like this, mooning like a schoolgirl over a man she had hardly met?

This sort of dissatisfaction wasn't like her at all. She would feel better in the morning, when the sun shone on the snow. Christmas was coming—it was her favorite time of year—and she would soon have plenty to keep her occupied. Still, she lingered a moment, seeing in her mind the way he'd pushed back the hair from his forehead. When she released the curtain it fell into place. Turning from the window, Mary crossed the hall.

"I'm coming, Grandfather. I'm coming now," she called.

## Chapter Two

JACK SPREAD BUTTER on a biscuit and took a bite, sighing with satisfaction as the richness rolled over his tongue. The taste brought back memories of childhood and home—as did the aroma of sweetness that had drifted from beneath the kitchen door and snaked up the back stairs, all the way to the third-floor room that he was sharing with Gray. Gray was still sleeping off the effects of last night's late hours, but the smell had awakened Jack and coaxed him from his bed, hurrying through his ablutions and leading him downstairs to the dining room. There a basket of light-bread biscuits awaited him on the table, and an urn of almost-warm coffee on the sideboard. He imagined that the kitchen would produce more if he asked, but something about the way the morning light slanted through the tall windows made him opt instead for plain biscuits and solitude.

Jack spread the second half of the biscuit with blackberry jam that he knew without having to taste it would be homemade as well. He remembered how it was cooked in big pans in the kitchen, simmering at a slow boil, then set out to cool on the worktable, absorbing the ruby brightness of the morning sun. It had been a long time since he'd tasted homemade jam. Too long, he thought with an unexpected pang of nostalgia. A rising young lawyer in Boston hardly had time to spare for eating, let alone for tasting his food, and even the time he had off from the office was most often spent advancing his career.

The last time he'd left Boston had been six months ago, and that had been only for a weekend at Mr. Clyburn's house in Maine. Mr. Clyburn was a senior partner in the firm. It had been a mark of favor to be invited to his house, and Jack had shown his appreciation by squiring Mr. Clyburn's daughter about, though many of the other young ladies would have made better company. There had even been one rather well-preserved wife who had let him know by look and by innuendo that she would welcome the diversion of a weekend's dalliance. Another man in his position might have been seduced, but instead Jack had put her off with just the mixture of humbleness and good humor that would keep her from becoming an enemy while preserving her as a friend. He might be country-bred, but he'd learned...he'd learned. He knew where he was going, and he knew how to get there, as well. He was going to be rich—as rich and as respected as Clyburn himself.

Strange to have traveled so very far from his roots. If someone had told him at age twelve that this would be his life, Jack would have laughed in his face. He had seen the future with a complacent eye then. He had thought he would grow to manhood in the house his grandfather had built, farming the same acres his father had cleared. Then, when he married, he would buy land of his own—since his older brother, Ned, would surely inherit the farm—and raise upon it a home as happy as the one in which he had been born.

But then his father had fallen ill. It had begun with a stomachache that Jack's mother had dosed with all the old remedies. But the ache had dragged on and little by little his body had succumbed, until he moved about stooped over like an old man. By the time he had seen the doctor, the wasting had gone too far, and there had been nothing left to do but dull the pain for what time was left.

Perhaps the farm would have survived if the war with the South had not come. Ned had been drafted, and Jack, then just fifteen, had stepped into his brother's place, with only his mother beside him. He had done the best he could, rising in the darkness and working past dark every night. But there had never been quite enough hours in the day, and every time he had looked up something else had gone wrong. The stock had taken ill, the rains had failed, the spring thaw had come too soon. Bit by bit they had borrowed against everything they had, holding on until the day Ned would return.

Then had come the telegram informing them that Private Gates had died a hero's death, and within the same month the bank had moved to foreclose. By the day of the auction, Jack's mother was dead—of pneumonia, the doctor said, but in truth of a broken heart. In a daze, Jack had seen the land his grandfather had claimed from virgin woods sold away, and he himself hired out to the local lawyer as an errand boy.

In time the numbness had faded and Jack had found himself faced with the choice of taking what fate had dealt him or trying to better it. He had chosen the latter course. Working even longer hours than he had on the farm, he had scratched out as much of an education as the lawyer's books could afford. Then, turning his back on Wisconsin, his birthright and his dreams, he had struck out for Boston, where the real learning was. Five more long years of toil had earned him a law degree, and a job in the respected firm of Clyburn and Scott. To some the job would have been a triumph in itself, but to Jack it was but one more step up to the top—to the pinnacle of power on which he meant to stand.

Experience had taught Jack that only power and wealth could ensure the security he craved. Someday he intended to own that security. He meant to be like Mr. Clyburn, with a Back Bay mansion and a summer house in Maine, and weekend parties, and servants and carriages. It wasn't enough to be well-off, as the Hillyers so obviously were. He wanted more than that. He wanted people to point him out when he drove by, murmuring to each other, "Look, there goes Jack Gates." Jack meant to beat the bankers at their own game.

He meant to, and he would. It was worth the long hours, the hurriedly bolted meals, the constant politicking and the courting of homely girls. It was worth all the imposition in order to reach the goal. And he was sure he would reach it, for his feet were set upon the path, and surely such single-minded ambition as his would earn its just reward.

"MOTHER, I was thinking—"

A voice broke into Jack's thoughts, and he recognized it even before the kitchen door swung back to disclose the flushed face of Mary Hillyer. She had been speaking as she'd entered, but now, at the sight of Jack, she stopped, and her confusion mounted as he rose to welcome her.

"Miss Hillyer. Good morning."

"Mr. Gates! What are you doing here?" Then, hearing the tone of her question, she added hurriedly, "It's just that I thought to find my mother alone. Emily brought her breakfast not fifteen minutes ago. Have you been here waiting? I didn't hear you ring."

"Because I didn't ring. I came downstairs for breakfast and, finding the table set, imposed upon your hospitality by simply helping myself. Would you care to join me?" He gestured to the place that had been set opposite.

"No, thank you. Please sit down. I can't think what has happened to Mother. She usually stays for a while."

"Perhaps she heard something calling," he suggested with a smile so thoroughly friendly that she could not take offense. Today he was wearing a charcoal-gray morning coat and a pearl-gray waistcoat and trousers; they were the same color as the light that filtered in from the snow yard. She felt a rush of pleasure to find that he was as handsome by day as he had been the night before.

"Yes, perhaps," she agreed. "I suppose that Gray has told you about Mother's beliefs. It's been her single interest ever since Father died. Some people think it silly—my sister Sophia for one. She believes that communing with spirits is nothing but hocus-pocus. Perhaps she is right, I can't say for sure, but I think people often discount what they do not believe. And if it brings happiness—'' She stopped and shook her head, astonished and bewildered by the way she was rattling on about something in which Mr. Gates likely had no interest at all—not to mention interrupting his meal. "But I have kept you from your breakfast. Those biscuits must be cold.... I will warm them for you. And what will you have besides? Ham and eggs, or fried steak? Whatever you prefer.''

He stayed her with a gesture, touched by her earnestness. "I thank you for your kindness, but the biscuits are enough. And as for your mother's interest—whatever gives her the will to remain among the living is worthy of respect.''

She paused, caught off guard by the sincerity of his tone and the directness of his gaze. Then her eyes, losing courage, slid to the table, where his hand lay so slim and strong along the snowy cloth. Although she knew she ought to go and leave him in peace, she felt drawn to stay. The cloth beyond where he was sitting had been rucked up, as if someone had brushed by it with full skirts. Without thinking, she reached out to smooth it, sensing his eyes upon her.

"Is . . . is your mother still alive?''

"No,'' he answered, and saw her start slightly at the bitterness of his tone. The quickness of her motions, her shy brown-eyed way, made him think of a doe caught by surprise. Once, as a boy, he had come upon a doe in the forest. He had been hunting, and he could have killed her, but instead he had held his fire and watched as she'd moved away into the underbrush. Now Miss Hillyer raised her head in exactly the same way the doe had.

"I—I am sorry to hear it. Is it a recent loss?"

"Not at all. She died years ago, when I was just a boy. Ancient history—and surely not a thing to think of on such a lovely day!" he said, flashing her a smile that achieved its purpose of drawing hers in response. He realized that she must have been helping with the cooking of the sweets, for as she moved closer the aroma clung to her. "Tell me what you've been cooking?" he asked, sniffing the air.

"Oh!" She cast that quick glance at him again. "Toffee and peppermint drops, to give away for gifts. They don't really need me—" she nodded towards the door "—but I do enjoy it—the toffee especially. Do you like toffee, Mr. Gates?"

"More than anything on earth! When I was a child, my mother cooked pans at Christmastime. Then she'd bar us from the kitchen so that we couldn't taste. But we would always persuade her to take a kinder view. Tell me, Miss Hillyer, do you take a kind view?"

"I?" she answered, shivering at the intimacy of his voice, which seemed to reach out and lay a finger upon her skin and sent chills racing down her spine. "My sisters would say so," she heard herself saying in an oddly breathless voice, "for they complain that I spoil their children when they come for the holiday. If you like, I shall cut you some toffee as soon as it has cooled."

"I would like that very much." He smiled, at once amused and touched by the innocence of her charm.

He was used to women who played sophisticated games, and he prided himself upon being able to match them point for point. But the limpid brown eyes she raised to him now held neither subterfuge nor bluff, only a genuine gratification at having pleased. On impulse, he invited her to join him again, but once more she refused.

"No, I couldn't, really, not in this old dress, all treacle from head to toe."

His attention called to it, he considered her dress. Caught by other impressions, he had not noticed it before, but now he saw that it was unusually plain—a high-collared white bodice and a dark wool skirt. Something about its design struck him as different. For an instant he pondered; then he knew what it was. Of late, fashion had demanded full bustles, but her skirt hung unbroken from her waist to the floor, giving her slender figure a clean delicacy that he found not only refreshing but also surprisingly attractive.

"I like your dress," he said, nodding approvingly. "I think if you were to wear it out on the street you would spur a change in fashion—and perhaps a welcome one."

"Mr. Gates, you are very kind—" she began, flushing deeply. Just then there was a sound like a pile of bricks crashing to the floor above. At the sight of Jack's expression, Mary had to smile. "It's Grandfather," she explained. "His room is right above. He taps the floor with his cane when he wants me during meals."

The ogre . . . He had forgotten. Then he recalled, as well, what Gray and Eveline had said about Mary liking to stay in. They had spoken with conviction, yet he could not believe that anyone would prefer nursing to amusement. "He must be demanding. It's not much of a life."

He had meant to be sympathetic, but her response was defensive. "I have no complaints," she said quickly, drawing herself up. "I have plenty to keep me busy, and Grandfather's not so bad."

"I only meant—" The bricks fell again, louder and more insistent than before. As he had the first time, Jack cringed instinctively. "Not so bad, eh?" His brows rose skeptically. She opened her mouth to deny it, then surprised them both by laughing aloud instead. For the first moment Jack watched her; then his laughter joined hers. The old man must have heard them, for the cane beat an angry tattoo.

"I'd better go," said Mary, smiling regretfully. "Just ring the bell for Emily if you should need anything."

He sat listening to the fall of her retreating steps, the biscuit, still half-eaten, lying upon his plate. Now he put the remaining bit into his mouth, but though it had lost no richness, his thoughts were no longer upon the taste but were rather upon the girl whose laughter still rang in his ears. Woman, he corrected, for she was past her first bloom. Yet, but for the fact of the household being balanced upon her shoulders, there was still something about her that made her appear very young, untried and innocent.

She intrigued him. Gray had described her to him as an old maid, and from the description he had expected something tired and dry, but as far as he could determine she was neither of those things. Raising the cup to his lips, Jack drank thoughtfully, contemplating the attractions of Mary Hillyer. They said that still waters ran deep; he wondered what he would discover if he probed her depths. Perhaps only a nice, simple, quiet small-town girl—the type of girl he would have said was not his cup of tea. Jack's eye was attracted by sophistication and style, for such things in a woman would enhance his position. Clearly Mary Hillyer lacked both of those things, and yet...

And yet. Leaning back in his chair, he remembered the way she'd smiled, the way she'd flushed when he'd mentioned her dress. The way she'd laughed. She was like a frightened doe, but she was also like the purple gentian that grew in the woods back home, hiding its beauty beneath plain leaves so that you had to search. When you found it, you felt a special thrill, the feeling that it had been waiting just for you.

A familiar set of footsteps sounded outside the door, which burst open to disclose Gray, freshly groomed and eager to get on with the day.

"Where has Mary gone in such a rush?" he asked, flipping back the napkin to inspect the basket's contents.

"Up to your grandfather. He was pounding on the floor."

"Was he?" Gray broke a biscuit in half and popped it in his mouth. "He's an old brute, isn't he? Rich as Croesus, though you'd never know it, he's so tight with his funds. I've just been in to see him.... You know, keep up the good work. I suppose that's what has gotten him all worked up. Well, if he's in a state by now, we'd best make ourselves scarce. We'll go down to Main Street. Everyone will be in the shops—including Annabella Woodcross, who seemed to catch your eye last night." He winked and downed the remains of the biscuit. Tucking two more in his pocket, he turned to Jack. "Well, then, are you coming—or shall I claim Annabella for my own?"

"Heaven forbid!" Jack laughed, recalling the green-eyed beauty with whom he had danced the night before. Mary Hillyer intrigued him, but she would still be there later. In the meantime, pleasure beckoned, and Jack was not one to turn away. He meant to enjoy this well-earned vacation. Tossing his napkin on the table, he said, "Lead the way!"

"*FAUGH!* IT'S POISON, I say! Likely I'd be better without a bit of it—Then again, if I dropped dead, you'd none of you be sad!"

"Now, Grandfather," Mary said soothingly, recapping the brown bottle. "You know that's not true."

"Not true, eh?" The old man turned shrewd eyes upon her. That was the trouble with aging: his mind was still sharp enough to put in a fourteen-hour day; only his body was failing, and it was failing miserably. If living weren't such a habit, he'd have died long ago. God alone knew why he kept at it; he had little enough enjoyment. At least he had the satisfaction of knowing he'd lived a full life—fuller than most people could ever wish to live.

Take the girl, for instance. In her place he wouldn't put up with a cranky old man. He'd have poisoned the patient or he'd have up and left. But she did neither; instead she cared for him, day after day, when other girls were marrying or gadding about like birds. He wondered why she did it. Feebleminded, most likely... but, even as his mind uttered the judgment, he recognized it as the product of a pain-filled night. She wasn't feebleminded. Quite the opposite: if she lacked a real life, he was the one to blame. Well, he'd make it up to her. He'd drawn his will to leave her the best part of his fortune, and done it in a trust so that she would not end up giving it all to the rest—as he had no doubt they could convince her to do.

"That brother of yours, for one," he said, following his thoughts. "He was just in to see me—only stopped by to make sure that I don't forget how to spell his name when I make my will! All top hat and smiles and 'How well you look, Grandfather.' Well! Ha!" the old man barked. "I haven't looked well in over twenty years. If that's how he talks to his clients, he won't go very far."

"Gray has done very well." Mary pulled the covers tight at the end of the bed. "They've given him a bonus and two weeks' vacation for the work he's done. I'm sure he only meant to be encouraging."

Isaiah Hillyer continued to study his granddaughter. Yes, she would see one day that he'd appreciated her care. But what of the meantime? What of suitors, and marriage? He knew that he'd lessened her chances by keeping her in, away from the parties and social occasions where courting was done. Perhaps it was unfair, he thought, struck by a sudden qualm, but he needed her. Nobody understood how it was to be stuck in bed, at the mercy of whoever decided to look in. He could depend on Mary, and if he let her go the rest of his bat-brained family would likely let him starve.

And besides, he continued, pursuing his own defense, it wasn't as though he kept her from showing her face on the street. If a young man was interested in carrying on with her, he would surely try to steal her away—and if he had enough gumption, he would surely succeed.

"That's the way I did it," he said, thinking aloud again. "I snatched your grandmother from beneath her father's nose. He didn't think I was good enough for his girl, but I had my convictions and I acted upon them. Good enough... Ha! Why, I made enough money to buy him twenty times over!"

"And Grandmother was worth it, wasn't she?" Mary moved from the bed to the table, tidying as she went.

"Worth it and more, she was! She was as fine a woman as God has set upon this earth—and as pretty a one, as well. And tiny! Shoes like a doll's slippers, and she danced like a butterfly. All the young men wanted to dance the last dance with her, but I told her that she'd better save it for me. And so she did, though her father almost hit the roof. But I told her that I'd handle him, and in the end I did!" Isaiah chuckled to himself. Mary smiled with him, but she wasn't listening, he could see from her eyes, and the way her head was tilted, as if she were listening to something else. Cocking his head, Isaiah heard the front door slam, and voices below on the steps. "Who is that?" he demanded.

"What?" She turned from the table, then she realized what he had asked. "Oh, it's only Gray and Eveline, and a friend that Gray's brought home—a Mr. Jack Gates. A gentleman." She knew that it was foolish, but she could not resist the temptation of speaking his name out loud.

As she had expected, Grandfather pounced upon her. "Caught your eye, has he? Well, I say he's not worth it!"

"Grandfather, what an idea! I hardly know the man. Nor do you, I might mention, though you judge him most harshly."

"And with good reason! If he was worth the salt on a pickled herring he'd have stayed right here at home with you instead of going out gallivanting with that no-account brother of yours! Ha! Haha!" he barked, pleased with himself for having caught her on the point. But Mary, being Mary, did not protest. She turned back to her fussing, hiding her face from him. He watched her for a moment; then, at last, he gave up, for talking had made him tired, that and the medicine. That was the trouble with young men, he thought, closing his eyes. That was the trouble with everything, everything, these days.

Mary gave up on the row of bottles and smoothed her skirt with fingers that were still shaking from Grandfather's questions. I like your dress, he had told her, smiling that smile of his that made her feel special, important, unique. And Jack Gates was more than pretty compliments, she thought, remembering the intensity of his tone when he had defended her mother and spoken of his own. He had known sorrow, for all his dashing airs. It drew her heart to him, made her want to comfort him.

They had laughed together. The thought warmed her heart. Jack was different from other people, though she couldn't have said why. On him the simplest gesture glowed so very vividly. Perhaps it was the force of his vitality that made him seem more real, more alive. And then there was the way he looked at her, as if he saw something more than plain Mary Hillyer. Whenever Jack looked at her, she felt that she was more, like a brand-new person whom no one had ever met. She had known him less than one day, and yet she could recall his every word and gesture with perfect clarity. Already, without thinking, she had begun to build a store, a trove of precious moments to be kept for when he left. She would take them out on long winter evenings and pastel spring twilights, to try to dull the yearning that never seemed to die.

Behind her, Grandfather had begun to snore. Leaving the table, she moved to the bed, looking down at the old slack face, the lines of pain and age that seemed to be etched into the bone. Yet there was more there, much more, that she could not see, experience and pleasure, a life's worth of success. She wondered what she would have when she reached his age. Perhaps only the satisfaction of knowing that she had helped. Well, if so, then that must be enough. She touched the gnarled fingers that lay on the counterpane, then turned away and moved silently to the door, leaving the room on tiptoe so as not to disturb his rest.

# Chapter Three

MR. GATES, you skate as well as you dance." Annabella Woodcrosses' green eyes were coolly appreciative. "Don't tell me you have time for such things in your Boston life."

"Had I a partner as fair as you, I would surely make the time," Jack replied smoothly, swinging Annabella to the left in order to avoid two boys racing across the frozen pond. The snow that had been falling at his arrival two days before had left a good eight inches behind, and a thick coat decorated the surrounding shrubs and trees. This morning, it being Saturday, a number of the young men had come down armed with brooms and shovels to clear the pond's surface, and now, just short of noon, a crowd had collected. Young girls showed off their turns to the boys, who did their best to impress with speed and daring, and couples glided hand in hand in what space remained.

Annabella smiled at Jack's chivalrousness. "Mr. Gates, you are gallant, yet I find it hard to believe that Boston cannot produce a single pretty girl."

"Perhaps one," he allowed, returning her smile. "But I don't think I've been skating since I was a boy in school. Then I was on the ice as often as at my books—and some things, happily, one does not forget." He swung her wide again, and her skirts swirled in a graceful arc, showing a generous ruffle and a trim ankle beneath. Annabella wore a green velvet walking dress—picked to match her eyes, he imagined— and a tiny bonnet perched high upon her curls. Beyond doubt, she cut the finest figure on the ice, and the tilt of her head informed him that she knew it well. Her family, according to Gray, was the wealthiest in town. Jack had danced with her last night and the night before, though what claim she might lay to him would not outlast the holiday. He'd steered a clear course in Boston, and he would do so here, as well; pretty women were a pleasure, but marriage to one of them was not a part of his plans at present.

She laughed now as he pulled her back towards him, her smile at once girlish and knowing. "Are you enjoying your vacation? I wonder what you make of the Hillyers? Do you not find them a most peculiar bunch?"

"Peculiar?" he repeated, wondering at her choice of words.

"Not Gray or Eveline, of course, they are as normal as you or I—though Eveline can be excessive when it comes to men. But the mother is another thing. Everybody knows that she spends more time speaking to her dead husband than to anyone left alive!" As before, her laughter invited a response from Jack, but, though he managed a smile, it was not genuine.

"Many people believe in spirits," he said, surprised to hear a sharpness in his voice. "Likely more people than not. And if it brings her happiness..." Even as he spoke, he recalled his conversation with Miss Hillyer.

"Oh, she is harmless enough," Annabella agreed. "More so than that old tartar, her father-in-law. And then, of course, there is Mary—though one hardly thinks of her."

"So it seems," murmured Jack, frowning to himself, missing in his musing the curiosity in Annabella's upward glance. "But," he continued, still in the same tone, "she is not bad-looking. Nor is she unpleasant company. I wonder what it can be that has kept her from marrying."

"Disposition, perhaps," Annabella said with a shrug. "My mother says that some women are born to be old maids. She says that they must be, or there wouldn't be men enough to go around. Thank goodness, that has never been a worry of mine!" she concluded with a smile, one that seemed to be lost on him. Instead, he was apparently still considering her previous statement, and with real interest.

"You think that Miss Hillyer was born never to wed?"

"That is just what Mother thinks. How can one ever know?" she replied, trying to keep her irritation from her voice. She scarcely intended to waste her time listening to him pondering the fate of Mary Hillyer. "What a gloomy subject to discuss on such a lovely day! Isn't the morning splendid now that the sun is out?"

"Splendid," Jack agreed. Indeed, the sun did cast bright diamonds across the snowy fields, and the air was bracing, and Annabella was light on her feet. All the requisite ingredients for a perfect day. Then why this restless feeling, this longing to be gone from the ice and even from Annabella, pretty as she was? Why this preoccupation with Mary Hillyer?

Since their talk yesterday morning, he had hardly laid eyes on her, but this morning, when he and Gray and Eveline had been leaving for the pond, Mary had come into the hall to inquire if they planned to be in for lunch. From the open door behind her had come the heady scent of pine, from which Jack had concluded that she must be decorating—perhaps tying boughs into long ropes to be draped around the room, just as his mother and he had done every year at this time.

The vivid warmth of memory had flooded over him, just as it had the day before, and he had realized in surprise that he had thought of his childhood twice in two days. He never did that. The darkness of his adolescent years had so obliterated the early happiness that he had put all such thoughts from his mind, not only of the times that were best forgotten, but also of the good days that had come before. Happiness was rooted in far more recent things: in pursuing his ambitions, and in such fleeting pleasures as parties and flirtations with pretty women. But now, standing in the hallway, his eyes on Mary's face, he had felt for the first time in years the real joy of Christmastime. He had smiled at the memory, and Mary had smiled at him. At the time, he had seen only her smile. Now he recalled her eyes, as well . . . so very brown and wistful as she had wished the three departing skaters a good morning on the pond.

Had Mary's eyes been wistful or was he imagining it? According to Gray and Eveline, they could not have been, for Gray and Eveline were quite certain that Mary preferred to stay at home. And hadn't Mary said the same just yesterday morning? Then what gave him the impression that she was reaching out, perhaps not to him directly, perhaps to something beyond?

Annabella was speaking. He realized that he had not heard her. "I beg your pardon," he said, shaking his head. "I fear that all the fresh air has gone to my head. My thoughts seem to wander.... What was it that you said?"

"Only that they say it will snow again tonight. I hope so, for we are planning a sleigh ride tomorrow evening. Of course you and Gray will come.... I'd invite you to join our party, but I know that Gray will want to take his own sleigh. Well, after we stop for refreshments, perhaps we shall be rearranged.

"Have you had enough skating?" she added, for, despite his apology, he seemed preoccupied still. "If you have, we can collect the others and go have something warm to drink. I think that Hetty Pickering is expecting to take us all home. Gray and Eveline will be coming—and Justin Harris, of course, as it seems that Eveline is permanently attached to his arm!" Annabella laughed, partly at her own joke and partly with pleasure at the thought that Eveline was so smitten with Justin as to show little interest in Jack. It was not that Annabella really feared competition, just that Eveline had an unfair advantage, for Jack was staying with her family. But Eveline's preoccupation left the field open, for, according to Gray, Jack had no Boston sweetheart to occupy his thoughts.

"Well, then," she concluded, "are you ready to go?"

"Yes, I am." He nodded as if he had come to a sudden decision. Gripping her arm firmly he steered her towards the edge of the pond. "Only I am afraid that I cannot join you and the rest. I'm afraid that I have . . . some work I must complete."

"Work!" Annabella's tone expressed her disbelief. "On such a lovely morning?"

"Even so," he said, wondering at himself at least as much as she was. Was he mad to leave the party just as it was getting under way? It was utterly unlike him. And yet here he was stooping to unlace his blades with hurried fingers, bidding her goodbye as quickly as he could, so that he could be away before Gray realized and came after him. Perhaps it was madness. Why this eagerness . . . as if he were a child who'd been promised some special treat if he came straight home without stopping after school? Why this light-hearted joy? His blades over his shoulder, Jack made his way up the bank without a backward glance.

Annabella watched him go, torn between irritation and mounting puzzlement. Was it truly work that had taken him away? What else could it be? Not another girl, surely, for all the girls who mattered were right here at the pond. Then it must be work. She could hardly fault him for that, for, although it was not pleasant to be abandoned thus, still she must admire the ambition that took him off. She could understand ambition, for she shared it herself. And Gray said that Jack was sure to go far, that he was a favorite with the seniors at the firm. He'd be the sort of husband who did not spend much time at home, and yet, she thought, five minutes of Jack Gates's time would be worth five hours of another man's.

Yes, she concluded, turning back as he disappeared beyond the trees, he would be worth it. Well, there was a week to Christmas, still plenty of time. Plenty of time to maneuver him to where she wanted him to be: down on his knees before her with a proposal on his lips. There was still a week to Christmas, she thought with a smile.

"A LITTLE MORE TO THE LEFT, miss. Yes, that's it. My! How pretty it looks already!" Emily, the downstairs maid, clasped her hands together, admiring the effect of the holly cluster Miss Hillyer had just fastened to the rope of evergreen that decorated the top and sides of the parlor mantelpiece. She and Miss Hillyer had been working since breakfast that morning, breaking the pine boughs into pieces, then tying them to the length of rope with bits of copper wire. It was tedious work, but it was enjoyable, both for the finished product, and for the company. Emily liked working with Miss Hillyer, who was clear in her directions, unlike Mrs. Hillyer, and never lost her temper, unlike those other two. As a rule, Miss Hillyer was companionable, as well, not chattering six to the dozen the way some ladies did, just a well-placed comment now and then.

This morning, however, the comments had been fewer than usual; nor was Miss Hillyer smiling and humming beneath her breath as she did each year when they strung the pine ropes. Everyone knew how

fond Miss Hillyer was of the Christmas season, and
yet this morning she seemed silent and preoccupied, as
though the best part of her mind were fixed on something else, something troubling.

Emily wondered what it could be. Surely not family
trouble, for she would have heard—there was little in
the household that the servants did not know, and,
besides, none of the others seemed the least bit out of
sorts. Mrs. Hillyer was lost among the clouds, and the
old gentleman was his normal grouchy self, while Mr.
Gray and Miss Eveline seemed in top spirits, gadding
about like jaybirds with that handsome Mr. Gates
who'd come home with Mr. Gray. Yesterday it had
been shopping and then a supper party, and up again
this morning and off for ice-skating and goodness
knew what else, for they'd told Miss Hillyer that they
wouldn't be dining in. She'd run out to catch them as
they'd passed in the hall, and Mr. Gray had told her
that they'd be gone all day. Now that Emily thought
back upon it, Miss Hillyer's dark mood had seemed to
begin after that. Frowning, Emily pondered this new
idea. What could it be, she wondered.... So intent was
she upon her thoughts that she missed the ringing of
the bell until Miss Hillyer spoke her name.

"Emily, there's someone at the door. I wonder who
it could be," she added. "I heard no carriage or
horse."

"Perhaps the postman with a special letter from one
of your sisters," Emily volunteered over her shoulder. But it was not the mailman who stood on the
brick porch, but rather Mr. Gates, whose smile of
gratitude warmed the chilly air.

"I had enough of skating," he offered as she took his Inverness coat—as though he must explain his presence in the house. She expected him to go upstairs, but instead he followed her across the hall to the parlor, hesitating a moment just outside the door.

Mary heard his momentary pause and felt her heart stop for fear he would turn back. She had heard him speak to Emily at the door, and had sat as if cast in stone these last two minutes, a half-woven wreath of holly forgotten in her hand, her whole mind repeating: "Please, let him come, let him come!"

And then there he was, framed in the doorway, his cheeks flushed from exercise, his eyes such a brilliant blue that she could hardly look at them. She felt her lungs collapsing.

"Mr. Gates," she wheezed.

"Good morning, Miss Hillyer." He seemed to hear nothing unusual in her voice; he looked about him, inhaling the rich smell of the pine. When at last his glance reached her, she melted beneath its warmth. "You have been doing good work—as always, I should say."

"You are too kind," she managed, feeling her cheeks beginning to burn. Jack noticed her color, and so did Emily.

Could it be, Emily wondered, her eyebrows drawing up, that even our Miss Hillyer is not immune to Mr. Gates's charms...Miss Hillyer, who has never shown a shadow's care for a man? Why, just last week in the kitchen Mrs. Parker was commenting that perhaps Miss Hillyer didn't care any more for men than men seemed to care for her. Wouldn't Mrs. Parker be surprised when she heard about this!

"It is less work than a pleasure," said Mary, and suddenly she meant it, for the cloud that had been weighing her down had lifted with his appearance. The world, which had been so dark, now seemed full of charm and bright promise. "You are back early from skating. I hope nothing is amiss."

"No, nothing. It was only that I . . . had some work to do."

"What a pity. And on your vacation." She smiled sympathetically, wondering why he looked almost embarrassed. His eyes, which had been on her, circled the room again, and landed upon the rope of pine that lay across the table.

"Here, let me help you hang it," he offered, advancing.

"Oh! Thank you for your kindness, but there is no need."

"But I would enjoy it."

"What about your work?"

"Work?" His face went blank for a moment. Then, flushing, he shook his head. "Oh, that is no matter. It will surely keep." Mary was baffled, but she was too glad to care.

"All right, then, I'd like that." she said, rising. "We'll hang this one on the mirror." Lifting one end, she turned, and that was when she noticed Emily standing at the door, eyes bright with an interest that was all too transparent. Mary felt her color rising as it had before. "Emily, Mr. Gates and I can manage this. I think perhaps Mrs. Parker could use your help with the meal. Thank you for all your help.''

''Yes, miss. Very good.'' With a bob and a half-hidden smile, Emily left the room, full of what she would tell Mrs. Parker and Betty and Tom. Of course, very likely Mr. Gates was only being kind, for what should a handsome gentleman like that want with Miss Hillyer? Still, it was nice for Miss Hillyer to have a little flutter now and again.

Jack was tall enough to drape the mirror without a chair. Mary stood beside him, holding up the ends, while he tucked the rope around the corners, fluffing the fullness of the branches out over the wood. Then she brought the holly wreaths from the table for him to attach as trim.

''Just above the corner. That's it.'' She nodded approvingly as he fastened it. ''It looks so pretty.... I sometimes wonder if I don't enjoy the preparation as much as the day itself.''

''Or more, perhaps.'' He reached for a second wreath. ''I remember, when I was a child, feeling such a letdown when the last of the treats were eaten and no more surprises were left. I remember that once I burst into tears over my empty plate, and when my parents asked me what was wrong I couldn't think of what to say. They concluded the problem was too much plum pudding, but I knew that wasn't it—I suppose it was the letdown that I was feeling. The bubble grows slowly bigger, and then the bubble bursts, leaving nothing but crumpled wrappings and dirty dishes behind.''

"But what of the presents?" she reminded him. "Even when the pudding is eaten, the presents still remain."

"Yes, but they lose their magic once they are taken from the tree. Then they are no longer presents, but instead only things— Why do you smile that way?"

"You argue like a lawyer."

"Heaven forbid!" He laughed, feeling again the lightheartedness he had felt upon leaving the pond. The sun, which had been shining, had disappeared behind the clouds, but to him it seemed to be the other way around, as if the sharpness he had missed had now been restored, here in this paneled parlor fragrant with fresh-cut greens.

Mary stood behind him, watching as he worked, obviously unaware that he could see her in the mirror. Today she was wearing a day dress of deep cinnamon wool; it was not a color he would have chosen, yet it suited her well, as did the simple way in which she dressed her hair. He felt a surge of pleasure, a pleasure that was inextricable from the scent of the pine and the brightness of the holly berries and the steadiness of her gaze.

"You were up late last night. I . . . heard you when I came in."

"Yes. Grandfather had a bad night. It helps when I read aloud." He had heard her, too! Her heart leapt at his words, as if he had reinforced some secret bond between them. For of course she had heard his tread on the stairs, and had paused in her reading to listen as he passed. She had hardly seen him that day, for he had been out with Gray and Eveline all day, and all night, as well. Sitting with Grandfather, her eyes on the book, she had longed to run out into the hall, just to see how he looked, so carelessly handsome in his good broadcloth, his hair rumpled from the evening and the ride home, his eyes dark with fatigue.

Watching her in the mirror, Jack saw the same wistfulness he had seen before steal into her eyes again. *And then, of course, there is Mary,* Annabella had said, *though one hardly thinks of her.* He turned.

"Come out with me!" he said.

"What—now?" She looked around them, at the half-finished room.

"No not now..." he cast about, too, feeling strangely giddy. "Not now, but tomorrow evening— There's to be a sleigh ride. Everyone is going.... You'll enjoy yourself."

"No, really, I could not," she said automatically. "Who would care for Grandfather? His nights are often hard."

"Why not your mother?"

In spite of herself, she smiled, and, realizing the ineptness of his idea, he smiled, as well.

But still he persisted. "Then why not one of the maids? Someone must care for him when you do your errands." Pausing then, he added, "Tell me, how long has it been since you've been on a sleigh ride?"

He regretted the question as soon as the words were out, for he saw her stiffen and draw her shoulders up. It must be bad enough to lead the life she did without some passing stranger rubbing her nose in it.

"I'm sorry," he said quickly. "It's only that I do want you to go."

At that she looked up, her eyes searching for the expected pity, but finding only compassion and a strange eagerness. She did not understand it, could not understand why he should want her to go out with him when he could have any girl in town. It was a dream, a miracle, a made-up Christmas tale. And yet it seemed to be happening....

"Please, will you come?" he asked.

"Yes. All right." She nodded, wondering how she would manage to leave Grandfather.

"Then it is decided," he said. "Only promise you won't change your mind. Promise me you'll come, and everything else will work."

"I promise," she whispered, and wondered if the whole world could hear her heart shouting for joy.

# Chapter Four

NOT THE BLUE. No, definitely not. The style is out-dated and the color makes you look washed out.''

Eveline, normally so indecisive, spoke with finality as she ran her fingers through the clothing in Mary's wardrobe, scarcely aware of Mary, who waited patiently, her hair bound up in the rags that Eveline said would increase its curl.

"Which leaves the light brown," Eveline concluded, drawing out the gown. "My goodness, I cannot fathom how you can make do with only two evening gowns—and the blue's the one you had made when Florence was married. That's almost four years ago!"

"I don't go out too often," Mary reminded her.

"That's so," Eveline agreed, her eyes, still not approving, fixed upon the second gown. "What a pity that you are taller than me, or I would lend you one of my own. Perhaps if we called Mrs. Lindstrom she could let down a hem. We do have time," she continued, but Mary shook her head.

"You're sweet to suggest it, but I don't think I'd look well in one of yours."

This Eveline considered and accepted with a nod. "Yes, I see your point. Well, perhaps this one will do. I don't like the color much, but it looks well on you. With the right jewelry..." She held the gown away from her, raising the gauze draping from the honey-colored silk below.

Mary was considering the gown, as well. "Eveline," she ventured, "don't you think a ball gown is too much for a sleigh ride? Perhaps just a dinner gown, or even a walking dress..."

Eveline's glance mixed pity with affection. "Of course it's too much for a sleigh ride. But it's what the others will be wearing, so you must wear one, as well. I'll be wearing my dark green, and Annabella Wood-cross will wear her peach silk, with her grand-mother's cameos. If you wear a day dress, Annabella will laugh at you."

"Surely it can make no different what Annabella thinks—and anyway, how is it that you know what dress she will wear? I had the impression that there was no love lost between you two."

"Nor is there." Eveline smiled to herself at the thought of Annabella's face when Jack appeared this evening with Mary as his date! "Annabella told Sarah Harris, and Sarah told me. Sarah is sure that Justin will propose this evening."

"Will you accept if he does?"

"Perhaps. I don't know. I'll have to see how I feel at the moment."

"It seems a strange way to approach the most important decision in one's life," Mary said with a shake of her head, but Eveline only smiled, thinking to herself how very much there was that Mary didn't know—and doubting she would ever learn half of it. She wondered what had prompted Jack to ask her sister out. Was it gallantry, or pity, or a combination of the two? Eveline frowned, hoping that Mary would be able to carry this off.

Mary saw the frown and guessed its meaning, and her heart plunged from the clouds into the abyss. She had been like this all day, ever since she'd first awakened. Yesterday she'd been enveloped in a benumbed daze, still not quite able to believe that he'd asked her out. She'd gone to sleep serene, but with today's dawn the numbness had ended and her moods had fluctuated, ascending into ecstasy only to plunge into despair. Even now, as her nerves tingled at the very mention of his name, she groaned before the vastness of her inadequacy.

Rising, she went to the window, if for no other reason than to steady her nerves. The snow had begun again this morning, and had fallen steadily all through the day, covering the yard and rooftop with a new blanket of white. She wondered if it would still be snowing when they left for the ride; in her mind she saw them driving through the curtain of white, the horses' manes and the carriage robes gilded with fresh snow. And Jack would be beside her. She would feel him at her side; perhaps he would put his arm around her to protect her from the cold and she would nestle down closer, into that heaven on earth.

Then the image faded. "It won't work," she said. "What will happen when Grandfather calls for me and they say I've gone out? I really have to tell him, I can't just sneak away. He'll go on a rampage, and then what will they do?"

"Give him a spoonful from the brown bottle—as you've told them two dozen times. And if he won't take it from Betty, there's always Emily. One of them can hold him and the other spoon it in. If you tell him first you know he'll tell you that you can't go, and you'll never have the nerve to stand up to him." Eveline frowned, hands on hips, looking like a lecturing governess, but Mary was too overwrought to see the moment's humor.

"I don't know." Biting her lip, she glanced about the room. Catching sight of herself in the mirror, she took a step nearer, searching, as if there might have been some wondrous changes in her appearance. But there was only Mary, just as she had always been, neither pretty nor ugly. Even a gown of spun gold would not change who she was. Her fingers found each other, twisting around themselves. "I'm sure he's regretting that he asked me at all. He'd probably be greatly relieved to hear that I'd changed my mind."

"Nonsense!" asserted Eveline, the heartiness in her voice masking her belief in what Mary had said. Well, he had asked her, and he'd have to see it through. At least he was too much of a gentleman ever to let on such a thing. "Come now." She patted the back of the chair. "It's time to take the rags out and begin on your hair."

She had almost finished when Betty opened the door.

"Your shoes, miss," she began. "I've—" then she stopped, staring at the curls gathered high on Mary's head, falling in a glossy cascade down towards her slender neck.

"Oh, miss!" Betty sucked in with admiration. "I'd hardly have known you. Really, it makes such a change!"

Looking at the maid's bulging eyes, Mary wasn't sure whether she should laugh or cry at the compliment. She frowned instead.

"You're sure you'll remember his medicine...the biggest brown bottle, the one on the shelf by the bed? He may refuse to take it, but you must insist. You must!" she repeated, and saw Betty and Eveline exchange a glance.

"Of course she'll insist. Won't you?" Eveline held out her hand. "Give me the shoes, that's right. Now go to my bedroom and fetch my amber necklace from the dressing-table drawer."

Mary, about to renew her protests, was distracted by this last. "Your amber necklace! Oh, Eve, how kind! How can I ever thank you for all you have done today?"

Eveline laughed. "Why thank me? I haven't had so much fun in years!"

"Fun!" Mary groaned in a way that made Eveline cluck.

"Yes, fun, and when I've finished you won't recognize yourself. Only do sit still and stop moaning, or it will take all night, and I still have my own toilette to finish by 8:30!"

AT 8:30 BY THE CLOCK, Jack stood in the hall, watching Mary come down the stairs. Eveline was behind her, but tonight was unlike the first evening. Tonight he was conscious of nobody but Mary; his mind was filled with wonder and with emotions he could not have named. She looked like a stranger, and yet he knew it was her, for above all the ruffles, the netting, the bustled poufs, shone the same brown eyes whose shy glance had touched his heart and touched him again now, tonight, as she came towards him, her lips trembling with uncertainty until he smiled at her. Then she blossomed, like a flower opening in his hand.

Her dress was golden silk trimmed in velvet that was the same liquid brown as her eyes. The basque, undraped, showed her slender figure to perfection, as did the gauzy cloud of her twin muslin overskirts, looped in a drifting double tier and aproned to show the deep flounce of her silk underskirt, then drawn back in a bustle that rustled as she descended. One gloved hand rested on the banister, the other guided her skirts, and her eyes were shining with unrestrained happiness.

"Mary!" Gray had exclaimed when Jack had told him this morning. "Why did you ask *her*? What of Annabella? What will she make of this?" But then Gray's eyes had narrowed, and he had laughed aloud. "Now I understand you . . . you old sly fox! You want to make her jealous, that's why you've asked Mary out! And that's why you left her stranded high and dry at the pond yesterday! Telling stories about working—I knew it must be a joke!"

When Jack had protested, Gray had only laughed, leaving him with a heavy feeling of dread and regret. Now that feeling faded before Mary's shining eyes, and he felt once again the pleasure and eagerness she seemed to arouse in him.

How handsome he is! Mary thought as she came down towards him. He was dressed in black broadcloth, just as she had imagined him, the starched white of his shirtfront bringing out the blue of his eyes, his hair just combed back, though already she could see the rebel lock beginning to fall forward again. Earlier she had worried that she might trip on the stairs, but now she walked on cloud feet and could do no wrong, not with his smile lighting the way. For this one night she had her heart's desire, and even if there was no tomorrow, still she was the happiest girl alive. As she reached the last step, he held out his hand.

"Miss Hillyer, you look so lovely!" he said as their fingers met, and she felt her heart leap. He did not release her hand, but rather raised it to his lips, and in one dizzying moment she realized his intent. Holding her breath, she awaited the touch of his lips on her skin, her errant heart trembling within her so that she thought that she might faint.

But the touch never came. Instead, a crash from above brought his head up like a shot. There was a sound of running feet, and Jack raised his eyes to the landing just as Mary and Eveline turned. A scarlet-faced Betty appeared at the head of the stairs.

"Oh, dear, miss! Oh, dear!" Shaking her head, Betty looked from one to the other of them, tears welling up in her eyes. It took Mary a moment to emerge from her daze; then she sprang forward.

"Grandfather!" she exclaimed, but Betty shook her head violently.

"No, miss, there's nothing wrong with Mr. Hillyer's health. Only he says that he will not have his medicine from me. He says— Oh, dear!'' She gasped as another crash echoed down the hall, followed by the thin, rising outraged voice.

"Sending a servant to try to poison me while she tries to sneak out! Where is Mary? Where has she gone to? Send her to me at once!"

"Oh, dear!" Glancing behind her, Betty wrung her hands. Eveline laid a hand on Mary's arm, but Mary shook it off.

"It's all right," she said, catching up her skirts once more. "Perhaps after his medicine..." Passing Betty on the staircase, she patted her on the arm. Betty watched her vanish around the turn in the stairs.

"Poor Miss Hillyer," she murmured, tucking up a tumbled lock of hair as she came down. "I'm afraid he's worked himself into a rare state this time."

"The old goat," said Eveline. "How like him to do this to her. After I spent all day making her look beautiful!"

Only Jack made no comment. His eyes still dwelled on the space left empty by Mary's passing, and his mind was still upon the moment when their hands had met. His own was shaking; he pressed it against his side, wondering what had happened that had touched him so deeply. He had squired a hundred women since he had come to Boston, bowed low over a hundred hands, yet his had never trembled from a woman's touch. He felt as if someone had dealt him a sharp blow to the chest. Staring at the empty landing, he tried to understand what there was about this moment that set it apart thus.

Lost in reflection, he did not hear the bells, but Eveline heard them and turned to the door.

"That must be Gray and Tom with the sleigh. The others will be waiting, we ought to be off. Perhaps Mary can calm him.... Betty, please, our wraps."

"Yes, miss." Betty ran to do as she was asked just as silk rustled above them and Mary reappeared.

"Mary—just in time!" Eveline beckoned to her, but she shook her head.

"I'll have to stay with him. You go on without me."

"I knew it!" exclaimed Eveline. "I knew he'd do this to you! You oughtn't to have gone up! Betty should have said that you had already gone!'

"Perhaps if we waited with you..." Jack took a step towards Mary, but she stayed him with a shake of her head.

"I would only hold you back. It may take an hour before he is settled in.... It may take all night."

Jack turned to Eveline. "Then you go without me. I'll stay with Miss Hillyer. Then, later, perhaps—"

"No!" Mary heard the desperation in her own voice and felt the mounting pressure of unshed tears. Oh, pray, let him leave before she broke down! It was hard enough to give up her one chance at a fairy tale without having to watch him suffer through Grandfather's company. Though her heart was constricted with pain, she managed a smile. "No, you are kind to suggest it, but really, you must go."

"It is not kindness—" he began as Gray opened the front door, letting in with him a draft of cold night air.

"Here we are!" he cried. "And eager to be away. Where are your wraps, ladies? Jack, have you seen a ghost? I say, is that Mary? You look quite ravishing! Ah, here is Betty," he added as the girl appeared with the coats. "Now, quickly, into them. We are holding everyone up." Tossing Jack's cape to him, he held Eveline's for her.

"Mary can't come," said Eveline, slipping her arms in the sleeves. "Grandfather's found she was leaving and gone into a fit."

"Oh, too bad." Gray clucked sympathetically. "Well, perhaps next time. Look, we must be going. We were to meet at nine!" He took hold of Eveline, drawing her to the door. Jack's eyes were still on Mary.

"Are you sure, Miss Hillyer?"

"Yes, absolutely. I—I hope you have a nice time."

"We shall do our best!" cried Gray, reaching out with his spare hand to pull Jack along with him. The door banged behind them, and then they were gone, leaving Mary on the landing and Betty in the hall below, clutching Mary's good coat and her good fur muff.

"It's a pity, miss," she said. "Perhaps I should have told him that you were already gone."

"No, you did the right thing. It is I who should have told him earlier today. Well, there is no point in discussing it. You can put my things away."

"Yes, miss. Very well." Betty watched Miss Hillyer disappear up the stairs, contemplating the great unfairness of life. Poor Miss Hillyer got out precious little.... You'd think the old gentleman would take pity on her. And her looking like a princess in her gold dress. Why, just this morning Mrs. Parker was saying that maybe Miss Hillyer would be married yet. But it hardly seemed so, not with the way her luck went. Outside, the sleigh bells sounded as the sleigh drove away; with a sigh, Betty turned away and went to the cupboard.

MARY, STANDING IN her darkened room, could still hear the sleigh bells jingling, but she did not move to the window to see them driving off, for she thought that if she did she would not survive the pain. They were leaving, and this time, as always, she had been left behind. She thought despairingly that this was what they must mean when they spoke of a broken heart, for there was a throbbing pain exploding in her chest. Two tears formed beneath her lids and spilled hot down her cheeks. She wiped them away with the back of her hand, biting back the rest. If she started crying, she knew, she would not stop. And in a very few minutes Grandfather would call for her and she would have to go to him.

But not yet. Not yet. First she must take off her dress, undo her hair, destroy each shred of evidence of what was to have been, so that it could not remind her of what she had missed ... and yet part of her wanted to keep everything in place, to go back to that moment when he had held her hand, to seize it and hold it and keep it forever. To refuse to let it go.

Her fingers curled into fists, and she thought of all the poets, all the writers who had told of love—of Tennyson, for instance, who believed that it was better to have loved and lost than never to have loved at all. Was it? she wondered now. But then, Tennyson was speaking of one who was loved in return, he was not speaking of love nipped in the very bud, so that one party remained forever unaware of its existence.

Did she love Jack Gates? How could she, when she had known him only a handful of days, and yet how could her heart be breaking if she did not? Oh, to return to the pleasant, humdrum life that had been her existence before he had appeared! But even as her mind uttered the thought, her heart was longing to be with him again, to see the way he smiled, to hear his voice, to feel his fingers on hers.

"Oh, Jack!" she whispered to the darkness, and the whisper disappeared, and once again there was nothing but the trembling of her breath.

Grandfather was waiting, he would be impatient for her, and the sight of her grieving would only upset him more. Uncurling her fingers, she reached back for the first of the hooks that she had fastened with such gladness only an hour before, while somewhere in the distance sleigh bells tinkled merrily.

# Chapter Five

OH, MOTHER, you should have seen it!" Eveline shook her head, glancing across at Gray, whose eyes were sparkling with glee. "They had built a fire by the stream in Wilson's Dell. You know the place I mean, just up from the fishing hole. We stopped there for hot chocolate—though they served it in tin cups that were too hot to hold and half of mine spilled on Justin's boot."

Eveline paused, then caught up her thread again. "Anyway, you know that fur-trimmed bonnet Hetty Pickering is so proud about—the one she bought with her mother when they were down in New York? Well, Hetty was so busy making eyes at Asa Webb that she stood too near the horses, and one of them snatched the bonnet right off her head. You should have seen her expression! You should have seen the horse's face! Either one was enough to make you burst your sides!"

Eveline and Gray exploded in peals of laughter that their mother greeted with a smile of bemused affection. They were all at breakfast, Eveline, Gray and their mother clustered about the table's end, with Jack and Mary placed by chance opposite each other. Having spent a long and sleepless night, Mary had considered not appearing for the meal, but good sense had informed her that she would have to face Jack sometime and that the longer she waited the worse it would be. He had greeted her politely, and she had responded in kind. He had not mentioned the previous evening, and she had been grateful for that. Thus far, she had managed to keep her emotions under control, though she was not certain for how long that control would last, as every word Eveline spoke struck like a blow to her heart.

A fire down in the Dell... Yes, she could see it all, the sleighs drawn in a circle at the clearing's edge, blankets spread on the fallen logs, the gay bells resounding with every shake of a horse's head, as the revelers mingled, laughing and talking among themselves. She could taste the richness of the chocolate steaming in the mugs, hear the uproar of hilarity as Hetty lost her hat. She could hear Jack's laughter rising free above the rest, just the way she'd heard it on the first morning. Tears stung her eyes, and she willed them away. This would not happen; she must not let herself think. She must be the Mary who took everything in stride.

"Well, Jack!" she heard Gray say. "Have you got a headache? You look down in the mouth. Try some of Mrs. Parker's biscuits, they'll perk you up!"

"I don't know," Jack glanced at Mary's downcast head. "I was there the whole time and hardly found cause to laugh."

"To laugh!" Gray shook his head. "Well, I never— Come now, old man, you roared with the rest of us, you and Annabella! We're out of marmalade, Mother, you'll have to ring for more."

"I'll get it," said Mary, grateful for the excuse to rise from the table. Grasping the empty dish, she blundered towards the kitchen door, tears blurring her way. Annabella Woodcross . . . Somehow that made it worse, for Annabella was so pretty and so very sure of herself. Jack would not have missed her at Annabella's side; likely he had forgotten her long before the Dell.

Gray chuckled as Mary disappeared. "Hetty Pickering." And who will ever forget the sight of Asa rising to her aid? Yes, Jack, what is it now? You look as though someone's gone and buttoned your boots together!"

"I think perhaps Miss Hillyer might prefer not to hear about last night."

"Mary? Why ever not?"

"Perhaps she's disappointed at having been left behind," Jack answered, taking care to keep his voice low, lest Mary overhear, for he thought she would not like to hear them discussing her. But the idea did not seem to have occurred to Gray.

"Oh, not Mary. She takes everything in stride. Though," he added, frowning in the direction of the kitchen door, "I can't imagine what could be taking her so long. By the time she brings the marmalade my toast will be cold. Did someone say that Sophia was arriving today?"

"Our oldest sister," Eveline explained for Jack's benefit. "She lives in New Haven."

"And has a hundred children who all shout at once." Gray pressed his hands to his head in mock dismay. Then he removed them, brightening. "Is that someone at the door? Perhaps it is Sir Asa, come for another chaffing!"

Their caller, as it turned out, was not Asa Webb, but rather Mrs. Maria Judd, whose husband owned the Northampton Dry Goods Emporium and whose son delivered coal. What gossip failed to find its way to the Emporium was scooped up by the coalman on his daily rounds, to be brought home to mother like choice scraps to a pet. A morning call from Mrs. Judd often heralded portentous news—and today's visit seemed no exception, for her plump cheeks were flushed scarlet, while her false curls fairly trembled with repressed excitement.

"Mrs. Judd! Mother, ring for Emily to set another place," Eveline directed, but Mrs. Judd forestalled her.

"Oh, no, I cannot stay. I wouldn't want to impose. I have some information I thought you ought to know. Good morning, Mary," she added when Mary came through the door, the marmalade dish in her hand.

Seeing Mrs. Judd's agitation, she asked, "Is something amiss?"

"Mrs. Judd has some information she thinks we ought to have," said Eveline. "She was about to tell us when you came in."

"Please." Mary indicated a chair, but Mrs. Judd shook her head.

"It's about your cousin, Mr. Amos Hillyer."

"Cousin Amos?" Mary set the marmalade down beside Gray. "Has something befallen him?"

"Befallen?" Mrs. Judd appeared to ponder the word. "Well, perhaps it's befallen, but if you ask me I'd say that it was more his own idea." Then, having exhausted her store of suspense, she said, "He's abandoned the Old House!"

"Abandoned?" Gray withdrew his knife from the marmalade. "You mean he's gone?"

"Lock, stock and barrel," she replied with great satisfaction. "Took all his own things with him—and things not his, besides. My Seth stopped there this morning to deliver him his coal—though the good Lord knows Amos still owes for November, but when Seth asked me should he stop I said you can't let a man freeze. And besides, I told him, the family will surely back him up."

"Well, I wouldn't say—" Gray began, but Mary brushed him aside.

"Of course we will pay for the coal that Cousin Amos used. Are you sure that he has gone? Perhaps he has gone visiting, for the holidays?"

"With all the furniture, not to mention such bric-a-brac as your Aunt Alice left? No, not a chance of it! Must have left before the snowfall, from what Seth said, because there was no sign of his wagon tracks in the snow, and he must have had a wagon, to cart off what he did. According to what Seth could see, the rooms were almost bare!"

"Gone!" Eveline exclaimed. "But his lease on the Old House ran through the spring, and he was to have paid rent in repairs."

"Well, you won't have it from him, not now," Mrs. Judd declared, setting her wool bonnet more firmly on her head. "I'll be going now. I won't keep you from your meal. Good day, Mrs. Hillyer. Good day to you all."

"Rushing off to be the first to spread the dismal word," Gray added in a whisper when she had left the room. Then, raising his voice, he added, "I always said it was no good to let Amos have the house. He's never turned an honest hour's work in his life."

"But Aunt Alice would have wished it," his mother pointed out. "You know how very fond she was of him—and he was not a bad boy. Why, just last month I saw him when I was shopping on Main Street, and he told me how much he still missed her. I suggested that he might stop by some evening and we would try to reach her through the Ouija board. He thanked me for the offer and said that he surely would—only I don't suppose he'll be coming now."

"Not likely," Gray agreed. "Which leaves the Old House with no one to care for it. What a pity that Grandfather is so keen on keeping it."

"What is the Old House?" asked Jack, who had been trying without great success to follow the proceedings.

Eveline answered. "A horrid old wreck of a place. But Grandfather was born there, so he is stubborn about holding on to it. After he made all his money he had this house built, and then Aunt Alice lived in the Old House alone."

"She was your father's sister?"

"No, Grandfather's," said Gray. "Grandfather would have been glad to have her live here with him, but she preferred to live out there. She didn't like the new ways, kept the old place as it was.... When she died last winter, she left it in a sorry state. We all expected that Grandfather would sell it then, but in-

stead he decided that it should be kept in the family—
only no one in the family wanted to live in it, except
for Cousin Amos, and now even he has fled."

"It could be fixed up." Mary's quiet voice was almost lost in the conversation. "With a little effort it
could be a pretty place."

"Pretty!" Eveline sniffed. "Well, if you love it so
much you'd best go over and see what damage Amos
has left behind."

"Of course." Mary's tone was wry. "Who else did
you imagine would go?"

"I will," said Jack. He rose even as he spoke, tucking his napkin beneath his plate. Then, seeing the
expressions the family turned on him, he smiled and
explained, "I've always had a weakness for old
houses."

"Here's chivalry!" Eveline cried, applauding, but
Gray only shook his head.

"There's old and there's old— You don't know
what you're saying, you'll ruin your good trousers
only walking through—and then there's the skating
down on the pond, and dinner afterwards. Everyone
will be there."

"Then you'll make my excuses. My mind is quite
made up."

"It's all right," Mary murmured, her eyes on her
folded hands. "I don't mind going alone."

"And I don't mind going with you— I *want* to go,
in fact." His tone was so definite that she could not
help but look up, and she saw him smile when she did.
He held his arm out to her. "Shall we be going?"

"Refreshments at the Woodcrosses', in case you're finished by then!" Gray called after him as they left the room. "He'll be sorry," he muttered as the door swung shut.

"I think it's rather romantic," Eveline replied. "The handsome knight rising to the aid of the fair damsel."

"Mary as Lady Elaine?" Gray gave her a skeptical look, then laughed good-naturedly. "He's got a knack for it. Why, last summer he spent a whole weekend with Mr. Clyburn's daughter, who has a face like an ailing horse. Now Mr. Clyburn treats him like a son. Well, let him freeze his bones at the Old House. He'll see what I mean!" Laughing at his own wit, Gray helped himself to another slice of toast and more marmalade.

YESTERDAY'S SNOW had covered the rutted sidewalks and the trampled yards, hiding the soot-stained, dwindling banks beneath a thick fresh coat so that once again the world was clean and soft and white, glowing luminescent beneath a pale gray sky.

"I love this kind of morning. It's as if the whole world were holding its breath." Mary spoke in a rush of emotion, then stopped and turned her head, afraid that Jack might see the joy shining in her face.

"It's my favorite, too," he said. She thought that she would explode with happiness. Perhaps he had come only to be kind, or perhaps he really did have a fondness for old buildings, but she cared not for his reasons. What mattered was that she was driving down

Elm Street with Jack Gates at her side! It made up—
more than made up—for last night's disappointment.

He drove easily, as she had imagined he would, as
she imagined he must do everything. She knew that
her own movements were governed by competence,
but it was this graceful self-assurance that she admired
in Jack, this assurance that invested his every gesture
with a style and a specialness. Watching his hand on
the reins shot a little thrill through her, and despite her
shyness she glanced up at his face, if only to reassure
herself that this was not a dream.

She found his eyes on her. Meeting hers, he smiled.
"Are you warm enough?"

"Of course." She smiled back, for things like
warmth and coldness had no meaning for her. Had a
blizzard swept down Elm Street, had a tornado or a
flood, she would have watched them come with
serenity, knowing that nothing could touch her, not
when she was with Jack. The weight she had carried
since last night had ceased to be, leaving behind such
a buoyancy that she had to grip her seat for fear that
if she let go she would rise like a balloon. Her lips
curled in a secret smile as she imagined the startled
faces below as she drifted slowly, head over heels,
through the high gray sky.

Coming onto Locust Street, they passed Hetty
Pickering walking with Asa Webb, her skates in one
hand, her fur bonnet secure on her head. Hetty looked
startled when she saw who was driving with Jack. Asa
waved as they passed, and Mary smiled at him.

"Did the horse really grab her hat?"

Jack nodded his head. "Mmm."

"That must have been funny," she said with a chuckle.

"It was," he admitted, and, as he had not done this morning, he laughed with her. Gray had not been lying; he had laughed last night, as well, but that laughter had lacked the joyousness and freedom he felt now. All night he had carried with him the memory of her face, pale and drawn as she had looked down, refusing his offer to stay behind. He had felt that he had betrayed her, so he could not enjoy the sleigh ride that she had been forced to miss. Though he had laughed and smiled and flirted with Annabella, he had done so more from habit than from any real desire.

Was that why he had insisted on driving with her today—in order to relieve the burden of the guilt of his desertion? Or had it been in reaction to something more immediate—to her family's insensitivity to her feelings? Whatever it was, the heaviness that had oppressed him last night and at breakfast was gone, and he drank in the cold, damp air with gusto and appreciation. The smells and textures recalled him to Wisconsin, and he realized how long it had been since he had enjoyed good country air.

For they were in the country now. At Mary's direction, he had turned off the main street, and then a second time into a lane. Here the houses lacked the classic lines of the town's finest mansions but showed instead the plain substantiality of those built in the last century, when Northampton had still been a farm community. Orchards filled the space from one house to the next, and empty fields rolled away across the valley floor to the slate-and-purple mountains that rose in the distance. Wood smoke rose in twisting plumes from every chimney, and its good smell reached out to the road. In one yard they saw a farmer tramping toward his kitchen with a bucket of steaming milk; in another, several children were having a snowball fight, their shrill voices muffled by the vastness of the sky. Again Jack felt the sharp tug of nostalgia, felt the presence of old memories pressing close to him.

There were no sidewalks here, and but a few tracks in the road, which dwindled to the double one of Mrs. Judd's coal-dealer son, coming, then going again, and turning at last into the yard of a farm standing off to the left. Without needing Mary's directions, Jack turned off, as well, bringing the carriage to a halt in the space cleared by the coal wagon. He fastened the reins, then paused, letting his eyes take in the house and its surroundings.

The house was set back from the road, with a yard in front and the barn stretching out behind it, attached by a kitchen shed, so that the farmer could reach his stock when the snow lay deep. The house was built in the old style, three floors with a lean-to in back that made its steep roof look lopsided, being one story longer in back. A porch that must have been added during this century ran along the front, its shallow roof sagging beneath the blanket of snow. Nor did the the snow disguise the crooked shutters or the peeling paint, nor the general air of gentle delapidation.

"It *is* old," he murmured.

"Quite," Mary agreed. "Grandfather's great-great-grandfather built it when he first came here, in 1705.

Back in those days there were still Indian raids—I can show you the secret closet they built as a hiding place. It was standard practice back then."

"And did they have to use it?"

"No." Mary shook her head. "Not against Indians. But later, after the Revolution, it came in handy enough. While my great-grandfather and his neighbors had been off fighting against the king, their fields had lain fallow and debts had piled up. Afterwards, instead of rewarding their sacrifice, the government passed laws in favor of their creditors. That struck the farmers as an injustice, so when the constable arrived to try to put one of them out they met him with their guns. That turned back the constable, but it also brought criminal charges. So when word came that the constable was coming to arrest them, Great-grandfather and the others retreated into the secret closet."

"Good for them!" cried Jack, filling his lungs with cold, fresh air. Mary's story reminded him only too clearly of that morning twelve years before when the sheriff had come to the farm with the notice of the sale. Overwhelmed by anger and frustration, he had reached for his father's gun, but his mother, fore-seeing his impulse, had snatched it from his reach. "Good for them," he repeated. "And since this place is still your family's, I presume they won in the end."

"Yes, in the end they did." Struck by the vehemence of Jack's response, Mary had turned to him, but he didn't notice; his attention was fixed on the Old House, as though he were seeing it all for himself, the constable with his warrants, the farmers with their guns. Mary turned back, as well, adding, "They spent some time as outlaws in Vermont, but in the end the laws were changed and the governor pardoned them. It's been a favorite family story, passed down from father to son—and no doubt growing in drama with each generation," she added, smiling to herself. The smile faded when she looked more closely at the sagging porch, the peeling paint, the shutters hanging awry.

In spite of herself, she sighed, "Cousin Amos was to have done the painting and repairs instead of paying rent. It was all written in the lease—Grandfather's agents handled it," she murmured, wishing that Amos had not left just now, not when she was so busy, with so much else to do.

"Contracts are made to be broken." Pushing his memories away, Jack turned to Mary with a wry smile. "That's one of the first things I learned about the law. You pay a lawyer to write the contract, then pay him again to sue on it—though from what I've heard of your cousin, I doubt that a suit would be worthwhile."

"Hardly." Mary sighed again. "Amos never managed to hold on to anything—except Aunt Alice's affection, and that wasn't hard to do. She had a very tender heart."

*Like you,* thought Jack, his smile softening at the wistfulness in her tone—the same gentle wistfulness he had seen in her eyes. *People hold on to you, don't they?* he thought gazing at her. *They hold on as long as it pleases them, and then they let you down. Just as I did last night,* he added, feeling the guilt rise again.

As if she had followed his thoughts, Mary looked up with a smile. "I have no cause to complain. It is a pity, to be sure, that Amos has gone off. But still, it does give me a chance to visit this dear old place. It's been so long since I've been here—not since Aunt Alice died. Come," she said, gathering her skirts. "I'll give you the royal tour."

He sprang down from the buggy before her, then reached up to help her down, feeling the lightness and warmth of her fingers through the two layers of their gloves and feeling, as well, the same sudden, sharp contraction of his heart that he had felt last night. He saw from the way her eyes rose that she had felt it, too, and for a moment they stood together, hand in hand beside the wheel, and he felt himself melting in the softness of her brown eyes. She was like no other woman he had ever known, quiet, unassuming and yet with a hold on his heart he could not have explained. How easy it would be now to bend to kiss her lips, to gather her warmth in his arms and to touch his cheek to her smooth one, both cold and hot at once. Her eyes were wide and startled—a wren caught by surprise—and yet he knew that if he were to reach out she would not fly away.

The horse nickered and stamped, its breath rising in a white cloud in the cold air. Mary started at the sound, and her sudden movement brought Jack back to earth. Mary was a complete innocent, not the sort of woman to kiss on a whim. Her lack of experience could lead her to take such a spontaneous action as something more serious. And then there would be the kind of complications he meant to avoid. This was his vacation, his time for having fun. He would return to Boston and a life in which she could play no part.

Was there disappointment in her face when he let her fingers go? But what difference did that make? Turning, Jack nodded toward the house. "Shall we?" he asked. "I'll follow in Judd's footprints, and you follow in mine."

Mary walked slowly in the path that he had cleared, dazed from too little sleep and from what had just occurred. She had thought that he meant to kiss her. Perhaps he would have if the horse had not moved. She wished it had not; her heart still beat unevenly, and her legs shook just a bit as she made her way across the yard on the path that he cleared.

Jack kicked the snow from his boots, looking out from the porch, while Mary found the key in her pocket and unlocked the door. A maple tree, its branches covered with snow, spanned the front yard; now, as he watched, two blackbirds flew down, dislodging as they landed a section of snow, which showered silently to the ground. The blackbirds watched it settle, heads cocked to one side; then, in one movement, they rose up and disappeared back over the roof. A commonplace occurrence, one he had seen before... Perhaps it was the very commonness of it that touched him so deeply. As a boy he had tramped the forests and fields on days such as this, less to hunt squirrel and rabbit than to enjoy the tang of the air and the crunch of the snow-covered forest beneath his heavy boots. In going to Boston he had turned his back on that part of his past.... Now, in these surroundings, the memories flooded back with a clarity and a power that was almost frightening.

Mary had long since found the key and unlocked the door. It was standing open as she waited patiently.

Jack shook his head as if he were emerging from a dream. "I'm sorry. I don't know what's come over me."

"It's the house." She smiled. "Working its spell on you. I've felt it often myself. Mother would say it was the spirits trying to communicate. Watch your step coming in, there's a loose board right here."

He stepped where she showed him and found himself in a house whose basic floor plan was identical to that of his own family's farm. The four rooms on the first floor were divided by a central hall, with the stairs to the upper story rising opposite the front door. The walls of the hall were painted in some indeterminate shade, and, though the hall was empty, Jack could see from the patches of more brightly colored paint where furniture must have stood until quite recently. Some sort of small bureau, he guessed from the marks on the wall, and perhaps a grandfather clock. Glancing at Mary, he saw that she, too, was studying the blank spots. For a moment her gaze lingered on the place where the clock had apparently stood; then without speaking, she turned through the first door on the right. Jack followed her through the dining room and into a kitchen so like the one of his childhood that he felt himself overtaken by a strange light-headedness, as though he had left the present and stepped back in time.

Here were the same ample lines; here was the same massive stone fireplace, tall enough for a woman to stand erect at the highest point. Heavy hooks of iron had been driven through the roof and an oven cut into one side, its door blackened with age. Unlike the hall and the dining room, the kitchen contained furniture: a ponderous oak table, an old-fashioned bureau on which were piled at random all manner of implements, a half-dozen ladder-back chairs. A greasy wrought-iron skillet stood on the old cookstove, and the dishes on the table held the remains of a recent meal.

Mary's fingers touched the handle of the skillet, as though she meant to carry it to the stone washtub on the opposite wall. Instead, she left it where it was, letting her fingers slide along the stove's well-worn edge.

"Great-grandfather Hillyer bought this stove for his brand-new bride. In those days, a cookstove was considered quite a modern invention. All the neighbors were envious—they all came to visit on one pretext or another, and a good many of them expressed the opinion that it was likely to explode and carry the whole house away. They scared the bride so badly she refused to light the fire. Great-grandfather pleaded, but it was no use: she stood in the yard with her hands pressed against her ears while he cooked their first meal—wet cornbread and scorched venison steak!"

"A typical woman's story," Jack said with a laugh. Mary smiled in response, and the unaffectedness of the gesture drove the old ghosts away. "I've known plenty of men in my life who could cook a decent meal."

"Perhaps," she allowed with a shrug. "But none of them Hillyers. Aunt Alice was a wonderful cook. She used to bake brown bread in the brick oven. She'd fire it up with dry wood until the bricks were red-hot, then scrape out the embers and leave the bread to bake overnight, and in the morning it would be ready, all brown and crusty and warm. She said that one of the things she hated most about getting old was not having her own teeth to chew brick-oven bread." She smiled at the fireplace, seeing in her memory Aunt Alice kneading dough at the oak table and herself as a child, hanging over her aunt's side, watching as the sticky mass turned silky beneath her touch, then watching the red-hot shower as the embers were swept away and oak leaves laid down on which the bread would sit, while Aunt Alice explained as always that this was the way it was done.

Jack watched the soft lips curve into a secret smile and was seized by a sudden longing to be part of her life, to have her lips curve thus when she thought of him. To live in this house with her, to share the same happiness. To be worthy of such pleasure...to be worthy of her smile...

Crazy, he thought, shaking his head to shake out such thoughts. What was he thinking of? If he didn't know himself better, he'd think he was falling in love. But of course he couldn't be. He needed a wife who liked to mingle in society and who could play hostess in the mansion he meant to own someday. A woman like Annabella Woodcross, he thought, and was surprised by the distaste he felt. Mary had been right about one thing: this old place cast quite a spell. His gaze, disengaging from her softly curved lips, settled instead on the dishes, with their remnants of congealing food that must have been Amos Hillyer's parting meal.

"Was he her only child?" he asked, and felt Mary turn to him.

"Child?" Mary's eyes followed Jack's to the dirty dishes. "You mean Amos?"

Jack nodded without looking around. "Yes. I wondered if your Aunt Alice had children beside him."

"Oh. No." Mary shook her head, moving without thinking to gather the dishes up. "Amos wasn't her child at all. His mother was her cousin, and when she gave up on him, she asked Aunt Alice if she couldn't please try. So of course Aunt Alice did," she said, depositing the dishes in the stone sink. "Aunt Alice never married, most likely because she was the only girl in a family of boys and her mother died when they were only half grown. Men would try to court her and her father would chase them away, because what would he do without her?"

"Couldn't her husband have lived with her there?"

"Would a man do such a thing?" Mary turned to look at him. "I think that most men prefer their independence. There was one who swore that he would take her away, but when he met her father's resistance he, too, changed his mind. Still, she forgave him, and treasured his memory as she treasured all the things she loved—her rose garden, her piano, everything in this house. Aunt Alice never thought of herself as living alone. Nor did she, really, since there was always somebody else about.''

"Such as Cousin Amos.''

"Such as him,'' she agreed, but Jack shook his head, frowning.

"People imposing on one are are not the same as having someone to love.''

"And do you think that one cannot impose upon and love at once?'' she asked.

She met his eyes with a limpid gaze before which his own faltered. "I would have thought so,'' he said, "but then, I have not considered it. I suppose I was thinking of her father's heartlessness.''

"But was he really heartless, or was he only thinking of his little boys who needed a mother?'' She waited for a moment, in case he would reply; when he made no answer she turned and passed out of the room and across the hall. Jack stayed for a moment, pondering her words. Then, still frowning, he followed after her.

On this side had been a parlor, and perhaps a lower bedchamber, though little remained to distinguish one from the other, the few sticks remaining standing forlornly among piles of dust and debris and blank spots where pictures had hung and rugs had covered the floors. Mary passed from the first to the second room, her eyes moving here and there, as if seeking some scrap, some momento that had been overlooked. At last, with a sad shake of her head, she gave up her quest.

"He took nearly everything,'' she said with a small, hopeless wave of her hand. "The little sewing table, the family photographs…the stool that used to stand just here, beside the hearth…" Her voice trailed off as she caught her lip between her teeth. In the glint of brightness that dampened her lashes, Jack saw all the pain and bitterness of his own remembered loss. In the first instant, habit warned him to turn away, as he did from all signs of the past. But then habit faded, swept away by a fierce desire to take Mary in his arms, to ease away with soft caresses the tears she fought to hide. He took one step towards her, but in the same moment she drew a breath and straightened, firming her shoulders and stilling her trembling lips.

"Of course, it doesn't matter," she said in a tone that stayed Jack's advance. "What was of real value we'd already taken away. He could not take the house—and that is what matters, after all."

"If," said Jack, recalling the conversation at breakfast, "your grandfather is not persuaded to sell it now."

"If…" she repeated, her finger reaching out for the wooden wainscoting, then following its molding in a gesture of familiarity and affection that made Jack catch his breath. "As you heard, Gray thinks it should be sold. He was most adamant on the subject when Aunt Alice died. Grandfather resisted then, but perhaps he will change his mind, now that there is no one from the family to live in it." Her fingers lingered a moment, then fell to her side.

Jack's eyes followed her fingers, and he fought the urge to encircle them with his. Clasping his hands together, he said, "But that's not what you want."

"No, but it might be best. The house seems so lonely with no one to care for it. It would be better to have a family living here—a family with children, who could appreciate it. There used to be a long swing hanging from the maple out front, and in the back is the best berry patch in the whole valley. It would be nice to know that children were living here again."

"No!" Jack's voice echoed through the empty rooms. "No, you must not let it go! It is a part of your history. You must hold on to it!"

The sharpness of his tone brought Mary's eyes around; they were round and wide, with an amazement in them that made Jack's color rise. What was he thinking, crying out like a child? This was not his own farm, that had gone long ago, and no amount of mourning could bring it back again.

He forced a smile. "Forgive me. Old ghosts rising up. What right have I to tell you what you ought to do?" He tried to meet her gaze but found that he could not, so he turned to the window instead, letting the expanse of white soothe his shaken nerves.

Mary's voice came from behind him, as calming as the snowy fields. "You're speaking of your own life."

He opened his mouth to deny it, out of stubbornness. But instead he nodded. "Yes," he said. "I am." The fields were empty save for an occasional stand of skeletal trees. The view was so familiar, for a moment he felt the light-headedness creeping back. But then he became conscious of Mary watching him, and something about her presence moved him to speak aloud of the past as he had never done before.

"I grew up in a house like this—in western Wisconsin. My grandfather built it, with my father's help, when they'd outgrown the log cabin that had been their first home. It—it was a good house. It, too, had a berry patch. And it had a swimming hole—and a hayloft as high as a cathedral. The loft was my favorite place. I used to go there when something was bothering me. I'd lie back in the sweet-smelling hay, and after a while I'd see things a whole new way." Jack shook his head. "There are times in Boston I wish for that loft. Wouldn't Gray rib me if he knew?" He laughed joylessly.

Mary flinched at the sound. "What happened to that farm?" she asked, though she thought she already knew.

"I lost it," Jack said. "I swore to my father that I would hold on, but I lost it in the end. Of course," he added, "it was not my fault. There were so many debts from the very start, and then when the news came that my brother had died at Chancellorsville..." Stopping, he shook his head, in his mind once more holding the telegram that spelled the death of hope. "For us there were no farmers to stop the constable, nor a secret place to hide," he said, the window reflecting his ironic smile. "The bank took it and put us out. That killed my mother—that and everything else."

"How terrible!" Mary exclaimed. "How terrible all that must have been for you!"

"Yes, I suppose it was," he replied, at once yearning for her comfort and shrinking away from it. Pride straightened his shoulders. "But it pushed me ahead, as well. It made me do things I would never have attempted otherwise. I've come a long way since that day—and I mean to go farther yet.''

''I'm sure you will,'' she murmured, understanding his pride. ''But what of Wisconsin? Do you ever go back?''

''No.'' He shook his head. ''There is no time, what with my schedule.'' But, even as he said it, he knew it was just an excuse. The truth was that he feared confronting all the old pain—seeing people and visiting places that would bring it all back for him. ''There were too many ghosts,'' he said bitterly. ''And now it is too late.''

Jack's broad back blurred as Mary's eyes filled with tears. Her heart was aching for the boy he must have been—and for the man, as well. Blinking back, she murmured, ''It's never too late, you know. You could still go back.''

Her tone was as gentle as he imagined her hand would be smoothing the hair from his forehead—just as she must smooth her grandfather's bedcovers. Again he felt the yearning for the comfort she could bring, for the compassion. But he must not let her turn him from the path that he had worked so hard to clear. Again he pushed the yearning back, though this time with difficulty.

''No, it's gone,'' he said. ''I've made other choices, and those choices are right for me. Perhaps one day I will go back, as a rich, fat old man.'' He turned to smile at her, but it was a smile tinged wtih sadness. ''Who knows? Perhaps one day I shall have a house like this. Perhaps I shall retire to it, in my stout old age. But in the meantime I need what Boston can supply."

"And what is that?" she asked, conscious of her compassion condensing into a circle of pain that seemed to lodge and settle somewhere in her chest.

"Power, he said. "Success. Wealth and position— everything money can buy. And enough of them to ensure that I will never again know a day's insecurity."

"I understand," said Mary, though the pain continued to grow. "I suppose I would feel the same way, had I been through what you have."

"No," he said slowly. "I don't believe you would. I believe you'd trade Boston and all those other things for this old house. I don't believe you'd ever be seduced by wealth."

"And have you been?" she asked.

Had he? He frowned. No, it was not seduction, for his eyes were open wide, and yet, standing here in this empty room, he could not quite grasp the reason for his existence. For the first time in twelve years, the drive had disappeared—or perhaps the anger that had always pushed him on. It was a strange feeling, and a deeply disquieting one.

Mary was watching him still, her brown eyes thoughtful and kind. The sight of her eyes hurt him, though the pain was of a different sort from that which he had known before. Turning away, still uncertain, he said, "What of the upper floor? Are we going to see it, or have you had enough?"

Mary did not answer, and for a moment she did not move. But then, bowing her head in aquiescence, she led the way into the hall.

Upstairs were four bedchambers, one larger than the rest, its windows facing east, towards the mountains and the sun.

"This was Aunt Alice's room," said Mary, gesturing with her arm. "It had been her mother's and her grandmother's. All the Hillyer babies were born in this room. My father was born here. It does seem a pity that there will be no more—" She stopped, turning her eyes to the window to hide the tears that were rising up.

As a girl she had imagined that she would live in this house with her own husband and have her own babies in this very same room. Now, in the gray winter coldness, even the beloved house could not soothe the ache she felt before the certain knowledge of what she would not have. As Jack had spoken of his sorrows below, she longed to give voice to her own failed dreams. But of course she could not. If she spoke of marriage she would embarrass him. But, even as she closed her lips on the unspoken words, she was swept by a yearning to live here with Jack. She knew she was being foolish, but the yearning was so strong that she pressed her fingers to her lips for fear she would cry out.

Jack gazed down at Mary's bent head, wondering if it was possible that he could read her thoughts—or if not her thoughts, then at least her feelings. At breakfast this morning he had seen her distress and had cringed within. Now he felt no cringing, only the same desire he had felt below. And this time, when he moved towards her, she did not steel herself.

"Mary?" he murmured, and when she raised her head he found himself gazing into eyes liquid brown with tears. As before, her lips trembled, but this time he did not hesitate. As thirst draws one to the water of a cool clear spring, Jack's hands touched her shoulders and his lips sought hers.

They were soft, as he'd imagined, and sweet beyond all promise. He had imagined comfort, but he found lushness instead. The cold, bare room slipped away, to be replaced by green meadows bowered with wildflowers, and clear water, and the sun potent and hot upon his back. His hands slipped from her shoulders, down the curve of her back, he pressed her to him, seized by a fierce urge to love and nurture her. But at the same time he felt a familiar heavy sinking guilt. They could share this moment, and perhaps even this week, but he could not give her what surely she must want. He knew he would be doing her a kindness if he stopped at this moment; this his mind counseled, though his body refused.

Mary had never imagined a man's touch could be at once so gentle and so strong, for beneath the breathless velvet of his kiss throbbed the hardness of the body against which she was drawn and towards which she pressed with a will she hardly recognized as her own. Her hands hesitated, then slipped upward to touch the curling crispness of his hair, twining themselves within it, reveling in the way it felt, reveling in the moment, which must surely last forever, for no life could follow bliss such as this.

He pressed her closer, heard again the voice of reason. You do her no kindness, it said, but rather the reverse, and if this goes further you will harm yourself, as well. Whatever has come over you is an aberration. Your life is in Boston; remember that, my friend. Fighting against desire, he pulled his lips from hers, trying not to notice the yearning in her eyes.

Shaking his head, he murmured, "That spell is pretty strong."

"Spell?" Her voice was dazed.

"Of the house." As he spoke, she shivered. "You are cold."

"No, no." She shook her head. Her fingers, embarrassed, untwined from his hair and slipped down to hang empty and useless at her sides. Her gaze slipped, as well, unable to meet his, and she heard him draw a quick breath, then slowly let it out. "We should get back," she said. "Likely Sophia has already arrived. And Grandfather doesn't like for me to be gone for long."

"Yes..." He meant to move. Instead, he stood, feeling the words well up in him. He knew it was unwise to speak them, but they burst out anyway. "It is no life for you!"

She looked up in surprise. "What?"

"Living in that big house, shut in all the time! Never going out to parties, caring for that old man!" he said, embarrassed yet unable to stop.

"But," said Mary reasonably, "who else would care for him? And, even if there was someone, what else should I do?"

*Marry me,* said a voice in Jack's mind. He felt his skin go cold and his heart begin to pound. What had made him think that, what had planted such an idea? At a loss for an answer, either to Mary's question or to his own, he spread his hands and said, "You could live here, in this house."

Like Aunt Alice, Mary thought, and felt again the sadness of her failed dreams, and felt, as well, the yearning that had come with them. How she wished he might have said *"You could marry me!"* But he had not said it; nor would he, she knew, and she wanted Jack's pity no more than he wanted hers.

"Yes, perhaps—" she nodded "—if it is still here. If it is still empty when Grandfather is gone. Perhaps then we shall sell the big house and come to live out here."

"We?"

"Mother and I," she said, and managed a smile. "Surely Eveline will have selected the man of her dreams by then."

He returned her smile, but with no more conviction than hers had embodied. He wished he could say something that would make things right for her, wished he could make her smile as she had earlier, but he was afraid to speak, afraid of what he might say. So he stood, confused and useless, until she turned away, saying, "It must be close to dinnertime, besides." And then there was nothing for him to do but follow her, back down the staircase, as he had followed her up.

THE SKY WAS STILL OPALESCENT as they drove back to the town, both of them silent and lost in thought. The road before them was now well-worn with tracks, the yards and sidewalks were trampled, the front walks were shoveled flat. It must be close to dinner, for there were few people about, but as they came down Elm Street they saw a group on foot who, from their dress and their gay laughter, must be coming from the skating pond. As they drew nearer, Mary saw Eveline, as well as Hetty Pickering and Asa Webb—and Annabella Woodcross, who did not add her voice to the cry that rose up in greeting when they were recognized.

"Hello! Where are you going! We've had such a marvelous time! We're on our way to Annabella's—Why not come along?"

Jack pulled up the carriage, and the group clustered around.

"Why, hello, Mary. Mr. Gates!" cried Hetty. "Wherever have you been? We've all been reminiscing about the sleigh ride last night. We missed you at the skating, so don't let us down. You simply must join us.... Do say you'll come along!"

"That's up to Miss Hillyer," Jack replied, wondering if he was imagining that she had been slighted just now.

"I can't." Mary shook her head. "But I can drive myself home, if you'd like to go on. Honestly, I don't mind," she said, reaching for the reins, but he snatched them from her.

"Of course not!" he said, and saw her start at the roughness in his voice. Turning to the others, he managed a fleeting smile. "Thanks for the invitation. Perhaps some other time."

"We'll miss you . . . you'll be sorry!" They laughed as they moved on, except for Annabella, who lingered behind. "Perhaps you will come back after you've seen Miss Hillyer home. We won't be having dinner for an hour at least, and then we'll take our time." Without waiting for his answer, she turned after the rest, her high-bustled skirts swaying as she moved away.

For a moment Jack sat, watching her move off. Then, laying the reins on the horse's back, he urged it ahead with a violence that almost sent them skidding off the road.

What, he wondered, straightening their course, made the good folk of Northampton completely oblivious to the remote possibility that Mary might have human feelings—that she might like enjoyment as much as anyone? Perhaps their cruelty was not intentional, but that could not lessen the hurt it caused. His hands shaking with anger, he glanced at Mary, to find her face averted, her lips closed tight, as they had been at breakfast this morning while Gray and Eveline had dithered on—and once again he had allowed it all to pass without doing something to save her from the hurt. Recalling the cool assurance in Annabella's voice, he gripped the leather hard, resisting the urge to turn and call out after her that he would rather fast with Mary Hillyer than eat ambrosia with her.

Lord, what was happening? What was happening to him? First his outburst in the Old House, then the kiss, and now this rage— He felt as though another being had taken over his emotions and was playing him as a puppet beyond his control. Whatever happened to the coolheaded Jack Gates, who knew where he was going and let nothing block his way? What was happening to him, and where would it end?

At his side Mary was waging her own battle, trying to hold on a little longer to the joy of the kiss, but in view of what had just happened it was a losing fight. It would not have been so bad had he left her there to go off with the others. That she could have accepted. He had no obligations, no relatives to meet. He had done her a favor coming out to see the house, and she could understand him now wanting to have some fun. She knew that was what he had wanted, she had seen it in his face— Then why had he refused her offer to go on by herself? Why, when it made him so angry to think of missing the fun, had he nevertheless insisted on seeing her to her door? Again she cringed inside as she remembered the way he had snapped at her, the way the horses had skidded beneath the sharpness of his whip.

Tears sprang to her eyes, but she bit them back. True, she would have been sorry to see him go, but it would have been something known and acceptable. Then she could have driven on, still snug in her own happiness, with the memory of his kiss to warm her through the rest of the day and beyond. Then she might have cherished some dream of his caring for her, whereas now it was too painfully clear that he'd been moved by something less than affection—by whim, perhaps, or by pity, which was even harder to take. Pressing her lips together to keep them from trembling, she wished she could have held the pleasure a bit longer.

THE FRONT DOOR SWUNG OPEN as they came up the drive. Gray stepped onto the brick porch. Seeing them, he cried, "Jack, you are a genius—either that or a mind reader! I ripped my trousers skating and had to come home for a change. Mother's got the carriage on some errand or other, and I would have been late for Annabella's if I'd had to go on foot. Before you appeared I'd despaired of getting away and resigned myself to eating with the pygmy horde! No, no, don't even bother to climb down. Just stay up there—I'll give Mary a hand. What's taken you so long? Grandfather's been bellowing for you all this last hour."

Reaching up, he handed Mary down from the seat, just as a swarm of children rushed out through the open door to envelope Mary with embraces and cries of joy. They were followed by their mother, who called above the din, "Oh, there you are, Mary! Thank goodness, at last! That girl of yours insists that the children's nanny is to be on the second floor, but I know you meant for her to be upstairs, near the nursery! And do you have a button? Robin's popped one from his blouse."

"Hello, Sophia." Mary greeted her sister and scooped up the smallest child to carry up the steps; the others trailed along beside her, each holding a hand or a handful of skirt. "You may give your nanny whatever room you like, and if you show me the shirt I'll find one to match." Then, pausing, she turned her head to the buggy, which Gray had already mounted. "Mr. Gates, thank you for the lovely morning. Gray, will we see you for supper?"

"I hope not." Gray grimaced. Then, laughing, he added, "Goodbye, Sophia. Have a nice day, boys and girls! Drive on!" He turned to Jack again as Mary was borne off by the clamoring throng. "What are you waiting for?"

"I—thought perhaps I would stay."

"Stay? Are you mad, man? You'd go deaf in an hour! We'll go to Annabella's, then driving afterwards. Someone is sure to be giving a supper, or we'll eat in town— We'll stay out until after the monsters have gone to sleep! Now drive on, I say. We're already late for dinner, and Annabella does not like to wait!"

At the mention of Annabella, Jack felt his anger rise; he recalled how she snubbed Mary when they had met just earlier. He had no desire to spend the day with her, and yet it seemed that he had no real alternative. Gray was right about staying. Though the front door had closed, still he could imagine well enough what was happening inside. Everyone would be crying for Mary, and she would be answering them one by one with patience and good humor—deserved or otherwise. He wished that he could help her, but what could he do? He would look only foolish rushing to her aid. So, despite his reluctance, he raised the reins, and though the day was still lovely, he no longer noticed it.

# Chapter Six

CHRISTMAS APPROACHED. Sophia's brood had hardly been settled when Florence arrived with her two. The husbands, who were still working, would arrive on Christmas Eve. Now the house hummed with life and activity, and Mrs. Parker's kitchen had become high headquarters, turning out goodies in such volume and with such frequency that the children took to going about like hounds, with their noses in the air, sniffing the scents of gingerbread, plum pudding and apple-sauce cake.

Everyone was occupied, out shopping and visiting or at home making presents behind closed doors. Bits of ribbon and gold paper peeped out from hastily shut desk drawers, and telltale colored spangles clung to carpets and skirts. They would come together in the form of pen-wipers and fancy pincushions and book-marks to go into stockings or be hung on the tree. Emily's father, who had a farm in the country, deliv-ered another cartload of greenery, and festoons of pine and hemlock draped the mantels and banisters; the heady tang of the forest competed with that of the sweets, and little wreaths of mistletoe and holly were hung everywhere.

The children breathed ecstasy. Expressly forbidden to search for their gifts, they spent hours speculating on what they would receive. Robin, Sophia's oldest, longed for a model ship, and Amy wanted a doll, while the younger ones were not quite sure what Christmas was about. They sat, eyes as wide as saucers, while Mary read, "The Night Before Christmas." Then they listened to Robin and Amy debating the habits of old Saint Nick.

These days, Mary was lucky to find time in which to read, so busy was she day and night with an endless round of tasks: seeing to meals and arrangements, and preparing for Christmas Day. Then there were her own presents to be sorted, wrapped and stored, and Grandfather to be coddled through what he viewed as one vast imposition. The roster for each day's dinner alone was a Herculean task, sorting out who would dine in and who would be out with friends.

To add to the confusion, Sophia's nanny broke her ankle falling on the ice, thus changing from a helping hand to another invalid for whom trays must be carried and medicine dispensed. Her duties were divided between Betty and Florence's nurse, both of whom resented the imposition—to which Sophia responded that she was sorry indeed, but she did not intend to spend her holidays playing the nursemaid. So it was left to Mary to pacify her sister and mollify the overworked staff. This she did, as always, with grace and efficiency, and yet she went about her round of duties with her mind only half on her work. All that she was not using was fixed steadfastly upon Jack; nor would the best of her efforts turn her thoughts away from him.

These thoughts, thus focused, were deep and troubling—as deep as the emotions that he had stirred within her. If she had not known it, if she had harbored any doubts, his kiss had swept them away like chaff before the wind. She was in love with Jack Gates, beyond wisdom and reasoning. Simply to be near him—to see him, to hear his voice—pierced her heart with a happiness she had never so much as imagined before. She might tell herself that the wise thing was to turn away from him, to deny and avoid such feelings until they died a natural death, and yet he drew her to him as a magnet drew steel. Every moment spent in his presence was a precious gift to be folded away and guarded like jewels in a treasure chest, and the moments in the Old House were the most precious of all.

She felt she knew him, knew him as perhaps no one else did. From what she knew of him and of human nature in general, she doubted that he made a habit of repeating his life story—in fact, she believed he had never told it to anyone else. The trust he had shown her filled her with gratitude, and now she could not look at him without seeing in her mind the frightened, angry boy that he had once been. She loved him for both his self-assurance and his vulnerability, and she loved him all the better because he understood her. He knew what she felt for the Old House as nobody else ever had—as no one else had ever taken the trouble to do. In those still, unheated rooms, they had spoken from the heart, and the memory of it would live in her for all her days.

"Mary," he had murmured, and when she had looked up he had bent to her.

Yes, she loved Jack Gates, as she had never loved before, and yet, for all the strength of her secret passion, she had no illusions. They had shared a moment, but a moment was all that it had been. Jack might have told her things he had never spoken of, but, having seen his pride, she doubted that he would ever wish to speak of such things again. And the same must hold true for the kiss. She might consider the memory of that kiss one of life's lasting events, but in Jack's more varied existence it must be a commonplace thing. She wouldn't be surprised to learn that Jack had kissed another girl that very same day. Certainly he had rushed off quickly enough with Gray, and neither of them had come in until very late that night. And as much as such things might hurt her, she must accept their truth, for clinging to illusion would only lead to hurt. Jack himself had told her where his future lay, and she would do herself no good by pretending otherwise.

The important thing to remember—more important than joy or hurt—was that the truth of her feelings must remain locked within her heart, hidden not only from Jack himself, but from everyone else, as well. She shuddered to think what would happen if anyone guessed what she felt; how they would laugh at her, what a joke they would make. *Poor Mary's sweet on Jack.... Do you see how she moons over him?*

*Poor Mary.* Strange that, for all that she had spent her whole life in Northampton, among these same people, until now she had never noticed how she was treated by them. Strange that she had never minded her role before, while now, all of a sudden, it seemed to bear down upon her. She didn't mind serving other people's needs, but it pained her to be regarded as someone without a heart—and not only without a heart, but almost without a form, for she had the impression that if not for her many functions she would be invisible. Was something broken? Ask Mary, she'll fix it for you. Was someone missing something? Mary will search it out. But what about Mary? What of Mary's heart?

What of her heart indeed? Until now she had hardly been aware of the existence of that organ, but now it was awakened and craving sustenance; and, though she could not bring herself to wish that Jack had never held her in his arms, still she could not but dread what the future held in store. What would become of her after Jack went away? The probable answer seemed brooding and portentous, yet she was powerless to change what had happened or the way she felt. So she went about her duties, tidying, placating, hungry for each coming hour, and yet dreading it, as well.

AMONG OTHER THINGS, she was late in sending Christmas cards this year. She would find a bit of peace in which to sit down to work, only to be roused by some new emergency that could not be resolved without her attention. Wherever she was at the moment became the center of activity; her room came to resemble the public room of an inn, full of rowdy children and truculent governesses and whatever impedimenta was too much for the other rooms. The schoolroom, her accustomed haunt, had become the nursery, and the injured nanny was housed in the sewing room. Finally, four days before Christmas, she took her cards and her pens and sneaked down to the library, closing the door silently.

She opened the box and, spreading out the cards, set about matching pictures to the people on her list. The group of carolers would do well for Martha Washburn, with whom she had been at school, and Emily's family would like the one of the woodsman returning home. Her fingers moved to one of a child leaning out of a mullioned window, scattering crumbs to the redbirds that gathered in the snow below. One bird, smaller than the rest, perched on a holly bush, its head tilted sideways, as though it were not quite sure that the child was to be trusted, and yet one had the impression that it, too, would eat in the end, that no one would be left out by this act of compassionate grace.

Aunt Alice would have liked this one, Mary thought with a sigh. For a moment her fingers lingered; then she put the card aside. Later she would decide to whom it would be sent. Taking up the carolers, she opened the card and dipped her pen, considering the message she would write to Martha Washburn. But she had hardly completed the salutation and the date when the door opened and Sophia put in her head.

"Do you know where Florence has gone?"

"Shopping, I think," Mary said.

"Well, wherever she's gone to, she's taken that nurse of hers, as well. I'm invited to the Pickerings, they've simply insisted, and I've got no one to watch the children. Of course, Robin and Amy can practically care for themselves, but the little ones . . . Well, I asked Betty, but she says that you told her to do the silver now, and she can't shine silver and watch children at once—though I can't see the trouble, since they're both ready for rests, and if she only gets them to sleep she'll have practically all afternoon to do as she likes."

"All right." Mary sighed. "Tell Betty I said that she should do as you wish—though," she added to herself as Sophia went out, "it will probably end in my doing the silver myself. Oh, well . . ." She sighed and returned to the cards on the desk, but she had not yet dipped her pen when the door opened again. Oh, dear, she thought with another sigh, if things keep up this way, I shall never be done. But she managed a smile as she raised her head. Her heart leapt, as always, when she saw who it was.

"Miss Hillyer, forgive me, I thought to find the room vacant."

"Mr. Gates! Come in."

Today he wore fawn trousers, a matching fawn waistcoat and a frockcoat of chocolate brown—the very colors, Mary realized, that she would have chosen for him, had she been granted the right. A week's outdoor entertainments had replaced his city pallor with a ruddy health that fairly glowed above the rich brown of the coat, while the pale elegance of his trousers accentuated his long, lean lines. Realizing that she was staring, she made herself look away, down at the assortment of brightly colored cards lying on the desk.

Jack glanced at the cards, as well. "I have interrupted you."

"No, I was only trying to finish up." She noticed the papers beneath his arm. "You . . . have work to do?"

Jack nodded with a rueful smile. "I am afraid I have left it too long. It should have been done last week, but each time I thought of it there was always some excuse, something I would rather do."

"No wonder," she agreed, emphatic in her defense. "After the number of hours you must have worked this past year! Gray says that often he goes weeks without so much as a half-day to call his own!"

"Yes, the hours are long," Jack said, his smile softening at her indignant tone. How like her to leap to the defense of the ones she loved. Of Gray, that is, he corrected.

"But the rewards are sweet," he added, moving around the desk to examine more closely the cards spread before her. They were all evocative yet unsentimental; their delicacy of design and color was so very much like her. His eyes was especially drawn to one, of a child feeding birds in a snowy yard. Lifting it, he murmured, "I bet this was you. I bet you used to save your breakfast for the birds."

"I did," she admitted, with that quick shy smile of hers, as fleeting as a shooting star, and as lovely, as well. Hesitantly she added, "I was thinking how Aunt Alice would have liked this one."

"Would she have?" he wondered, returning the card to her, and she felt her hand tremble as she received it from him.

He stood very close to her, just at her side, his hips resting against the desk as he faced the window. Consciousness of his presence invaded all her senses at once; she heard him and she felt him, drank him in through her very pores. Time hung suspended, as it did whenever he was near, and her whole soul was focused on each breath he took, on the texture of his jacket, on the tiny scar on his hand. How she longed to touch it, to lay her lips on it, to feel its warmth and roughness, the life pulsing beneath the skin. And, even if she could not touch him, it was enough to have him near.

The children must be playing somewhere outside. Jack could hear their voices, though they were not within view in the snowy yard that the window overlooked. Although the morning had dawned bright and clear, the clouds had since moved in to cover the sky, and the sunlight filtered through them with a pale pearly light. Somewhere a woman's voice was calling, to the children, perhaps, and from the kitchen cutlery clattered, but those sounds fell away before the stillness that pervaded the room. It surrounded Mary with an aura, an aura in which she would always move. Even in hectic Boston she would create an island of calm, with her small hands folded, her neat brown hair shining. His eyes moving from the window to Mary's bowed head, he was filled with a sudden dread of the life to which he must return and with an equal yearning to remain where he was, safe and secure within her governance.

"I shall miss you when I'm gone." He spoke without intention and felt his heart leap without reason when her eyes swiftly rose.

*I shall miss you!* His words ignited an explosion of hope in her breast; and yet, as quickly as hope blos-

somed, she pinched it off, reminding herself sternly
that his words did not mean what she thought. It was
only his way of flirting, of passing the time with her.
Glancing at the card she still held in her hand, she replied, "Half the girls in Northampton will miss you in
turn."

"And you among them?" he asked, his very voice
a caress, as soft and as tantalizing as his remembered
touch.

Cast her eyes about the room where she would,
Mary could not lose the vision of his strong, slim
hands, and so great was her desire to feel them upon
her that she had to bite down on the longing to keep
from crying out. Of course I shall be among them! she
would have cried out to him. I shall remember you
with longing until the end of my life. Of course I shall
remember— How can you doubt that it is so?

"Of course," she heard herself answer, with a calm
she did not feel. "The house will seem so empty without you and Gray."

You and Gray. He must have been holding his
breath, for now he felt it release, and felt the clenched
muscles of his stomach go limp with disappointment.
Then, despite what had happened between them, her
thoughts of him had not changed; she saw him as her
brother's friend, no more than a holiday guest.

Why should that bother him? If anything, he should
be happy that she did not think of him as more, that
she had not blown their one kiss out of all propor-
tion, fashioning him as her suitor. He ought to be rejoicing that he was off the hook, instead of sinking
beneath the sensation that he had lost something

valuable—that he'd lost his one chance at true happiness.

What was happening to him? He wished he could understand. What made her so alluring, so desirable, that beside her image every other woman paled, that every voice seemed grating compared to her own low sweet tones? Just last night, at the party, the minutes had seemed to drag, and his partners had seemed as unwieldy as cows, loping about the floor, their dresses all too showy, their smiles all too brittle and bright. He had made himself talk and smile, but his eyes had searched the crowd for brown eyes as clear and as gentle as hers and his ears had listened for the sound of her voice. What had happened to him, to make him feel such things? It was as if the Old House spell were upon him yet. Indeed, the memory of that hour spent in the peaceful rooms was with him constantly, as were all the yearnings he had felt that day.

What did Mary feel, he wondered, looking down at her. When his lips had sought hers, she had responded with a willingness that had taken him by surprise, but he saw no trace of that passion in her present attitude. Most likely she regretted that embrace, and would find any mention of it offensive and embarrassing. Probably she had concluded that he kissed women all the time—which was an accurate assessment, and yet had no bearing at all on what had passed between them. He wished he could explain so that she could understand and would no longer harbor an ill impression of him. Finally, he wondered why it mattered so very deeply what she thought of him.

Yes, why indeed? he wondered, shaking his head sharply once, as if to drive such weakness away. Why should any of this matter, when he would soon be gone, away and back to Boston, back to his own goals and his own life? Whatever spell Mary and her old house had laid upon him would soon enough be broken, forgotten and cast aside. Three days until Christmas, and then he would go away, and likely by New Year's he would have forgotten her.

Mary had moved as he straightened, but still she did not look up. Pausing for a moment, his gaze still upon her bent head, he lifted his work papers, saying, "I shall keep you no longer. Please pardon the interruption."

"There is no need," she replied, and watched him cross the room, her heart aching with regret. She had no expectation that he would say more, so she was surprised to see him hesitate at the door.

For a moment he stood unmoving, his back still to her; then, turning quickly, he murmured, "What would it take, I wonder, to prove myself worthy of you?"

Too startled to answer, she could only stare at him. He lingered the space of two heartbeats, then turned again and was gone, leaving her to her confusion and her fledgling hope.

*What would it take, I wonder...* Had she heard him right, or had she only imagined him speaking those words to her? Her senses were still humming from his presence so close to her, so that everything looked brighter, sharper and larger than life. How could she have existed before he had entered her life?

A noise cut into her thoughts, a most peculiar noise, a sort of sliding skidding, like snow falling off a roof. A moment of silence followed, and then there was a low, rising wail that seemed to come from the snow-covered yard. Dropping the card on the desktop, she sprang up from the chair. Throwing back the latch on the window, she flung it wide open, and as she did the wail grew in pitch and in desperation.

"Help! Oh, somebody, help!" shrieked a child's voice, and, leaning out the window, Mary saw her niece Amy standing just beneath the roof of the kitchen porch, over what appeared to be a half-buried sack.

"Amy! What's the matter?" she called out, and Amy turned. Then, seeing her aunt at the window, she began to wail again.

"Help, Aunt Mary, help! Robin's killed himself! He went afer the gray cat, she was up on the roof, but there was too much ice and he must have slipped. He tried to hold on, but—" Amy stopped, since her Aunt Mary was no longer listening at the window. For a moment, she stood staring, tearstained and open-mouthed; then, glancing down at the crumpled form of her brother, she drew breath to cry again, but she had hardly released it before Aunt Mary was at her side.

For the first awful moment, Mary thought that Amy must be right, for Robin looked so still and white. He lay as he had fallen, limp as a broken doll, his knees pointed one way, his left arm outflung. His cap had come off and lay a short way off, and a spreading pool of dark red stained the snow beneath his head. The sight of it clutched at Mary's heart, and for a moment she stood by Amy, too afraid to move. Then the paralysis passed and she dropped to her knees, pushing up his right sleeve to feel for the pulse.

It was there, running quick and wild, but strong enough for hope. Laying the limp arm across his chest, Mary slipped one gentle hand beneath his head, probing the sticky warmth for the wound itself, while Amy watched, terrified.

"Is he dead, Aunt Mary? Oh, please don't let him be! He said it would be easy, but he didn't see the ice—"

Mary cut her off. "Get Betty. Or Emily or Mrs. Parker—whoever is about. Tell them to bring blankets, and something to carry him on. Quickly!" She used her free hand to give the little girl a gentle push in the direction of the house.

She could not judge without turning Robin how deep the wound might be, and she did not want to move him, in case he was badly hurt. They must fetch the doctor, as soon as Betty came, but in the meantime she had to stanch the flow of blood. The handkerchief in her pocket was a useless scrap of lace, but she wore an apron over her day dress. With her free hand she untied it and wadded it into a ball; then, using her already-bloody hand to raise Robin's head fractionally, she slipped the wadded apron between palm and skull. Bracing his head with her free hand, she pressed against the apron, and up against the wound. There was still a danger that the coldness of the snow might kill him through shock, but it would surely help to slow the flood of blood.

"Oh, Robin!" she murmured, her eyes on the ashen face. "Please don't leave me! Help is on the way!" But where? she wondered, glancing back at the house—and there, at last, was Betty, rushing across the snow, breathless and almost as pale as the boy at her feet.

"Oh, dear, Miss Hillyer! Is it true that Robin's dead? I told them to be careful, but I couldn't—"

"Have you brought no blankets?" Mary asked hopelessly. "Have you brought nothing at all?"

"I didn't think of blankets.... When Amy said what had happened, I—"

Mary cut her off. "Never mind. Only go now and fetch them, as many as you can. Amy, run to the stable to see if Tom's about, and if he isn't—" She stopped as a hand covered her shoulder and a man's voice spoke.

"Blankets and what besides?"

It was Jack! For once Mary's heart thrilled not with pleasure, but rather with relief, for, unlike Betty's, his eyes held only calm.

"Blankets and some sort of bandage, and something to carry him in. And someone should go for the doctor—"

"Send the girl," he said, and was gone.

"Dr. Millburn?" Betty asked, wringing her hands, her eyes still on Robin's face.

"Yes—or rather no, he's gone for the holidays. You'll have to get Dr. Brawley, over on Prospect Street. If he's with a patient, you'll have to go on and find him."

"Yes, ma'am, Miss Hillyer." She took one step and turned. "But what about the babies? Of course they are resting, but Miss Sophia said—"

"Don't worry about the babies, just go! And, Betty—run! Don't cry, Amy," she added, for the child had not moved, but stood hiccoughing softly. "You'll see, Robin will be eating sweetmeats with you on Christmas day!" she said, with far more conviction than she felt. If only Robin's face were not so deathly pale.

Betty had hardly vanished when Jack was back again, dragging behind him the old toboggan they had used as children. It had lain forgotten in the cellar for years, until Gray had resurrected it a few days ago. He and Jack had gone sliding with Eveline, and Mary had watched them go, imagining how it would be to ride leaning back against Jack, his arms warm and snug around her. With a thrill of relief, she saw the blankets and linen he had heaped upon it and realized he meant to use it as a stretcher.

He had brought Tom, as well, who spared only the briefest glance at Robin's still form before bending to rearrange the blankets on the sled, spreading them open so that they could be wrapped about the boy once he had been moved. Jack was already busy ripping a pillowcase to use to bind the wound.

"I didn't know where you kept the bandages, so I got this instead. Can you judge the hurt?"

"Not really," she admitted, lifting Robin's head again so that Jack could slip in the binding. "I think his left arm's broken, from the way it looks, but I can't tell about the rest. Still, I think we'd do him more harm leaving him here in the cold than trying to move him in.''

He nodded in agreement, tying the ends of the makeshift bandage. Then he and Tom moved the toboggan in close and, working quickly and gently, shifted the boy onto it, covering him securely. The last blanket they wrapped around the toboggan to hold Robin in place. He groaned when they raised him; it was a long sigh through parted lips.

''It's a good sign,'' Mary said, the lines in her forehead belying the conviction in her voice. ''Bring him to the parlor,'' she called as she went ahead to build up the fire and clear a place for him. Amy, still hiccoughing, trailed close behind.

They laid him before the hearth. As soon as he was settled, she sent Tom to the Pickerings to break the news to Sophia as gently as possible. Emily had appeared, and Jack sent her off for the hot potatoes which had been in the oven for lunch to wrap in the blankets. To Amy, Mary gave the job of unbuttoning his boots.

''His boots?'' Jack's tone was wondering, but Mary only shook her head.

''To give her something to do.'' She would have liked to know if the bleeding had stopped, but she didn't want to disturb the child unnecessarily. At least the blood had not soaked through the wrapping yet. If only he weren't so cold, she thought, chafing his right hand, which lay like ice between hers. Pray God he hasn't broken his back or his neck. Visions of Robin as an invalid for life brought a new wave of fear. "Perhaps I should have gone to the Pickerings myself," she said, but Jack shook his head.

"You'll do more good here. Look, his lips are moving."

And indeed they were, uttering unintelligible half sighs. His face, too, she noticed, had lost its awful pallor and a faint flush of color was showing beneath his skin.

"Will he be all right?" Amy asked in a quavering voice.

"Of course he will! How could he not be, with your Aunt Mary here?" Jack said, and the child was reassured.

"It wasn't my fault," she said. "I told him that old cat didn't mind being on the roof, but he said that she did. He said he could reach her if he went in through the house and out through Grandmother's window. But when he tried to grab her the cat bit his hand, and that's what made him slip. I don't know what happened to the cat," she added as an afterthought. "Maybe she ran inside. All I saw was Robin falling off the roof—but it wasn't my fault."

"Of course not," Mary said, glancing at the clock, wondering if Betty had found the doctor yet. As if in answer to her wondering, a carriage stopped in front.

It was Dr. Brawley, all business and no sentiment. Kneeling beside Robin, he drew the blankets aside, probing gently with his hands. Mary sent Betty upstairs with Amy to check on the smaller children, then helped Jack unfasten Robin's clothes so that the doctor could examine him. They watched in anxious silence until at last Dr. Brawley leaned back.

"Well, he's taken a crack on the head—but of course you know about that—and broken his arm pretty well. It's too soon to say how he is with perfect certainty, and for the next few days we can't rule out a brain fever, but the indications are that with some rest and careful feeding he ought to be all right. The depth of the snow saved him from more serious injury—and this must be your sister, home from her visiting."

It was Sophia. They could hear her voice as the carriage drove up before the door opened, and it grew stronger as she burst into the house.

"Where is he? Where is my poor baby? Where are they keeping him?"

Then Tom must have told her where Robin was, for a moment later the parlor door was flung back, and with a rustle of silk and buckram, Sophia rushed into the room. She would have flung herself upon Robin, had not Mary caught her arm.

"Dr. Brawley says he's all right. He's broken his arm and cut his head, but otherwise he's all—"

"Oh, my poor Robin! Let me go! I must go to him! Oh, how still and pale he is! This would not have happened, if I had stayed at home!" Breaking away from Mary, Sophia threw herself on the rug, her skirts rising about her in a sea of silk.

"Accidents will happen," the doctor said, speaking in firm tones, "regardless of intention. Perhaps, Miss Hillyer, your sister would do well with a bit of laudanum, just to quiet her nerves. I'd like to get the arm splinted before the boy wakes up. He's gone through enough today without the extra pain. Mr. Gates can stay behind. I can use his help.''

"Of course," Mary agreed, tucking her hand beneath her sister's arm. "Come now, Sophia, you can see him in a bit." She spoke as if to a child, coaxing her from the room.

She was still with Sophia when they brought Robin upstairs. She heard the thud of the toboggan banging against the wall. "Do you think he will die?" asked Sophia, her voice drowsy from the drug.

"The doctor says not," Mary replied. "Why don't you close your eyes and have a little rest? I'll go sit with Robin until you wake up."

"You won't let him die?"

"Of course not, my dear."

ROBIN LOOKED VERY LITTLE in the high bed where they had put him to sleep, his head and his left arm wrapped in a bandage, the latter looking like a huge white sausage resting across his chest. As Mary watched, he sighed deeply and turned his head to one side.

"The doctor says he ought to be waking up any time. How is your sister?" Jack asked from across the room. He had been with the boy when she had come in.

"Thank goodness she's asleep." Mary sighed and saw his smile flash. He stood at the window, outlined by the gray afternoon light. "I don't know how to thank you for everything you've done. I don't know what would have happened if you had not been here."

"You would have done everything yourself," he said. He paused then added, "You'd make a good lawyer. You stand up under pressure, so would do well in court."

"I doubt it—" she smiled, flattered "—but thank you for the compliment."

Robin muttered again. As one, they turned to him, watching the sleeping face. Three hours ago she would have felt the air charged with Jack's presence, but now she felt relaxed and easy, as if he were an old friend from whom she could draw comfort and in whom she could confide.

"I remember watching him this way when he was first born," she said, her lips curving at the memory. "I was still a girl, much younger than Eveline. He seemed such a miracle." She shook her head, harkening back to the time when she had first held him in her arms, the tiny, warm weight of him. She had sat for hours cradling him against her, imagining how it would be when she held her own firstborn. How sure she had been in those days that motherhood lay ahead—and how wrong. Her smile faded, and she heaved a sigh of regret.

Jack had been watching the play of emotion across her features. Now he said gently, "A penny for your thoughts."

"Oh..." Her smile was sad. "I was just thinking how differently life sometimes turns out from the way you expected. Children, for instance. I always thought that I'd have a half dozen at least."

"You may have them yet."

"Yes, of course," she agreed, and her courtesy cut him as rudeness could never have done. The soft gray afternoon light smoothed her shoulder and framed her cheek as his hand might have done. For a long, long, silent minute he stood gazing down at her, while his heart swelled and contracted with a sweet aching for her. He opened his mouth to address her but, finding no words to speak, at last turned away from her and left on silent feet.

She looked up from Robin at the soft click of the door to discover herself alone. Jack's retreating footstep sounded along the hall. She considered calling after him, but she lacked the energy, and in any event had no reason to bring him back again. Throughout this endless afternoon she had taken his presence at her side almost for granted, but now, when he left her, she felt instantly bereft—it filled her with dread of the week to come, when he would be gone for good. But there was no use dwelling upon such sorrows now, not when she was so tired, not with so much yet to do.

A chair stood against the wall. Drawing it over to the bed, she let herself sink down onto the cushions, limp with exhaustion and yet filled with a sadness greater than all her fatigue.

# Chapter Seven

TOM HAD UNHARNESSED THE HORSES from the carriage after he'd brought Sophia home. When Jack reached the stables, he was brushing the horses down.

"How is the little fellow doing?"

"The doctor says well," Jack replied. "Is there a horse I could take out?"

"I'll hitch up the buggy, if you like," Tom offered, with a willingness born of the day's experience. He'd taken this Gates fellow for a gay blade like Mr. Gray, full of himself and the ladies and good for little else. But he'd done his share and more with young Master Robin, earning Tom's admiration, and his respect, as well.

Jack met the offer with a shake of his head. "Thanks, but a horse will do fine. If you point me to the right one, I'll saddle up for myself."

THE CLOUDS THAT HAD HIDDEN the sun since midmorning were showing signs of breaking now, at the day's end, though the air held the peculiar dampness that often speaks of snow. Jack roused the bay mare to a canter over the hard-packed snow, keeping his eyes on the road, glad for the afternoon's rawness, which kept people snug at home. He had no inclination to be stopped by passersby; what he wanted was the cold air and some time alone.

Had he a destination? He had named none consciously, and yet he found himself turning and turning again, down roads that though remembered, were not yet familiar, until at last he saw the Old House standing to his left. Slowing the horse to a walk, he guided her into the yard.

It had not snowed again since he had been here last, and the snow was crusted brittle and hard on top. The horse's hooves broke through it as they came into the yard, the sound echoing loudly through the still, cold air. No one had come here since that day, so the prints they had left that morning had not been disturbed. He thought he saw the place where he had been first tempted to take Mary in his arms. At first the mare raised her head, awaiting his command, but, when she saw he meant to stay awhile as he was, she dropped her head to the ground to forage in the snow, stamping her feet from time to time as the chill rose through her hooves.

The sun, finding a breach in the clouds, poured down upon the snow, turning it first gold and then crimson, bathing the house in its glory, so that the narrow windows became bright copper squares and the icicles on the rafters gleaming ruby spears. The band of sunset widened, spreading splendor across the land; Jack watched it growing, felt it swell within. Feelings long forgotten came creeping back once more—that sense of seeing paradise, of feeling oneself blessed, of coming home at sunset across the snowy fields, wet and cold and glowing, through a blazing wonderland. He breathed in deeply the remembered smells of wet wool and wood smoke beckoning towards home, where dinner would be cooking and everything safe and warm. Boston and his real life seemed so far away.... Wisconsin was much clearer, and things from long ago.

What do you want? Mary had asked, and he had replied, Wealth, power and success. Now he heard those words without the familiar elation their sound had always evoked. Before this splendor those words rang hollow, all glitter and bright promise, like the piles of Christmas presents that, once they were opened, became only things. If he spent his life on them, he would indeed be wasting it.

The sun passed the horizon. Though the sky still glowed, the windows were darkened and the house stood empty and forlorn. He recalled what Mary had said about children living here, to fill it with life and laughter and love and family. For a moment he thought he saw the darkness vanish again and the windows light up. He saw the front door open and Mary appear on the porch; as he watched, she smiled and opened her arms, and then he was running, his breath coming in great clouds of steam, the snow crunching under his feet. Then the image faded, and again the house was dark.

Shivering, he looked around. The sunset was gone now; the first stars were twinkling, and the tracks in the crusty yard had turned from white to black. When he sighed, his breath exploded in a silent cloud of white. He watched it drift and scatter, knowing that he should go but, even so, remaining to watch the darkness spread over the silent land.

How long did he sit? He lost track of time, and only the horse's restless stamping brought him back to life. Had he reached a decision? Had he been seeking one? He was not aware of it, and yet he felt a lightness where there had once been a weight, although his fingers were freezing and his toes half numb. Guiding the mare in a half circle, he set off back towards town, the moon casting its unearthly brightness over the snowy fields.

## Chapter Eight

ROBIN OPENED HIS EYES that evening long enough to look around, but he felt too bad to do more than sip some of the broth that Mary fed him before drowsing off again. He woke again the next morning with an aching head and arm, but in sufficiently high spirits to recall a chocolate cake Mrs. Parker had been baking the afternoon before and to wonder if anybody had thought to save him a piece. At that his grateful mother would have produced a whole tray of cake, had not Mary prevented her.

Dr. Brawley, arriving just afterwards, examined him thoroughly before offering the opinion that Robin was a very lucky boy. To the still-nervous Sophia, he spoke in glowing terms, but in private he added to Mary that it was still too soon to rule out a fever and that they should keep Robin very quiet, at least through the next night. Mary, who had spent most of the night sitting up with him, received Dr. Brawley's words with outward calm; after he left, however, she retired to her room to soak her pillow with grateful, weary tears.

She was just bathing her face, preparing to go downstairs to arrange the day's assignments, when Eveline knocked on the door to say that she and the other sisters would see to Mary's tasks on condition that Mary try to get some rest. Too weary to oppose the offer, and telling herself that whatever chaos thus created could be sorted out later on, Mary changed into a wrapper and climbed into bed—and her last thought as she drifted off was to wonder if perhaps Jack had had a hand in it. Farfetched though the notion was, yet it persisted, and she drifted off to sleep with a smile on her lips. Nor did she open her eyes until late afternoon.

Robin passed another quiet night, waking the next morning clear-eyed and ravenous. Dr. Brawley proclaimed him past the danger point, and Robin was rewarded with a plate of ham and eggs. By that afternoon, things were back to normal once again—or as normal as they could be the day before Christmas Eve, with a houseful of excited children, and three invalids besides. Sophia, having taken Robin's accident very much to heart, turned down all invitations to go out visiting, instead ministering to the wounded with such expansive incompetence that at last Mary begged Florence to take her out to tea.

Amy and the younger children had set up camp in Robin's room, where once again the subject was Santa Claus. Robin, propped up on pillows, made the little ones cry by insisting that he would not come because all the fireplaces had been blocked off by Franklin stoves.

"Except for the drawing room," Amy pointed out, "where we hang our stockings."

"But Uncle Gray and Papa always build a great roaring fire there—if Santa tries to come down, he'll scorch his behind!"

"Will not!"

"Will too"

"Mother! Aunt Mary! Robin's being mean!"

In the end, Mary explained that Santa would not come until the fire had died down, and that he wore special boots to protect him from the coals. Then she shooed out the others to let Robin rest.

"That wasn't very kind," she chided, laying her hand upon his cheek.

"Yes, I know." He chuckled, not a bit contrite. "Will Papa come tomorrow?"

"In the morning, first thing. And your Uncle Porter, as well. Then we'll all be together."

"Yes, and Saint Nick will come." Beneath the thick white bandage, his eyelids fluttered shut. Then they sprang open again. "You don't think he'll forget me, because of what I said? I was only teasing—"

"Yes, I know." She smiled. "No, he won't forget you. Now close your eyes and rest."

She sat with him, stroking his hand until he fell asleep, her eyes upon the window. Twilight was gathering again, just as it had gathered two days ago, when Jack had stood across the bed, smiling at her.

Jack. She had not seen him since that afternoon, for by the time she had waked yesterday he and Gray had gone out, and today she had hardly strayed from the servant stairs. Yet, though she had not seen him, she had felt him near. She had a sense of his presence, as if she could reach out and touch his sleeve, as if she could see his smile, hear him speak her name. The bond woven between them during the afternoon at the Old House had remained within her ever since. She knew that he was leaving, that soon he would be gone—that it was very likely they would never again be alone—but somehow all this knowledge could not shake her mood. Perhaps she was just grateful that Robin was all right, or perhaps she was only shielding herself. She felt a certain sadness, yet the sadness was sweet, not the strangling aching that she had felt before. She was not empty-handed, as she had been the night when he had gone to the sleigh ride and she had stayed behind. He had left her with something, though she could not have said just what.

Beside her Robin sighed. Turning from the window, she saw that he was sleeping. For a moment she stayed as she was, savoring the light, but there was too much still undone for her to linger here. Laying Robin's hand on the covers, she rose and tiptoed from the room.

She heard Jack's voice as soon as she shut the door. Her heart lifted, and she turned towards the stairs, expecting to see him coming down from the room that he was sharing with Gray. Instead, to her amazement, she saw him emerge from Grandfather's room. She thought immediately that Grandfather must have called for help, but saw from Jack's demeanor that it could not be so. He showed no signs of rushing, and his expression, though sober, did not appear alarmed. If anything, he seemed to be lost in profound thought—so lost that he came towards her without looking up.

Without thinking, she laid her hand on the knob of Robin's door, intending to slip back inside so that Jack would not see her. But the door, which had been perfectly silent in closing, now uttered a whine of protest. Looking up, Jack saw her, and he started in surprise.

"Miss Hillyer!"

"Mr. Gates," she said, and paused, unable to come up with even a commonplace.

Jack seemed flustered, as well. Looking about, he noticed the door, half open at her back. "How is the patient?" he asked.

"Oh, very well, thank you. Well enough to be teasing his sisters about Santa Claus."

"Is he?" Jack smiled, but he looked distracted. Thinking he meant to be going, she pulled in her skirts to let him pass, but he did not move; instead, he stood looking at her with the same intensity she had seen on his face just before. Curiosity and discretion battled within her, and for once curiosity won.

"You were just with Grandfather..."

"Was I? Yes, I suppose I was." He glanced back at the door, and Mary was astonished to see his color rise. "I... thought I ought to thank him for his hospitality. It... it seemed the polite thing."

Mary tried to picture such an encounter. "And what did he reply?"

"You're welcome—or some such thing. A pity we didn't meet sooner. He's a fine old gentleman."

"Grandfather?" She saw him smile at her incredulity.

"And a hard-headed businessman. I hope that I've his command when I am his age."

"You were speaking business?" she asked, in the same wondering tone, and saw him flush again.

"In the most general way. Well!" He straightened, as if he were waking from a nap. "I'm sure you've got plenty to do. Tomorrow's the big day— I'll leave you to your work. Good afternoon."

"Good afternoon," she murmured, turning to watch him go. Then, her brow still furrowed, she went in to Grandfather.

He was sitting up in bed, staring straight ahead, with an expression strangely like the one she'd seen on Jack just now. He looked up when she spoke his name.

"Ah, so it's you! I thought you might have forsaken me for your other patients."

"Of course not, Grandfather. I was just with Robin. He's very much improved."

"Improved, is he? Well, he's lucky not to be dead. And as for his flea-brained mother—"

"It wasn't Sophia's fault. Boys will be boys, you know."

"Is that so? And what do you know about boys? You haven't got one hidden somewhere on the sly?"

"What an idea!" She flushed. Grandfather found this amusing, and he cackled to himself until she had to battle the impulse to flee the room. When she heard his next subject, she wished that she had.

"I've been thinking about the Old House."

"Have you?"

"Yes, I have." His fingers drummed a soundless tattoo on the counterpane, and his sharp, inquisitive eyes followed her movements as she drew the curtains and lit the evening lamps. "I'm thinking that perhaps I'll sell it. What do you think of that?"

Mary could not hide her dismay. "But I thought you meant to keep it! You said so when Aunt Alice died!"

"And so I did," he agreed. "But now I've changed my mind. What's the point in its lying empty until it rots to the ground? Then it would be worth nothing but the value of the land. Now there's a house, as well."

"But you don't need the money."

"Not need the money, hah! You sound like that brother of yours! Who else would pay to keep you if I ran out of cash?"

"That's not what I meant," she murmured, feeling the hot rush of tears.

"I know what you meant!" he replied. "I know what you meant, all right. Well, it's my decision, and I guess I can do what I like. Now stop fidgeting in the corners and come read to me. I'll have some of Mr. Boswell, if you haven't misplaced the book!"

AT LAST IT WAS CHRISTMAS EVE. Sophia's and Florence's husbands arrived at dinnertime, heightening the children's excitement to a fever pitch; it continued all afternoon, and climaxed that evening with the hanging of the stockings in the drawing room. Robin was carried down for this great event and allowed to stay with the others for a half hour of caroling. Then all the children were whisked off to bed, amidst the usual flurry of kisses and good-natured threats. When they were safely retired, Jack and Porter, Florence's husband, went out to bring in the tree from the woodshed, where it had been hidden since Emily's father had brought it that morning. The tree was a Douglas fir, dark green and luxuriant; its uppermost branches brushed the very ceiling.

"It's beautiful!" cried Eveline, clapping her hands. "I declare that we have never had a more handsome tree!"

"You say the same thing every year," Gray told her. "And now Sophia will go into rapture about the decorations."

These latter were in boxes, wrapped in soft paper: tiny bits of furniture cunningly fashioned in tin— chairs and polished tables, bureaus and eight-day clocks; finger-sized dolls and tiny animals; and bright balls of every color gilded with silver and gold.

"Mary, here's your favorite!" Eveline called out, holding up a silver sleigh hardly bigger than a dime, whose horses' bells jingled when given a shake. She passed it to Mary, who held it in her hand, seeing in its brightness a chain of Christmases stretching back through the years.

"How pretty. May I see it?" Jack held out his hand. The small bells tinkled when she placed it in his palm. He held it for a moment, then passed it back to her; their fingers touched briefly, joining warmth to warmth.

She was wearing the mauve silk he'd seen her in that first night, but her hair was dressed more fully, piled high on her head. Her skin was flushed from excitement and the heat of the room, and her eyes were bright—for a breathless moment he wished they were alone and not surrounded by the whole of her family. Yesterday, he had made a proposal to her grandfather, and ever since then he had thought of nothing else. The question was what Mary would say when she learned.

"Here are the candles!" Florence cried. "Mary, where are the holders?"

"I'll find them," Mary turned away, the sleigh still in her hand. Jack felt a disappointment, but also a rising suspense. Before the night ended, he hoped to know the truth.

To the old decorations, each added a new surprise—presents for the children, and for the grownups, as well: tiny crochet purses, charms of silver and gold, miniature paint boxes and toy soldiers with shining swords. Florence's husband, Porter, had brought a box of gold-leafed fruit, and Sophia one of bonbons wrapped in Christmas designs. Jack won a round of applause when he produced a half-dozen little men whose roly-poly bodies were filled with sugarplums.

"Too much! Too much!" groaned Gray, rolling his eyes in mock distress. "I'm too old to be bought off with promises of tomorrow and too young to swear off sweets!"

"But not the decorations," Eveline told him, laughing. "Look, here is Emily in answer to your prayers."

The answer was the heaping tray Emily carried in her arms, loaded with goblets of mulled wine and plates of sugared nuts and crisp ginger cookies studded with tiny currants. Setting the tray on the table, Emily turned to the tree.

"Why, it's a wonder—even without the candles lit!"

"Thanks to your father," Mary agreed, handing the glasses around. "Eveline vows it is the finest we've ever had."

"I propose a toast!" cried Gray, raising up his glass. "To Christmas and to family—may they long endure!" He would have drunk his wine then, but Florence stayed his hand.

"Wait, there is something more. Porter, go ahead." She looked to her husband, who smiled modestly.

"It's nothing, just my company seems to have bought Spofford Mill—"

"Spofford—here in Northampton?"

"Yes!" Florence cut in. "And they've asked Porter to manage it!"

"So you'll be moving back to Northampton!" Eveline added. "Will you buy a house of your own or live here with us?"

"I thought here, at least, to start— That is," Florence added, "if Mother doesn't object."

"Object?" Mrs. Hillyer seemed confounded by the idea. "But you'll have to ask Grandfather. It's his house, after all."

"Oh, I thought that Mary might do that for me. She'll know how to put it so that he'll agree. After all, he can't refuse his own great-grandchildren!"

"Hear, hear!" Gray applauded and raised his glass again. "To the proud homecoming!"

After the toast had been drunk and the sweets passed around, they gathered at the piano for caroling. Eveline questioned Jack on his singing voice and, upon hearing that he could produce a creditable tenor, insisted he sit beside her to turn pages while she played.

Mary watched them all. Their faces were all so bright, flushed from pleasure and from wine. Sophia was so grateful for Robin's recovery, and Florence was bursting with pride at Porter's promotion and full of the excitement of moving home again. No doubt she was already thinking of the fine house they'd buy with the money they would save by living here at home. Eveline was looking smug, as well as happy. Justin Harris had indeed proposed, and she was now savoring the pleasure of making up her mind. Mother, of course, always looked at peace, for she had opted for a life above worldly harm. And then there was Gray and Jack, who had chosen the opposite, and who stood so poised and ready, with everything lying ahead of them.

And her? What of her? She had happiness this moment because Jack was near—because he had asked to hold her tiny, beloved sleigh. But, just as he had returned the ornament to her, soon enough he would go away without a backward glance. She knew she could not blame him for having been born as he was. If he could have great things, why should he settle for less? Why should he choose a plain girl when he could have a beauty? He had shown her kindness, friendship and respect. It would be doing him an injustice to mistake those things for anything else.

And yet where did that leave her? There was no point in self-pity, and yet what else could she feel, playing such a minor role in the others' happiness? Once she had nursed the consolation that even if she never wed she would live one day at the Old House, tranquilly, as Aunt Alice had. But now Grandfather was saying that he meant to sell it away—which meant that she would live out her days as she was now, managing the big house as a family hotel, snatching bits of affection from her sisters' families. Florence would move in with them and Florence would move out again, but Mary would be Mary, day after day after day. She stood amidst her family, an arm's length from the man she loved and yet, for all the longing within her, she might have been standing on the moon.

"It came upon a midnight clear," the others sang, and Mary tried to sing with them, but the words stuck in her throat.

THEY HAD JUST STRUCK UP "Good King Wenceslas" when Jack noticed that she was gone. She'd been standing beside Porter when he'd last turned to her. He'd caught her staring at her mother with that yearning, wistful expression that had touched him from the first. His first instinct had been to speak her name—but he couldn't very well do that with everyone all around and Eveline wondering why he hadn't turned the page. There would be time later, he'd thought, turning back—but when he looked again she was no longer there.

He thought at first that she might be fetching something from the kitchen, but when the minutes passed and she did not return he decided to look for her himself. Pressing Gray into service as the page-turner, he made his way through the carolers and across the room.

Emily and Mrs. Parker looked up in surprise when he came through the kitchen door.

"Miss Hillyer? No, not since supper, sir. Perhaps you should try upstairs with the old gentleman—though he hasn't been calling, or we would have heard for sure."

"I'll try there. Merry Christmas."

"Merry Christmas, sir," they replied, exchanging a look that grew more meaningful when he left in a hurry and by the servants' stairs.

The old man's door was ajar. Jack paused just beyond it, listening for some sound that would tell him whether or not Mary was within. But he heard nothing, so he passed on. Mary's door was closed to him; this time he knocked.

There was no response. Did he imagine it, or had he heard a sound within, the sound of a breath catching, as if between sobs? He knocked again, more firmly.

"Mary?" he called.

There was a pause. Then a muffled voice said, "What is it?"

"Are you there? Can I come in?"

Again there was a moment's silence. "All right, if you want. The door isn't locked," she added, so he opened it and went in.

She sat in a low chair on the far side of the room. Only the lamp at the dressing table had been lit, and the room was dim. Still, he could see that she'd been crying and had only just stopped. When he pulled the door shut behind him, she stood, her skirts falling about her. They were the color of a summer's dawn.

"Is something wrong, Mr. Gates?"

"Do I need something, do you mean?" Jack shook his head; his smile was brief and bitter. "No, I haven't come to tell you that there's a task to be done. I noticed you were missing and I came to find out why." He paused, then added, "Why were you crying just now?"

He saw her start to deny it, but then the tears started afresh. Dropping her head, she murmured, "It's nothing, nothing at all. I don't know what's come over me. Oh, dear..." She started to sob, bringing her hands to her face to hide it from his sight.

He had no recollection of having crossed the room, but suddenly he was with her, gathering her up in his arms, as he had longed to do so many times before. Cradling her head in one palm, he drew her closer still, feeling her warmth within him, her trembling sobs.

"Is it because I am leaving? Is that what it is?"

"Yes, in part," she whispered, her voice muffled against him. "It's everything—Florence coming, and Grandfather selling the house. I know I should be thankful for everything I've got, but still, I can't help feeling—" She stopped, overcome by her tears.

"Oh, my dear," he murmured, his lips against her hair. "My poor little sweet one, I will take care of you." He pressed her closer to him, murmuring words of comfort and affection, until somehow her lips were beneath his and he was kissing her. She was as eager as the first time he had kissed her at the Old House, as soft and as sweetly yielding. He would do anything for her, anything in the world. In his whole life he wanted nothing but to love her and pleasure her. Yesterday he had known it, and this evening as well, but not until this moment had he felt the full force of the truth, and he, who had always prided himself upon maintaining control, felt only the humblest gratitude for having been granted love. Holding her head between his hands, he showed her with his kisses everything that he felt.

Mary was only able to think she was with him once again, swooning once more beneath the rough gentleness of his lips, tasting the sweetness of the spiced wine he had taken below when they had toasted Florence. They had toasted everything but her life then, but that no longer mattered. Nothing mattered except the fact that she was wrapped in Jack's arms, drugged by the slow wonder of his embrace. Her cheeks were still wet from crying, her eyes still swollen with her tears, but her happiness was no less for being bittersweet, for being shot through with the knowledge that this was all she would have. She must cling to this moment and not let herself think about the other women whom he had held before, nor about those who would know the paradise of his arms in days to come. He had whispered "my dear" to her, and that must be enough. Two weeks ago she would have been shocked at such sentiments, but tonight she would give gladly whatever he asked, if only for this one night on which to look back in the years to come.

Her two hands had somehow found their way to his neck; now he held one, drawing it to his lips, then pressing it to his cheek. The warmth of his breath, of his rough skin, shot sharp thrills through her, until it was a wonder that her legs could support her weight. He pressed her hand against his heart, then turned it in his palm, his lips tracing a line of fire from her wrist along her arm. When he reached the soft skin beneath her elbow, she moaned low in her throat, arching her body against his, seeking by instinct his hardness and his heat.

Her moan set his pulse racing and all his nerves tingling. He wanted to protect her, but he wanted her, as well, with a depth of passion he had never felt before. Raising his lips from her arm, he sought the warm curve of her throat, drinking in the fragrance of the scent she used, as delicate and inviting as the soft swell that rippled beneath the silk of her bodice. His fingers found the tiny row of hidden hooks down her back, and he felt her shudder as he unclasped the first; he thought that she might stop him, and so he stopped himself—though it cost him an effort he had not been sure he possessed. Then the shudder ended and she was his once again, and his lips moved lower, seeking their sweet reward.

His kisses were lighting fires in places she had never felt, so that her body shook like a young tree before the wind. His will was the tempest, the force by which she lived, and she would bend before it and welcome it. She loved him beyond reason, beyond even regret. If he did not feel the same things she felt, still it was enough that he was with her now.

It was enough, she told herself, willing all other truths away. But something was rising, swelling deep within. At first she tried to fight it, but it was too strong to resist. She prayed that it be pleasure, but instead it was tears, erupting in a fountain too abrupt to stem.

Jack felt her body shaking and, raising his head, saw the bright tears pouring and pouring down her cheeks.

"My darling, you are crying! I have made you cry!"

*My darling!* The words hurt as unbearably as the gentleness of his voice. They brought home all too clearly what she would never have. But she could have something, if only she had the nerve—if only she could manage to stem the hot flow of her tears. But it seemed that even this lay beyond her control.

"It's nothing. I'm sorry," she told him, sobbing. "I thought I could, but now I just can't. I can't." Heartbroken, defeated, she shook her head back and forth. She tried to keep her head down when he touched her chin, but at last she surrendered; she had nothing more to lose.

Tilting her face to him, Jack gazed down at her, wanting her with all his being, with his very soul—wanting her in a different way from that in which he had ever wanted anything in his life. Boston, wealth, ambition, all were pale ephemera before her strength and sweetness, her tender, loving heart. He could give up those things and hardly feel the loss, but to give up Mary would be to give up life itself. He thought he knew her feelings, but he had to know for certain.

"Can't what?" he asked, and at first he thought that she would not reply. Her lips trembled; he saw the effort by which she stilled them so that she could speak.

"Can't forget who I am. I want to, but I can't, even though I'll regret it after you are gone. I know I'll remember these moments and ask myself how I could have turned away from you. But still…" She shrugged with a hopelessness that at once hurt Jack and thrilled him.

"But, my dear, I would not have you be other than you are. Not for all the gold in the world."

"Yes, but you will leave." Her tears were starting afresh.

"Look at me," he said, and she obeyed with streaming eyes. Through the blur of her tears, his eyes looked almost black. "Do you want me to stay?" he asked, and despite all her sorrow she could not help but smile.

"How can you even wonder? How can you ask me that? But it makes no difference."

"No difference!' he exclaimed, and something in his tone struck hope within her heart. He saw her eyes widen as she gazed up at him. For a moment he stood, unmoving; then he dropped to one knee.

"Mary, will you be my wife? Will you marry me?"

"Marry you?" she repeated, puzzled and unbelieving. "What on earth would make you want to marry me?"

It was the very question he had asked himself two days before, but now that he heard it spoken it struck him as profane.

"Perhaps because I love you," he said, rising once again. "Because I could not be happy living apart from you, whereas being with you is all that I want in life—that and a half-dozen children, or a dozen if you like!"

Her expression had not changed. He could see that she was still baffled, that she was still clinging to her disbelief. His mind groped for the words that would wipe away all her doubt. Then he knew the answer—and it was so simple that he wanted to laugh.

"Wait here." He gripped her hands briefly, squeezing them as if for luck, then, dropping them, he turned and practically ran from the room.

He had left the door open, so she could hear that he had gone to see Grandfather, as he had done yesterday. Her bafflement increasing, she listened to their murmuring tones, sometimes rising above the caroling, sometimes lost within it.

"God rest ye merry gentlemen, Let nothing you dismay..."

He wanted to marry her. No, it could not be true. She must be dreaming. She would wake up in the next breath and find it was all a cruel hoax. She looked down at her hands, feeling the remembered warmth and strength of his grip.

Now the voices had stopped, and she heard Jack's step running down the hall, not towards her room but towards the servants' stairs. Where could he be going? What could he be about? She wanted to get up, but still she sat where she was, afraid that any movement would shatter the dream.

He was gone for what seemed an hour. She had almost given up when once again he was with her, grasping her hand to pull her from the chamber and with him down the hall.

"Where are we going?"

He laughed. "You'll see."

He pulled her through the kitchen, past the blur of pale faces, past Emily and Mrs. Parker who called out, "Merry Christmas!" Then he led her out through the back door and into the yard, where the sleigh was standing, the horses' bells jingling. Tom held the harness, a wide grin on his face.

"Merry Christmas, Miss Hillyer."

"Merry Christmas, Tom. My coat," she protested dazedly.

"Never mind," Jack told her. "The rugs will keep you warm." He tucked her in securely, then climbed in at her side. Tom stood waving as they drove from the yard.

"Where are we going?" she wondered a second time, though it was not truly a question, for, somehow, she already knew.

IT WAS BEGINNING TO SNOW AGAIN, a few fat, lazy flakes, just as it had the evening Jack had arrived, only this time she was driving in the sleigh, not standing at the window watching his shadowed face, oblivious to the houses passing on either side, aglow with decorations and holiday cheer, and to the sweet sound of carols drifting out through the cold night air. Now and again he would turn to smile down at her, and at some point he took her hand and tucked it through his arm. She stood poised on the precipice between hope and happiness, unaware, despite her protests, of the falling snow.

When they reached the Old House, he turned into the yard and pulled the horse to a stop.

He turned to her. "Merry Christmas."

She looked from him to the house, smiling in confusion. "I don't understand."

"The Old House is my present, I'm giving it to you—but on one condition. That you'll marry me."

"Then I wasn't dreaming," she whispered. "You really did ask me."

"Yes, I really did. Then what about the Old House—can we make it yours?"

"But what about Boston?" She shook her head. "What about all the things you've worked for so hard?"

"I've got them all right here," he said, bringing her hand to his lips. She watched him, breathless, until he raised his head. "Funny how long it took for me to understand. In a way, I think I knew it the very first time we spoke. For a while I tried to fight it, tried to tell myself it was just a passing whim. But Boston was the passing whim. This is what is real."

"But what will you do here?"

"Practice law, of course. They do have lawyers here in Northampton, don't they?"

"Yes, they do," she said, knowing that she was smiling, but unable to stop. "And what about the Old House? Has Grandfather sold it to you?"

Returning her smile, he nodded. "Does that surprise you so very much? Oh, I'll admit it—he was skeptical at first. 'How do I know that you don't just want her for my money?'" he said, in such a perfect imitation that Mary had to laugh. "He told me that he never trusted a handsome man."

"And what did you reply?"

"That I'd seen the portrait of him in his youth." He laughed with her, filled with a rising joy. The clouds of their breath mingled in the frosty air. "He said that I was a charlatan but he liked me all the same."

"Is that what you were doing when I saw you yesterday?"

"Yesterday I'd only begun to feel him out. He said he'd have to think it over, he'd have to let me know. Tonight I told him I meant to make you both mine.... I don't know who was more surprised, your Grandfather or I! What will it be then, Mary—will you marry me?"

"Oh, yes, I will," she whispered, her eyes fluttering closed as he bent to her. But his lips had not touched hers when hers opened again, filled with a new concern.

"But what about Grandfather? What will become of him? And Mother, and Eveline—"

"Bring them all along!" he laughed. "Or leave them in the big house with Florence. That would come as a surprise!"

"Yes, it would," Mary smiled, understanding him perfectly. "Only I can't leave Grandfather. Do you think you could live with him?"

"If he can put up with me, I can put up with him—so long as he promises not to thump his cane on my floor!" Mary was still laughing when he grabbed her hand again.

"Where are we going this time?"

"Into the house," he replied, throwing back the fur rugs to sweep her into his arms. "I mean to carry you across the threshold."

She laughed. "That's *after* the wedding."

"I'll do it then, too, if you like. I figured that once I did this you couldn't change your mind."

"I won't change my mind," she whispered. "I'll love you forever."

She felt the cold, wet kiss of a snowflake upon her forehead, and then, in the next instant, the soft warmth of Jack's lips, and this time there was nothing to interrupt their embrace. All about them the snow was falling, gilding the trees in the yard, gilding the sleigh and the horse's mane with twinkling fairy dust. And somewhere behind them, from the distant town, came the sound of the evening church bells welcoming Christmas Eve.

# A Note from Lucy Elliot

Like most transplanted New Englanders, when I moved to California I missed the changing seasons. I missed the balmy summer nights and the fall foliage, but most of all I missed the colors of Christmastime. Snow at Christmas was perfect, but even without white frosting the colors were special to me—the slates and purples of the hills, and the golds and browns of the bare fields. I missed that special damp coldness in the air and the shades of a winter sunset, incredible purples and pinks. Christmas in California seemed an arbitrary thing—until one afternoon about four years ago when my son, Daniel, and I went for a walk in the woods.

It was a cold dank day. The fog had been in for so long that we'd forgotten what sun was like, and at 3:00 p.m. it was almost dark. A perfect day to stay indoors, but Daniel had the idea of making a special Christmas wreath from things we might find in the woods.

The trail we followed was muddy from the damp, and drops of condensing water dripped from the trees overhead. A stream gurgled nearby, hidden by the underbrush. We walked along together, Daniel's hand warm in mine, speaking in whispers, for except for the sounds of water, the woods were very still. As we walked we gathered things—a bit of bright green lichen, like coral but more delicate; the small rose-shaped pinecone of the Japanese cedar; a handful of eucalyptus buttons, bright blue at that time of year; a sprig of tender-leafed bay, fragrant to the touch; a red leaf from the rare maple, and a blue jay's tail feather. We planned to glue them to a circle of cardboard in a pretty design.

It was dark by the time we got home. Daniel cut the

cardboard while I made hot chocolate. Then we sat at the kitchen table, drinking and decorating our wreath. The kitchen was warm and cozy, and as the wreath took shape, I realized that it was as lovely as the ones we had made back East—or perhaps even lovelier. Christmas in California was Christmas, after all.

*Lucy Elliot*

P.S. These wreaths are a tradition now and also make wonderful gifts. If you're going to make one, use corrugated cardboard and a thick sticky glue like linoleum adhesive.

# HOME FOR CHRISTMAS

*Heather Graham Pozzessere*

Since my father was Scottish, my mother is Irish and my husband and in-laws are Italian, Christmas dinner at our house is usually an unusual affair.

I love Christmas. With four children or more, the day is wild and woolly and wonderful. The house is all decorated, and we usually build a fire, even if it is eighty-odd degrees in South Florida that day. We tend to have a lot of family and friends every year, from thirty to fifty people, and my mother, sister, mother-in-law and everyone else cooks up something and brings it. We have turkey and gravy and potatoes and a big ham, and we also have lasagne and meatballs and Italian cheesecake.

One of my favorite Christmas recipes is a clam sauce I learned from my cousin-in-law, and it's a favorite recipe because it always tastes great and takes little time and effort. When unexpected company drops by, it can be whipped up in less than half an hour. It's also just about foolproof!

## COUSIN JIMMY'S CHRISTMAS CLAM SAUCE

*4 cans of chopped clams*
*2 ¼-lb. sticks butter or margarine*
*1 large garlic bulb (yes, that much!), chopped*
*1 tbsp olive oil*
*fresh parsley, chopped*

Sauté garlic in olive oil. Add clams and juice. (Use a little water to make sure all clams and juice are rinsed from the cans.) Add parsley. Heat mixture to almost boiling. Add butter or margarine and heat until the mixture bubbles lightly. Sauce can be served immediately or allowed to simmer on lower heat for about an hour.

Serve over linguine, tortellini or any other pasta of choice. It tastes even better when reheated.

I like to prepare the sauce using butter, but when I'm feeling health-conscious, I like it just as well made with margarine, or sometimes made with a stick of each.

Another Christmas tip:

For those who like stuffing cooked on the stovetop just as well as inside the turkey, cook the turkey without the stuffing. Instead, insert a stick of butter or margarine wrapped in a number of lettuce leaves. Cooking stuffing inside the bird dries out the turkey, while the lettuce keeps it moist, and the butter or margarine bastes the inside.

# Prologue

*Christmas Eve, 1864*

A SOFT, LIGHT SNOW was falling as Captain Travis Aylwin stood by the parlor window. He could almost see the individual flakes drift and dance to the earth against the dove-gray sky. It was a beautiful picture, serene. No trumpets blared; no soldiers took up their battle cries; no horses screamed; and no blood marked the purity and whiteness of the winter's day.

It was Christmas Eve, and from this window, in the parlor that he had taken over as his office, there might well have been peace on earth. It was possible to forget that men had died on the very ground before the house, that lifeless limbs clad in gray had fallen over lifeless limbs clad in blue. The serenity of the darkening day was complete. A fire burned in the hearth, and the scent of pine was heavy in the air, for the house had been dressed for the season with holly and boughs from the forest, and bright red ribbons and silver bows. Hawkins had roasted chestnuts in the fireplace that morning, and their wintry scent still clung lightly to the room, like the mocking laughter of holidays long gone. He had not asked for this war! He hadn't been home for Christmas in four long years, and no scent of chestnuts or spray of mistletoe would heal the haunting pain that plagued him today.

She could heal the wound, he thought. She, who could spend the holiday in her own home, at her own hearthside. But she would not, he thought. And no words that he spoke would change her feelings, for it was almost Christmas, and no matter what had passed between them, no matter how gently he spoke, Isabelle took up the battle come Christmas, as if she fought for all the soldiers who rested in the field.

From somewhere he could hear singing. Corporal Haines was playing the piano, and Joe Simon, out of Baltimore, Maryland, was singing "O, Holy Night" in his wondrous tenor. There was a poignant quality to the song that rang so high and clear. Two people were singing, he realized. Isabelle Hinton had joined in, her voice rising like a nightingale's, the notes true and sweet.

She had forgiven the men, he thought. She had forgiven them for being Yankees; she had forgiven them the war. It was only him she could not forgive, not when it came to Christmas.

The sounds of the song faded away.

He closed his eyes suddenly, and it was the picture of the past he saw then, and not the present. Not the purity of the snow, the gentle gray of the day. He could not forget the past, he thought, and neither could she.

He tensed, the muscles of his arms and shoulders constricting, his breath coming too quickly. She was there. He knew she was there. Sergeant Hawkins had told him that Isabelle had requested an audience with him, and now he knew she was standing in the doorway. He could smell her jasmine soap; he could feel her presence. She would be standing in the doorway when he turned, waiting for him to bid her to enter. She would be proud and distant, as she had been the first day he met her. And just as it had that very first time, his heart would hammer within his chest as he watched her. She was an extraordinary woman. His hands clenched into fists at his sides. It was almost over. The war was almost over. He knew it; the lean, starving soldiers of the South knew it; she knew it—but she would never concede it.

He straightened his shoulders, careful to don a mask of command. He turned, and as he had known, she was there. And as he had suspected, she was dressed for travel. Her rich burgundy and lace gown was dated; her heavy black coat was worn, and beneath her patched petticoats, he knew, she would be wearing darned and mended hose, for she would take nothing from him except the "rent" for the house, and that she put away each month behind a brick in the fireplace. Once she had put it away for two brothers, but now one of them lay dead in the family plot that was hidden by snow, and so she put the money away for Lieutenant James L. Hinton, Confederate States Artillery, the Army of Northern Virginia, in hopes that he would one day come home. She took the money because the United States Army had taken over her house. Because she was determined not to lose her home, she had no choice but to let them use it. The Hinton plantation lay very close to Washington, D.C., and though the army had been forced to abandon the property upon occasion when Lee's forces had come close, they always returned.

Isabelle knew that. That he would always return.

Travis did not speak right away. He had no intention of making things easy for her, not that night, not when he felt such a despairing tempest in his soul. He crossed his arms over his chest and idly sat on the window seat, watching her politely, waiting. His heartbeat quickened, as it always did when she was near. It had been that way from the first time he saw her, and now that he had come to know her so well...

She was pale that night, and even more beautiful for her lack of color. She might have been some winter queen as she stood there, tall, slim, encompassed by her cloak, her fascinating gray-green eyes enormous against the oval perfection of her face. Her skin was like alabaster, and the darkness of her lashes swept beguilingly over the perfection of her flawless complexion. Her nose was aquiline, her lips the color of wine. Tendrils of golden hair curled from beneath the hood of her cape, barely hinting at the radiant profusion of long, silky hair beneath it. Watching her, he was tempted to stride across the room, to take her into his arms, to shake her until she cried for mercy, until she vowed that she would surrender.

But he would not, he knew. He had touched her in anger before, had shaken her to dispel the ice from her heart. He held the power, and sometimes he had used it, in despair, in desperation, and once in grim determination to save her life. But he would not touch her tonight. He loved her, and he would not force her to stay.

"Good evening, Isabelle," he told her. He had no intention of helping her. He would let her go, because he had to, but he would not help her abandon him to the barren emptiness of another Christmas without her.

"Captain," she acknowledged.

He didn't say a word. She lifted her chin, knowing they were both fully aware of why she had come, and that he would not make it easy for her.

With soft dignity she spoke again. "I would like an escort to the Holloway place, please."

"The weather is severe," he said noncommittally.

"That does not matter, sir. I will go with or without your escort."

"You know that you won't go two steps without my permission, Miss Hinton."

Her lip curled, and her rich lashes half covered her cheeks. "You would prevent me from leaving, Captain?"

Why didn't he do it? he wondered. He could turn his back on her, could deny her request. If she tried to leave him, if she tried to ride away into the snow-bound wilderness, he need only ride after her, capture her, drag her back. It would be so easy.

But he had fallen in love with her, and he could never hold her by force. If she wanted to go, he would saddle the horse himself if need be.

"No, Miss Hinton," he said softly. "I will not prevent you from going, since that is your heart's desire."

He stood and walked to the desk, her brother's desk, his desk. It was a Yankee desk now, piled high with his paperwork, orders, letters, the Christmas wishes that had made it to him, the letters he had dictated to the parents and lovers and brothers and sweethearts of the men he had lost in their last skirmish, letters that had not yet been sent. He searched for his safe-conduct forms, drew out the chair, sat and began to fill in the blanks. Any Union patrol was to see to the safe passage of Miss Isabelle Hinton to Holloway Manor, just five miles southwest of their own location in northern Virginia. She would be accompanied by Sergeant Daniel Daily and Corporal Eugene Ripley, and she was not to be stopped, questioned or waylaid for any purpose.

He signed his name, then looked up. He thought he detected the glistening of tears behind the dazzle of her gray-green eyes. *Don't do this!* he longed to command her. Don't you see that in this very act you deny our love?

But she had never said that she loved him. Never, not while she was burning in the flames of desire, nor in the few stolen moments of tenderness that had come her way. And neither, God help him, had he ever whispered such words, for he could not. The war waged between them, and enemies did not love one another.

He stood, then approached her with the pass. Her gloved hands were neatly folded, but they began to tremble where they lay against her skirt.

"Isabelle..." He started to hand her the paper.

She reached for it, but her fingers didn't quite reach it, and it drifted to the ground. He meant to stoop to pick it up, but he didn't. His dark eyes locked with hers, and the room seemed to fill with a palpable tension. Suddenly he discovered that it was the woman he was reaching for, not the paper. He drew her into his arms and knew that she was not made of ice, that warmth flickered and burned within her. A soft cry escaped her lips, and her head fell back. Her eyes met his with a dazzling defiance, yet they betrayed things she would not say, that she would deny until the very grave if he allowed her.

"Isabelle!" he repeated, staring into her eyes, devouring her perfect features, his callused fingers coming to rest on the gentle slope of her cheek and chin. Once more he whispered her name, and he felt the frantic pounding of her heart just before he kissed her. He touched his lips to hers, and the fire seemed to roar behind him as he delved deeply into her mouth, stroking the inner recesses with his tongue and evoking memories within them both. His lips caressed and consumed hers, and flames lapped against his chest, his thighs, his loins, until he thought he could bear no more. Her breasts thrust explicitly against his cavalry shirt as he filled himself with the sweet taste of her, a taste that would so soon be denied him.

If she had thought to fight his touch, he had quickly swept that thought from her mind. In the power of his arms she did not—could not—deny him. The kiss evoked memories. Memories of blinding, desperate passion and need, memories of tenderness, of whispers, of golden, precious moments out of time, when love had dared and defied the reality of war.

The kiss was hungry, and it was sweet, and in those stolen seconds it meant everything to him that Christmas should. It simmered with passion, yet reminded him deep inside his heart of the times when they had laughed together. Of the times when he had held her against the world. It had begun in tempest, and yet it whispered of peace and the commitment of the soul. It promised years together, evenings before an open fire with children on their laps and the sweet sounds of Christmas carols dancing in their ears. It was everything that a Christmas kiss should be....

"No!" she cried softly, breaking away from him. Her small gloved hands lay against his chest, and the tears that had glazed her eyes now dampened her cheeks. "Travis, no! I must go! Don't you understand? I have to be with my own kind for Christmas, not in the bosom of the enemy!"

"By God, Isabelle! Don't you see? You *are* home. *This* is your home—"

"Not with you in it, Travis!" she interrupted, backing away from him. "Travis, please!" The desperate sound of her tears was in her voice. "Please, let me go!"

He felt as if his body was composed of steel, taut and hard and rigid, but he forced himself to breathe, and, watching her, he slowly forced himself to bend for the paper. He handed it to her, and their fingers brushed as she reached for it.

"Don't go, Isabelle," he said simply.

"I have to!"

He shook his head. "The war is almost over—"

"I cannot be a traitor."

"Loving me would not be turning your back on your own people. The war will end. The nation must begin to heal itself, to bind up its wounds—"

"The war is not over."

"Isabelle! Lee's men are wearing rags and tatters. They're desperate for food, for boots. Don't you see? Yes, they've fought and they've died, and they've run the Union to the ground, but there are more and more of us, and we have repeating rifles when half the boys in gray are dealing with single-shot muskets! I didn't make this war, and neither did you! Isabelle—''

"Travis, don't! I don't want to hear this!"

"Stay, Isabelle."

"I can't."

"You must."

"Why?" she demanded desperately.

"Because I love you."

She froze as he spoke the simple words, her cheeks going even paler. But she shook her head in fierce denial. "We're enemies, Travis."

"We're lovers, Isabelle, and no lies, no heroics, no denials can change that!"

"You're a Yankee!" she gasped. "And no gentleman to say such things aloud!"

A pained smile touched his features. "I tried, but a gentleman could not have had you, and I had to have you. Don't leave. It's Christmas. You should be home for Christmas."

"No!" She shook her head fiercely and spun around and hurried toward the door. She went through, then slammed it in her wake.

"Isabelle!"

Travis charged after her. He heard her lean again the door, and he paused, fingers clenching and unclenching.

There was nothing left to say.

"You should be home for Christmas," he repeated softly.

He heard her sob softly, then push herself away from the door.

And then she was gone.

At length Travis wandered into the room and sat down before the fire. The flames leaped high, and he saw her face in the red-gold blaze. Come home! he thought. Come home, and be with me tonight.

He leaned back. It had been almost Christmas when they met, he thought.

From far away, he heard the piano again. The men's voices were raised in a rendition of "Silent Night." The fire continued to burn, and beyond the window the delicate flakes of snow continued to fall.

He could go after her, he thought. Maybe he should.

It had been almost Christmas, an evening like this one, when they had first met.

He closed his eyes, and he could see her again. See her as she had stood on the front steps, a woman all alone, ready to defy the entire Union Army.

# Chapter One

*December, 1862*

THE SNOW HAD FINISHED FALLING, but the house sat like an ice palace, like something out of a fairy tale. Rain had glazed over the white, newly fallen snow, and when the sun came out, the house and grounds seemed dazzling, as if they were covered with a hundred thousand diamond chips. The landscape seemed barren, a painting from a children's book. It was a place where the winter queen should live, perhaps—it certainly seemed to have no bearing on real life.

But real life was why they had come. Since the first shots had been fired at Fort Sumter, everyone had known that northern Virginia was going to be a hotbed—and that certain areas were going to have to be held by the Yanks if Washington, D.C., was to be protected.

Now, with the war raging onward, it was becoming more and more important to solidify the Union presence in Virginia. The Hinton house was just one of the places that had to be taken over. The little township was already filling with his men, and from studying his maps looking for strategic locations, Travis had known that the Hinton house would be the best place for his headquarters. His occupancy would keep the Rebs away, while he would still have easy access to the town nearby if it became necessary to pull back. In addition, he would be in a good position to join up with the main army should he be called.

The day seemed very cold and still. Travis could hear only the jangle of harness and the snorts of the horses as his small company of twenty approached the house. The breath of men mingled with the breath of the horses as they plowed through the snow, creating bursts of mist upon the air. He reined in suddenly, not knowing why, just staring at the house.

It was such an elegant structure, like a grand lady in the crystallized snow. Great Grecian columns rose high upon the broad porch, tall and imposing. The house was white, and the white, diamondlike snowflakes caught on the roof and the windows. Even the outbuildings were covered in crystal. Through one window he could see a flicker of red and gold, and he realized that a fire was burning, warm and comforting against the snow and cold.

"Captain? It's mighty cold out here," Sergeant Will Sikes reminded him.

"Yeah. Yeah, it's mighty cold," he said. He nudged Judgment, his big black thoroughbred, forward. His men, cold and quiet, survivors of Sharpsburg and more that year, followed in silence. Everyone had thought the war would be over by May. A few weeks. The Yanks had expected an easy victory, while the Rebs had thought they could beat the pants off the Yanks—which they had done upon occasion, Travis had to admit—but they hadn't counted on the tenacity of Mr. Lincoln. The president had no intention of letting the nation fall apart. He was going to fight this war no matter what. So the North had learned there was to be no easy victory, and the South had learned that the war could go on forever, and here it was, just a few days before Christmas, and they were all preparing to bed down in Virginia instead of returning home to their loved ones.

Of course, for some, Christmas was destined to be even gloomier. For some, the war had already taken its toll. Fathers, lovers, husbands and sons, many had returned home already, returned in packages of pine, wrapped in their shrouds, and for Christmas they would lie in their familial graveyards, home for the holiday.

He was becoming morose, he reminded himself, something he couldn't allow. He was in charge of this group of twenty young men and the hundred he had left behind in the town. He had no intention of letting morale fall by the wayside, nor was he of a mind to shoot any of his men for desertion.

"Seems a fair enough place, eh?" he called out, lifting himself out of his saddle to turn and view the troops. He was met with several nods, several half smiles, and he turned once again to face the house.

That was when he saw her.

She had come out to stand on the porch. She had probably heard the jingle of the horses' trappings, and she had known that men were coming. She must have hoped it was a Confederate company, yet it seemed she had suspected Yanks, for she had come out with a shotgun, and Travis was certain it was loaded.

For the life of him, at that moment, he couldn't care.

She was clad in blue velvet, a rich, sumptuous gown with puff sleeves and a daring bodice that left her shoulders bare and gave a provocative hint of the ivory breasts that surged against the fabric. She wore no coat or cloak against the cold, but stood upon the top step of the porch, that heavy gun swept up and aimed hard at him even as a delicate tumble of sun-gold curls fell in a rich swirl against the sights. She tossed her hair back, and he knew that she was young, and though he couldn't see the color of her eyes, he knew they would be fascinating. He knew that he had never seen a more beautiful woman, more striking, more delicate and fine. For several seconds he lost sight of duty and honor, even of the fact that he was fighting a war.

"She looks like she intends to use that thing," Will muttered, casting Travis a quick glance. "What do you think, Captain?"

Travis shrugged, grinning. She couldn't be about to shoot them. One lone woman against a party of twenty men. He lifted a hand and twisted in the saddle to speak. "Hold up, men. I'll do the talking and see if we can't keep this polite."

He urged his mount forward, leaving the others by the snow-misted paddocks and gate. She aimed the shotgun straight at him, and he pulled up his horse, lifting a hand to her in a civil gesture.

"Stop right where you are, Yank!" she commanded. The voice matched the woman. It was velvet and silk. It was strong, but with shimmery undertones that made her all the more feminine.

"Miss Hinton, I'm Captain Travis Aylwin of the—"

"You're a Yank, and I want you off my property."

He dismounted and headed for the steps that led to the porch. His heavy wool cape flapped behind him, caught by the breeze. He tugged his plumed hat over his forehead in acknowledgement that he had come upon a lady, but before he could take the first step he discovered himself spinning in astonishment. She had fired the rifle and just skimmed the feather on his hat.

"Son of a bitch!" he roared.

Behind him, twenty rifles were cocked.

"Hold it! Hold it!" he shouted to his men. He jerked off his singed hat and sent it flying down on a snowdrift, then glared at this southern angel, his dark eyes flashing with fury. "What the hell is the matter with you? If you had hit me—"

"If I had intended to hit you, Captain, you'd be dead," she promised softly, solemnly. "Now, get your men and move off my property."

He threw back his cape, set a booted foot on the first step, placed his hands on his hips and clenched his teeth. There was no easy way to take over a person's property, but this was war.

"So you didn't intend to hit me, huh?" he demanded.

"Don't you believe me, Captain?" An exquisite brow rose with the inquiry.

"Oh, yes, ma'am, I believe you. If I didn't, you'd be tied up and on the backside of a horse right now."

He watched her eyes narrow and a slow crimson flush rise to her cheeks. She started to aim the rifle again, and though he wanted to believe that she wasn't stupid or vicious enough to shoot a man—even a Yank—he didn't want to take any chances. He leaped up the remaining steps, sweeping an arm around her waist to wrest the rifle from her grip. A soft gasp escaped her, but her grip was strong, and his efforts to dislodge the weapon sent them both reeling off balance. Suddenly they were tumbling down the steps and careening into a snowdrift. Travis instinctively attempted to keep his body lodged beneath hers. He didn't know why—she wanted to shoot him. Maybe he just couldn't bear the idea of such a beautiful creature being hurt in any way.

When they landed, she was still seething and fighting. He wrenched her beneath him, securing her wrists, and spat out an oath. There was no nice way to do this, no nice way at all.

"Lady, in the name of the United States government—"

"The U.S. government be damned! This is the Confederacy! Don't threaten me with the U.S. government!"

"Lady," he said wearily, "this is war—"

"Get off my property!"

"In the name—"

"Get off me! I will not listen to a government that—"

He jerked her hands hard, dragging them high above her head, and leaned very close to her. "Don't listen to the government, then, listen to me. Listen to me because I'm twice your size, ten times your strength—and because I have twenty armed men behind me. Is that logical enough for you? Listen, now, and listen good. I'm taking this house. It's called confiscation, and it is something that happens during times of war. I'm sorry that your property happens to be so close to the border, but that's the way it is."

She blinked, and he noticed snowflakes clinging tightly to her eyelashes and dusting her cheeks. She was very white, and she was shivering beneath him. He didn't know whether it was the cold that made her shiver, or if she was trembling with rage. She moistened her lips to speak, and he found himself staring in fascination at her mouth, her pink tongue as it moved over her lips. They were wonderful lips, well defined, full, sensual, beautiful. He wanted to touch them. He wanted to feel the sizzling warmth he knew he would find within the recesses of her mouth.

He blinked, straightening against the cold of the day.

She spoke then, the breath rushing from her in a gust. "You're not going to burn the house?"

He almost smiled. She might hate having a pack of Yankees on her property, but she did want her property to survive.

He shook his head. "I'm taking the house for my headquarters. These fellows will bunk here—I have another hundred men in town. We'll do our best to compensate you for what we use."

She was still staring at him, unblinking now. Her velvet gown was wet with snow, her golden hair lying like curious rays of golden sun against it, and her gray-green eyes were startlingly bright and deep against the pallor of her cheeks. He felt her tremble again and saw that the snow was touching her bare shoulders and her breasts where they rose above her bodice. Little flakes fell deep into the shadowed valley between them. Lucky snowflakes, Travis thought, then he realized that she was freezing and silent in her misery. He thought with a sudden, unreasoning fury that she was what the South was made of, that she would suffer any agony in silence, that her pride was worth everything to her. This war would go on until eternity because of all the damn Southerners just like her. They had something that all the Yankee weaponry and numbers could not best, that sense of pride, of honor.

"Get up!" he snapped suddenly.

"I can hardly do that, sir, when you're lying on top of me!" she returned, but he had already thrust himself upward and reached down to help her. She didn't want to take his hand, but he allowed her no nonsense, taking hers. He drew her to her feet and swept his cloak from his shoulders, then threw it over hers. "I don't need Yankee warmth!" she protested.

"Whether you need it or not, you'll take it!" he growled and prodded her toward the steps. "Who else is inside?"

"General Lee and the entire army of Northern Virginia," she said sweetly.

"Sergeant! Draw a detail of five and shoot anyone inside that house who lives and breathes!"

"No!" she cried out in protest. She spun around, caught within his arms, but meeting his eyes again. "I'll tell you who's inside!" she snapped. "Peter, the butler, Mary Louise, my maid, Jeanette, Etta and Johnny Hopkins, all of them house servants. In the barn you'll find Jeremiah, the blacksmith, and five others, field hands. That's it. Just the servants—"

"Just the slaves?"

She lifted her chin, smiling with such a supreme sense of superiority that he wanted to slap her. "My parents are dead; and my brothers are fighting. The *servants* are all free men and women, Captain. My brothers saw to that before they left for the fighting. All free so that they could leave if trouble came—and not be shot by the likes of you!"

Her blacks were far more likely to be shot by rene-
gade Confederates, but he wasn't going to argue the
point with her. He turned around, trusting her suddenly, because she had no more reason to lie. "Sergeant, bring the men in. It's getting damn cold out
here. Oh, excuse me, Miss Hinton." He bowed to her
then bent to pick up his hat from the snowdrift. He
started up the steps, then paused, for she was staring
at him with pure hatred. "Lead the way, Miss Hinton."

"Why, Captain? I'm not inviting you in."

He walked down and caught her arm, a growling
sound caught in his throat. He had assumed that the
Southern belle he had to wrest the house from might
have the vapors, or faint at the sight of a Yankee detail. He hadn't expected her to come after him with a
shotgun, nor had he expected this defiance.

"Fine. I can escort you elsewhere."

"What?" she said.

"I can see that you are sent elsewhere, if that is your
wish. I can pack you south, Miss Hinton. Where
would you like to go? Richmond, New Orleans, Sa-
vannah, Charleston?"

"You intend to throw me out of my own house?"

A tug-of-war was going on within her beautiful
eyes. She didn't want to be near him—but neither did
she want to desert her home. He smiled. "Lady, the
choice is yours."

"Captain, you're not going to be here long enough
to do anything to me."

"I won't be?"

She smiled serenely. "Stonewall Jackson rides these parts, sir. And Robert E. Lee. They'll come back, and they'll skewer you right through."

He smiled in return. "You hold on to that thought, Miss Hinton. But for now . . . well, you can talk to Peter about something for dinner, or I can send my mess corporal down to raid your cellars. My men are good hunters. They can keep you and yours eating well. Just don't interfere."

"Interfere—"

"God in heaven, woman, it's cold out here!" He grasped her arm hard and jerked her along, opening the door to the house and thrusting her in before him.

The servants she had spoken of stood along the elegant carved stairway that led from the marble-floored foyer to the second floor above. Doors lined a long, elegant hallway to the right and another to the left, but Travis was certain that she hadn't lied, that the servants were the sole occupants of the house. They were all staring at him now with eyes wide. That must be Peter, a tall, handsome man dressed in impeccable livery, and that would be Mary Louise at his side. The others were peeking out from behind them.

"Hello." He doffed his hat to them, smiling, aware that Sergeant Sikes was coming up behind him with half the men. Peter nodded gravely, then looked at Miss Hinton.

"Speak to them," Travis suggested.

She moistened her lips. "Peter, this is, er, Captain Travis Aylwin." He thought she was about to spit on the floor, but the manners she had learned long ago on her mammy's lap kept her from doing so. "Oh, hell! The damn Yanks have come to take over the house."

"They're not a-gonna burn us—" Peter began.

"No!" she said quickly, then shot Travis a furious stare. "At least, the captain has promised they're not."

"I don't remember promising anything," he said pleasantly. "But, Peter, it is not my intent to do so. Not unless your mistress is a spy. She isn't, is she?"

Peter's eyes went even wider. "No, sir. Why, you can see how it is here, winter and all. You can hardly go house to house in these parts, much less find an army to spy for!"

Travis laughed. He had to agree. They were just about snowbound for the moment, except that he was going to have to get word through to intelligence about his location and the situation here. "There are twenty of us here, Peter."

"And we're colder than a witch's teat and hungry as a pack of bears!" Sergeant Sikes said.

"Sergeant!" Travis barked.

But Sikes already appeared horrified at his own words. He was staring at their unwilling hostess as if he were too mortified for words. Travis found himself grinning. "I'm certain Miss Hinton has heard such words before, even used a few herself, perhaps, but an apology is in order."

She cast him a scathing glare, but her lips curled into a curious smile. "If I haven't used such language, Captain, I'm quite sure that I shall before I have seen the last of you."

"Supper, Miss Hinton?" Peter asked.

She lifted a hand. "Feed the rabble, since we must, Peter." She pulled away from Travis's side, letting his military cape fall to the floor. "Do excuse me, Cap-

tain, but I choose not to watch your ruffians eat me
out of house and home."

She started up the stairway. He watched her warily
as she went, but he did not stop her. She might very
well be going up to find a bowie knife or a pistol, but
for the moment, he would just let her go. It was time
to settle in.

"Where is Miss Hinton's room, Peter?" he asked.

"Second floor, second door to the left, sir," Peter
said uneasily.

Travis merely nodded and smiled. "Thank you,
Peter. Sikes, you find a room in the house, and find
one for me, too. As for the men—"

"The barn has a full bunkhouse," Peter advised
him. "Fireplace, wood-burning stove, all the ameni-
ties, sir. Sleeps thirty easily."

"But that leaves Sergeant Sikes and me alone in the
house, doesn't it, Peter? You wouldn't be planning
something, would you?"

Peter shook his head.

"But your mistress might be."

Peter lowered his head, but not before Travis saw
acknowledgement in his eyes. She was dangerous,
Miss Fairy-tale-princess Hinton. But he could handle
the danger. "Fine, Peter, thank you. The men will take
the bunkhouse. Sikes and I will find rooms here, and
if you value your Miss Hinton's life, you'll take care
to see that she behaves."

Peter nodded, but Travis had the feeling that he
wasn't at all sure he was up to the task.

"I'll sure try, Captain. I'll sure try," Peter told him.

Travis started to walk along the hallway to find a room he could use as an office. He paused, turning back. "Why?" he asked Peter.

Peter grinned, his white teeth flashing as he smiled. "I don't want to see her shot up by you Yanks, Captain, and that's a fact."

Travis nodded, grinned and started down the hallway. He waved a hand. "See to the men, Sikes. And to yourself. Peter, when's dinner?"

"I can fix you up in an hour, Captain."

"An hour. Everyone in the house. It isn't quite Christmas Eve, but we'll pretend that it is. Everyone at the dining table except for a guard of two."

"Only two, sir?" Sikes asked.

"Only two. The enemy lurks within the house tonight," he warned, then wandered down the hallway.

ISABELLE HINTON didn't appear for dinner. The men ate, warming their hands by the fire and gazing at the fine plates and silver and the crystal goblets as if they hadn't seen such luxury in years. It had been forever since they had sat down to this kind of meal. It seemed as if they had spent the entire year in battle. The worst of it had been at Sharpsburg, by Antietam Creek. Travis had never seen so many men die, never seen the bodies piled so high, never smelled so much blood. Great fields of corn had been mowed to the ground by gunfire. Yankees and Rebels had died alike, and that battle alone had taught them all that war was an evil thing.

While the men were in the parlor playing the piano and singing Christmas carols, Travis retired to the den he had found to use as his office. He sipped from a snifter of brandy and rested his booted feet on the desk, staring at the flames that burned in the hearth. He closed his eyes, and for a moment he felt the sun again as he had that day at Sharpsburg. He remembered how eerie it had felt to lead a cavalry charge, then watch as the men were mown down around him. He had taken grapeshot in the shoulder himself and wondered if it wouldn't be easier just to die than to wait for infection to set in. But he hadn't lost the arm, and he hadn't died—he'd lived to fight again.

The men were singing a rousing rendition of "Deck the Halls." The warmth of the fire enveloped Travis, and the pain of battle drifted slowly from his memory. He wondered what he would be doing if he was home. Well, he wouldn't be at his own house. Since his wife had succumbed to the smallpox, he had avoided his own house for the holidays, but never his family. He would have headed into town to his mother's house. There would be a huge turkey roasting, and the scent of honey-coated ham would fill the house. His sister Liz would be there with the kids, and Allen would be asking him all about West Point, while Eulalie would want a horsey ride on his knee. Jack, his brother-in-law, would talk about the law with his father, and all the voices would blend together, the chatter, the laughter, the love. They would go to church on Christmas Eve, and they would all remember, even in the depths of the deepest despair, that it was Christmas because a little child had been born to rid the world of death and suffering. And somehow, no matter how dark an hour they seemed to face, he would believe again in mankind. And even now, even here, far from home, he knew that Christmas would always convince him that there could be love again. He just wished that he were home.

The men were no longer singing; the house had grown quiet. Travis set his brandy snifter on the desk, rose and stretched. He had a pile of maps on the desk, but he would get to them tomorrow. Right now, he wanted to get to bed.

He found Peter in the hallway, returning the last of the crystal glasses to a carved wooden rack on the wall. "Upstairs, Captain. We done give you the master suite, third door to the right."

"Thank you, Peter. Sikes?"

"He's gone up, sir. Third floor, first door to your left."

"It's a big house, Peter."

"Lordy, yes. Needed to be, before the war. There was parties galore then, cousins coming from all over the countryside to sleep for the whole weekend. Why, around now, at Christmas..."

Peter's voice trailed away. Travis clapped an arm on the man's shoulder. "Christmas is kind of hard all around right now, Peter. Good night."

Travis climbed the stairs and found the door to his room. The master suite. It was a huge room, with a four-poster bed against the far wall, two big armoires, a secretary facing a window and a cherry-wood table with a handsomely upholstered French chair beside it by the fire.

He draped his sword and scabbard over a chair and unhooked the frogs of his jacket, then cast that, too, over the chair. His shirt followed. Then he sat to tug off his boots and socks before peeling away his breeches. He would have slept in his long underwear, but there was a big pitcher of water and a bowl on a small washstand by one of the armoires, so he stripped down to the flesh and found that the water was still a little bit warm. There was a bar of soap there, too, supplied by Peter, he was certain, and not his hostess. It didn't matter. He scrubbed himself the best he could, then dried himself, shivering, before the fire, before slipping into the bed. It wasn't quite home, but it was a good soft mattress and an even softer pillow, and it was, in fact, so comfortable that he wasn't sure he would be able to sleep.

He closed his eyes, and he was just starting to doze when he heard the sound. He opened his eyes, then closed them again swiftly, before allowing them to part slightly. Firelight danced on the walls, and for a moment he didn't know what he had heard. The door to the hallway had not opened.

But he wasn't alone. He knew it.

He waited. Then he sensed the soft rose fragrance of her perfume, and he knew that she had invaded his bedroom, though for what purpose he didn't know. He could see her through the curtain of his lashes. All that lush blond hair of hers was free, flowing like a golden cascade over her shoulders and down her back. She was dressed in something soft and floor length and flannel, but the firelight ignored the chasteness of her apparel, playing through the material and outlining the alluring beauty of her form. Her breasts were high and firm, her waist slim and tempting, her hips and buttocks flaring provocatively beneath it. She carried something, he saw. A knife. And she was right beside the bed.

He snaked out an arm, capturing her wrist, pulling her down hard on top of him. She gasped in surprise, but she didn't scream. Her gray-green eyes met his with a fear she tried desperately to camouflage, but with no remorse. He tightened his grip on her wrist, and the knife clattered to the floor.

"What good would it have done to kill me?" he asked.

She tried to shift away from him. He gave her no quarter; indeed, some malicious demon within him enjoyed her flushed features and the uncomfortable way she squirmed against him. He hadn't dragged her into his bedroom; she had come of her own accord.

"I wasn't going to kill you!" she protested.

He skimmed both hands down the length of her arms, then laced his fingers through hers and drew her to his side, leaning tautly over her. She swallowed and strained against him, but still she did not scream, and she tried very hard not to look his way. "I see," he said gravely. "You came to offer a guest a shave, is that it?"

Her eyes fell to his bare chest. He could feel the rise of her breasts, the outline of her hips, the staggering heat coming from her skin. He knew that she was aware of the desire rising in him. She couldn't help but feel the strength of him hard against her.

"I—I just . . ." Her voice trailed off.

"You came here to murder me!" he snapped angrily.

"No, I . . ."

"Yes, damn it!"

Suddenly her eyes met his. They flashed with fury, with awareness, then fear. Then something more. "All right!'' she whispered. "I—I thought that I would kill you before you violated my home! But then..."

"Then what?" he demanded.

She moistened her lips. Her lashes fell, and she was so beautiful he could barely restrain himself. He wanted to live up to the reputation Yankee soldiers were given in the South; he wanted to wrap his arms around her, to have her, to make love to her at all costs. He would have traded every hope he had of heaven just to fill his hands with the weight of her breasts; he would have sold his very soul to the devil to feel himself within her.

"I realized that you were a man, flesh and blood.... I..." Her words trailed away, and her eyes met his. She had never seen the deaths at Sharpsburg; she hadn't watched them fall at Manassas. But tonight she had played with death, and she had discovered that it was not glorious, not honorable.

She had recognized him as a human being.

"I still wish you were dead!" she snapped, surging against him suddenly as if she was horrified that she had forgotten their fight. "You're still a damn Yank and—" She broke off, breathing raggedly. He smiled, because they were both all too aware that he was human, and very much a man.

"Please, Captain, if you would be so good as to let me up now...?"

He started to chuckle softly. She could still be such an elegant, dignified belle, so regal despite their position.

"Sorry," he said.

"Sorry!" she gasped, realizing that he had no intention of letting her go. "But—but..."

"I can't take the chance that you might decide you're capable of killing me after all," he said, rolling over and dragging her with him. He had to forget modesty to bring her along with him so he could find a scarf. She tried to fight him, to look anywhere but at him, but he was ruthless as he pulled her along in his footsteps until he found a scarf, then brought her back to the bed, where he tied her wrists together, then laid her down with her back against him.

She swore and she kicked and she protested, and she wriggled and fought until his laughter warned her that her movements were pulling her gown precariously high on her hips.

Then she merely swore. Like a mule driver. Sergeant Sikes could have learned a thing or two.

"Go to sleep!" he warned her at last. "Aren't you afraid I'll remember that I'm a raiding, pillaging, murderous—raping—Yankee?"

He heard her exhale raggedly. She didn't know how close she had come to forcing him to discover that a desperate monster lived in every man.

But in time she slept, and so did he, and when he awoke, his arm was around her, his hand resting just below the fullness of her breast. His naked leg lay entwined with hers, while the golden silk of her hair teased his nose and chin. It felt so good to hold her. To want her, to long for her. Even to ache. Just seeing her, just touching her, evoked dreams. Dreams of a distant time, dreams of a peaceful future. In those first seconds of dawn, she seemed to be the most wondrous present he had ever received.

She twisted in his arms, instinctively seeking warmth. She cuddled against his chest, her fingers moving lightly across his skin, her lips brushing his flesh. He pulled her against him. As the morning light fell into the room, her lips were slightly parted, slightly damp, as red as wine.

Carefully he untied her wrists, freeing her hands.

Then he kissed her. He touched his lips to hers, and he kissed her. A soft sound rumbled within her throat, but she didn't awaken right away. Her lips parted farther, and his tongue swiftly danced between them, and he tasted, fully and hungrily, everything that her mouth had to offer. Heat rose within him, swift and combustible, swamping him, hurting him, making him ache and yearn for more. His fingers curled over her breast, and he found it as full and fascinating as he had imagined. He touched her nipples beneath the flannel that still guarded them and he felt her stir beneath him as he drew his lips from hers.

Her eyes opened slowly, and he realized that she had been lost in her own dreams. Their gazes met, then a horrified whisper left her lips. She suddenly seemed to realize what the situation was, and she twisted violently away from him.

And he let her go. She leaped away from the bed, her fingers trembling as they touched her lips, her arms wrapped tightly around herself. She stared at him in fury. "You...you Yank! How could you, how dare you, how—"

"You tried to murder me, madam, remember?"

"But you tried to—" She broke off. He hadn't really used any force against her. "You know what you did! You are no gentleman!"

"I never make any pretense of being a gentleman when I'm in the midst of trying to stay alive!" he told her angrily.

"A Virginian, sir, would have been a gentleman to the very end. A Virginian—"

She broke off as her gaze fell over him, over his nakedness, and she turned to run.

He caught her arm and pulled her hard against him. His eyes burned into hers. "I *am* a Virginian, Miss Hinton. And trust me, ma'am, nothing has hurt so bad as this war. I have cousins in blue, and cousins in gray, and do you know something, Miss Hinton? Every single one of them is a gentleman, a good, decent man. And sometimes I wake up so scared that I can't stand it because I just might find myself shooting one of my very decent cousins someday. My gentlemanly cousins. Most of the time I wake to my nightmares. This morning I woke to see you. It was like a glimpse of paradise."

The blood had drained from her face, and when her eyes met his they were filled with a tempest of emotion, but she did not try to pull away. For the longest time they just stood there, then he lightly touched her cheek. "Thank you. It was just like a Christmas present."

She didn't move even at that. Her hand rose, and she touched his cheek in turn. She felt the texture of his skin, rough from lack of shaving.

Then suddenly it was gone, that curious moment when they were not enemies. Her hand fell away, and she seemed to remember that she was flush against a naked Yankee. With a soft cry she whirled and headed across the room, and he discovered that there was a door in the wall, very craftily concealed by the paneling.

She disappeared through it without a word.

LATER THAT DAY she found him in her den, which he had taken over as his office. She wore a bonnet and cloak, and her hands were warmed by an elegant fur muff.

"You said that I could go where I chose, Captain."

His heart hammered and leaped as he looked up from his work. It would be best if she left. He would cease to dream and wonder; he would be able to concentrate more fully on the war.

He didn't want her to go. He would never know when she intended to pull a knife again, but he was willing to deal with the danger just to enjoy the battle.

"Yes," he told her.

"I wish to go to a neighbor's."

"Oh? You're not going to stay to protect your property?" he said, trying to provoke her. His eyes never left hers. Her lashes fell, and she reddened very prettily. She was remembering that morning, he thought, and he was glad of the flush that touched her cheeks, just as he was glad of the totally improper moments they had shared.

Her eyes met his again. "Don't worry, Captain. I'll be back. I just don't care to spend Christmas with the enemy."

He looked down quickly. She was going to come back. He opened his drawer, found a form and began writing on it. He looked up. "I don't know your given name."

"Isabelle," she told him.

He stared at her. "Isabelle," he murmured, a curious, wistful note in his voice. In annoyance, he scribbled hard. "Isabelle. Isabelle Hinton. Well, Miss Hinton, where is this neighbor?"

"Not a mile on the opposite side of town."

He nodded. "Sergeant Sikes and one other soldier will serve as an escort for you. How long do you plan to stay?"

She hesitated. "Until two days after Christmas."

"Sergeant Sikes will return for you."

"I hardly see why that will be necessary."

"I see it as very necessary. Good day, Miss Hinton."

She turned and left him.

CHRISTMAS DAWNED gray and cold. Restless, Travis went out into the snow with a shotgun. He brought down a huge buck and was glad, because it would mean meat for many nights to come.

At the house, Peter and the servants were almost friendly. There was a long and solemn prayer before they started eating the Christmas feast, and there was general good humor as the meal was downed. Travis tried to join in, but when he realized that his mood was solemn, he escaped the company of his soldiers and returned to the den. He did not know when Christmas had become so bleak. Yes, he did. It had become gray and empty when Isabelle Hinton left.

HE DIDN'T HEAR HER RETURN. He had spent the day poring over charts of the valleys and mountains, pinpointing the regions where Stonewall Jackson had been playing havoc with the Union Army. A messenger had arrived from Washington with orders and all kinds of information gleaned from spies, but Travis tended to doubt many of the things he heard.

By nightfall he was weary from men coming and going, as well as from the news of the war. Peter had brought him a bowl of venison stew and a cup of coffee, and that had been his nourishment for the day. Exhausted, he climbed the steps to his room, stripped off his cavalry frock coat and scrubbed his face. Then it seemed that he heard furtive movements in the next room.

His heart quickened, but then his eyes narrowed with wariness. He hadn't forgotten how she had come upon him that first night, even if she had stopped short of slitting his throat. Silently he moved across the room, wondering what she was up to. He found the catch of the secret door and slowly pressed it. The door opened, and he entered her domain.

A smile touched his features, and he leaned casually against the door, watching her, enjoying the view. Miss Isabelle Hinton was awash in bubbles, submerged to her elegant chin, one long and shapely leg raised above the wooden hip bath as she soaped it with abandon. Steam rose from the tub, whispering around her golden curls, leaving them clinging to her flesh. From his vantage point, he could just make out the rise of her breasts, just see the slender column of her throat and the artistic lines of her profile.

Then she turned, sensing him there.

Her leg splashed into the water, and she started to sit up straighter, but then she sank back, aware what she was displaying by rising. She lifted her chin, realizing that she was caught, and from his casual stance against the door, she knew he wasn't about to turn politely and leave.

"Welcome home," he told her.

She flushed furiously. "What are you doing in my room, Captain?"

"Seeking a bit of southern hospitality?"

She threw the soap at him. He laughed, ducking.

"No gentleman would enter a lady's bedroom!" she snapped angrily.

"Ah, but no lady would venture into a man's bedroom, Isabelle, and it seems that you did just that to me. Admittedly, you came to do me in, but you barged in upon my, er, privacy nonetheless."

Ignoring him, she demanded, "Get out, or you shall be gravely sorry."

"Shall I?"

So challenged, he strode across the room toward the tub. Her eyes widened, and she wrapped her arms around her chest, sinking as low as she could into her wealth of bubbles. He smiled, crouching beside the tub. She stared at him in silence for a moment, then called him every despicable name he had ever heard. He laughed, and she doused him with a handful of water, but he didn't mind a bit, since her movement displayed quite a bit of her.

"I'll strangle you!" she promised. But he caught her wrists when her fingers would have closed around his throat, and then, even as she struggled, he kissed both her palms. Then he stood, releasing her and stepping back.

"Damn, I forgot to be a gentleman again," he apologized. "But I was just wondering whether you had a knife hidden under that water or not. Do you?"

She inhaled sharply. "No!"

"I could check, you know," he warned.

Her look of outrage made him laugh. He gave her his very best bow, then returned to the door that separated their rooms.

"I'm changing rooms!" she called to him.

He paused in the doorway, looking at her. "No, you're not. You chose it this way the night you planned my early demise. So now it will stay."

"I'll move if I choose."

"If you move, I'll drag you back. Depend on it. If you stay, I promise that we're even. I won't pass through the doorway unless I'm invited. A threat, and a promise, and I will carry out both, Miss Hinton."

Thick honeyed lashes fell over her eyes. She was so lovely that he ached from head to toe, watching her. "You will never be invited in, Captain," she said.

"Alas, you have a standing invitation to enter my room, Miss Hinton. Of course, I do ask that you leave your weapons behind."

Her eyes flew to his. He offered her a curiously tender smile, and she did not look away, but watched him. She was as still and perfect as an alabaster bust. Her throat was long and glistened from the water. Her golden curls clung tightly to her flesh, and if she were to move, he knew she would be fluid, graceful, a liquid swirl of passion and energy.

I'm falling in love, he thought.

"I missed you on Christmas, Isabelle," he told her. She did not answer, and he slipped through the door, closing it behind him.

# Chapter Two

ISABELLE HINTON had never wanted to like the Yankee commander who had come to take over her home. She spent hours reminding herself that the boys in blue were causing the war, that the South had just wanted to walk away in peace. She reminded herself of all the atrocities taking place; again and again she remembered that her brothers were out there, facing Yankee bullets daily, but nothing that she could tell herself seemed to help very much. He'd never claimed to be a gentleman, and indeed, his behavior had been absolutely outrageous at times. But still, as the days went by, he proved himself to be a true cavalier underneath it all.

She tried to ignore all of them at first. But one evening, when she knew that he was dining alone, her curiosity brought her to the table. Though she tried to bait him, he was calm and quiet during the meal, the flash in his dark eyes the only indication that she touched his temper at all. He was a good-looking man—she had admitted that from the start. His eyes were so dark a mahogany as to be almost coal black; his hair, too, was dark, neatly clipped at the collar line. He was the perfect picture of an officer when he set out to ride, his cape falling over his shoulders, his plumed hat pulled low over his forehead, shading those dancing eyes. Beneath the beard, his features were clean and sharp, his cheekbones high, his chin firm, his lips full and quick to curl with a sensuality that often left her breathless, despise the condition though she might. Even his tone of voice fascinated her; his words were clear and well enunciated, but there was something husky about them, too, just the trace of a slow Virginia drawl. And, of course, she was very much aware of the rest of him; even if she didn't see much daily, the picture lived on vividly in her memory.

She hadn't had a great deal of experience with men's bodies, but she did have two older brothers, and after a few battles she had gone to the makeshift hospitals to help with the wounded. She had gone from ladies' circles, where she and others had rolled bandages, to being thrust right into a surgeon's field tent, and she had learned firsthand a great deal of the horror of war. She had cleaned and soothed and bandaged many a male chest, but none of them had compared to the very handsome chest that belonged to Captain Travis Aylwin. His shoulders were broad and taut with muscle and sinew, and the same handsome ripple of power was evident in his torso and arms. His waist was trim, and dusky dark hair created a handsome pattern across his chest, then narrowed to a thin line before flaring again to...well, she wouldn't think about that. She had been raised quite properly, she reminded herself over and over again, but that didn't keep her from remembering him, all of him, time and time again. She couldn't cease her wondering about him, nor could she keep him from intruding upon her dreams.

She always awakened before anything could happen, though her cheeks would be dark with a bright red blush, and there was a burning behind her eyes as she longed to crawl beneath the floor in humiliation.

She tried hard to stay away from him. He respected the distance, as he had promised when he had left her room after Christmas, but she always knew he was there at night, just beyond her door. His men were perfectly courteous and polite, and they were good hunters; there was always plenty to eat. So much so, she knew, that when she mentioned that some of her neighbors were facing hard times, the Union officers were quick to leave a side of venison before a door, or a half dozen rabbits, or whatever bird had ventured too close to the hunters. It was Travis's leadership that led to their generosity and care, she knew. Travis did not relish war.

She began seeing him and his troops not as faceless enemies but as men, just like the friends who had come to her parties, just like the young Southerners who had come to her home to laugh and dream, to fall in love and plan a future. She had to tell herself that they were the enemy, and that she did not want her enemy to be flesh and blood.

It was late January when she came down to dinner with him again. He had been reading some papers, but once he masked his astonishment at her appearance, he quickly set them aside, rose and held out her chair. She sat, quickly picking up the glass of wine that had just been poured for him and swallowing deeply. He sat down again, a touch of amusement in his eyes. He must have been a true lady-killer back home, she thought. He was full of warmth and laughter, a quiet strength and a subtle but overwhelming masculinity. His eyes held so much, and his lips were so quick to curve into a smile. But he could be ruthless, too, she knew. She had learned that the first night, when he had held her beside him until dawn.

"To what do I owe this honor?" he asked her softly. He barely needed to lift his hand. Peter was there with a second setting almost immediately. More wine was poured for him. Peter glanced her way worriedly. She winked, trying to assure her servant that she was, as always, in charge.

"The honor, sir? Well, actually, I was hoping that the snow would be melting, that you might be marching out to do battle again soon."

He sat back, watching her. "Perhaps we will be. Will that really give you such great pleasure?"

She rose, not believing that he could make her feel ashamed for wanting the enemy to fall in battle. She walked around the room, pausing before the picture of her family taken by Mr. Brady just before the war. Her brothers stood on either side of her, and her parents sat before them. But already the boys were dressed in their uniforms, and every day she prayed that they would return. If they sat in some northern house, would a girl there wish them into the field of battle, to bleed, to die?

"I just want you out of my house," she told him, turning back.

He had risen and was staring at the picture, too. He walked around to it. "Handsome family," he told her. "Your parents?"

"They died in 1859, a few days apart. They caught smallpox. My brothers and I were safe, I think, because we had very mild cases as children. Neither Mother nor Father caught it then, but one of the

neighboring babies came down with it and then..."
She left off, shrugging.

"I'm very sorry."

"It's a horrible death," she murmured.

"I know," he said, turning from her. He stood behind his chair. "Shall we have dinner?"

She sat. Peter served them smoke-cured ham from the cellars, apricot preserves and tiny pickled carrots and beets.

"Where is home, Captain?" she asked him.

"Alexandria."

Alexandria. The beautiful old city had been held since the beginning of the war because of its proximity to Washington, D.C., but many of its citizens were Unionists. It was a curious war. Already the counties in the west had broken away and a new state had been born, West Virginia.

"You're going to get your home back, you know, Miss Hinton," he told her.

"Am I?"

"Of course."

She set her fork down. "How do I know you won't decide to burn the house down when you leave?"

He set his fork down, too. "Do you really believe I intend to do that?" he asked her.

She watched him for several long moments. He buttered one of Peter's special biscuits, then offered it to her.

"General Lee lost Arlington House," she said. "And, I admit, I'm quite surprised that you Yanks haven't burned it to the ground."

He set the biscuit down and sipped his wine. "It's a beautiful house," he said softly. "And it overlooks the capitol. General Lee knew the moment he chose to fight for the South that he would have to leave his home. His wife knew, his family knew, and still he made his decision. Some people were bitter. Some of the men who had fought with him or learned from him before the war wanted to burn the place down. It is Mrs. Lee I pity—she grew up there. And as George Washington's step-granddaughter, she has always had a great sense of history. She's a magnificent lady." He paused, as if he had said too much. Then he shrugged, setting down his wineglass. "They're not going to burn the house down. They've been burying Union soldiers there since the beginning of the war. The land will become a national cemetery."

"And Lee will forever lose his home."

"The South could still win the war," he told her.

Startled, she stared at him. She hadn't realized that she had displayed such a defeated attitude. "The South *will* win the war!" she assured him, but then she frowned. "You sound as if you're quite taken with the Lees."

He pushed back his chair. "The general is my god-father, Miss Hinton. We all lose in this war. He made his choices, and so did I. A man must do what he feels is right. And yet I tell you, Miss Hinton, that this fratricide must and will end, and when it does, if we are blessed to live, then he will be my friend and mentor again, and I will be his most willing servant."

She jumped up, wrapping her fingers around the back of her chair, staring at him in fury. It was almost blasphemy to speak so of General Robert E. Lee; he was adored by his troops, by the South as a whole.

He was a magnificent general and a soft-spoken gentleman.

"How dare you!" she spat out, trembling.

He took a step toward her, grabbing her wrist, holding her tight when she would have fled his presence. "Would you make monsters of us all?"

"I've read about the things that have happened. I know what Yankees do."

"Yes, yes, and *we've* all read *Uncle Tom's Cabin*, but I've yet to see you whip or chain or harness your slaves. By God, yes, there is injustice, and some horror is always true, but must we create more of it ourselves?"

"I'm not creating anything." She jerked free of him and spun around, hurrying from the room, but he called her back.

"Isabelle!"

She turned. He stood tall and striking in his dress frock coat and high cavalry boots, his saber hanging from the scabbard strapped around his waist. His eyes touched her, heated and dark.

"I am not a monster," he told her.

"Does it matter what I think?" she demanded.

A rueful smile touched his lips. "Well, yes, to me it does. You see, I . . . care."

She gasped in dismay, "Well, don't, Yankee, don't! Don't you dare care about me!"

She fled and raced up the stairs.

THAT NIGHT and every night after that she lay awake and listened to his movements, but he never touched her door, and he never mentioned anything about his feelings again. He was always unerringly polite to her, and though she felt that she should keep her distance from him, she couldn't. She came down to a meal occasionally, usually when Sergeant Sikes or one of the other men was joining him.

Sometimes he disappeared for days at a time, and she suspected that he had ridden away to supply information about troop movements, or to receive it.

At the beginning of April Isabelle awoke to find that the house was filled with activity. The way the men were bustling around, coming and going from the office, she knew that something was going on.

She came down the stairs and presented herself in the den. Travis's dark head was bent over a map in serious study. He sensed her presence and looked up quickly.

"What's happening?" she asked without preamble.

He straightened and studied her as thoroughly as he had the map, a curious shadow hiding any emotion in his eyes. "We're pulling out. There's a company of Rebels headed this way."

"You're going into battle?" she asked him.

"That's what war is all about," he returned, and there was just the slightest trace of bitterness in his voice. He sat on the edge of his desk, still watching her. "You should be pleased. Maybe we'll all die."

"I don't want you to die," she said. "I just want you to go away."

He smiled and lifted a hand in the air, then let it fall back to his thigh. "Well, we're doing just that. Tell me, Isabelle, will you miss me at all?"

"No."

He stood and walked toward her. She stepped back until she was against the door. It closed, and she leaned against it, but he kept coming anyway, until he stood right before her. He didn't touch her, just laid his palm against the door by her head. "You're lying just a little, aren't you?" he whispered.

She shook her head, but suddenly she found that she could not speak, that her knees were liquid, that her palms were braced against the door so she could stand. He smelled of soap, of leather and rich pipe tobacco. His eyes were ebony coals, haunting her; his mouth was full and mobile.

"I could die a happy man if you would just whisper that you cared a little bit," he told her, the warmth of his breath creating a warm tempest against her skin while the tenor of his voice evoked a curious fire deep within her.

She kept her eyes steady and smiled sweetly. "I'm sure you say those words to every woman whose home you confiscate."

He smiled slowly. "Yours is the only home I have ever confiscated." He leaned closer. "And you've known for some time how I feel about you."

She wanted to shake her head again, but she discovered that she couldn't. His lips brushed hers, and then his mouth consumed hers as the roar within her soul came rushing up to drown out the rest of the world. She fell into his arms and felt the overwhelming masculine force of his lips parting and caressing her own; she felt the heady invasion of his tongue, so deep it seemed that he could possess all of her with the kiss alone. His hands, desperate, rough, massaged her skull, and his fingers threaded hungrily through her hair, holding her close. But she couldn't have left him. She had never known anything like that kiss, never known the world to spin in such delirious motion, never known the hunger to touch a man in return, to feel his hair, crisp and clean, beneath her fingers, to feel his body, his heat and his heartbeat throbbing ferociously against her breasts. The sweet, heady taste of his mouth left her thirsting for more and more, until sanity returned to her, some voice of reason screaming within her that he was the Yankee soldier who had taken over her home, a Yank who was leaving at last.

She pulled away from him, her fingers shaking as she brought them to her lips.

He watched her, his eyes dark and enigmatic, and sighed softly. His rueful smile touched his lips again. "Will you care if I come back, Isabelle?"

"You're a Yank. I hope you never come back," she told him. She wiped her mouth as if she could wipe away the memory of his kiss, then turned and hurriedly left the room.

But later, in her room, she lay on her bed and knew that she had fallen in love. Right or wrong, she was in love with him. In love with his eyes and his mouth and his voice...and with all the things he said. And he was riding away. Perhaps to die.

She rose when she heard the sergeant call out the orders, and she raced down the stairs two at a time. She forced herself to slow down and walk demurely out to the porch. There he was at the head of his troops, his magnificent plumed hat in place, sitting easily on his mount.

He saw her and rode closer, his horse prancing as he came near. He touched his hat in salute and waited.

"Well, I do hope that you don't ride away to get killed," she told him.

He smiled. "Not exactly a declaration of undying devotion, but I suppose it will have to do." He leaned closer to her. "I will not get killed, Isabelle. And I will be back."

She didn't answer him right away. She didn't remind him that she could hardly want him to come back, for if he did, it would mean that the Union was holding tight to large tracts of Virginia.

"As I said, I hope that you survive. And that is all."

His smile deepened as he dug his heels into his horse's flanks and rode hard for the front of his line.

Isabelle watched the troops until they were long gone.

NEWS CAME TO HER in abundance as spring turned to summer. There was a horrible battle fought at Chancellorsville. The Union had over sixteen thousand troops killed, wounded or captured; the South lost over twelve thousand, and though the South was accepted to be the victor, she had received a crippling blow. Stonewall Jackson was mistakenly shot by one of his own men, and he died on May tenth from his wounds.

Isabelle prayed for more news. She volunteered for hospital duty again. She worked endless hours, fearful that every Confederate soldier might be one of her brothers, anxious that any Union soldier who fell into their hands might be Travis.

She was working in the hospital in July when news came through that a horrible battle had been fought in a little town in Pennsylvania called Gettysburg. The losses in human life were staggering. And General Lee and his Army of Northern Virginia were in retreat. Men whispered that it was the turning point of the war. The South was being brought to her knees.

Isabelle hurried home, anxious to hear about her brothers, anxious to hear about Travis. In town she waited endlessly for the lists of the dead, wounded and captured to come through, and when she was able to procure a sheet she eagerly sought out her brothers' names. When she did not find them, she thanked God in a silent prayer, wincing as she heard the horrible tears of those who had lost sons, fathers, lovers and brothers.

She swallowed tightly, wondering about Travis, and prayed that he had made it. Shaking, she drove her carriage home. And that night she admitted in her prayers that she loved Travis Aylwin, and that even if he was a Yankee, she wanted God to watch over him always.

In September she was busy picking the last of the summer vegetables from her small garden when she heard Peter calling to her anxiously. She came running around the house, wiping her hands on her apron. Peter was on the porch, anxiously pointing eastward. Isabelle shaded her eyes from the afternoon sun. Riders were coming. She could see them. Her heart began to beat faster. There were about twenty or thirty men on horseback. In Union blue.

Her heart thudded. Travis was alive!

But what if it was not Travis? What if it was some other Yankee who lacked Travis Aylwin's sense of right and wrong, even in the midst of war?

She turned toward the porch and raced up the steps, shoving Peter out of her way. At the end of the hallway she tore open the gun case and reached for her rifle. With trembling fingers she attempted to load it. A hand fell on her shoulder, and she screamed, spinning around.

"You're going to shoot me again? Damn, I didn't survive Chancellorsville and Gettysburg just to be shot by you, Isabelle!"

He was thin, very thin and gaunt, and yet his dark eyes were alive with fire. She started to move, and the gun rose with her movement. His eyes widened, and he grabbed it from her, sending it flying across the floor. Then he swept her into his arms and kissed her hard, and she couldn't begin to fight him, not until he eased her from his hold. He clutched her tightly to him, his fingers clenched around her upper arms. "Tell me that you missed me, Isabelle. Tell me that you're glad I'm alive!"

She swallowed hard. She was a Southerner. A Virginian. Her heart was alive, and it seemed that her breath had deserted her, but she could not surrender while the South fought on. She pulled away from him. "I'm glad you're alive, Yank, but I wish heartily that you were not here!"

She ran upstairs, where she paced her room while the Yankees settled in. When darkness fell, she listened to his footsteps in the room beside hers. She heard them come close to her door; she heard them retreat. Again and again.

IT WASN'T TWO WEEKS LATER that the Yankee rider came racing to the house. He slammed his way into the house, then hurried into the den with Travis. Isabelle came hurrying down the stairs, wondering what was happening. Men were rushing into her house, knocking glass from the windows, then taking up positions with their rifles at the ready. Travis came out of the den in time to see her at the foot of the stairway. "Isabelle, you've got to get down to the cellar."

"Why? What's happening?"

"Rebels. Clancy's brigade."

"Clancy's brigade?" she said, her face paling.

"Yes, Clancy's brigade," he repeated. "They're on their way here. They heard that Yanks were holding this house and the town, and they want a battle."

She was going to fall, she thought. She was too weak to stand.

"Isabelle, what is it?"

"Steven is with Clancy's brigade. My brother Steven."

She saw in his eyes that he felt her pain, but she saw, too, that at that moment he was in command of his men, that this was war, and that he had to fight to win. "You've got to get down to the cellar."

"No!"

Travis turned to the butler, who had just come on the scene. "Peter! Peter, I don't know who is going to win or lose here today, but I'll be damned if I'll let Isabelle become a casualty of this war! Get her downstairs."

Peter put his arm around her and rushed her toward the cellar stairs. Dazed, she let him force her down them.

When she heard the first cannon roar, she screamed and clapped her hands over her ears. Then the house shuddered, and she heard a burst of fire and shells, and the screams of horses and men. She never knew what goaded her, but she couldn't bear it, knowing that Steven was out there, bombarding his own house. She escaped Peter and hurried out, ducking as bullets whizzed through the open windows. She didn't know what she hoped to accomplish—of course she wanted the Confederates to win. But there was Private Darby with his freckles, crooked teeth and easy smile, and there was blood pouring out of his shoulder, and he looked as if he was in shock. Isabelle crawled swiftly to the window by his side, ripping at her petticoat, finding cloth to bind up his wound, to staunch the flow of his blood.

"Thank you, Miss Hinton, thank you," he told her over and over again. She stretched him out on the floor; then she heard Travis shouting her name in fury.

"Isabelle!" It was a roar. He came rushing over to her, spinning her away from the window, pressing her against the door. "You could be killed, you little fool!"

She didn't hear his words. She was looking out the window, and she wanted to scream. Steven, in his battered gold and gray, was coming nearer and nearer the house, sneaking toward the rear. He looked so close that she could almost reach out and touch him. Then he stiffened, and red blossomed all over the gray of his cavalry shirt, and he fell onto the grass.

"Steven!" She screamed her brother's name and jerked free of Travis to race toward one of the windows. She felt nothing as she slipped over the windowsill with its shattered glass. She knew no fear as she raced across the battle line to her brother's silent form. "Steven, oh, Steven!" she cried desperately.

"Get down!"

Travis was behind her, throwing himself on top of her, bringing her down to the ground. Bullets flew by them, lodging in the house, in the ground so very near them. "Fool! You'll get shot!"

"That's my brother, I will not go back into the house without him!"

"You have to!"

"He could die!"

"Get in the house! If you go, I'll bring him back. I swear it. By all that's holy, Isabelle, I have a chance! You have none!"

He rolled her away with a shove. Then, before she could protest, he was up himself, racing across the lawn to reach Steven. A Confederate soldier stood up, his sword raised for hand-to-hand combat. Travis was unprepared, and he fell with the man onto the verdant grass. Isabelle bit the back of her hand, repressing a sob. Then she saw Travis again, saw him reach Steven, saw him lift her brother and stagger toward the house.

When he neared it, several of his own men hurried out to meet him. Steven was carried in and set on the floor of the parlor. Isabelle fell beside him, ripping open his shirt, finding that the bullet had pierced his chest, frighteningly near his heart. She staunched the flow of blood, discovered that the bullet had passed cleanly through him and wrapped the wound, with her tears falling down her cheeks all the while. She realized suddenly that the sound of the battle had re-

ceded, that no more guns blazed, no more shouts or
Rebel yells rose upon the air. She turned toward the
doorway. Travis stood there, leaning in the door
frame, watching her.

She moistened her lips. The Yanks had held their
ground, but he had brought Steven to her. She owed
him something. "Thank you," she told him stiffly.

He smiled his crooked smile, doffing his hat. "It
was nothing, ma'am, nothing at all."

But then he suddenly staggered and keeled down
hard on the floor, and she heard herself screaming as
she saw the blood pouring forth from his chest.


TRAVIS WAS GOING TO LIVE. The Yankee surgeon
promised her that, although he had lost a good deal of
blood, he was going to live. He was tough that way.
Steven's injury was by far the worse of the two.

The Yank worked hard over her brother. And he
seemed to be an enlightened man, using clean sponges
for each man, washing his bloodied hands with regu-
larity. She could not have asked for better care for her
brother. The Yanks had morphine, and they kept him
out of pain. They gave him their best.

But that night Steven died anyway. She held him in
her arms as he breathed his last, and then she held him
until dawn, sobbing. No one could draw her away
from him.

She was only dimly aware, when morning dawned
at last, that Travis was with her. In breeches and bare
feet, his chest wrapped in bandages, and none too
steady on his feet, he came to her. He curled his fingers over hers, and she slowly released her grip on the
brother she had loved. He whispered to her, he

soothed her, and she fell against his shoulder and allowed her tears to soak his bandage. Then she realized who was holding her, and she tried to pull away, slamming her fists against him. She didn't see him wince at the pain, and, indeed, it meant nothing to him. Though he had seen men die time and again in war, he'd had little opportunity to see what it did to the loved ones left behind.

And he loved Isabelle Hinton himself.

"Let go of me, Yankee!" she ordered him, but he didn't release her. And finally her sobs quieted. In time he lifted her into his arms, and carried her upstairs, where he laid her on her bed.

It was hours later when she awoke. And he was still with her. Bandaged and in his breeches, he stared out the window at the September fields where the war had come home. Where the blood of her brother still stained the grass.

"Travis?" she whispered, and tears welled in her eyes, because she wanted to believe that it had all been a dream, a nightmare. He came to her bedside, silent and grave. He stared into her eyes and found her hand, squeezing her fingers. "I'm sorry, so very sorry, Isabelle. I know you would have rather it had been me, but I swear that we tried—"

"Oh, God, Travis, don't say that, please! I—" She broke off, shaking her head. Her tears were very close to falling again; she felt that she had been destroyed in those moments when Steven had breathed his last. "Thank you," she said primly. "I know how hard you tried to save him. And you—you shouldn't be up. You're wounded yourself." Indeed, he seemed drawn and weary and haggard, and he had aged years in the months since he had been gone.

"I'm all right," he told her.

She nodded slowly. "So am I," she whispered.

"I'm always here if you need me."

"I *can't* need you!" she whispered.

He inhaled deeply, but he released her hand, turned and left her.

That afternoon they buried Steven. They stood by his grave, and the chaplain said that he had been a brave soldier, fighting for what he believed. Then Travis ordered that the musicians play "Dixie." Isabelle wasn't going to cry again, but she did. Then she ran away from the grave site and retired to her room. She spoke to no one for days. Peter brought her food on a tray, but she ate very little of it.

Steven had been dead for almost two weeks when a sharp tap on her door and then a thundering brought her from her lethargy. She swung the door open, furious that her privacy was being abused, but when she would have protested she fell silent instead. It was Dr. Allen Whaley, the surgeon who had tried so hard to save Steven. He looked grave and worried.

"The captain is dying, Miss Hinton. I thought you should know."

"What?" she gasped incredulously. "But he was fine! I saw him. He was fine, he was—"

"He shouldn't have been up. He lost more blood, and he courted infection. Now he's burning up with fever."

Isabelle raced to the door connecting her room to Travis's. She thrust it open and raced to his bedside.

He was burning up. The bandage around his chest had been curtailed to cover just the wound, and the flesh all around it was slick and hot. Sergeant Sikes had been sitting by him, ineffectually dabbing at his flesh with a wet cloth.

"Up, Sergeant!" Isabelle ordered quickly. She took over the task of soothing Travis's forehead and face with cool water. She touched his wrist and felt for his pulse. She flinched from the fire of his skin and glanced toward Doctor Whaley, who nodded his approval of anything she might try. She bathed Travis from his waist to his throat with the cool water. She began to talk to him, and she talked until she was hoarse.

Later Doctor Whaley came and they rebandaged the wound. The doctor lanced it, and they drained the infection, then wrapped it again. And still his fever burned on.

"Tonight will tell," Doctor Whaley told her. "If you would pray for a Yank, Miss Hinton, pray for this one tonight."

She tried to pray, and she kept moving. She soaked him again and again, trying to cool him. She wiped his forehead and his cheeks; she saw where the war had engraved lines around his eyes, and she thought of how dearly she loved his fascinating, handsome face. If he died, he would have died for her, she realized. She had wanted Steven. He had gone for Steven for her.

"Don't die, don't die, damn you! I—I need you!" she whispered fervently to him.

It couldn't have been her whisper. It really couldn't have been. But he inhaled suddenly, a great ragged breath, and then he went so still that she thought he had died. She laid her ear against his chest and heard his even breathing. She touched his flesh, and it was perceptibly cooler. She started to laugh as she sank into the chair by his bedside. "Oh, my God, he is better!" She breathed the words aloud.

And then Doctor Whaley was by her side, lifting her up. "Yes, he's better, Miss Hinton. And now you'd best get some rest before you fall apart on us!"

He led her away, and when she slept that night, she slept soundly, a smile curing her lips for the first time since Steven had died. There *was* a God in heaven; Travis had lived.

HE STAYED IN BED for a week before he summoned sufficient strength to stand. Isabelle kept her distance from him, not trusting herself with him anymore.

She heard him, though, the day he first rose. He shouted now and then when one of his men seemed to think he needed more help getting around than he did. His soldiers walked around that day with pleased grins, ignoring his tone. They were just glad to have him up.

Isabelle wanted to see him, but she couldn't bring herself to do so. She avoided the dining room; she avoided his office. She was afraid of getting too close to him.

November faded away. December came, and Isabelle made her plans to leave for Christmas. She was packing when she realized that someone was watching her from the open doorway.

That someone was Travis.

He was completely healed now. He was still gaunt, but his features were so striking that his thinness only accentuated the clean lines of his face. His eyes followed her every step, and wherever they fell, she was touched with warmth, with fire. He was striking in blue wool breeches, his high boots and regulation cavalry shirt, his officer's insignia upon his shoulder.

"What are you doing?" he asked her.

"Packing."

"Why?"

"I'm leaving for Christmas."

"Why?"

"Because it is not a holiday to be spent with the enemy."

"I am not your enemy, Isabelle."

She shrugged and kept packing.

He slammed the door shut and strode across the room, catching her by the shoulders, wrenching her from her task. His eyes bored into her like ebony daggers.

"Let me go!" she cried.

"Why, Isabelle?"

"Because, because—"

"No!" he cried, and he tossed her leather portmanteau to the floor, bearing her down upon the bed. His fingers curled around hers, holding her hands high over her head.

"Travis, damn you!"

"I need you, Isabelle. I need you!"

She wanted to fight him. She wanted to deny everything that had happened, everything she felt, but then she thought that perhaps it had always been coming to this, from the very first, when they had fallen together to the snow. She opened her mouth to swear, to protest, but his whisper was already entering her mouth.

"I need you, Isabelle, my God, I need you!"

Then his lips were on hers, his kiss fervent, building a fire within her. He whispered against her mouth, and his lips burned a fiery trail across her cheeks, to her throat, against her earlobe, then back to her mouth again. His tongue teased her lips, then delved between them.

She wrapped her arms around him, her fingers burrowing into his hair, and she came alive, rejoicing in the feel of his hair, in the ripple of the muscles in his shoulders and back. She wasn't sure when it happened, but it seemed that his shirt melted away, and she was torn between laughter and tears when her hands moved across his bare flesh, luxuriating in the warmth of him, in the feel of life. She touched the scars where war had torn his flesh, and she placed her lips against them as tenderly as possible. But after that few things were tender, as the tempest flared between them with a sudden swirling desperation. Her bodice had somehow come undone, and his face lay buried against the valley between her breasts. And then he was taking one into his mouth, his lips and teeth warm upon one pebbled, rosy peak, and the sensation was shattering, sending tremors of fire and yearning through her. She gasped, clinging to him, then she gasped again as she felt his hands upon her naked hips, then between her thighs. She moaned, closing her eyes, shuddering and breathing deeply against his neck as his touch became bold and intimate, stroking, delving, evoking need and searing heat and molten pleasure...

His breeches were shed; her gown was a pile of tangled froth around them; his features were both hard and tender as he rose above her. He gently pulled and tugged away the tangle of her clothing until she lay naked and shivering beneath him. And yet she trusted him, the enemy; he saw it in her eyes. He laid his head against her breasts, then he shuddered with a frightening force. "My God, I've needed you, Isabelle. I may be your enemy, but no enemy will ever love you so tenderly. No friend could swear with greater fervor to be so gentle...."

She cried out, finding his lips, drowning in his kiss. As they kissed, his hands traveled the length of her. He touched and stroked her endlessly, boldly, intimately....

And gently, tenderly.

Finally passion rose swiftly, wantonly, within her. Desire had bloomed so completely and surely in her that she knew nothing of distress or pain, and everything of the driving, blinding beauty of being taken by a man who gave her love. She knew the fury of his passion and the wealth of his rapture as he brought her to a peak of ecstasy so sweet that it was heaven on earth before he shuddered violently and fell beside her, the two of them covered in the fine sheen of their own sweat.

They were silent for the longest time. Then he reached out and touched a curl against the dampness of her cheek. "I'm sorry, Isabelle, I had no right...."

She caught his hand. "No! Shh. Please don't say such things, not now!"

He rolled over, stroked her cheek and stared unabashedly at the rise and fall of her breasts. "I love you, you know."

"No! Don't say that, either!"

She tugged away from him, trembling as she reached for her clothing.

"Isabelle," he said, rising, trying to stop her.

She didn't know why she was so upset. She wanted him—she had wanted him desperately! And she loved him, too.

But there was a war on.

"Travis, leave me alone. Please."

"Isabelle, I didn't—"

"No, Travis, you didn't force me. You didn't do anything wrong. You were—you were the perfect gentleman! But please, leave me alone now. I have to be alone."

He turned angrily and jerked on his shirt and breeches, then his boots. "I'll expect you at dinner tonight," he told her.

She watched him leave, then she washed and dressed and finished her packing. She walked down the stairs and into his office.

"I want to leave for Christmas, Captain," she told him.

He stood up, staring at her across the desk. "Don't leave, Isabelle."

"It's war, Captain."

"Not between us."

"I can't stay! Don't you understand? I can't spend Christmas with the enemy!"

"Even if you sleep with him?"

She slapped him. He didn't make a move, and she bit her lip, wishing she hadn't struck him. She didn't know what she was doing to either of them anyway. It was just that the sound of Christmas carols made her cry now. She wanted so badly to be home for Christmas, but she didn't know where home was anymore.

"I'll write you a pass immediately," he said curtly. "Sergeant Sikes will see to you."

"Thank you."

He scratched out the pass and handed it to her, then looked at the work piled on his desk.

Isabelle turned and headed for the door, then hesitated. She wanted to cry out to him; she wanted to run back.

But she couldn't. Something deep inside her told her that it just wasn't right. She might be in love with the enemy, but it was still wrong to spend Christmas with him.

# Chapter Three

ISABELLE SPENT CHRISTMAS and New Year's Day with Katie Holloway. Katie's place was an old farmstead, and Katie was as solid and rugged as the terrain that surrounded her. She had watched the British siege of Fort McHenry during the War of 1812, and she had lived long enough to say and do and think what she wanted.

"It's dying down now, mind you, Isabelle. This war, it's almost over."

"That's not true! Our generals run circles around theirs. Time and time again we've won the day with far less troops and—"

Rocking in her chair, Katie clicked her knitting needles and exhaled slowly. "When our men die, there's none left to replace them. Aye, we fight fine battles! None will ever forget the likes of Stonewall Jackson. But he and many of his kind are gone now, cut down like flowers in the spring, and we cannot go on without them. Not even Lee can fight this war alone. It's over. All over except for the dying."

Isabelle didn't feel like arguing with Katie; she just felt like crying. She didn't know how life would change when it was all over; she only knew that she had seen enough of it, and she was ready for it to end. She had buried one brother; she wanted the other to live.

She wanted Travis to live.

"I think I'm going to go home tomorrow," she told Katie. It was late January, the snow was piled high, and she wasn't supposed to go home alone. Sergeant Sikes or one of the men came by every couple of days to see if she was ready to leave. No one was due for a few days—she had been determined to say that she wasn't going back. Not until the snows melted. Not until the men went to war again.

But now, suddenly, she didn't want them to go to war. She didn't want *Travis* to go to war.

She hopped up and kissed Katie's weathered cheek, then she hurried into the bedroom to do her packing.

It was the end of January, and not even high noon brought much warmth. Despite Katie's protests that she shouldn't travel alone, Isabelle was going to ride home.

"You should wait for an escort! Captain Aylwin is not going to be pleased."

"Well, Katie, they haven't won the war yet. I can still do as I please," she assured her friend.

She mounted her bay mare and drew her cloak warmly around her. She determined not to go through town—there were too many Yankee soldiers she didn't know there. So she headed east, past small farms and decaying mansions. Everything was winter bleak, and her mare snorted against the cold, filling the air with the mist of her breath. Trees were bare, and the landscape was barren. It was always like this during winter, she told herself. But it wasn't. It was this barren because of the war.

She had ridden for an hour when she came upon the deserted Winslow farm. Thirsty and worried about her mare, she decided to stop to see if the trough had frozen over. She dismounted into the high drifts and led the mare toward the trough. She sighed with relief, because the water had only a thin layer of ice over it. She broke through with the heel of her boot, then patted the mare as she dipped her head to drink. Then she heard a noise behind her and turned around.

A soldier had come out to the porch. He was dressed in ragged gray and butternut, his beard was overgrown, and his eyes were hard and hostile and bleary. At first her heart had soared—one of her own. But as the man leered at her the sensation of elation turned to one of dread. She knew instantly that he was a deserter, and he was here hiding from the Confederates and the Yanks.

She pulled the reins around swiftly, ready to mount, but to no avail. The man threw himself against her, dragging her down into the snow. She pounded her fists against him desperately, and her screams tore the air, but neither had any effect on him. His breath was horrible and rancid, he was filthier than she had ever imagined a man could be, and the scent of him terrified her beyond measure. She knew what he intended, and she thought wildly that she really might rather die than let him touch her. But she was unarmed; she'd had no reason to travel with a weapon— Travis had always seen to her safety.

And now she was alone.

"Hey, ma'am, I'm just looking for some good old southern hospitality!" he taunted.

She freed a hand and smashed at his face. A hard noise assured her that she had hurt him. She took the advantage and kneed him in the groin with all her strength. He screamed with the pain, but took hold of her hair and wrenched her to her feet, then dragged her toward the house. She started screaming again, but it didn't matter; he dragged her up the stairs and through the doorway. A fire was burning in the open hearth, and he tossed her down before it. She tried to scramble up, but he pounced on her. She twisted her face, frantic with fear, when he tried to kiss her.

Then, suddenly, the man was wrenched away from her and tossed hard across the room. Travis was there. Travis, in his winter cape, his dark eyes burning with an ebony fury. As Isabelle scrambled away, she saw the Rebel deserter draw his pistol. "Travis!" she shrieked in warning. She heard an explosion of fire, but Travis did not fall. A crimson stain spread across her attacker's shirt, and she realized that Travis, too, had pulled a pistol. He wasted little time on pity for the Reb but strode quickly to Isabelle, jerking her to her feet.

"What were you doing out alone?" he demanded.

"I was coming home."

His hands were on her. He was shaking; he was shaking her. "Fool!" he exploded, and he wrenched his hands away from her, turning his back on her. She wanted to thank him; she wanted to tell him that she was grateful he had come. She even wanted to cry out that she loved him, but she couldn't. He was the enemy.

"Thank God I decided to come for you myself this morning! Damn it, Isabelle, don't you know what could have happened? He could have raped you and slit your throat and left you in the snow, and we wouldn't even have known it!"

She moistened her lips. She couldn't tell him that she had been anxious to come home because she had been anxious to see him. He caught her arm and pulled her along with him until they got outside. Then he lifted her up on her mare before mounting his own horse, and they started off in silence. The silence held until they reached the house, where he dismounted and came over to her before she could get down herself. He lifted her down, his hands fevered and strong. Her hair tumbled in reckless curls around her face, golden beneath the sun. "What?" he asked suddenly, angry. "Are you upset that I killed the Reb? He was one of your own, right? A good old Southern boy!"

"Of course not!"

"Friend or enemy, is that it, Isabelle? And am I forever damned as the enemy?" His eyes were alive with fire, and his fingers were biting into her upper arms.

"What do you want from me?" she cried.

His grip relaxed slightly, and a slow, bitter smile just curved the corners of his lips. "Christmas," he told her quietly. "I want Christmas."

And suddenly Christmas was everything—everything he wanted and everything she could not give. She pulled herself from his arms and ran into the house.

TRAVIS DAMNED HIMSELF a thousand times for the way he had handled things. But finding her in the arms of that deserter had scared him to the bone, and he trembled to think that he would not have been there if he hadn't determined that morning to go to Mrs. Holloway's himself and bring her back.

And he had done that only because his orders had come. They were pulling out again. He was to lead his men to ride with Sheridan. Grant was in charge on the Eastern front now, determined to cage the wily Lee, whatever the cost. Grant knew that the other Union generals had been overmatched by Lee's abilities—and overawed by his reputation.

He had only a few days remaining to him here. Right or wrong, he was in love with her, and after the endless months of torture, he had found that she was not all ice and reserve, but that she could be fire and passion as well. He wanted a taste of that fire upon his lips when he rode away again.

But it was lost now, he thought.

He sat in the dining room alone, waiting for Peter to serve him. But then he grew impatient with himself, with her. He slid from the table and strode up the stairs to his room, and, once there, he burst through the connecting doorway.

He paused sharply, for he had found her this way once before. She was cocooned in a froth of bubbles, one slender leg protruding from the water as she furiously soaped it. Her eyes met his as he entered the room, and a crimson flush rose to her cheeks. But she didn't deny his presence, and she even smiled softly. "I was coming to dinner," she said quietly. She bit her lower lip. "It's just that I felt so...dirty after today."

Golden-blond ringlets were piled on top of her head, some escaping to dangle softly against her cheeks and the long column of her neck. He had no answer for her other than a hoarse cry and the long strides that brought him to her. He didn't reach for her lips, but paused at the base of the bath, smiling ruefully as he dropped to his knees, then caught the small foot that thrust from the bubbles, and kissed the arch, teasing the sweet, clean flesh with the touch of his tongue. His eyes met hers, which were shimmering with mist and beauty, and he heard the sharp intake of her breath. Her lashes half fell, sensual, inviting. Her lips parted, and still her gaze remained upon him. He stroked his fingers along her calf, soaking his shirt as he leaned into the water, but he didn't care. Brazenly he swept his hand along her thigh. Then he lifted her, dripping and soap-sleek, from the tub. He held her in front of the fire, kissing her, before he walked with her to the bed, cast aside his sodden shirt and breeches and leaned down over her.

No woman had ever smelled so sweet; no skin had ever felt so much like pure silk. She was the most beautiful thing he had ever imagined, with her high firm breasts, slender waist, undulating hips. He kissed her everywhere, ignoring her cries, drinking in the sight and taste and sound of her, needing more and more of her.

That night she dared to love him in return, stroking her nails down his chest, dazzling him with her fingertips. Dinner was forgotten. The night lingered forever. He didn't leave her, didn't even think to rise until the sun came in full upon them and he heard a knocking at his own door.

He kissed her sweetly parted lips and rose. Scrambling into his breeches and boots, he hurried to his own room and opened his door.

There was a messenger there from Sheridan, Sikes told him. He was needed downstairs right away.

He found a clean shirt and hurried down the stairs, where he closeted himself with the cavalry scout and received the latest news.

He had only until the fourteenth of February to meet up with other troops north of Richmond.

ISABELLE CAME DOWN LATER. She wore her reserve again, as another woman might wear a cloak. "You're leaving?" she asked coldly, sitting down across from him.

"Soon."

Her fingers curled around her chair, her lashes lowered. He rose and came to stand before her, then knelt down, taking her hands. "Marry me, Isabelle."

"Marry you!" Her eyes widened incredulously. Gray-green, brilliant against the soft beauty of her face, they were filled with disbelief.

"I love you. I would die for you. You know that."

She swallowed painfully, then shook her head. "It's not over yet. I can't marry you."

"Isabelle, you love me, too," he told her.

She shook her head again. "No. No, I don't." She paused for a second, and he sensed the tears behind her voice. "I *cannot* love a Yankee. Don't you understand?"

She leaped up and was gone. She didn't come down to dinner, and he wouldn't go to her. He ate alone, then drank a brandy, before he finally dashed the glass into the fire and took the stairs two at a time. He burst in upon her and found her clad in a soft white nightgown of silk and lace, a sheer gown, one that clung to the exquisite perfection of her form. She was pacing before the fire, but when she saw him, she paused. He strode over to her, wrenching her into his arms, shaking her slightly so that her hair fell in a cascade down her back, and her eyes rose challengingly to his. "If you can't marry me," he said bitterly, "and you can't love me, then come to bed with me and believe that I, at least love you!"

At first he thought she would lash out at him in fury. He bent over, tossing her over his shoulder, and the two of them fell together onto the bed. Her eyes were flashing, but she only brushed his cheek gently with her palm.

"I cannot love you, Yank!" she whispered. But her lips teased his, her breath sweet with mint, and her body was a fire beneath him. Her mouth moved against his. "But I *can* need you, and I need you very much tonight!"

It remained like that between them for the days that remained. By day she kept her distance, the cool and dignified Miss Hinton, but by night she was his, creating dreams of paradise.

But neither paradise nor dreams could still the war, and in due course he rode out for his appointment with battle. She stood on the porch and watched him as he mounted his horse. And then, as he had before, he rode as close as he could to where she was standing on the porch.

"I love you," he reminded her gravely.

"Don't get yourself killed, Travis," she told him. He nodded and started away.

She called him back. "Travis!"

He turned. She hesitated, then whispered, "I'll pray for you."

He smiled and nodded again, then rode away. The war awaited him.

THEY SAID THAT THE SOUTH had been losing the war since Gettysburg, but you couldn't tell it by the way they were fighting, Travis thought later.

At the end of February, when Travis was joining up with Sheridan's forces, General Kilpatrick staged an ill-conceived raid on Richmond. Papers found on the body of Colonel Dahlgreen indicated an intention to burn the city and assassinate President Jefferson Davis and his cabinet. Meade, questioned by Lee under a flag of truce, denied such intentions vigorously, and Lee accepted that the papers were forgeries. Travis was glad to hear that both sides could question something so heinous, and that even in the midst of warfare, some things could be discussed.

In May, Travis and his troops were engaged in the Battle of the Wilderness, which would stand out in his memory forever. Rebels and Yanks alike were caught, confused and horrified, in the depths of the forest. Soon the trees were ablaze, and more men died from the smoke and fire than from bullets.

From there the survivors moved to the Battle of Spotsylvania. Next Travis followed Sheridan into the Battle of Yellow Tavern, where the cavalry, ten thousand strong, met up with Stuart's southern troops on the outskirts of Richmond. Stuart brought over four thousand men, and the fighting was pitched and desperate, but Travis managed to survive. The great Confederate cavalryman Jeb Stuart was mortally wounded, however. He died in Richmond days later.

LATE IN JUNE Isabelle became aware of a man approaching the house on foot. She was upstairs in her room, and she watched from the window. She bit her lower lip, perplexed. He wore a gray uniform, but she couldn't trust Confederate soldiers anymore, not after what had occurred on her journey home from Katie's.

Travis had given her one of the new repeating rifles, and she hurried downstairs to the gun cabinet to get it. She loaded the gun and hurried to the window, but her worry fell away when she saw the man coming closer. With a glad cry she set the gun down and raced outside, flinging herself into the man's arms. It was her brother, James.

"Oh, my God, you're home!" She kissed him, and he hugged her and swung her around, and she laughed, and then she cried. And then they were in the house, and Peter was there, and the other servants, too, all eager to welcome him home. He only had a few days' leave; he was a lieutenant in the artillery, and he had been lucky to receive even that much time.

Isabelle was determined to make his time at home perfect. She ordered him a steaming bath, dug out his clothes, supervised dinner, and when he was dressed and downstairs again, she was ready to sit with him for a meal of venison stew. He smiled at her, a very grave young man with her own curious colored eyes, slightly darker hair and, now, freshly shaven cheeks. He started to eat hungrily, as if he hadn't seen such a meal in years. Then he suddenly threw down his fork and stared at her, his eyes filled with naked fury.

"This is Yank stew!"

Isabelle bolted back in her chair, sitting very straight. She stared at her hands.

James stood, walking around the room behind her. "I just realized what this means. The house is standing, and there's food in it. What did you pay for those concessions, Isabelle?"

She gasped and leaped to her feet. "I didn't pay anything for concessions!" Guilt tore at her, but she had never paid for anything. She was protected, yes, but she had never paid for that protection. She had simply fallen in love. "They use the house as their headquarters—that's why it's still standing. And there's food in the larder because they bring it in, for their own use, and ours, too."

"And you stay here!" he accused, his hands on his hips.

"I stay here, you fool, for you and Steven! I stay so that they won't burn the house down around us. I've even taken the Yankee dollars Sergeant Sikes gives me as rent, and I've stowed them away to keep this place alive so that you and...and Steven would have a home to come back to!"

He strode from the dining room, down the hall and into the den. With a fury he pushed Travis's papers from their father's desk. Something fluttered to his feet, and he bent to pick it up. It was a record of her safe conduct form to the Holloway home for Christmas. He stared from the form to Isabelle. "What is this?"

"Safe conduct. I—I always leave for Christmas."

Suddenly he started to laugh, but she didn't like the sound of it. "Oh, this is rich! You play the whore all

year, but then you leave for Christmas! Oh, Isabelle!''

She itched to slap his face, but he was too gaunt
from all he'd been through, and besides, she felt the
horrible truth of his words. She turned, a sob tearing
from her, and raced up the stairs. She burst into her
room, where she lay on her bed and sobbed. It was
odd, she thought. It was Christmas she was suddenly
crying for, and not the war, the death, the pain. It was
the peace of the holiday that had been lost, the peace
and the gentle dreams, and the belief that man could
rise above his sins.

Her door opened. James came in and sat beside her
on the bed, then scooped her into his arms. ''I'm
sorry, Isabelle. I'm so sorry. The war has warped me.
I know you, Isabelle. You're the sister who bathed all
my cuts and bruises when I thought I was too big for
my friends to see me cry. The one who stood by our
parents. The one, Peter tells me, who ran out in the
midst of a barrage of bullets to reach Steven. Isabelle,
I love you. If some Yank has kept you safe, then I'm
glad. Can you forgive me?''

She hugged him tight, because no words were necessary between them. Then they went down to their
cold dinner, and when they had eaten, Isabelle took
him out to Steven's grave, and she told him how odd
it had been to hear Yankee musicians playing ''Dixie.''

He slipped his arm around her, then gave a silent
salute to Steven before they walked to the house together.

Over the next few days he drew her out. He listened
to the accounts of his brother's death, and he listened
when she haltingly told him about the deserter who

had attacked her. He also listened to her talk about Travis. He gave her no advice, only warned her, "Isabelle, you're in love with him."

She shook her head, watching the fire. "Even now he could be dead. He's fighting somewhere south of here." She swallowed. It was the front that James would soon return to.

James leaned toward her. "You *are* in love with him. And it sounds like he loves you."

"He is still the enemy."

"Will he marry you?"

"James, I cannot marry the enemy!"

"The war can't go on forever, even if it seems so. But it has taught me that life and love are sweet, and too easily stolen from us before we can touch them."

James left the next day. She forced herself to smile as she buttoned his coat and set his hat on his head. "You'll be home soon for good!" she told him.

He smiled. "Yes, I promise. I promise I'll come home for good." He kissed her cheek, and she walked him as far as the porch. He had to go a few miles on foot, since he was in Yankee territory. Somewhere to the south he would be picked up by a transport wagon. Horses were rare now, and he refused to take her mare. "They'll just kill her down there, Isabelle. Let her survive this thing. I may need her when I come back!"

She hugged him one last time, fiercely, and then he started out. She watched him from the porch, and he suddenly turned around. "Isabelle, don't marry him, if you feel you can't. But give him Christmas. He deserves Christmas."

Then he walked away, and she prayed that the war would soon be over. She assured God that she really didn't care in the least if the Yankees won, just so long as someone ended the damn thing.

THE BATTLES WERE FOUGHT fast and furiously on the eastern front as summer progressed. Women were desperately needed to nurse the wounded, and Isabelle found transport south to the outskirts of Cedar Creek, where an old church was being used as a field hospital. A horrible battle had been fought on October nineteenth. The South had nearly taken the day, but in the end the Union had prevailed.

Rebels and Yankees both were being brought in, and Isabelle was grateful to see that no injured man was being left on the field. Still, each time she saw a blue coat with a cavalry-red stripe on it, her heart sank. Travis had ridden away to join Sheridan, and Sheridan's men had won this battle. Had Travis, too, ridden victoriously away?

At last she discovered that he had not, for she turned to a sheeted form one afternoon to discover it was Travis.

His face was as white as death, and he was barely breathing. She ripped open his uniform to discover that a saber had savagely slashed his side.

Isabelle turned to search out one of the surgeons. She wanted Dr. Hardy, a man with a keen belief in hygiene. If the wound didn't kill Travis, infection might.

"His pulse is good, his breathing is steady and, so far, no fever," Dr. Hardy told her a little while later. "Keep his wound clean, and he should make it."

She did as he'd said. She was careful to tend to all the men, but she reserved time daily to wash and re-bandage Travis's wound.

On the third day he opened his eyes. He stared at her incredulously; then his eyes fell shut again. The effort to hold them open was too much. "Water," he croaked.

She dampened his parched lips, warning him not to drink too quickly. He managed to open his eyes again, and she tried not to smile. Despite his long hair, he was still so handsome. His dark eyes filled with dismay when he realized that he was in a Confederate hospital.

"You might as well let me die," he told her.

"Don't talk like that."

"Andersonville *is* death," he reminded her sharply, and a cold dread filled her heart, because rumor said it was true, that Union soldiers died like flies in the Confederate prison camp.

"You're far too ill to be sent to Andersonville now," she told him, then moved away.

The next morning she was dismayed to find that Travis had stirred an interest among the Southern women helping out as nurses. She was unable to find him alone. If he was going to get that much care, she decided, she was going to keep her distance.

He healed more quickly than anyone had expected. Two weeks after his arrival, she was making the bed beside his when his fingers suddenly clamped around her wrist, and he pulled her to face him.

"What are you doing here?" he demanded sharply of her.

Her brows arched. "Helping!" she snapped.

He shook his head. "You should be home. Oh . . . I see. You want to find your brother."

"My brother is well, thank you very much. He was home on leave during the summer." She pulled away. "Perhaps I was looking for you, Captain," she told him quietly. Then she left him. It was becoming altogether too disturbing to cope with him.

She didn't have to cope with him much longer. Three days later, when she came in, he was gone. Trembling with raw panic, she asked Dr. Hardy what had happened to him.

"The Yank? Oh, he's gone."

"Andersonville?" she whispered in horror.

Hardy shook his head, watching her closely. "He escaped. Not that we have many men to watch the prisoners around here. He just slipped away in the night."

Three days later Dr. Hardy called her, and when she turned, he took her by her arm and led her outside. She held her breath, terrified that he was going to tell her that Travis had been shot during his attempt to escape.

But Hardy hadn't called her about Travis. He cleared his throat and squeezed her hand as they walked along the barren meadow. "Isabelle, Lieutenant James Hinton is on our list as a prisoner of war. He was taken at Petersburg."

"No!" She screamed the word, then sank to the ground, denying Hardy's news with everything in her. She wanted to scream, to keep screaming, to make the words go away.

Hardy knelt beside her. "Isabelle, listen—"

She didn't listen. She grabbed his arm. "Was he injured? Are they taking him west? Do you—"

"He wasn't injured, he was just forced by overwhelming odds to surrender. And he's being taken to Washington. Isabelle, he's alive! And well. He'll probably even be able to write to you. Isabelle, many men died at Petersburg! Be grateful that he's alive. He might be better off in that Yankee prison. He might have Christmas dinner."

She tried to smile, tried to believe Hardy.

Two weeks later, December was upon them and the place was just about cleared out. The injured men had been sent home to recuperate, or back to the battlefield, or they had died.

Hardy called Isabelle into his makeshift office and handed her a sealed document. She looked at him. "You're going home, Isabelle. Confederate soldiers will escort you to the Union line. That letter should give you safe conduct. You need to go home. The war is digging in for winter. I'm moving on to Petersburg."

He stood and kissed both her cheeks. "Merry Christmas, Isabelle."

She kissed him in return. "Merry Christmas."

He smiled and slipped something from his pocket, then handed it to her. "I was afraid you wouldn't think it was a very merry Christmas. I just received that letter two hours ago. It's for you. From your brother, James. He'd heard that the Yanks were in and out of the house, so he wrote through me."

She stared at him, then ripped open the letter, tears stinging her eyes. He was alive; he was eating; he was lucky, considering what could have happened to him.

He ended his letter with a command: "Merry Christmas, Sister! Have faith in the Father, and who knows, perhaps next Christmas will bring us all together again."

She kissed Dr. Hardy again, then she ran out, pressing the letter to her heart.

As Dr. Hardy had promised, she was escorted to the Yankee line by two cavalry soldiers; then her papers were handed over, and she was given an escort through the lines to her doorstep. She had worried the whole way about Travis. He must have been weak after his ordeal; he hadn't been strong enough to return to battle. She hoped fervently that he would be there when she reached home.

He was.

Travis was waiting for her on the porch. The Yankee sergeant with her papers saluted him sharply and respectfully, and said that he had brought Miss Hinton home at the Union's command, and that he needed permission to return to his own unit. Travis quickly granted him permission, saluting in return. He stood tall and straight as he watched Isabelle dismount, then ordered one of his men to take her horse. When she walked up the steps, she saw that his eyes were alight with a pleasure that belied his solemn features.

She walked past him and entered the parlor, shedding her worn travel cloak and hat and tossing them on a chair. Seconds later Travis was behind her, pulling her against him, pressing his lips to her throat, whispering things that were entirely incoherent.

She turned, ready to protest, ready to reproach him, but no words would come. She didn't give a damn who was in the house, who saw what, or what they might think. Not at that moment. She wrapped her arms around his neck, and he swept her into his arms, then carried her into the huge master suite that he'd claimed as his own. A fire was burning in the hearth, hot and blazing. Darkness was falling, but the fire filled the room with a spellbinding glow. Travis laid her down on the bed, his fingers shaking as he removed her clothing. Then he shed his own and straddled her, and the loving began.

The fire cast its glow over them as the night passed. In that curious light he was sleek and coppery, and she couldn't keep her lips from his skin or her fingers from dancing over his rippling muscles. More scars were etched now across his flesh, and she touched them gently, kissed them with tenderness. She had wanted him so badly, and now he was hers. Right or wrong, she loved the enemy.

When morning came, Isabelle made no pretense of denial. She kissed him eagerly by the light of day, met his eyes openly, honestly, and smiled at his hoarse cry as she was swept into the ardent rhythm of his love-making.

She dined with him that evening. He told her about the battles, about Wilderness, about Cold Harbor, Chancellorsville. There was so much sadness in him. She kept a tight rein on her own emotions as she told him that James had been taken prisoner at Petersburg, but that she had heard he was in Washington, not Camp Douglas, in Chicago, which the Rebs feared so greatly.

Two nights later the men started playing Christmas carols. They came in and used the piano, and they played their sad harmonicas. She felt for them, for their longing to go home.

She didn't run away when they sang, and when Sergeant Sikes prodded her, she even rose to sing herself. To the tune of "Greensleeves" she sang about the Christ child's birth, and when she was done, the room was silent and still, and the eyes of every man in the place were on her. At last Sikes cleared his throat, and Private Trent laughed and said that he had made a wreath, and he went out and brought it in. She told them that they could find the household decorations in the attic, and they raced up to bring them down. Soon the place looked and smelled and glowed of Christmas.

Travis, who had watched her from beside the fire, turned and left the room. She heard his footsteps on the stairs.

Rising, she determined to follow him.

He was in the room they shared, staring down at the half-packed portmanteau she had set in one corner. She stared at him in silence as his eyes challenged hers.

"You're leaving again?"

"Yes."

He walked across the room to her, pinning her against the door, his palms flat against the wood on either side of her head. He searched her eyes for a moment, then walked away to stand in front of the fire, his hands clasped behind his back.

"There's something for you on the table," he told her.

"What is it?"

"Go see for yourself."

She hesitated, then walked across the room to the round oak table by the window. There was an official-looking document there wrapped in vellum and red ribbon.

"Travis . . . ?"

"Open it," he commanded.

She did so, her fingers shaking. There was a lot of official language that she read over quickly and in confusion, and then she saw her brother's name. Lieutenant James L. Hinton. She kept reading, trying to make sense of the legal terms and the fancy handwriting. Then she realized that James was to be exchanged for another prisoner, that he was going to be sent home.

She cried out and stared at Travis. She didn't know *how* he had arranged it, only that he had. She started to run toward him, then she stopped, her heart hammering.

"Oh, Travis! You did this!"

He nodded solemnly. "Merry Christmas. You never let me give you a gift. This year I thought you might."

"Oh, Travis!" she repeated; then she raced into his arms. He kissed her, and it was long and deep, and as hot and glowing as the fire. Breathless, she pressed her lips against his throat. "Travis, it's the most wonderful gift in the world, but I have nothing for you. I would give you anything—"

"Then marry me."

She was silent. She saw the fever in his dark eyes, the shattering intensity.

"I—I can't," she said.

Disappointment banked the ebony fires. His jaw hardened, and she could hear the grating of his teeth. "And tomorrow afternoon you will come down to the office as if we were perfect strangers, and you will ask my blessing to leave."

"Travis . . ."

"Damn you! Damn you a thousand times over, Isabelle!" He turned away from her.

"Travis!" she called again, and he turned to her.

He stared at her for several agonizing seconds, and then his long strides brought him to her, and he wrenched her hard into his arms. His kiss was laced with force and fury, and his hands were less than tender as he touched her. She didn't care. She met his fury.

"Isabelle!" Her name tore from him raggedly as his fingers threaded into her hair. In the end, the loving was sweet, agonizingly sweet, and accompanied by whispers that he loved her.

Lying with her back to him, she repeated the words in silence. *I love you.* But the war was still on; he was still the enemy. She couldn't stay, and she couldn't tell him how she felt.

Not even for Christmas.

TRAVIS LAY BY HER SIDE and watched the moonlight as it fell on the sleek perfection of her body. Her back was long and beautiful, and the ivory moon glow caressed it exquisitely. Her hair was free and tangled around him, and he thought with a staggering burst of pain about how much he loved her, how much he needed her. And perhaps God was good, because he *was* alive and able to hold her, and she was here with him. And, damn it, he knew that she loved him!

But he knew, too, that tomorrow would come, and that she would indeed enter the study and demand safe passage.

Suddenly he smiled ironically. He could remember being young, could remember his parents asking him to choose the one thing he wanted most for Christmas. He would think carefully about it, and they always gave him the gift he chose.

If only someone would ask him now. He wouldn't need to think. There was only one thing he would ask for.

Isabelle.

He mouthed her name, then rose, dressed and stepped into the hall. The smell of roasting chestnuts was in the air, along with the scent of the pine boughs the men had brought in.

Tomorrow would be Christmas Eve. She would come down for her safe-passage form, and he would give it to her.

HE HAD BEEN RIGHT. At noon Sergeant Hawkins came to tell him that Isabelle had requested an audience with him.

And now he was alone.

# Chapter Four

*Christmas Eve, 1864*

WITH HER SAFE-PASSAGE PERMIT in her hands, Isabelle closed the door to Travis's office behind her and leaned against it. Didn't he understand that it hurt to leave him, but that it was all that she had left? She was among the nearly beaten, the bested. She was a part of the South. Once she had thrilled to the sound of a Rebel yell; once she had believed with her whole heart that Virginia had had a right to secede; once she had followed that distant drum.

It was true, perhaps, that the end was near, but the South had yet to surrender, so how could she do so?

She hurried along the hallway. Sergeant Sikes was there, waiting for her with his light blue eyes clouded, his face sad and weary. "So, you're leaving, Miss Hinton. I had hoped that you might stay this year."

She adjusted her gloves, and smiled. "It's Christmas, Sergeant. We should be with our own kind, don't you think?"

"It ain't up to me to think, ma'am. I'm just the sergeant." He turned, opening the door for her. "Seems to me, though, that Christmas means we ought to be with the ones we love. Yes, ma'am, that's what it seems to me."

"Sergeant," Isabelle said sweetly, stepping onto the porch, "didn't you just tell me that you weren't supposed to do any thinking?"

"Um." He whistled, and their horses were brought up by one of the privates. She mounted without his assistance, and he sighed and mounted his horse. They started out, Sergeant Sikes riding behind her. Even so, he was determined to talk. "We celebrate a day when a little baby was born. Oxen and lambs flocked around him!"

"Right, Sergeant," she called back.

"There were angels floating around in heaven. Wise men made a journey following a star. Why, ma'am, God looked down from heaven, and he actually smiled. Miss Hinton, even God and the army know that Christmas is a time for peace!"

She turned around, smiling. "You love him a lot, don't you, Sergeant?"

"Captain Travis? You bet I do, ma'am. He's a great officer. I've known him for years. I've watched him put his personal safety behind that of his men every time. I've seen him rally a flagging defense with the power of his own energy, and I've seen him demand that the killing stop when the war turned to butchery. Damn right—'scuse me, ma'am—I do love him. And you do, too, don't you?"

She opened her mouth, not at all sure what she was going to say. In the end she didn't say anything at all. She only stared across the snow-covered fields and saw that another party was out that day, three Union soldiers heading south, trailing a hospital cart behind them. They were headed for the farmstead where she had been attacked the year before.

"Sergeant! There's a man on that cart."

"That's the way it looks, Miss Hinton."

"Come, then, let's see if we can be of help!"

She urged her horse on, then realized that she had forgotten the men were Yankees. Maybe it was Christmas magic that made her so concerned for the unknown soldier in the cart. She didn't know.

Her mare plowed through the dense white snow until she was nearly on top of the first soldier. "Sir! What's happened? I've been a nurse, perhaps I can be of some assistance."

The young officer paused, reining in, looking back as one of the other soldiers lifted a body from the cart and headed for the house. "I don't think so, ma'am. The old fellow isn't going to make it. We found him on the trail, barefoot and fever-ridden, and we've been trying to help him along, but, well, it doesn't look very promising."

Isabelle stared at him, then dismounted, tossing the reins over the porch railing. She caught up her skirts and hurried along the steps and inside.

One of the soldiers was working diligently to start a fire. The other was beside the old man, who he had laid on the sofa, and was holding a flask to his lips.

Isabelle stepped closer, and the Yankee soldier moved politely away. She gasped when she saw that the man on the couch was not a Yankee at all, but a Reb dressed in gray, with gold artillery trim. He was sixty, she thought, if he was a day, yet he had gone out to fight, and he had tried to walk home through the blistering cold with nothing but rags on his feet.

She knelt beside him, pulling the blanket more tightly around him. "I've done what I can," the Yank beside him said. He inclined his head politely. "Frederick Walker, ma'am, surgeon to the Ninth Wisconsin Infantry. I promise you, I have done all that is humanly possible."

She nodded quickly to him, but she didn't leave the old man's side. She took his hand.

"He wanted to get home. Home for Christmas. We were trying to see that he made it, but . . . well, sometimes home is a very long way away."

"Is he comfortable?" Isabelle asked.

"As comfortable as I can make him."

Suddenly the old man's eyes opened. They were a faded blue, rimmed with red, but when he looked at Isabelle, there was a sparkle in them. "God alive! I've gone to heaven, and the angels are blond and beautiful!"

Isabelle smiled. "No, sir, this isn't heaven. I saw the Yanks bring you in and came to see if I could do anything. I'm Isabelle Hinton, sir." She flashed a look at the doctor, wondering if she should be encouraging the old man to talk. The doctor's eyes told her that it was a kindness.

The old man wheezed, and his chest rattled, but he kept smiling. "What are you doing out on Christmas Eve, on a day like today? You should be warm and safe at home, young lady."

"And you shouldn't have been walking in your bare feet!"

"They weren't bare. They were in the best shoes the Confederacy has to offer these days!" he said indignantly. He sighed softly, then caught her eyes. "Oh, girl, don't look so sad! I knew my game was up. I was just trying to see if I could make it home. These nice young fellows tried to give me a lift." He motioned to her, indicating that she should draw near. "Yanks!" he told her, as if she hadn't noticed. Then he smiled broadly. "The doc here knows my boy Jeremy. Jeremy is a doc with a West Virginia division. They've worked together on the field. In Spotsylvania and Antietam Creek. Even at Gettysburg. Isn't that right, Doc?"

"Your son is in the Union?"

"One of them. Both my boys with Lee are still alive, and my daughters, they're back home. But you know, Miss Hinton, every year, whoever could get leave came home for Christmas. Not that we could get many leaves but . . . no matter what, we all wrote. My boys all wrote to me no matter what, no matter what color uniform they were wearing. And having those letters, why, it meant everything. It meant that I was home for Christmas." He broke off, coughing in a long spasm. Isabelle worriedly patted his chest. The young Yankee doctor offered him another drink. It soothed the coughing. Then he lay back, exhausted, but he looked at her worriedly. "Don't you fret so, girl. I'm going to a finer place. I'm going where the angels really sing. Can you imagine what a Christmas celebration is like in heaven? Where the war don't make no difference? Quit worrying about me. Go home. Go home for Christmas."

She shook her head, swallowing. "I—I don't want to leave you."

His eyes closed, but he smiled, his lips parched and dry. "Then stay with me. But when I'm gone, promise me that you'll go home."

"I don't know where home is," she whispered beneath her breath.

But he heard her. His eyes opened, soft and cloudy, but she knew that he was seeing her.

"Home is where there is love, child. Surely you know that. It don't matter if it's a shack or a palace or a blanket beside a fire, home is where love is."

His eyes closed again. Isabelle squeezed his hand, and he squeezed back. Then his lungs rattled again, and the pressure of his hand against hers faded.

Tears flooded her eyes and spilled over his blanket.

Someone was touching her shoulder. Sergeant Sikes. "You come on now, Miss Hinton. Let me get you to Katie Holloway's place."

She let him lead her to the door because she could hardly see. She couldn't bear the injustice of it, that the old man had to die so close to home.

She shook free of the Sergeant's touch and turned back. The old man seemed entirely at peace. The lines had eased from his face. He even seemed to be smiling.

She walked into the snow. Someone came to assist her into the saddle, and Sergeant Sikes remounted, too.

They could go on. She could go to Katie's for the holiday.

Or she could go home.

She cried out suddenly, pulling the reins with such force that the startled animal reared and pawed the air, spewing snowflakes everywhere.

"Miss Hinton—" the sergeant began.

"Oh, Sergeant Sikes! He hasn't died in vain, has he? He's in there smiling away, even in death. Because he's home. And I'm going home, too. It's Christmas, Sergeant!"

Let the Yanks think that she was crazy. It was true that the war wasn't over yet. But for her it was. At least for Christmas.

She felt that she was flying over the snow. It was a day that promised peace to all mankind.

The snow was kicked up beneath the mare's hooves, and the wind whipped by them as she raced across the barren countryside. Sikes was far behind her, but he needn't have worried. She knew the way.

At last she saw the house. Through the window she could even see the fire that burned in the hearth in the office.

She leaped from her mare and raced, covered in snow, up the steps. She tore open the door, leaving it ajar, and flew on winged feet to the den. She didn't knock, just threw open that door, too. And then she stopped at last, completely breathless, unable to speak.

Travis was behind the desk. He stared at her in astonishment, then leaped to his feet, coming quickly around to her. She sagged into his arms.

"Isabelle! Are you hurt? What's happened? Isabelle—"

"I'm not hurt!"

"Then—"

"Nothing has happened."

"Then—"

"I'm just home, that's all. I've come home for the holidays. Oh, Travis, I love you so much!"

He carried her to the hearth and sat before the fire, holding her on his lap, his eyes searching hers. He whispered her name and buried his face against her throat, then repeated her name again.

"I do love you, Travis. So very much."

He shook his head, confused. "I think I've loved *you* forever. But you left...."

"I had to stop. Some Yanks were taking an old Rebel home, but he didn't make it. He died, Travis."

"Oh, Isabelle, I'm sorry."

"No, Travis, no. He was satisfied with his life. He'd known all kinds of love and...and he'd never cared about the color of it. It's so hard to explain. He just made me see... Travis, love is fragile. So hard to come by, so hard to earn. As fragile as a Christmas snowflake. Oh, Travis!"

She wound her arms around him, and kissed him slowly and deeply. Then her eyes found his again. "I—I'd like to give you something. What you did, getting James freed, was wonderful."

"Isabelle, you're my Christmas present. You're what I have wanted forever."

She flushed. "Well, I was hoping you would say that. Because I don't have anything to wrap for you. I've been so stubborn, so horrible."

"Isabelle—"

"Travis, do you really love me?"

"More than anything in the world, Isabelle."

"Then may I be your Christmas gift?"

"What do you mean?" He started to smile, but his eyes were suspicious.

"I mean, well, it would be a present for me, too, really. You—" She paused, took a deep breath and plunged onward. "You said you wanted to marry me. Our minister has gone south with the troops, but your Yankee chaplain is with you, and the church is just down the lane. Travis, I'm trying to say that I'll marry you. For Christmas. If you want to, that is."

He was silent for the longest time. Then he let out a shriek that rivaled the heartiest Rebel yell she had ever heard. He was on his feet, whirling around with her in his arms. He paused at last to kiss her; then he laughed and kissed her again.

When his eyes finally met hers again, they were brilliant with the fires of love, and his hands trembled where they touched her.

"Isabelle, there has never, never been a greater Christmas gift. Never. God knows, there is no gift so sweet or so fine as the gift of love."

She smiled, winding her arms more tightly around him. "And the gift of peace, Travis. You've given me both."

IT WASN'T HARD TO ARRANGE. The men tripped over themselves to decorate the church, and though little else could be done on such short notice, they did manage to bring old Katie Holloway in for the ceremony.

Isabelle stood at the back of the church, while Katie insisted she take her mother's pearl ring. "Something borrowed, love. You must wear the ring."

Isabelle smiled. Her dress was light blue silk, her undergarments were very old, and her love...her love was new. She was all set to become a bride.

"I wonder what's taking them so long!" she said, looking toward the back of the church. Travis was outside in the snow, along with half his men. He turned around suddenly, saw her and ran into the church. To her amazement, he dragged her out into the snow. "Isabelle! Do you believe in Christmas?"

"What are you talking about?" she demanded. "Travis, you're behaving like a madman."

He started to laugh, then he shoved her around in front of him. "Isabelle, all we were lacking was the proper person to give you away. Now, well, we have that, too."

For long moments she stared at the man in the gray uniform standing in front of her. Then she screamed with happiness and tore away from her prospective groom to catapult into the newcomer's arms. Travis, tolerant of her display of affection for another man, watched the dazzling happiness with which she greeted her brother.

"Isabelle!" James hugged her, then looked around at the blue uniforms surrounding them.

"Well, Yanks, is it a truce, then, for a wedding?"

Hats were ripped off and went flying into the air. A cheer went up.

Moments later they were all inside the church. James led her down the aisle and handed her over to

Travis. The chaplain began the service, and she and Travis stated their vows. And when they were solemnly promised to one another, the chaplain stated, "On this date, Christmas of 1864, with the power invested in me by God and the state of Virginia, I declare Travis and Isabelle husband and wife. Captain, kiss your bride."

He kissed her and kissed her. And kissed her.

Sikes had found rice to throw at them, and James was quick to join in. Laughing, the newlyweds ran from the shower of rice to the supply buggy that had brought them, then headed to the house.

Peter had made the most sumptuous Christmas and wedding dinner imaginable, given the state of their larder, and though his feelings would change with the coming of the new year, James seemed willing enough to ignore the fact that the men in his house were Yankees, and the Yanks were more than willing to accept him as one of their own.

It was Christmas.

LATER, WHEN MOST of the soldiers had gone to their sleeping quarters, when Sikes and James were half asleep in front of the parlor fire, Isabelle realized that her new husband was nowhere around.

She found him out on the chilly porch, looking up at the sky. She hooked her arm through his, and he smiled at her.

"What are you doing out here?" she whispered.

"Following a star," he told her softly. He brushed her hair from her face. "I thought I was far away from home for Christmas, but now I know I'm not. I am home. Wherever you are, love, that's where I live. Forever, within your heart."

She said nothing, and he lifted her into his arms, preparing to carry her from the cold porch into the warmth of the house, and then to their room.

But he paused just before he stepped through the door, and he stared at the North Star, whispering a silent prayer.

Thank you, God! Thank you so much. For Isabelle . . . for Christmas.

# Christmas

Christmas in South Florida is, by nature of the weather, different from much of the rest of the country. Some newcomers aren't fond of the fact that the landscape doesn't resemble a Currier and Ives picture postcard. I've never thought much about it. As long as I can remember, Christmas has come without snow and, most of the time, the day is warm enough for swimming.

Christmas cards and Christmas movies, however, are always full of scenes of knee-deep snow and sleds and sleighs and reindeer flying high above fields of frost—causing children to wonder and worry.

In the first home we had with our four small children, there was no fireplace and no chimney. We explained to them that in Florida, Santa Claus came through a window. Then, several years ago, my oldest son noted that many houses in Miami had crime bars on the windows. We explained then that Santa Claus was onto the situation—most parents went ahead and gave him a key to the house.

The children were all delighted when we moved into an old house in the Gables—one with a fireplace and chimney. It seemed a much more traditional way for Santa Claus to enter.

During our first year in the house, I was surprised by my second son's eagerness to attend church services as Christmas drew near. Each Sunday, Shayne would kneel down with his hands folded, deep in prayer. In our new parish, our church was old, beautiful, and traditional. I thought at first that maybe the appearance of St. Theresa's had made an impression upon him.

I told him how nice it was that he was looking forward

to Sundays and that he was so conscientious in prayer. But then his older brother, Jason, blithely informed me about the truth of the situation.

"Oh, he's deep in prayer, all right. He's praying that Santa Claus is going to be able to get his round belly down that dark, narrow chimney of ours."

*Heather Graham Pozzessere*

# *Harlequin Superromance*®

## LET THE GOOD TIMES ROLL...

Add some Cajun spice to liven up your New Year's celebrations and join Superromance for a romantic tour of the rich Acadian marshlands and the legendary Louisiana bayous.

Starting in January 1990, we're launching CAJUN MELODIES, a three-book tribute to the fun-loving people who've enriched America by introducing us to crawfish étouffé and gumbo, zydeco music and the Saturday night party, the *fais-dodo*. And learn about loving, Cajun-style, as you meet the tall, dark, handsome men who win their ladies' hearts with a beautiful, haunting melody....

Book One: *Julianne's Song*, January 1990
Book Two: *Catherine's Song*, February 1990
Book Three: *Jessica's Song*, March 1990

# CHRISTMAS IS FOR KIDS

Spend this holiday season with nine very special children. Children whose wishes come true at the magical time of Christmas.

Read American Romance's CHRISTMAS IS FOR KIDS—heartwarming holiday stories in which children bring together four couples who fall in love. Meet:

*Frank, Dorcas, Kathy, Candy and Nicky*—They become friends at St. Christopher's orphanage, but they really want to be adopted and become part of a real family, in #321 *A Carol Christmas* by Muriel Jensen.

*Patty*—She's a ten-year-old certified genius, but she wants what every little girl wishes for: a daddy of her own, in #322 *Mrs. Scrooge* by Barbara Bretton.

*Amy and Flash*—Their mom is about to deliver their newest sibling any day, but Christmas just isn't the same now—not without their dad. More than anything they want their family reunited for Christmas, in #323 *Dear Santa* by Margaret St. George.

*Spencer*—Living with his dad and grandpa in an all-male household has its advantages, but Spence wants Santa to bring him a mommy to love, in #324 *The Best Gift of All* by Andrea Davidson.

These children will win your hearts as they entice—and matchmake—the adults into a true romance. This holiday, invite them—and the four couples they bring together—into your home.

**Look for all four CHRISTMAS IS FOR KIDS books available now from Harlequin American Romance. And happy holidays!**

XMAS-KIDS-1R